DONNELLY'S WAR

DONNELLY'S WAR

by

David C. Brown

An alternate-history novel of a modern man plunged into a parallel world of Civil War era technology, slavery, drugs, and competing colonial empires.

International Standard Book Nr: 978-0-9997994-2-0
Library of Congress Control Nr:
1 2 3 4 5 6 7 8 9 0

Cover Design by: Mark R. Hayes
www.DavidCBrownAuthor.com

Previously Published Works:
Concrete Girl
Serendipity Hollow
Gap Hollow
Sandlick Hollow
The Trashman's Daughter
Boilermaker
Caroom's Raid
Nitro Wild

♠ Scott Depot, WV ♠

Chapter 1

The last thing Rex Knight clearly remembered on Earth was the sudden onset of intense cold. He'd just completed leveling his Topcon instrument in preparation for surveying the property. Looking about for the source of the chill, he glanced up. An eerie, rapidly expanding spherical black void appeared above him in the beautiful, clear-blue May sky.

There had been no indication of a developing storm. No lightning, no rain, and no wind, nothing but a sudden drop in temperature as the sun vanished, then a crash as blackness washed over him and the wooded hillside exploded upward. Leaf mulch, dust, small rocks, green leaves that had ripped off the trees along with dead limbs, even wooden construction-survey stakes, all of it swirled violently about him. The debris pelted his arms; the dust blinded him as he tried to protect the equipment. *A dry microburst* Rex thought as he lost consciousness.

The sun was bright and the air warm as Rex's awareness returned. His first thought was that an IED had nailed him. Then he remembered he'd been in West Virginia, not Afghanistan. It had been a microburst. The tangle of broken tree limbs he was lying in beside the root ball of a toppled tree confirmed that. He'd been very fortunate. Though roughed up, he was not seriously injured, just dizzy, cold, and confused.

Three large birds circled overhead in a crystalline blue sky. Vultures, Rex decided, as his wits cleared and the spinning sensation faded. The warm sun felt wonderful. Still lying on his back, he looked again at the massive tree. He could smell the fresh soil. The still-dripping loamy material from the exposed tree roots meant that whatever had happened had just occurred.

The realization that this tree hadn't been there prior to the storm snapped him out of his mental fog. Disoriented, and now worried, he sat up and looked about. A forest of enormous trees surrounded him. Parts of the Topcon survey equipment lay scattered among the tree limbs. His backpack dangled from one of the roots of the felled tree.

Rex got up and stumbled around the edge of the crater that the enormous root ball had created. He wanted to investigate the tree and retrieve the backpack. The tree's main trunk was six feet in diameter. He had never seen a tree to equal its size in West Virginia. The tree wasn't an oak or a poplar. The leaf looked a bit like a chestnut, but blight had wiped out the American chestnut trees a century ago.

Though perplexed as to his location and amazed such trees could existed, he decided to retrieve his backpack before trying to make sense of it all. Reaching the backpack required climbing through broken limbs to access the toppled tree trunk, where he then walked back along the massive trunk to the roots and his backpack. Standing on the trunk by the tree's roots, Rex turned around, hoping to see a recognizable sight or discover an explanation for the sudden change. Hadn't he just been admiring the panorama of the magnificent state capitol complex at Charleston from this ridge?

A small plume of dark smoke to the west, about where the Elk and Kanawha River's confluence should have been located, marred the stunning vista of the primeval hardwood forest. Was that smoke cause for concern or hope? Flustered, Rex took a wrong step and nearly fell off his perch by the tree's roots. He was awake. This place wasn't a dream. It was a mystery.

Rex recovered his balance and backpack and climbed off the tree. Some mysterious event had occurred. This wasn't his world. Everything manmade seemed to have vanished, yet the terrain looked familiar. *My god*, he thought, looking around, *there's the rock.*

One of his survey projects for the morning was to place the cut-fill stakes for the subdivision entrance road. The developer had wanted the road to split and loop around a cubical, barn-size, sandstone boulder. Now a similar monstrous rock loomed in front of him among the large trees on this mysterious forested ridge. Except for the trees, it looked identical to the rock he had planned to survey around. It even had that overhang of gray cap rock that made the boulder look top-heavy.

He looked at his hands, nothing different about them. His shirt and pants appeared the same; his legs and body felt the same as a few minutes previous when he was looking at the state capitol. Inspecting the area, he realized his hardhat was gone, along with his truck, phone, and laptop. Hell, everything was gone. No, a flash of sunlight reminded him that the smashed Topcon aluminum tripod was under the tree.

Proof he hadn't hallucinated surveying. So what happened? Where did the trees come from? How could that boulder be here? What would his mother think, his family, when he didn't show up for dinner? Had he vanished or had his world?

The abruptness seemed beyond strange. There had to be an explanation. After slowly turning around while looking at the surrounding silent forest, he decided answering that question would be his goal. The source of that black smoke down the valley would be a good place to start his search for answers.

Regardless of what had happened one thing was clear. Unless he was experiencing the most incredible dream, ever, he was alive in a wilderness, yet still standing on the ridge where he had been surveying a housing development. That made no sense to him, but another look around verified he was in uninhabited country that might be home to bears or other dangerous creatures.

Bears made him nervous; he never knew how to respond when he encountered a bear during a survey. Rex had no desire to hurt a bear, but he also did not intend to be its lunch. So far, the three bears he had encounter during past surveys had always turned away. He needed a weapon.

The pistol, he remembered his pistol. He tore open the backpack and discovered his Ruger pistol. In fact, everything he always carried on field surveys, the pistol, ammo, a small survival kit, a fire starter, a bottle of water, and a knife appeared to be undamaged. The two unopened boxes of 22-LR ammunition that he bought on the way to work for Saturday's event at the Putnam County Gun Club appeared undamaged. Then he laughed. The comfort he felt from possession of his small-caliber target pistol was unjustified, considering the large carnivores that were apt to roam this wilderness. He needed his 357-magnum revolver.

A gunshot from the valley, Rex stopped moving and listened. After a moment, the forest sounds resumed, but the gunshot gave him hope along with concern. Someone was out there. He wasn't alone, but was the party friend or foe, even human?

Well, standing there in bewilderment would accomplish nothing. He picked his way through the broken tree branches to the edge of the ridge and looked for a way into the valley. A dense forest canopy blocked his view of the ground between his location and the river, except for a few gaps in the tree canopy near the edge of the riverbank. There appeared to be a primitive road or animal trail visible through the gap. The trail meant traffic along the river. Curiosity and a sense of adventure were nudging aside his initial shock as he considered his next move.

The gentle breeze shifted back from the west, and Rex heard the murmurs of voices and a horse nickering. Sounds carried far in the quiet river valley, a fact he needed to remember. He didn't want to announce his presence inadvertently to strangers. The voices made him hopeful he would learn where on Earth he was, or even how he'd gotten there. However, Rex remained wary. Someone had just fired a gun and he didn't want shot. Before making his existence known to anyone approaching on the trail, he needed to know if he, she, or it was friendly.

Remembering the smashed survey equipment, he hurried back through the tangle of debris to the overturned tree to check on the condition of the instrument's scope. A quick check showed the unit's optics had survived the tree's impact. It would make a fine telescope. He jogged back to the cliff's edge and dropped to the ground. The sun was overhead and unlikely to reflect off the lens and give away his presence, so he propped the scope on a half-rotten log to watch the trail.

Searching through openings in the tree canopy, Rex spotted a horse with a rider. The rider appeared to be human, a middle-aged Caucasian male, and that discovery cheered him. At least he wasn't alone. The rider looked normal: not tall, a bit fat, and clean-shaven. The man wore a light blue coat and a black hat with a wide, circular brim. The rider's coat and hat had a military aspect, reminding him of a Union officer's uniform from the American Civil War, except the blue was a shade lighter. A rifle in a holster was hanging from the saddle. The rider's horse, tack gear, even the saddle, looked normal.

After a moment, two men walked into his view carrying rifles. He focused the scope on those weapons. The rifles carried by the two scruffy-looking men weren't modern magazine-feed types or ancient flintlocks. Instead, the rifle had the appearance of an old Remington rolling block single shot. Rex couldn't think of any country that still used such antiquated weapons.

Rex scanned the area behind where the guard was talking to the man on the horse. A file of thin men and women, chained in a column, waited along the forest trail, an ominous sight anywhere. And a scene he never expected to witness in America. It had to involve something evil.

The chained prisoners appeared to be a multiracial mix of no specific lineage. Rex's racist grandfather would have called them half-breeds. The tattered clothing worn by most of the prisoners appeared to be the remnants of buckskin pants and leather vests with bead decorations, suggesting a strong Native American influence. The prisoners displayed numerous wounds and were filthy. Their ages ranged from young to old, with several just past childhood.

"Unlock the hag and get the column moving. Clem will think we got lost," the man on the horse bellowed. The rider appeared angry.

Clem? Was he their leader? Did that mean there were more of the bastards? Worried, Rex paused to check the ridge behind him to make sure no one was sneaking up on him, before returning his attention to the tragedy unfolding below his location.

The younger guard who had been talking to the rider ran back along the column of prisoners, shouting, "Unchain the bitch. Get them moving!"

The commands in English startled Rex. Where could he be? He watched, in growing abhorrence as two other guards met the front guard and helped him unlocked a collar that freed the collapsed older woman from the prisoner column. She appeared to be dead.

A shot rang out. The front horseman had pulled his rifle and shot in the air.

"I'll shoot the next one of you animals that delays us," the lead rider said. The livid man ejected the spent casing and inserted a gleaming brass-colored cartridge into the rifle. All the while, the rider watched the prisoners.

Rex had watched the rider work the rifle's action. It operated like a single-shot Remington, and, based on the smoke from the shot, the cartridge had used black powder. No government police force on Earth still used black powder in its firearms. Where was this hell?

The guards dragged the woman's body off the trail as their comrades used their batons to get the column moving again. The violence and treatment of the captives disgusted him. He counted fourteen women and sixteen men in the chained column. Two more guards, on foot, followed at the column's rear. Another older man with a gray beard and an impressive potbelly followed them on a horse. He wore a blue coat and hat similar to those the first rider wore and led two brown packhorses loaded with several canvas-wrapped bundles.

None of the riders, guards, or prisoners appeared tall. Rex at 6'4" and 220 pounds, would tower over them. The guards appeared well fed. None of the prisoners had excessive fat, and the men looked fit. Rex wondered if he had just witnessed the results of a slavery raid on an indigenous people.

Well, wherever he was, at least the residents were human, Rex thought as the packhorses and column disappeared in the forest. The casual murder of the old woman and one group exploiting another group was all too typical of human behavior.

The strangers in blue coats were dangerous and not the ones to approach and ask where he was. The scene reminded him of the early nineteenth century. The glimpse he had just witnessed of this place's ethos had disheartened him. He had hoped the pristine environment meant an enlightened government. Instead, the place's culture appeared brutal and exploitive. From his military experience, Rex knew a man had better be prepared and able to defend himself in such an environment.

He found the crone's corpse; a bullet had killed her. Probably the first gunshot, he had heard. Were the men in blue coats slavers? But arthritis had twisted the elderly woman's hands, so why would slavers bother with such an unfit person? The discrepancy added to his apprehension that the inhabitants of this country embraced beliefs foreign to his.

Unsure whether more guards might happen along, Rex left the corpse undisturbed and searched for the empty rifle cartridge in the weeds along the trail. He found it. It was a center-fire cartridge about the size of his thumb, similar to the old 45-70 buffalo round. The spent cartridge was a good indication that this country's technology was mid-nineteenth century. Putting aside how he got there, the more he learned about this world, the more unfathomable was his situation.

The day was getting late, but after four years in the US Army with two tours in Afghanistan, night didn't bother him. Starting down the river trail, he wondered if the moon would be out tonight. He wanted to reach the place where he saw the smoke. The primitive trail took advantage of the side hollow formed by the brook that drained a swampy area. The west bank of the ford was a steep, muddy chute that traffic from the west slid down and traffic from the east crawled up, using roots and brush for handholds. The lack of a simple footbridge and steps convinced him this was just a game trail.

Rex was just starting up the chute when he heard another horse whinny. Aware of the murderous behavior of the earlier riders, he drew his pistol and looked for a place to hide. A brush pile jammed against the creek's west bank and several yards below the ford appeared large enough to offer concealment if he crawled under it. He considered dashing for the mouth of the hollow a hundred feet away and using the riverbank to shield him from the rider. But when he heard a horse snort above the ravine bank, he knew he was moments from discovery and slipped under the brush jam instead. Now he was soaked.

A lone horseman wearing a blue coat paused at the top of the chute and yelled, "Keep up, you damn animals, or I'll drag your sorry asses through the creek!"

English! Rex had heard right earlier from the rock overlook. At least language wouldn't be a problem. Then Rex watched the brutal behavior of the rider.

The horse and rider plunged down the muddy bank, dragging four filthy prisoners. Short sections of chain connected the neck collars in a line. The front two prisoners in the column were dead, a girl and a boy. The other two rear prisoners were girls.

The guard stopped in the stream and pulled the chained captives toward him. The man wasn't tall, but he was strong. He used the chain to lift the boy's body within his reach while remaining in the saddle. With a key, he opened the collar, freeing the boy's lifeless body from the chain.

"Let that be a lesson to you; keep up or get dragged," the guard said. "It makes no difference to me." The rider dropped the corpse. The body rolled into the creek, and he dragged the next chained body, a young girl, to where he could reach her collar.

The lone live prisoner was a muddy, sobbing girl who asked, "Why couldn't you have stopped? Let them get up?" The rider offered no comment as he unlocked the second collar.

The rear girl had collapsed at some point prior to the muddy chute and been dragged for a ways. She also looked dead. The man on the horse studied his remaining live prisoner.

"It'll be dark soon," the rider said, pulling his rifle from the scabbard. "I want out of these woods before dark, which means I have to hurry. Think you can keep up, or should I just shoot you now?"

What a heartless bastard, Rex thought. Should he intervene? The girl made his decision by flinging a rock with surprising force that hit the rider in his face. With a cry, the rider dropped his rifle, but not the end of the chain. With a curse, the man kicked his horse and it galloped out of the creek, dragging the screaming prisoner.

Rex heaved away the brush he had been hiding under, stood up, and aimed at the back of the rider's head. He was an exceptional marksman. Genetics had blessed him with a hand-eye coordination that allowed him to hit flying targets such as a tossed pop bottle cap with a bullet from his Ruger pistol. He fired one shot. The man fell off the horse still holding the reins and the horse stopped halfway up the ravine's slope.

By killing the bluecoat brute, Rex had cast his lot with the prisoners. He ran over to check the rider and the girl who had been jerked her off her feet and dragged about fifty feet. She wasn't moving, and he feared the chain had broken her neck.

He searched the rider's body and found a billfold, three keys, several odd coins, and half a dozen cartridges for the rifle. He noticed a small knife in a leather sheath protruded from the rider's right boot and made a mental note to get it after he freed the girl. A moan gave him hope as he approached her.

"What's your name?" A set of green eyes watched him in silence as he unlocked the slave collar. "It's a miracle the bastard didn't break your neck. You're tough."

She was the sole survivor. The muddy and barefoot girl wore the remains of a brown leather vest and pants. She was a bit over five feet tall, had short dark brown hair, and was in her early teens. She had a hint of breasts, a high straight forehead, an attractive straight nose, and she was wiry and muscular. Trying to look past her bruises, bloody neck from the cruel iron collar, the mud, grime, bug bites, scratches, and rank odor, Rex figured she had a light brown skin tone and would grow into a beautiful woman if she survived.

"Can you stand? I'm not going to hurt you. What's your name?" Rex asked, trying to start a conversation, after freeing the silent, watchful girl and backing away to give her room. Her answer was a mute stare. "Well, young lady, I can understand your lack of trust."

Rex went back to the rider's body and removed the boot knife and its sheath. His action seemed to alarm her, so he tossed the knife and leather sheath to her. "There. I mean you no harm."

The girl, now on her knees, deftly caught the package but remained silent. Shrugging, Rex went to the horse and searched the saddlebags. He was delighted to find two full boxes of ammunition with twenty rounds each. He'd already decided the manufacturing quality of the rifle was excellent. Somewhere in this strange place were factories and civilization--and answers.

A slight noise made him look up to see the girl sprinting into the woods away from the river. Rex went back to studying the paper ammo boxes. The printing was in both English and German. The size of the cartridge was 11.6 x 65mm. The manufacturer was Bismarck Chemical. He shook one of the brass cartridges out of the box and examined it. The round had a substantial heft. The centered primed brass case was loaded with a heavy .45-caliber round nose lead bullet. The saddlebag contained a neat brass cleaning kit for the rifle. He stored the treasures in his backpack.

The other saddlebag had food items, two Beckman's 100-gram chocolate bars-*Is Beckman's this place's Hershey?* Rex wondered-and several small linen cloths that someone had used to wrap hard biscuits and crackers. A waxed paper sealed 200-gram block of orange cheese was also in the saddle-bag, along with a leather pouch that held a handful of tobacco, a folded paper with a half-dozen dark colored walnut kernels, and a pack of cigarette papers. A glass tube, sealed with a cork, held several large wooden matches.

The contents of the saddlebag made it clear that this strange country operated on the metric system. Rex ate one of the hard biscuits while he and the horse studied each other. It would soon be dark. If he was going to hide evidence of what had happened to the rider, he needed to act.

Rex left the girls' bodies at the edge of the trail and, carrying the rifle, he dragged the shorter chain back to the dead rider by the ford. He looked around, spotted no sign of the girl, but he feared leaving the rifle unattended. Plus, bluecoats or warriors from the girl's tribe might arrive at any moment. He didn't want to be unarmed if one of those unlucky events happened.

After fastening the boy's collar around the dead rider's neck, Rex dragged the body down the creek to the river. He wrapped several loops of the chain around the body, stopping to clamp a collar on the rider's left thigh. He figured that if he hid the brute's body, his comrades might not connect him with the man's disappearance, and was dragging the corpse and chain bundle out into the river when the surviving girl yelled from a clump of brush on top of the riverbank.

"No! There are eels!"

"Eels, so what?" Confused by her sudden reappearance, Rex stopped in waist-deep water.

"The black eels are in the river. Get out!" The frantic girl yelled. "What's wrong with you? They'll kill you."

Rex remembered that this probably wasn't West Virginia, though it might look the same. He thought of Amazon piranhas. Alarmed, he abandoned the rider's body and splashed back to shore. He stood on the sandy shore, breathing hard, and wondering if he had overreacted. A sudden turbulence erupted on the water's surface about where the body had sunk. Shaken, he realized the river was not the Kanawha River he had known. He looked up at the ready-to-bolt girl, and said, "Thanks, I didn't know."

"Who are you?" the girl asked. "Are you a Prussian?"

"No, I'm an American." He thought of the men on horses. "His buddies will be back to check on him. We need to be gone. Where's your family?" The girl vanished without answering.

Rex, holding the rifle, hurried back up the ravine to find the horse. He was no horseman. His first thought was to walk the animal off the path far enough to be hidden and shoot it, but the horse had seemed glad to see him. No way could he murder the animal. Instead, he stripped off the saddle and tack gear, which he then carried into the woods and hid. The horse was free to go wherever it wished. His hope was the dead rider's comrades would think the horse had run off.

Having no way to dig, Rex left the dead girls and boy along the trail after dragging them out of sight into the weeds. He considered a test shot to check the rifle's sights, but a careful inspection showed no sign of damage to the gun, and he decided not to risk alerting any searchers to his location.

The sun had set by the time he had finished those tasks and had clawed his way to the top of the ford's west bank. He had proceeded only a short distance down the trail from the muddy ravine when he noticed the girl. She was carrying the bedroll he'd left with the saddle, following warily thirty-some meters behind him.

A chilly rain hit about an hour after sunset. The night was dark, and Rex wondered if the weather would clear later. If he could see the stars, especially the constellation Ursa Minor and find Polaris, the North Star, he could determine the latitude. Rex noticed the girl had been closing the distance between them as the night had become darker, until now, less than several meters separated them. He again asked her name.

"I have the knife," the girl said. She'd been crying, but defiantly held up the rider's knife. "I'm Indira Hopkins, a Wapiti."

"I'm Rex Knight. Where's your family?" He commenced plodding along the muddy trail in the rain, looking for shelter and waiting for the skittish girl's response.

"That was my brother back there. He killed him. I'm glad you shot him. Are you a deserter? Is Donnelly after you?"

"No, never heard of him. I want to rest for a while until the rain stops." Rex figured the girl was talking about the boy at the creek. He had a thousand questions for her but held back until she had a chance to decide he meant no harm. Instead, he looked for a shelter. A storm-toppled tree with its trunk held off the ground by the root ball had created a sheltered space under the broad trunk. He stopped on the trail and addressed the girl.

"We'll be warmer together under that tree and wrapped in the blanket you had the sense to bring." She looked exhausted, but still leery of him. "Well, I'm stopping and going to wait out the rain under that tree," Rex said pointing at the tree. "You're free to do what you wish."

"There is a panther out there," Indira said. The girl pointed away from the river, toward the dark ridge. "Without a fire, it's not safe at night." The girl appeared perplexed and had stopped a dozen meters from Rex. He figured she was deciding which was her greater danger, the panther or trusting a large male stranger.

"A fire will make it easy for any of those men searching for you, to find you," Rex said. "I have a rifle; the panther won't bother me, even with no fire. Trust me, I'll keep you safe."

The girl cautiously approached him sitting under the tree, and after more scrutiny by those intense eyes, she handed him the blanket. Rex wrapped it around his shoulders and motioned for her to sit beside him.

"If the knife makes you feel safer, keep it handy. I can understand your lack of trust."

"You look like a Prussian, but you don't sound like one."

He shrugged, holding the blanket open to allow her to ease in beside him with her knife. He finished wrapping the dirty wool blanket around them with the rifle in his lap and his pistol handy. Somewhere along the way, she had washed herself and no longer reeked. He probably didn't smell so great, either. Fleas and lice might be another matter. After a few wiggles and some squirming, the girl relaxed against him, asleep.

Bears had been Rex's concern. The panthers must be fearsome creatures to force a young, abused girl to trust him.

Rex woke up cold and needing to urinate. The girl was still asleep under his left arm and didn't stir when he crawled from under the tree. The sun wasn't up but the sky had started to lighten in the east. The rain had stopped. The stars were visible, including the constellations Ursa Major, the big dipper, and Ursa Minor, the little dipper with Polaris. The pole star was where he expected it. Rex lacked equipment, so he could only guess at the vertical angle from the horizon to the star, but around thirty-eight degrees seemed reasonable, which matched the Charleston area latitude.

Rex was mulling that unexpected information when the clip clopping of several horses along the trail alerted him. The tree's large root ball shielded them from the trail, but its location between the trail and high riverbank was a trap if the bluecoats discovered them. He saw the girl sit up.

"Don't make a sound," Rex whispered.

Three riders were slowly walking their horses along the trail, studying the surface. The horse from yesterday had a rope around its neck that the rear horseman was holding. Rex hoped sparing that horse wouldn't cost him his life.

The girl didn't listen. Instead, she panicked and bolted, running through the woods parallel to the trail.

"There she is! I'm on her," the lead horseman yelled. He was. The man grabbed the rear of Indira's vest and yanked her up. "I got the brat," he yelled, slamming her in front of him on the saddle.

The other two riders reined in their horses and stopped to watch. They appeared amused by his struggles to control the girl. The rider, holding the spare horse's rope, said, "Let's flip for first dibs."

"Like hell. I caught the bitch. I'm first after she tells us what happened to Zack," the rider said. Rex could see he had a chokehold on Indira's neck with his left arm, which made a shot risky. Her captor turned his horse to rejoin his comrades. "Boys, we're going to enjoy this sweet thing, before letting Clem have her," the smiling rider said.

Who was this Clem, Rex wondered. Then the rider screamed and flung the girl to the ground. He saw the blood and boot knife handle sticking out of the rider's thigh. Indira was on her feet, running. The other horsemen were pulling their rifles. Rex shot the farthest rider. The rider holding the horse looked stunned at seeing his pal fall out of the saddle. The stabbed one fumbled for his rifle.

"How'd you miss her?" The rider who had captured Indira shouted. "Kill the bitch! Don't let her escape."

The man hadn't realized that Rex had made the shot, probably thinking one of the other riders had shot at the girl. Taking advantage of the rider's misunderstanding, Rex shot him in the back. The remaining rider made a hasty shot that hit the root ball, and then he turned his horse to flee. Rex's third shot dropped him about a hundred feet down the trail. His rider-less horse galloped east on the trail.

What violence. Events of the last twenty-four hours had Rex remembering that night the Taliban overran his platoon's position on the hillside in Kandahar. Then, as now, he wondered if he'd survive.

The girl, to Rex's surprise, had returned to her captor's horse. She obviously knew horses and soothed the nervous animal. Rex, curious about her next move, watched as she then warily toed the fallen rider sprawled on his back in a puddle of water and blood.

"He's dead," she said, looking toward Rex. She then pulled her knife from the rider's thigh and cleaned it on his pants leg.

"Grab his rifle," Rex said. "Shouldn't you tie the horse to a tree? Do these bastards ever use dogs for tracking?"

Indira draped the horse's reins over a bush before walking toward him. She looked disconcerted. "I'm sorry I panicked, I ..." Rex had difficulty connecting the embarrassed teenager standing in front of him with the hellion who had just stabbed a man twice her size.

"And here I thought it was a clever move to distract the bastards so I could shoot them. How old are you?"

"Fourteen. Well, I'll be next month," she said.

"I would have guessed younger. Help me drag their bodies to the river. The eels are hungry. We need to keep moving. Where's your family?"

"My father and mother are down the river trading. I don't know where my sister or grandmother is," the girl said. After a pause, she added, "Bobby, my brother, we can't leave him to the animals." Then she paused again, before adding. "My family lives a day's travel up the Hopkins River, at one of many settlements along the river," she said.

"Is there another river near where the smoke was?" Rex asked.

If there was, then he knew the Hopkins River as the Elk River. The confluence of the Elk and Kanawha Rivers was another Charleston landmark, which meant something damn strange had occurred. He needed time to think, but first he wanted to hear Indira's story.

She nodded yes to his interruption, before continuing. “Smoke? I don’t know. Maybe they burned the camp. Every year we set up a fishing camp to salt and smoke the black eels. I’m old enough, so I’m allowed to fillet the bigger eels for the smoking rack,” Indira said. She noticed the knife was in her hand and returned it to the sheath in her boot.

“I spotted smoke at one place in the valley yesterday,” Rex said.

Indira nodded. “Probably was the camp,” she said, walking over to look at the dead man lying on the trail. “He’s one of them who attacked our camp yesterday morning. They work for Donnelly. No warning, but several of us escaped them and then hid nearby in the woods. Bobby and I wanted to try to steal a rifle.”

“Who’s Donnelly?” Rex asked after Indira’s silence had lasted for a minute. She had been staring at the corpse.

“You’ve never heard of him? He’s a monster, deals in slaves,” she said and walked back to Rex. “The men you just shot were all members of his gang of slavers who raided our camp.”

A local warlord, Rex gathered.

Standing by their tree shelter, a teary Indira added, “The man you shot yesterday was the one that kept shoving Grammy’s hand into the bed of glowing coals of the main campfire. His name was Zack.”

“Why, what did he want?”

“They wanted Bobby, my brother. The man was mad because we had escaped,” the girl said. “The man I stabbed had stayed to help him find Bobby. My grandmother refused to talk even as her hand was burned.”

“God almighty, what cruelty,” Rex said. Tears silently ran down Indira’s face as she stared at her feet.

“We surrendered,” she said. After a long pause broken by more sobs, she whispered, “He cut her throat and dragged her to the river and the eels...”

“Christ, such mercilessness, I’m glad I shot the bastards.”

“So am I. They all deserved to die,” Indira said while petting the muzzle of the horse that had walked over to her. *The wonder is that the girl trusted any man*, Rex thought. She went on telling of her experience in an eerily unemotional voice.

“Afterwards, Zack chained the four of us in neck collars. The one who murdered Grammy then left Zack by himself. That one,” she said, pointing to the rider who had grabbed her. “Zack didn’t like it and kept going too fast, causing us to trip and fall. My brother’s neck broke during a stumble. He didn’t deserve that. Zack murdered him.”

“You think your sister and other grandmother are in the first group of prisoners?” He thought of the old woman, hoping she wasn’t the girl’s other grandmother.

“I pray they haven’t hurt her. My sister’s nineteen, trained to teach school.” She started crying again.

“I’m so sorry, Indira. We’ll bury your brother when we finish here. Then we need to disappear before they return with dogs.”

Rex walked over to the trail and dragged the rider who had been holding Zack’s horse to the riverbank and went back for another. Looking over the bank’s edge, he realized they had one fortunate break. In this location, the river was undercutting the bank below where they stood. The bodies would drop directly into where the current was strong and deep. Indira had managed to drag the posse’s leader, the torturer of her grandmother, about a meter during the time it took to dispose of the other two dead riders.

“I’ll get the body. Go check the other saddlebags for ammo and settle down the horses,” Rex said. He took a better look and decided the man was the same rider who had shot the old woman yesterday. This gave him an idea. He stopped and removed the dead man's jacket and hat before dragging the body to the riverbank's edge. "Indira, where were they taking you and the other group?"

"First to the stockade," Indira said. "They lock up their captives until they're sorted."

"Sorted? What's that about?" Rex asked, as he rolled up the blue coat and placed it in a saddlebag. He examined the hat for lice and seeing none, tried it on. The hat proved too small; he cut the hatband so he could wear it.

"I'm not sure, but some of the people are sent up the river and some down the river, depending on who's buying," she said while opening the saddlebag.

"A slave market, is that what it is?"

What a barbaric country he'd landed in, where a thirteen-year-old girl talks dispassionately about the capture of her people and their enslavement.

"Well, it's more a fort." She was inspecting a Beckman chocolate bar she had found with the three boxes of ammo in the saddlebag on the horse waiting on the trail. "Mom would beat me if she caught me eating this. What's a dog?"

Rex was having a hard time keeping up with the girl's mercurial moods. However, he couldn't allow her sugar comment to pass without an explanation. He learned that Indira's family avoided sugar and ate swamp greens to protect their teeth.

"I've never heard of such a thing. Do you brush your teeth?" To lighten the mood, he added, "And take baths with soap?"

Indira bristled. "Yes, but I didn't have chance yesterday to pack my tooth stick." She placed the ammo into his backpack as well as the rest of the chocolate bar after she took a large bite from it.

"Why don't you keep the bar? I already have one," Rex said. Without a word, she pulled it back out and crammed it into her grimy left vest pocket. "What greens?" Rex asked. He knew about watercress and wondered if that was the swamp green. Then he wondered what fruit grew in the area. “Do apples grow around here?”

“Well, yeah, but not now. They just blossomed. Mom makes us eat and drink the water from cooking swamp greens. She calls it tea. Tastes hideous, but she says it’s good for our teeth,” Indira said. She inspected him and added, “What’d you drink for those teeth?”

How did they get on the subject of dental care? “From eating greens and apples,” Rex said.

He’d finished cleaning out the dead men’s pockets and had a number of small metal coins and folded pieces of paper that he figured served as money in this world. He handed it all to Indira.

“What’s this worth?” Rex asked as he rolled the third body off the bank. The first body to go into the river was now about twenty meters downstream. The swirling water and bobbing body indicated something was tearing pieces from it. The other body had vanished shortly after hitting the water.

“You can’t count. Where are you from?” a concerned Indira asked. He hadn’t asked the amount, and before he could explain, she said, “Two hundred seventy D-marks, enough that you could buy a cheap pack horse or musket.” She then inspected and bit a gold coin about the size of a quarter before adding, “You have a five hundred D-mark coin. You’re rich. You have almost eight hundred D-marks.”

“A dog is an animal, looks like a small wolf,” Rex answered, remembering her question and wishing to avoid the where-are-you-from question.

“Like a fox?” Indira asked. She handed the coins and bills to him.

“More like a wolf,” Rex said, putting away the money.

“A few men have pet wolves,” she added, trying to be helpful.

Rex realized she had never seen a dog, so probable neither had the bluecoats. Glancing toward a swirl in the water, he had a momentary glimpse of a large, dark, snake-like creature. The sight of the eel and the thought of the now-missing bodies left goose bumps on his arms. *No way am I swimming in that river.*

The two girls who Donnelly's man had killed were unlucky neighbors caught in the raid on the Hopkins fishing camp. He dug the hole for Indira's brother and the two girls, using a small spade he'd found tied behind the lead slaver's saddle. He then helped her placed the three bodies in the shallow grave off the trail.

"I'll fill it. You don't have to watch."

They had nothing to use as a shroud and Rex didn't want her to witness the shovels of soil landing on her brother's body.

"Wait, hold my hand," Indira said joining him at the open grave. "I commend my brother to you, Lord," the tearful girl said in a breaking voice. "Now that my beloved Bobby has passed from this life, may he live on in your presence. I ask this through Thee O' Lord and God."

After that Christian-sounding prayer and short chant for her brother's soul, a forlorn Indira sat on a log while he filled in the grave.

After Rex finished scattering a cover of leaves to hide the burial site, Indira stood and said, "We should head downriver and look for other fish camp survivors, but, if we do, it would leave my sister Lily with the monsters. If they send her down the river, she'll never return. No one ever does. I'll never see her again."

Rex hated to put the young girl through another burial, but she was the one who could identify the body. "There's one more body that I need to bury."

The elderly woman wasn't Indira's other grandmother but an old neighborhood friend she had known all her life. The harmless old woman's murder brought on another round of tears from Indira and renewed worries for her sister's life.

"We can't just leave my sister with them. Help me find them. I can crawl into their camp and use a collar key to free them," Indira said. Each dead rider had had a key, and Rex knew the girl had pocketed at least two of the keys.

"Freeing your sister, grandmother, and neighbors from those killers won't be that simple. Those men shoot first and ask questions later. If they discover you, they'll kill you and anyone with you."

"I'm not afraid. I can sneak in."

"You just told me the prisoners are kept chained in a walled stockade. You think those murderers are going to leave the door open and not be watching?"

Indira glared at him defiantly, though an uncharitable person might have called it mulish. Regardless, he preferred it to her earlier tears.

"Let's find their camp," he said. "An idea might come to one of us on how to free your sister without getting killed in the attempt."

Indira was right to be concerned about her sister and grandmother. Rex was convinced that the men in the blue coats were ruthless savages after the gunfight on the trail that morning and having just buried three young children and the elderly woman. Their murderous behavior infuriated him. Eradicating any of the bastards who threatened him or the girl wouldn't trouble his conscience.

Defending himself in an unprovoked attack was one thing; deliberately seeking a confrontation with the blue-coated savages to free strangers was another matter. He had no illusions that those killers couldn't fight. Besides the fact that they were on their home territory, Rex was a stranger in this violent country. This returned his thoughts to the location question. Where were they?

The land appeared about as Rex imagined the Kanawha Valley had looked before Charleston, dams and locks, and interstates. He supposed he could mistake one forested valley in Appalachia for another, but not that cubical rock on the ridge. It was the same rock, which meant what?

Everything he'd encountered-from the immense American chestnut trees, those flesh eating eels, murderous slavers, to the sparkling clear water and atmosphere and lack of roads and buildings-all said it was a different world. Yet from his surveying work around Charleston, he was familiar with the terrain. That knowledge, along with the rock and the location of Polaris and the constellations in the night sky, had convinced Rex that he was still in the Charleston area.

That was his quandary: how could this be true? Had he gone back in time and was still on Earth, or had the mysterious phenomenon hurled him to a parallel universe and a different Earth like planet? This was the science fiction nonsense that he had always thought entertaining but ridiculous.

Rex knew enough North American archaeological history to know that no evidence existed of inhabitants prior to the Paleo-Indians, which supported his growing belief that time travel wasn't involved. He was in a different world. Dead vanished to his family and friends on Earth. Christ, what would his mother think happened to him?

And Rex suspected his experience hadn't been unique. What other explanation could there be for the inhabitants' use of metric measurements and English, except that other Earthlings had in the past survived the same mysterious passage to this twin of Earth? A one-way passage, Rex feared.

Chapter 2

Rex's "prisoner" had wanted to wait until dark. A dubious Indira stood on the trail beside his horse. He chambered a round. Satisfying himself that the pistol was ready, he shoved its barrel under his left leg and against the leather saddle, a position where he could hold it out of sight, yet reach it in a moment. Indira, after another sigh that teenage girls do so well, handed him the end of the short section of chain attached to the iron slave collar around her neck.

"Trust me," Rex said. "Approaching in broad daylight is best. I want them to see us, but it's your call. Still game?" He smiled encouragement at her.

"Let's get it over with, and please don't get killed," Indira said. A moment later, after he was certain she had nothing to add, he started the horse forward. They left the forest cover and entered the clearing before the stockade.

The previous few hours, they had been busily watching the stockade area and considering rescue schemes. The crudely built rock structure that dominated the center of the area appeared to be a furnace. Two long, low woodsheds sat near the furnace. Rex could see several fit, shirtless, barefoot, tanned men who appeared to be laborers.

"They're not part of Donnelly's gang," Indira said to his unasked question.

"Who are those men carrying split logs, slaves?"

"Indolent laborers," she said, snatching the Topcon scope resting on the bank in front of Rex.

"They're working quite steadily to be called indolent laborers."

"Oh, I did not say that. I said *indentured* laborers," Indira replied. Her smile put the truth of her assertion in doubt. She then said, "They're feeding Donnelly's brine furnace. That circular pen made of logs is the stockade, the pen for holding captives."

Salt? If Rex's suspicions about his location were right, they would be near what was on earth was Malden and the location of the old J. Q. Dickinson Salt Works.

"Are they making, salt?" he asked. Indira nodded and she returned to studying the stockade through the scope while he reflected on that additional proof he was on a twin of Earth, though at a different stage of development and a society with a merciless frontier ethos. Perhaps he had died and this was hell.

Enough of those depressing thoughts, Rex refocused on their mission to liberate Indira's sister. Whoever had built the stockade had constructed it in the shape of a ring formed by standing numerous large tree trunks on end and side-by-side with one end of the trees buried in the ground. A twelve-foot high, fifty-foot diameter wall, he estimated, before remembering that this world operated on the metric system. He corrected his thoughts to four meters by sixteen meters.

"Who is Clem?" Rex asked. "I heard that rider mention his name."

"Clem Hubbard, he runs the brine furnace and stockade. He hates Wapitis. "Zack and those men worked for him. He's Donnelly's main overseer."

After an hour of sharing the Topcon scope and studying the stockade, Rex figured it was around mid-day when activity on the wall caught their attention. Three of the bluecoats had dragged a young Wapiti man with his hands tied behind his back onto the walkway. One of the guards then put a hangman's loop over the struggling man's head.

"Oh God, it's Jeff. They can't," Indira whispered as she looked through the scope. They did. The three guards had lifted the thrashing man over the wall and dropped him. The short length of rope snapped tight about a meter below the top of the wall, ending his beseeching screams.

Rex watched, horrified, as Jeff's kicks withered away over several minutes, his feet about a meter above the ground. Their hiding spot put them too far away to clearly hear the guards, but the meaning of the laughing and shouting of taunts into the stockade was clear. Indira vomited.

"If we're going to try a rescue, now is the time, before more raiders showed up," Rex said after deciding her retching was finished. "I counted nine men yesterday. We know four of those men won't be returning. That leaves at least five men, plus whoever normally guards the place."

"Poor Jeff. Why?" A tearful Indira asked. He had no answer and after a moment she said, "You're right. It's time. Besides, I've only seen three guards. Can't you handle three? You just killed three this morning."

Rex wondered if homicide was this blighted world's favorite sport.

"You do appreciate that other guards could be sleeping in the tents, in the sheds, or inside the log ring with the prisoners, or even be across the river watching?"

Despite the earlier killings and burials, he still wasn't certain he had accepted this world was real. Though he had to admit that the sunrays felt warm, the ant on his arm appeared real, and the smell from the grass and weeds around them seemed real.

Time wasn't his friend in this effort to rescue Indira's family. He liked the girl and suspected he'd be more comfortable among the Wapitis than with their tormentors. The wickedness of the bluecoats' conduct had deeply offended his sense of righteousness. Observing the slaying of helpless people had traumatized his Christian morality and awakened the violent temperament that had served him so well in Afghanistan.

The laughter of the guards had further provoked a perhaps foolish but still powerful desire to visit retribution on those psychopaths amusing themselves by hanging and dragging to death defenseless prisoners. Mounting a rescue of the Wapiti prisoners would provide him such an opportunity. Rex had several advantages: total surprise, an automatic pistol in a world used to single-shot firearms, and a foe not expecting the victim to fight back. He was confident he could handle the current five guards, but not if another half dozen raiders returned.

"I have a plan. It's dangerous, and it requires your help. If I'm willing to risk my life to save your sister, a total stranger, then I don't believe asking you to risk your life in the attempt is unreasonable. I need a distraction that will allow me to approach the stockade. You would be perfect as my prisoner in a slave collar."

"Me? In broad daylight, you want me to wear a slave collar and walk up to the guards?" she said. "They have three rifles, maybe more. You have one."

"Those guards would never expect a Wapiti warrior to risk a young girl. They'll think I'm Zack. Besides, the guards will be too busy looking at a pretty Wapiti girl to worry about her guard."

Indira didn't share Rex's opinion of her looks, or his certainty, but her desire to rescue her family had overcome her initial skepticism. Another hour was lost backtracking to get a slave collar and a short piece of chain from the pile of fetters by the graves.

Rex split the back of the raider's blue coat so he could fasten the front buttons. The cut hatband allowed it to fit. From a distance, if he didn't turn, he figured he'd look the part of Zack returning. Rex had a bit of trouble holding back his horse to Indira's less than enthusiastic pace as they crossed the clearing.

"I hope that guard has poor eye sight," she grumbled. The disguise worked. The lone guard on top of the stockade wall noticed them and waved.

About thirty meters from the stockade, as agreed, Indira screamed and fell down. Rex stopped and dismounted as if confused about why his prisoner had collapsed, all the while shielding his pistol from the guard's view.

The man peering over the wall asked what had happened. Rex shrugged as he prodded Indira with his foot. He had stopped by the small swale that ran toward the river. It would offer Indira an escape route if his scheme blew up. His hope was that the other guards would leave the stockade to investigate and help with the prostrate prisoner. To Rex's relief, two guards hurried from around the edge of the pen.

"Where have you been? Where is everyone? The rest of the prisoners?" asked the older guard who yesterday had been leading the two packhorses. "Wait, who are you?"

Each guard carried a rifle. The older one said, "Hold up, Bud. I don't know this guy." He put his arm out to stop Bud.

"I'm Rex, a new guy. Zack said to bring her here."

"So where's Zack?" the older guard asked, suspicious. "Clem said he should have been here last night."

The guard on the wall asked, "What's wrong with the girl?" Bud appeared likewise interested in Indira. Smart girl, she let out a pitiful moan and mumbled, "Snake."

"Did she say a snake bit her?" Bud asked, pushing past the older guard and walked toward her. The older one appeared more puzzled than alarmed and stopped several meters away to wait for Bud to locate the snake.

Rex's response was to shoot each guard in the head and dash to the wall before the upper guard, who had also been watching Indira moaning and thrashing on the ground, could react and aim his rifle. Rex waited against the stockade wall for the guard to lean out over the wall to locate him, which the guard did a moment later. The shot sent the guard falling backward into the stockade. The guard's rifle dropped outside the stockade wall.

Indira, instead of waiting for Rex's signal, bolted from the swale, flinging the hated slave collar into the weeds. Moments after the guard's rifle hit the ground, she was on Zack's horse galloping away. Rex hoped she would remember to wait with their other horses at the clearing edge until he waved that it was safe to return.

Securing the stockade before other Donnelly men arrived was critical. He raced around to the riverside, found the stockade door open, and looked in. Chained prisoners lay in groups on the ground inside the stockade. A few of them appeared alert to the rescue attempt. They'd be no help in a fight, but at least he didn't see any guards among the prisoners or in the stockade. Two guards were missing. Rex decided he'd better check the four small tents in a row parallel to the riverbank's top edge before entering the stockade.

Using the barrel of Zack's rifle, Rex warily lifted the front flap of each tent to inspect the interior. The first two were empty. Sleepily, a guard in just his pants stuck his head out of the third tent as Rex approached and asked, "Who's shooting?" He shot him.

A moment after the shot, another guard in his long johns burst out of the last tent with a rifle. Rex, in the process of reloading, flung himself to the ground as the guard's rifle roared. No pain, so the guard had missed. Rex scrambled to his knees.

The guard was running for the open stockade gate, yelling, "Help, man the gate! Shoot the bastard!" The man was trying to run and reload his rifle.

Slamming closed the rifle's breechblock, Rex fired at the guard's back just as the man jerked the stockade gate closed. Watching the top of the wall for the appearance of a guard, Rex crept along the stockade wall, looking for another door. The two log huts near the stockade that Indira had said were jail cells seemed abandoned. The men at the furnace had stopped working and started walking toward the stockade. He didn't need them getting in the way.

"Get back to work! Donnelly's not paying you to gawk. He'll be here shortly."

The indentured laborers hurried back to the furnace. By then, he had decided that the stockade had only one entrance and walked back to it. The gate was unlocked. The guard he was pursuing lay just inside the stockade gate face down. The earlier wall guard lay on the upper walkway.

Rex climbed the stairs and verified that the upper guard was dead. He then cut the rope holding the hanged man, Jeff, before hurrying down the rickety stairs to free the Wapiti prisoners who watched him in silence. He started unlocking the collars on the men closest to the walkway stairs. The women Rex had spotted in yesterday's column weren't among the chained prisoners sprawled across the stockade floor.

"Where are the women?" Rex asked the prisoner as he unlocked his collar. The freed prisoner, a sinewy young man with a dirty head bandage, wore leather pants and a vest similar in style to Indira's outfit.

"We need water," the young man said. "These bastards refused to give us water. They just laughed at our pleading and murdered Jeff."

"I don't have any water. Can you make it to the river?" Rex asked.

The freed man nodded and wandered toward the gate. The other two freed men just moaned and lay on the ground beside their open collars, unable or unwilling to rise. Rex continued to unlock collars. The lack of response during removal of their collars made clear that many of the prisoners were dead or beyond rescue. Two of the younger men had had their heads smashed in. The guards had shot three more Wapiti men. All five were dead. Rex didn't bother with those bloody collars. The slavers' ghastly treatment of their captives made no sense unless they were in fact running a Nazi-style death camp.

Yelling from the gate told Rex his young partner, as usual, hadn't listened and instead had returned. Racing through the gate, Indira went straight to the prisoners and started unlocking the remaining collars. She addressed many of the prisoners by name in an attempt to rouse them. From the few he'd opened, Rex knew the dirty, corroded collar locks didn't turn easily. In several of the collars, he had to strain the key until he worried it would snap off.

Indira, determined girl that she was, managed to open most of the collars she tackled. Rex had to help her on two collars. Between the two of them, they soon had all the collars removed. By then Indira was crying. There was much moaning for water from the prisoners.

"Tell them the river is just outside."

"See if you can find a bucket and bring the water here," Indira suggested. He remembered seeing a wooden bucket on the dilapidated wood dock and left to get it.

"Rex, they say there are prisoners in the huts," Indira yelled from inside the stockade. That girl had a voice that carried. He heard her clearly while standing fifty meters away on the river's shore.

The first freed prisoner had made it to the river. Rex tossed him the wooden bucket. "Help her get water to the other freed prisoners. I'll check the two huts."

Neither of the huts had a window nor an exterior lock on their only door. The six-meter-by-six-meter hut construction of notched logs with a shake roof of wood shingles looked sturdy. The huts reminded Rex of log cabins from the pioneer days. He considered the odds of a guard waiting inside the hut to shoot the person who opened the door.

"Hey, Wapitis, are any of Donnelly's men in there?" The prisoners surely would tell him if there was an ambush waiting.

The shouted question triggered an outburst of help requests and assurances that opening the door was safe. The hut nearest the river contained the missing women chained together to the hut's rear wall. He gave his key to the young woman he'd just unfettered and said, "Finish unlocking their collars."

The second hut contained several healthy men from their late teens to middle age. The slavers had provided water to the occupants of both huts. Again, Rex thought of death camps. The Nazis, Khmer Rouge, and Islamic State had separated useful prisoners, those able to work and sexually attractive women from the young, old and weak prisoners, whom they then murdered. Here, Donnelly didn't have a gas chamber, and he apparently didn't want to use firing squads, instead he let abuse kill them.

"Who are you?" the oldest man in the room asked. "Did Manuel Prado send you?" His facial structure was angular with a light brown complexion, reminding Rex of someone with Indian ancestry.

"No, don't know him," Rex said. Using his other key, he unlocked the men's collars. The freed prisoners all vacated the fetid huts, then milled around outside.

"You need to help the other prisoners," he added, pointing toward the stockade.

The occupants from both huts rushed to the stockade except for the man who asked Rex who had sent him. The man had a commanding appearance, and he wondered if he was some sort of chief, though the man's fearful glances toward the dead guard by the tent casted doubt on that being the case.

"Why'd you have to kill them? Donnelly will go crazy. Who are you?"

Rex thought the man's concern for his jailers misplaced and said. "Indira asked me to help free her sister, Lily. They got in the way."

"The younger Hopkins girl?" the man asked. He appeared puzzled. "Are you a Prussian deserter?" Rex's expression must have alarmed the man. "Where are my manners? Thank you for helping. I don't understand why they wouldn't allow us food. The Prussians must have told them not to."

"Food? Hell, those people didn't even get water," Rex said as he pointed toward the stockade.

The few surviving stockade prisoners were moving faster toward the river, helped by Indira and the group of men and women from the huts. Indira reminded him of a border collie herding confused sheep toward water. The girl, all energy, paused in her efforts to aid the survivors and ran over to Rex.

"Chief Chin, Rex, my sister isn't here. They sold her and Tara. We need to save her."

Rex was confused. This man was a chief, and who, he wondered, were the Prussians? All that had to wait.

"The first thing is to clear out of here before the other raiders return. Who knows how to use a rifle?"

Chief Chin spoke up. "We all do, at least a musket, though we normally use atlatls when hunting. I think Scott Belcher has broken the law and has used a Prussian army rifle. Regardless, Scott's a good shot with a musket, assuming he isn't dead. He made trouble, and they left him in the stockade. You do know that the Prussians hang anyone they find with an unlicensed firearm east of the mountains."

"Licenses …." Rex wondered why a man just saved from slavery or even death would give a damn about firearm licenses. Then, remembering Indira's sister and his purpose, he asked, "How many women were sold to these Prussians?" Just two, he learned, as several of the women answered his question.

"Indira, find Scott Belcher. I need him," Rex said. She had a fretful look. "I haven't forgotten your sister, but first deal with this. Now go," he ordered. The girl looked ready to argue but turned and left. He then asked the chief to verify Indira's information. "Who employed these bastards? Donnelly?"

"Yes, they're his men. He must have had a deal with the Prussians for they took Lily Hopkins. She had just finished her Jesuit education. I had her scheduled to start teaching our children. The man who bought her looked like you. I figure he works for Ruffner. Who do you work for?"

"Prussians," Rex asked, and then remembered to be cautious. The man looked surprised by the question, but before he could comment, Indira's shout attracted their attention. They both looked toward the river where the first man he had freed was following the girl.

"This is Scott," Indira said by way of an introduction.

Scott wore a grimy leather shirt and pants, which he'd tucked in brown rough-leather knee boots. Rex would guess that Scott Belcher was about his age, but shorter, maybe 1.7 meters. He had a wiry muscular physique. Scott had a number of bruises and a hand size scab on the back of his head where part of his hair was missing. The head bandage was gone. The man was still a bit shaky as he kept taking drinks of water from a leather bag.

"Scott knows my sister and Tara Smith. Even better, he'd overheard the negotiation between Clem and the Prussians," Indira said.

"One of them I've met," Scott said. "He was the gofer for the Prussians who bought Tara and Lily. The bastard works for Ruffner. His name's Hans."

"How do you know? Did he say he did?" Chief Chin asked. He seemed a bit offended that Scott was freely volunteering information to a girl and stranger.

"No, but he was with Ruffner last winter when we sold them the blue-nuts."

"I thought Donnelly was the only one who dealt in slaves. The council is not going to like hearing that Ruffner is trafficking in slavery," the chief said. "The Ichneumons promised to stop Donnelly's raids. Could this be Ruffner's operation?"

Rex wondered if he had misheard. "Wouldn't your council be upset with anyone who sold Wapitis into slavery?" he asked. He also wondered who the Ichneumons and Prussians were.

"What? Of course, but council business isn't your concern."

Indira looked ready to comment but didn't.

"Anyway, the feldwebel was in a hurry to go," Scott said. "He told that dead bastard lying by the gate that he needed to deliver them to a buyer in Roanoke." He then noticed the dead guard in front of the tent and studied Rex for a moment. "Are you a deserter from the Prussian army? Forget it. I'm just happy you freed us. How many did you kill?"

"Several," Rex answered. "What do you mean by *feldwebel*?"

"Several? Donnelly will kill all of us," Chin said.

"Not if we kill them first," Scott said. "Never heard of a feldwebel? Well, I guess you're not a deserter."

"Our York ancestors used the term *sergeant* for such a Prussian solider," the chief said. "In the territories, most retired Prussian military men you'll meet are former feldwebels." Apparently, the chief felt the need to enlighten him, or perhaps to frighten him because he added, "You don't want to mess with a feldwebel. They're the emperor's killers. Where did you say you were from?"

Emperor of what Rex wondered. And Roanoke, that name for a town on the east side of the mountains couldn't just be coincidental. How many people have survived the same ill-fated trip from Earth? Rex pondered while considering his next move.

"How did you kill…?" Scott started to ask.

"You think he'll go through Narrows or cut across the hot springs?" The chief asked, cutting off Scott's comment about the dead slavers. The man's rudeness snapped Rex's attention back to the discussion as the freed warrior answered that he figured the Prussians would follow the river.

"I'll call a meeting to organize a posse to go after them."

"Don't bother. I've heard enough. There're only three of them, and they can't be but a few hours ahead of us. Even better, the Prussians shouldn't be expecting pursuit. Get something to eat, Scott, while Indira finds you a horse to ride," Rex said before turning back to the chief who appeared offended.

"The council needs to be involved. I don't want some stranger making it worse. Scott, stay here. Your help is needed to get us to Smithtown."

"The two of us can handle it," Rex said. He wasn't at all sure of that, but after all the mayhem he'd precipitated to free Indira's sister, he intended to complete the task.

"Sorry, chief, but I'm going with him to ensure that Tara isn't left behind," Scott said.

Indira was not happy to learn that Rex and Scott would pursue Lily and Tara's abductors without her help. The chief wasn't happy with Scott's disobedience.

"You'll get them killed, rushing after them without a plan. Indira, you're not going. I'm not taking a chance losing both Hopkins girls. You're staying here. Now, before you two rush off and make a blunder that gets Lilly killed, wait until I find other men to help."

"No offense, Chief, but I don't want more men. Indira, the chief's right. You need to help with the horses and your ill grandmother." Staying to help her grandmother appeared to sway the obstinate girl.

"I'm keeping the rifle." Indira had earlier grabbed one of the guards' rolling block rifles.

"Have you ever shot a rifle?" Rex asked. "It's not safe to run around with a gun and strangers. Listen to the chief." He figured that wasn't the best advice to give her, but Chief Chin was the one in charge. He looked around for his horse and spotted it over with the Donnelly horses in the corral near the river, its reins wrapped around the saddle horn. The girl apparently didn't believe in hitching horses.

"I've shot a musket. You couldn't have fooled the guards without my help."

"Indira, you're not coming. Go help your grandmother. First, help Scott pick a horse out of our collection, and tie mine up before it wanders off."

Chief Chin and Scott appeared amused by Indira's willfulness. Her mulishness, along with their amusement, irritated Rex. Indira's help might prove useful, but he was finished endangering that courageous girl. He even felt a bit of guilt for using her earlier as bait.

"Chief, I wouldn't delay getting your people out of here. There have to be more of those bastards across the river who may return at any moment. Also, I'm leaving those other two horses in Indira's care. Is that a problem for you?"

"Those horses have a D brand. They're Donnelly's property, and he hangs anyone who steals one of his horses. You want to put the Hopkins girl at risk of hanging. Donnelly doesn't care how old the thieves are; they're just horse thieves to him."

Rex didn't have a response, and the chief added, "Do what you want. I need to talk with the furnace manager. Then we're headed to Smithtown." The chief turned and started to walk off, shaking his head as if he couldn't believe such foolhardiness.

"Before you go," Rex said, "Scott and I each selected two rifles to take. I want to have a spare in case one develops mechanical problems, such as a broken firing pin. The other four rifles, you hand out as you think best."

The two boxes of ammo pilfered from the slavers' tents brought Rex's supply of ammo for the rifles to a hundred rounds; he didn't share those rounds.

Chief Chin and two other men then walked over to the salt furnace to talk with the workers. Clenching her rifle, Indira slipped off to round up a horse for Scott. Rex let her keep the rifle after he made sure it was unloaded. A wasted effort, he figured, since she hadn't objected to him checking the rifle's breech. Undoubtedly, that resourceful young lady already had pocketed a box or two of ammo.

Some of the freed Wapiti women had discovered a ten-liter keg of schnapps and the slaver's food stores. Several of the women had quickly whipped together a venison stew using the guards' fire and supplies. The delicious aroma reminded Rex he hadn't eaten anything but a few hard biscuits since landing in this strange world yesterday.

He whistled for Indira's attention. She warily trotted her horse over. It crowded in and grabbed some of the oats Zack's horse was munching. Oats the Wapitis had found inside the stockade.

"Indira, it was a pleasure to work with you. Please be careful, and help the chief get everyone home safely. When I get back with your sister, I'll show you how to shoot."

"Can my grandmother use the other horse?"

"Well, I'd hope you wouldn't make your grandmother walk," Rex said. "They're your horses, your share of the spoils of war." A radiant smile was his reward. In a few years, Indira would be a beautiful woman, Rex thought, then cautioned, "Don't let Donnelly's men catch you. The chief said he hangs horse thieves."

"After what happened here, horse theft is the least of our worries. He'll kill or enslave every Wapiti he catches. Don't worry about us; free my sister," Indira said. She leaned over from the saddle and gave Rex a hug, then started tearing up.

"Come on, girl, stop crying. I'll find your sister. Besides, if you're crying, you might not see the tree branches and get knocked out of the saddle." That got a laugh out of her. If any of the Hopkins made it back to their home, Rex figured it would be her. "Oh, by the way, you ought to share some of your ammo with the chief."

The girl just grinned at him.

Rex then walked over to the stockade wall to retrieve the split blue coat and hat he'd shed before climbing the wall. He might need the disguise again. Scott had watched him while he gathered and dusted off his clothing. Rex saw Scott's puzzled look and told him, "Never hurts to confuse the enemy. Get something to eat; then find one of those dead slavers' blue coats and hat to wear. Hurry, I don't want the slavers getting too far ahead of us."

Dealing with the dead delayed their start. Rex and Scott helped load the Wapiti dead and injured in Donnelly's flat-bottom riverboats. The few healthy young men from the hut would paddle the boats to a Wapiti village down river for proper care and burial. Fearing Clem's return, Rex suggested that the Wapitis leave

Donnelly's dead and abandon the stockade. Clem could deal with the dead guards.

The size of the trees encountered along the river trail meant they'd reentered the virgin forest. As their horses trod along the shaded trail under the massive trees, he realized that his new friend was the talkative sort. The young Wapiti would probably be willing to tell him all about the Prussians, but Rex hesitated to ask. He feared the attention his ignorance of common knowledge might attract.

"What do you do for a living? I need to find employment."

"A little bit of everything, but mainly timbering and blue-nuts," the Wapiti said, while studying the trees, and then added, "It's going to be a good year for squirrels."

For sure, it seemed everywhere Rex had been in the last two days, he had heard squirrels chattering. He asked about the blue-nuts.

"They're the valuable winter-sloe, our money crop. In the fall, the tree has a plum-sized fruit with a nut-like pit. Crack open the nut and you'll find two blue colored kernels. That's what everyone buys."

"What does the nut taste like? Sounds like a lot of work opening the nuts. Is there any money to be made?"

"You've never seen blue winter-sloe kernels? Where're you from?"

"Don't ask. Are there any of those trees nearby?"

Scott appeared a bit irritated by his refusal to answer a common question. To smooth feelings, Rex added, "I'm not trying to be mysterious. Just accept that my home is on the other side of the empire and I'm not at liberty to talk about it. I can tell you that winter-sloe trees don't grow there."

"Really, I'd never have guessed," Scott said. Rex had to laugh. Suddenly the warrior turned serious. "Lord, you're not one of those people the church warns us about, a false prophet?"

He didn't like the sound of that, or his look. "I've no idea what you're talking about."

"Jesuit Wilhelm visits every fall and always asks about strangers who claim to be from other worlds."

Rex felt a chill, as the Wapiti studied him for a moment and then added. "The church pays a ten thousand D-mark reward for such a person."

"They pay a reward for crazy people? Why?" Rex asked. What a mad, evil world fate had hurled him. He hoped his face didn't look as alarmed as he felt.

"No idea," Scott said, looking perplexed. "I've heard the priests take them to Berlin, question them, then burn them. I have never heard why or of anyone like that around here. Still Jesuit Wilhelm comes ever year and asks the same question."

"Burns the poor souls? What a way to treat a disturbed soul."

"There must be something dangerous about such a person for the church to be concerned enough to pay a large reward Do you think there could be other worlds?"

"Beats me, I have enough trouble with this one. The nonsense churches worry about . . . tell me about the winter-sloe business. I need a job when we get finish chasing these bastards."

Rex now hoped Indira didn't tell people he claimed to be from America. He had been lucky in his selection of clothing that fateful day, tattered gray coveralls, now filthy, and old slip-on brown leather boots that looked similar to Scott's boots.

"Okay, I owe you my life, so no more questions, stranger. Ask whatever you want. Your mystery is safe with me." Scott soon had him educated on the local money crop of blue nuts. In the process he demonstrated, as had Indira, that the Wapitis were a literate people.

"The pit, or nut, contains a kernel similar to a walnut in size and shape. Bootleggers buy the raw kernel. I've heard it's a complicated process, but they can make cocaine from it. Roasting the kernel changes something and it can't be used to make cocaine."

"The Wapitis use cocaine?" Rex asked.

"We're human. Here's what the nuts look like," Scott said. He opened a small tan-colored drawstring cotton bag and poured out several blue nuts. He offered two to Rex, who then remembered those nuts he'd mistaken for walnuts in Zack's saddlebag. "Chew the nuts and you'll feel a mild shot of energy."

Rex did. After a few minutes, he felt a slight increase in his alertness, similar to what he'd expect from a cup of coffee. This world's caffeine, he reckoned. The taste reminded him of peanuts. Since this world, or at least the Wapitis, hadn't yet discovered coffee, Rex planned to find his own stash of winter-sloe nuts. The thought nagged him that he should learn more about the active alkaloid that provided the stimulant effect. Caffeine was fine; an alien cocaine precursor might not be.

"A person who eats a few roasted kernels won't feel any euphoria or high from cocaine," Scott said. "The effect lasts for an hour or two. Drug dealers don't like our roasted winter-sloe nuts." Rex thought that amazing information.

The eels that Indira had cautioned him about, he learned, had finished spawning. The eels arrived with the winter and spent several months eating everything that fell into the river. After spawning in late spring, the eels disappeared back down the river. Scott figured that by next week, all the black eels would have left the river above the Hopkins River junction. Rex learned that a mature black eel reached two meters in length and fifteen kilograms in weight. He also learned the name of the river they were following. The Wapitis called it the Southern River.

"Those black eels can drag a horse under. Still, they're good to eat; just be careful removing the hook," Scott laughed. He looked at the sun's location. "We'd better ride faster and talk less. It'll soon be dark, and we have a ways to go."

"Will the Prussians stop at dark or keep going?"

"Stop, no one travels at night. I think the Prussians will stop at the falls tonight and cross the North River in the morning. If Donnelly's men find out about your massacre of his men, we're all in danger."

"Even the kidnappers?" Rex asked while wondering about Scott's night travel remark. Were panthers the reason?

"For sure, that's the reason the chief went over to the salt furnace, to ask Donnelly's workers to send a message. He was going to tell the saline workers that Ruffner's men killed the guards, allowing the Wapitis to escape. He fears the bastard will be even more brutal toward captured Wapitis if he thinks we've started murdering his guards."

"What a boneheaded move," Rex said. "It'll endanger the women. Besides, the chief's wrong. Animals like Donnelly only respect those who fight back. If the Wapitis want peace, they need to fight back. Slavery's an evil business that deserves no quarter. Chief Chin, of all people, should know better after wearing an iron slave collar himself."

"The chief is a believer in not responding to oppression and insults with violence. I'm not," Scott said. "I've always argued we should fight back, but Pete and many on the council are afraid to. The Jesuits don't help with their teaching that violence begets violence. They say trust God to deal with people like Donnelly. I agree with you; kill the bastards."

Rex then remembered Scott's comment that the chief had sent a message. Did the salt works have a telegraph? "Won't the chief's message take a few days to reach Donnelly?"

"No, the salt furnace has pigeons. I figure he'll know by evening."

"Homing pigeons, you're kidding." Scott gave him a questioning look. "Ah, don't the hawks around here just eat them?" Rex asked, remembering where he was.

"Occasionally, but these are smart and fast pigeons, and the hawks rarely bother them. Don't your people use them?"

Think before talking, Rex reprimanded himself. Excellent advice anywhere, but in a strange world with inhabitants whose taboos he hadn't yet learned, it was extra important. Scott didn't need to be thinking that his partner was a dangerous alien.

"I was never around them much. What's Donnelly's business?"

"Lord, I thought everyone used pigeons?" Scott said. "Where are you …? Oops, sorry. You asked about his business, he's in anything that turns a profit. His business used to be trading furs, winter-sloe nuts, and purple ginseng. Now it's grown to include whiskey, tobacco, red-salt, tracking down runaway slaves, and, of late, kidnapping Wapitis."

After another sip of water, Scott added. "His main operation is near where the Sulfur River meets the Southern River. The man also spends time in Roanoke and has business there."

Rex figured that Scott was referring to the Greenbrier River, the New River, and Hinton. "Any other trails the kidnappers might take?"

"Sure, lots of trails, but the Prussian is unaware that we escaped. He has no reason to think he's in trouble with Donnelly or that we're following him. Using one of the other trails through the mountains west of the river to reach Narrows, where Ruffner has his base would add several days to his trip. Then there's always the risk he meets one of Cinnabar's bands of marauders or some angry Wapitis or Clovis chased out of the Jarrell River by Donnelly's other raiders."

"I hope Chief Chin has enough sense to leave before those raiders return," Rex said, thinking of Indira.

"Don't worry about that. That fearful old weasel won't waste any time getting back to Johnson Village."

Scott's use of the Clovis name for the native inhabitants solidified Rex's belief that he was just one of many people from Earth who had survived the transit between worlds. He asked who Cinnabar was.

"The rumor about Cinnabar is that he's an Ichneumon. Regardless, he's a murderous creature who heads a tribe of cannibalistic savages and fugitives from both empires. They live like animals in those mountains south of here, but they're nothing to worry about along the river. They never come this far north." The Wapiti warrior waved in the direction where Boone County would be on Earth.

"What kind of weapons do they use?" Rex asked and wondered what Scott meant by *Ichneumon* and what the other empire was.

"They'll use axes and clubs, but prefer flintlock muskets and bows. There's a spring up ahead, let's stop," Scott said.

The foul-tasting water from the canvas bag Rex found at the stockade had him wishing he had a good stainless steel water bottle. He didn't need diarrhea or some intestinal parasite incapacitating him. Spring water sounded good.

"But Cinnabar isn't our worry," Scott said. "Our problem is that Donnelly's men can travel down the Southern River a lot faster than we can travel up it. Plus, there's always the chance the small stockade at River Falls has pigeons and Donnelly sends them a warning. So we need to find the girls tonight."

Rex agreed, and they pushed the horses harder after drinking from the spring.

Chapter 3

Franciscka Weidman, studying her surroundings, wondered what out there made the retired Prussian Army feldwebel nervous. The man was nearly two meters of massive muscle. She couldn't believe a bigger man existed in this wilderness, nor one with more experience in surviving fights and wars. Feldwebel Burgdorf had stopped their column about two kilometers from River Falls and sat on his horse studying the trail ahead through the forest.

"Why'd we stop, Herr Burgdorf?" she asked. Nothing appeared different about the trail ahead from the last thirty-some kilometers they'd covered. Behind them were the captives and Hans, a more normal-size man, but he was sinewy and tough. He had thrown those bounded Wapiti girls onto the horse as if they were made of feathers. Unlike Feldwebel Burgdorf, who was always polite, Franciscka thought Hans repulsive, even treacherous, with his suggestive sexual comments about her and the captives when the feldwebel wasn't near.

Franciscka knew little about the slave business, but the cruel, senseless treatment she had just witnessed at that horrific slaver's stockade made no sense. Emperor Schnabel needed to get serious about enforcing anti-slavery laws in the territories and borderlands. She damn well intended to make Berlin aware of Donnelly's operation when she got back to Roanoke.

The feldwebel ignored her question. Waiting for the man to decide their next move, she thought about the gift. Based on the lateness of the day, the slavers should have finished off their present, a keg of fine schnapps, and should be in no condition to trouble them tonight. Franciscka thought that a clever move. Feldwebel Burgdorf finally made a decision. He turned off the trail toward the riverbank.

"Herr Burgdorf, why didn't we go on to the stockade? Is something wrong?" Franciscka asked.

The feldwebel didn't explain his odd action of stopping about two kilometers below the outpost by the falls. Franciscka was in no position to challenge his decision. After a moment of ignoring her, Burgdorf said, "There's nothing to worry about. I like this spot. Now help me hide our tracks. Hans, set up the camp on a sandy section of the riverbank."

"Should I collect wood for a fire after I cover the tracks?" Franciscka asked. It was getting rather dark.

"No, we'll skip a fire tonight. Instead, help Hans tie the captives to those trees." The feldwebel pointed to two sycamore trees on opposite sides of the campsite. "It'll present a more dispersed target for any potential rescue attempt. Hans, you sleep close to the horses. I'll stay near one girl captive, and Franciscka, you stay by the other. Both of you keep your rifles handy."

So much for nothing to worry about, Franciscka thought.

The gnats and mosquitos ruined an otherwise beautiful camping spot as she settled in for a miserable night. Franciscka Guderian Weidman hoped her father, a wealthy Berlin banker, didn't learn of her trip into the interior of this untamed territory. She had graduated with a master's degree in economics from Heidelberg University and accepted a position with the Imperial Revenue Service.

The IRS, for reasons known only to them, had assigned Franciscka to a three-year tour of duty in the Guderian Province of the Royal Western Territories. She loved the assignment, figuring it would be a great adventure before she had to settle down and consider starting a family. She had been betroth to Archduke Habsburg's eldest son, Rudolf as a child. The Archduke and her parents weren't pleased with her decision, but Rudolf from whom she had expected a fuss, was supportive of her plan. An uncharitable person might even term his attitude as indifferent. She suspected that didn't bode well for his fidelity in their future relationship. Emperor Schnabel needed to discourage these loveless arranged marriages among the aristocrats.

After a several months in the IRS New Hamburg office, Franciscka had learned of an IRS investigator position opening in Roanoke and had volunteered. Tired of audits, she wanted adventure. Her new boss in Roanoke, Joe Hansen, had supplied one.

"Franciscka, I heard a rumor that James Donnelly is planning a raid on a Wapiti eel fishing camp, presumably to catch slaves."

"Where you hear that? From your network of snitches and moles?" she asked. Her boss had ignored her question.

"I figure if a certain two Wapiti girls were among the captives, Len Ruffner will dispatch a crew to bring the girls back to their purchaser, Heinz William."

"Heinz?" Franciscka asked. "If the rumors are true about his reprehensible behavior, you need to stop Ruffner."

"Me? I'm not the sheriff," Joe said. "I have an idea, Franciscka, but it's dangerous. I was thinking of asking Len to allow a young engineer to travel with his next group going to the salt furnace. I'll tell him the IRS wanted an engineer's opinion on the feasibility of building a toll road along the river from Narrows to the saline works. The idea of building a road would be popular with Herr Ruffner. The engineer would be in a position to know what happened, if she was willing."

"I'm willing, but I know nothing about engineering."

"Neither does Len," her boss said. "Talk to a couple of engineers and pick up some construction lingo. Rape is my worry. There truly are savages out there. Can you manage an androgynous look? Handle a pistol?"

The full moon lit the valley in a silvery light that made following the Prussian trail easy, but as Rex appreciated, the light would make it easy for the Prussians to spot them.

"Those Prussians will stop at River Falls. I want to stop now, to avoid detection," Scott said.

"How far do you figure to the falls?"

"A kilometer or so, it's not far."

"I'm more concerned about leaving our horses, ammo, and extra weapons unguarded. I'm no expert on horses, but could they walk with us, or are they too noisy?"

"Damn, that's a point to consider," Scott said. "We'd better bring them."

They walked with their horses the remaining kilometer's distance to the edge of the clearing around the river crossing and little stockade. As Rex and Scott neared the edge of the River Falls clearing, shouts erupted from the men in the log ring camp. Men were shouting to a boat illuminated by a sudden flaring of the campfire on the riverbank.

"That's the fort crew," Scott whispered. "Someone is coming down the river."

Rex handed Scott his horse's reins and sprinted up the trail to reach the edge of the clearing while the men were distracted by two boats landing. He stopped in the last dark shadow area before the clearing, but close enough that he heard the half-dozen men in the boats asking if the Prussians had arrived. Rex quickly realized from the excited conversations that the hawks had missed a meal and the pigeons had delivered the news of the massacre at Salt Furnace. He also learned the Prussians hadn't arrived at the crossing.

"The Prussians haven't arrived," Rex said on returning to the horses.

"How'd we get ahead of them?" Scott asked, while petting his horse's neck. They both studied the surrounding area.

"I missed their cutoff, I just hope they didn't cross the river," Rex said. "At least we were lucky, they didn't bushwhack us. Let's back track and find their side trail. If their leader saw us, or hears this commotion, he'll know something's not right. If he's smart, he'll avoid the fort until he knows what Donnelly's thugs are planning. If it was me, I'd climb the mountain, and find a high path to use for slipping by the fort, unobserved."

"The guy is a retired feldwebel and dumb ones don't live to retire. Let's ease back down the trail and try to ambush them. A sandy beach area is about two kilometers back down the trail. Others occasionally use it for a camp, maybe the Prussians did. I don't think Donnelly's men will move till sunrise."

"We're in a damn precarious spot," Rex said. "Armed men above us, and who knows how many Clem will bring up from the salt furnace? We know the Prussians are hiding somewhere nearby. I don't want Indira's sister killed in a cross fire." Rex's reminder stopped Scott's turn back down the river trail.

"Nor do I want Tara Smith killed. You're the man with the magic; what's your suggestion?"

Good question, Rex thought. At first light, there could be several groups of confused armed men shooting at each other. That couldn't be healthy for the two women.

"I'm not interested in freeing Lily by getting her killed. Instead, we'll help the Prussians escape this trap, give them a day or two to settle down, then hit them at night."

"Ah, man, I like that. Besides, we can't kill too many of those slavers. So do we hit the gang at the falls now or ambush them on the trail in the morning?"

Such bloodthirstiness, Rex thought. "The men at the falls, who are they?"

"Those bastards, they're part of Clem's raiders. He put them there to block any Wapitis from escaping up the river. They're every bit as mean as those guards at the stockade."

That would take some doing, in Rex's opinion, thinking of the cruelty he had witness at Salt Furnace. Scott sensed his tentativeness and added. "I understand you're new to the valley, but trust me, all of Clem's men are rapists and killers, or he wouldn't have them."

"Let's watch the trail for an hour or so and see if the Prussian goes for the high ground. That'll give this gang time to bed down; then we'll decide." Rex said, still reluctance to start killing again.

About an hour later, a shadowy figure emerged from the woods about 200 meters down-river from their hiding spot. The shadow paused and studied the trail in both directions. About a minute after the shadow vanished, five men and seven horses stole across the trail and disappeared up the hillside.

The Prussians response encouraged Rex. Perhaps his reasoning wasn't that alien and he could blend in among the inhabitants. He waited another hour for the dead of night; then he poked Scott awake, and they walked back to the falls. Their horses left to graze.

The leader of Donnelly's men had posted two guards on the trail below the falls, but the guards were careless. They were sharing a clay pipe and talking between puffs, gossiping about their planned ambush of the Prussians and the recovery of the Wapiti women. After several minutes of eavesdropping, Rex realized their real concern was that Clem might make them wait until after everyone else had had their turn with the women. Scott was beside him listening to the guards. Rex could about sense his "I told you so."

Disgusted with the guards' plan, he whispered. "What will happen, if we take out the two guards and shoot up the camp? Will the survivors attack, flee, or hide?"

"They'll panic and head for the boats where we'll be able to get most of them," Scott answered. They were among several large boulders at the toe of the hillside and about thirty meters from the guards. "How about you take out the guards and while the camp's in an uproar I run up the hill to that tree where I can look down into the camp?"

Rex liked that idea. In answer, he laid out five cartridges on the rock, nodded to his partner, and drew a bead on the farthest guard.

The first guard never knew what hit him. The camp exploded, men screaming and firing wildly as Rex shot the second guard before he could reach the stockade.

"Hey, you assholes, we're Donnelly men," someone from the stockade yelled. After no response, he added, "Who are you? What do you want?"

In answer, Scott then fired four shots over the next few minutes. Whether those shots hit any of Donnelly's men, Rex couldn't tell. However, the return gunfire from the stockade stopped, the campfire suddenly extinguished.

Scott returned to Rex's location by the boulder a few minutes later. "Should I tell him who we are?"

"No, let them stew," Rex said and asked, "How many?"

"I hit two for sure and two maybes. They didn't run for the boats as I had expected. Now what," Scott asked while munching on a rock-hard biscuit from one of the saddlebags they had grabbed at the stockade.

"Is there another river on the right a couple of kilos from here?" Rex asked, thinking of the Gauley River on Earth.

"It's not that far," Scott said. "I wonder if our Prussian knows about it."

"Well, he came down the river, so I suspect he does," Rex said. "He needs to get past the river-crossing garrison and head south along the river, not take a northern detour. He may lie low today, try slipping past River Falls tonight or work his way along the ridges until he's past River Falls and can safely drop back onto the river trail."

"His danger will be running into more Donnelly men coming down the trail," Scott said. "I don't think he knows Donnelly believes he's the one who killed his guards. Which means going to the man's hideaway would be a fatal mistake for the Prussian. So he's trapped, just doesn't know it. What now?"

Rex had to admit Scott had raised a good point.

"Your chief's message stopped the Prussians, but it endangered Lily and Tara. We have to stop them and free the women before they stumbles into Donnelly's men who may shoot with no warning and accidently kill the women. Let's get the horses and swim the river before the sun is up. We'll await developments on the other side. The eels are gone, right?"

Franciscka never received an answer from her boss, Herr Hansen, on whether Feldwebel Burgdorf was in on their plans to free the two teachers. So far, the feldwebel acted as if he intended to deliver the women as captives to Herr Ruffner. Why, otherwise, haul the women to Roanoke before releasing them when their home was just down the river? Or did her boss, Joe Hansen, have another plan that he hadn't shared with her, such as a plan to hold them as hostages in order to induce the Wapitis' cooperation with the IRS's cocaine investigation.

Franciscka had almost worked up the nerve to ask Burgdorf his intentions when the worried feldwebel stopped the column. Now a half hour later she could hear shouting coming from up the river near the little fort at the falls.

"Why would Donnelly's men be shouting?" she softly asked Burgdorf.

"Who knows?" the feldwebel said. "Hans, we're breaking camp. Get the girls ready to move and make sure their gags are tight."

One reason Franciscka vacillated in confronting Burgdorf was her orders. Joe Hansen had told her to stay in character as an engineer interested in toll road locations. Let events unfold without getting involved or taking sides, a strategy that had seemed plausible in a comfortable Roanoke office. Her boss didn't want Ruffner worrying whether she might be a potential witness to his and Heinz William's flouting of various laws. Events had made those two criminals the least of her worries now that the Wapitis or Donnelly's men might be after them for blood. The Wapiti warriors would never believe her story.

"Get out of my way," a panicky Hans said. He shoved Franciscka's horse out of his way and tossed the Smith girl across the saddle like a sack. "Make yourself useful. Hold these reins while I get the other bitch."

The creep tossed her the reins for the horse the Smith girl was on and went to fetch the Hopkins girl. The full moon allowed her to see clearly their prisoners. They were miserable, hands bound behind their backs and a filthy piece of hemp rope tied cruelly across their mouths. Mosquito bites covered them with countless red marks.

"What's the matter, Hans? Fear her father might catch you?" Franciscka said. She needed to stop needling the jerk before he lashed out. She had enough enemies.

Burgdorf waved her over. "No talking. Now, pick a path up that hillside. We'll hide behind the ridge-top. Lead your horse. It's too steep to ride. Hans will tie the prisoners to the saddle and lead those horses. Keep your rifle ready, but don't shoot unless I tell you. I'll be the rear guard and cover our trail. Any questions?" Franciscka shook her head. "Good. Now go and don't stop until you hit the ridge top."

The gray-green Prussian field uniform Feldwebel Burgdorf and she wore blended into the shadows from the moonlight. Hans wore yellow leather pants and a yellow shirt, but the dirt and grime on the clothes did a credible job of blending him into the shadows. They were across the trail in a flash, and she saw no one.

The hillside was just short of being a cliff, and Franciscka had a tough time breaking a trail. Going straight up the slope wasn't possible; the horses couldn't get a purchase in the soft soil and leaf-mulch surface. The rocks had a moss covering that the horse's hoof slipped off. The conditions forced Franciscka to travel sideways at a slight upward gradient around the hillside to a ravine that allowed them to make a more direct ascent toward the summit.

About an hour after crossing the trail by the riverbank, gunfire started near the falls. They were too far up the side ravine to see the falls area. She had no idea who was fighting, but it didn't bode well for them.

Three hours later, exhausted, Franciscka cleared the summit and started looking for a spring to camp by. She hoped Burgdorf was successful covering their tracks and had some idea of who was after them. She had figured that the Wapitis had stumbled into Donnelly's men at River Falls. About hundred meters down the back slope of the summit, she located a small spring and decided they would stop there.

Franciscka helped Hans untie the prisoners from the saddles and remove their gags, and after he left to check on Burgdorf, she untied their hands.

"Go drink and clean up. Say a word and I'll tie you up again," Franciscka said. She was bigger than both Wapiti girls were, and they had suffered terrible abuse over the last two days. As a result, she didn't think they were in any condition to escape her.

"Who are you? Where are you taking us?" the girl called Lily asked.

"No questions. Take advantage of the chance to wash off before they return."

After the prisoners had cleaned up a bit, she handed each of them half of a chocolate bar and a hard biscuit for a meal. She figured the no-fire rule was still in effect and sat down to wait for the feldwebel's return. The horses found some grass below the spring. The men arrived just ahead of a beautiful sunrise.

"What are they doing loose? Hans get them tied and gagged," Burgdorf said.

"They won't be worth much to Ruffner with gangrene hands or dead from dehydration," Franciscka said. The big Prussian studied her a moment, then told Hans not to tie the knots too tight.

"I'm going back down where I can watch the trail, see who's shooting who. Hans, keep the captives quiet, and both of you stay off the ridgeline. We'll head out tonight. And no fires," Burgdorf added. He grabbed several hard biscuits and headed back over the ridge.

Finishing with the weapon cleaning, Rex watched the dawn gradually light up the valley. It promised to be a beautiful May morning. Since the chance of returning to Earth was none, he needed to resolve several pressing issues of personal hygiene, such as dental floss, soap, a bath, a shave, clean clothes, and dry boots. The sound of horses interrupted his thoughts of a hot shower.

Nine horsemen thundered by on the trail across the river. The five riders in the lead wore light blue coats and black felt campaign hats. The other four were dressed in an assortment of skins, leathers, and raggedy clothes. Several of the shabby-looking riders carried flintlock rifles; the other riders in the blue coats had the modern rolling block rifles. None of the riders looked familiar, and Rex asked, "Who are they, the group that had been in the Jarrell River?"

Scott eased in beside him on the rock and spotted the Topcon scope. "May I?" He indicated the Topcon, and Rex scooted out of his way. "Oh man, this is the best telescope I've ever used. Where'd you get it?"

"Off the Internet . . . ah, from a trader. Recognize any of those riders?" Rex said. He slid his cleaned Ruger pistol into the backpack to keep Scott from spotting the pistol and asking questions he wasn't prepared to answer.

"I do. The big ugly bastard with the turkey feather in his hat is Donnelly's man over the salt furnace and stockade, Clem Hubbard. You have anything to eat. Oh, while I think of it, be careful around that rattler on the ledge below the rock."

Rex had a live and let live philosophy toward snakes. If they didn't bother him, he didn't kill them and this one was ignoring them.

"I have a small bag of nuts in my horse's left saddle bag, if the river didn't mess them up. Hand me your rifle and I'll clean it while I have the cleaning kit out." He unloaded Scott's rifle and ran a cleaning patch through the barrel while the Wapiti warrior continued to study the far hillside with the Topcon.

"I found the Prussian," Scott said. "I'll bet you're right. They're going to try sneaking by River Falls tonight. He's by that double-stacked rock pillar near the ridge top. I'll bet he has the women stashed just over the ridge."

Rex was studying the Prussian through the scope when Scott tapped his shoulder.

"Trouble, three of Clem's men are rowing across the ford. I'll beat they're checking for horse tracks. If they walk down past the falls, they'll spot ours. What do you want to do?"

The odd sound disturbed her sleep again, like a whimper. Franciscka had found a sunny, warm spot near the ridge top. She was dreaming of a hot bath. Then a cloud blocked the sun just as she heard that odd sound again. Suddenly she was alert, remembered where she was, and sat up to check the prisoners. Hans had pulled off Tara's pants and was trying to pry her legs apart without making any noise. The Wapiti girl's writhing made it clear that Hans intended to rape her.

Franciscka got soundlessly to her feet while picking up her rifle. She tiptoed to Hans and slammed her rifle butt down on his head. He collapsed onto Tara. She feared for a moment that her blow had killed him. He stunk, though in fairness they all did. Still, she hated to touch him, but she couldn't chance he'd start screaming. She twisted Hans's hands behind his back and tied them. One thing for sure-on this trip, she was getting proficient at tying up people, she thought as she gaged him.

Tara was trying to get back into her pants, but her tied hands interfered with the effort.

"Just wait. He needs to see what Hans did," Franciscka said.

The naked Smith woman had a venomous scowl. Tara had started her menses, which added to her woebegone appearance. They all needed a bath. Even the gnats were starting to avoid them.

Events had ended Franciscka's hope of gaining the two Wapiti fräuleins' trust by saving them from that pervert William. It had been a ludicrous idea. Her new priority was to survive the fiasco. If Burgdorf took offense at her attacking Hans and ran her off, then she was in trouble. If the Wapiti men found them, could they defend themselves with only two rifles? The shooting last night suggested the Wapitis were hunting for the girls. Franciscka wondered if she'd end up a slave in some mountain hovel picking blue nuts. She wished she had saved one of her chocolate bars.

Franciscka watched Friedrich Burgdorf creep from tree to tree until the ridgeline shielded him from watchers along the river trail. He stopped on seeing the half-naked Tara and the bound Hans.

"Explain yourself," Burgdorf said in a low voice that frightened her. "Those slavers have found our trail and will attack as soon as the sun sets, might even now be trying to sneak around the ridge to cut us off, and you do this."

"He was trying to rape her. What else could I do? Should I get the horses?"

"That's why the prisoner has her pants off? Hans did that?" Burgdorf glared at the Smith woman, ending her hateful stare, and making her cower. "Does he know who hit him?"

"Yes. I used the rifle butt."

"He won't rest until he kills you. Damn rapist." Burgdorf gave Hans a solid kick in the ribs that woke him. "Help her get her pants on," the feldwebel said as he cut Hans's gag.

"Untie me. I'm going to kill that bitch," Hans said as Franciscka untied Tara, who immediately pulled on her pants.

"Ruffner didn't want these women molested. You knew that, so why did you try?"

"They're just animals. You know Donnelly's men have already raped them, so what's the harm? Now, untie me, or I'll start screaming, and you can tell Chem why you're so sweet on these savages. Look at that dirty slut." Hans tried to kick Tara in the face, and Burgdorf held him back.

"You threatened to scream, give away our location?"

"Damn right, I've have had enough."

"Is that so," Burgdorf said and slashed the man's throat. Blood poured over the Prussian's arm as he held Hans up for a minute before casting his body aside. "That son of a whore won't be screaming now."

The murder had horrified the two Wapiti women and alarmed her. "Time to end this nonsense," he added. "Ungag the prisoners."

Franciscka was suddenly fearful. Did he intend to kill the women, even her, then slip off by himself to escape, unburdened by human luggage? She reached for her rifle.

"Don't worry, fräulein, that's not my plan." After a pause, Franciscka put her rifle down and untied the women.

"Hans and I were hired by the IRS to free two school teachers from Donnelly's slavers, Tara Smith and Lily Hopkins," Burgdorf continued. "You're those two, right?" The wary Wapitis nodded as Franciscka cut their ropes, freeing them. "Hans worked for Ruffner, same as I. She's an engineer, works for the toll road survey. We had to pretend to be slavers to escape the salt furnace area. I was going to release you at the falls. Why Donnelly's men turned on us, I don't know, makes no sense to me. Ruffner and Donnelly had always gotten along just fine. Doesn't matter now; they've found us and will come tonight. We need to be gone before dark."

"You'll let us go?" The Hopkins woman asked. She appeared doubtful. "We're free to walk away right now?"

Franciscka had picked up her rifle. Lily wasn't the only woman with doubts about the feldwebel's change of heart. With her thumb on the rifle hammer, ready to cock it, she stepped back to gain some space in case the man turned violent.

"You can even have the horse, but remember, a dozen angry slavers are waiting at the bottom of the hill," Burgdorf said. "We'll all have a better chance of surviving by staying together. My original plan was to cross the river and go south through Narrows and on to Roanoke. The Jesuit organization would get you home. Now I'm thinking of heading north to the headwater of the Hopkins River to avoid Donnelly's men. After you're safe, Franciscka and I will find a way to Roanoke. Do either of you have a better suggestion for us escaping this trap?"

The Wapiti women appeared flabbergasted but managed to shake their heads in the negative. Several shots rang out down by the river, interrupting their discussion.

"Lord, I wish I knew who that other party is. It has to be someone with the Wapitis; though I didn't think those wimps had the nerve," Burgdorf said, and then added, "Let's hope they're not one of Cinnabar's war parties." He bent to wipe his knife clean on Hans's vest.

"Maybe they'll kill each other," Franciscka said. The two Wapiti women looked just as puzzled as she felt. She didn't know what to think. Maybe her boss had hired Burgdorf, but he had chosen to keep the information from her. More likely, the retired feldwebel feared the Wapitis might catch him and had decided to abandon Ruffner's plan, pretend he was on an IRS rescue mission, not transporting slaves.

Donnelly's men in the boat had spent several minutes half-heartedly searching the ford ramp while casting fearful glances toward the silent, dark forest hillside looming over them. Finding no fresh tracks, the men paddled back across the river and held a conference with Clem. A few minutes later, four horsemen galloped on up the river trail. Several of the riders started digging graves in the sandy beach area above the falls. Clem Hubbard and three riders went back to the area were Rex and Scott had left the trail and the Prussian gang had crossed the road last night.

"Their boss must suspect the Prussians didn't make it by the stockade, else the whole gang would have gone up the river," Rex said.

"I'll bet their order is to block the trail near Rainelle. That way, in case the Prussians try to swing north around River Falls, they're still trapped," Scott said while standing his rifle against the rock and taking a piss.

"The trail of five horses up a hillside wouldn't be easy to hide. If we call attention to ourselves, can we escape?"

"There's a small hollow where our horses are. It would be slow going up the hollow to the ridge top, but once there it would be easy to evade any pursuers and disappear. Finding the Prussian afterwards might be a problem; hard to tell which way he might go."

"Is this most of Donnelly's men?" Rex asked while studying the far shore through the scope.

"He'll have more men at the Rainelle and Hinton stockades, but he won't want to use them to chase us, so I figure this is the bulk of his available men," Scott said, returning from his business. "Let me take a look."

He then watched Clem through the Topcon scope. Rex's vision was good enough to see the men across the river without the scope. They watched the slaver walk back down the river trail and stop.

"Oh hell, Clem has found the Prussians' trail up the hillside. If we're going to do anything, it needs to be now." Rex agreed and shot at the man.

The Roanoke IRS office rarely received visitors from New Hamburg, the great port on the Atlantic Ocean that served as the Prussian Empire's capital for the Guderian Territory. Joachim "Joe" Hansen's visitor was the Royal Governor's chief of commerce, Stan Blankenship, one of those charismatic, amoral men who seemed to head up many of the Empire's agencies. Joe didn't trust the fixer but enjoyed his company. The governor's man had invited him to a private dinner at the swanky Royal Hotel in Roanoke where a steak cost 200 D-marks and the potato was extra; a bottle of wine, don't ask. Joe wondered what New Hamburg wanted from him to justify this meal.

The initial dinner topic concerned the source of the bootleg cocaine. Joe started to explain Fräulein Weidman's mission, but he hesitated and instead told Stan he was working with Len Ruffner to learn the source of the illegal cocaine.

"Ah, that'll sort itself out after we deal with the Wapitis." Joe didn't like the implication of that remark. Stan explained, "I don't need to tell you the problem holding the empire back is the lack of workers. The Pentons and Southern Textile Trust are developing several large cotton plantations in Myrtle Territory to supply their mills. They need ten thousand workers to man the planned expansion."

"There aren't that many extra workers in all the territories. What are they planning to do, turn the new world into a giant cotton plantation?"

"Well, sure, that's what the territories are for, raw material and markets for Prussian products," Stan said.

Joe realized he was dangerously close to getting into a policy debate against Berlin's mercantilism. "Stan, please, we all understand that, but Prussia needs more than cotton. So where does the cotton trust hope to find the workers?"

"The governor and I were hoping you could convince James Donnelly and some other enterprising men to clean out the Wapitis. Southern Textile's plantations will buy all the Wapitis available as slaves. Plus, everyone likes the younger Wapiti females; they're worth a fortune. I figure there are several thousand savages in the mountains. It would also solve the illegal cocaine trade with no one left to harvest the winter-sloe berries."

"Nuts, not berries. We're talking about the Wapitis with a vast wilderness to hide in, and they may start resisting with something besides arrows and a few flintlocks. Besides, didn't Emperor Schnabel outlaw the slave trade last year?" Joe asked. His delicious steak was suddenly tasteless. "I suppose the management at Southern

Textile hasn't considered paying a decent wage and just hiring workers?"

"Now you're teasing me. You know as well as I that such a move would force the territory's businesses to pay higher wages to keep their workers. As for the legalities of the slave trade, the attorney general issued a ruling that criminals can be fined and allowed to work to pay off the fine and reduce the length of their sentence," Stan said. He waved the waiter over and ordered a gin and tonic. Joe passed.

"I wondered why the lethargic dupe issued that ruling. Is Berlin aware of his unique approach to, ah, imprisonment and enforcement?"

"Now be nice. The emperor has enough concerns. The attorney general suggested the governor deputize the slavers to arrest the Wapitis as drug dealers; then the magistrates will hit them with large fines. To pay those fines, we'll lease the prisoners to the cotton plantations and the young fräuleins to bordellos and use the rental fees to pay off their fines and court costs. It's a win-win for us."

It's an idiot's dream, Joe thought. How such well-educated and clever people could be so stupid amazed him. He picked at the piece of lemon-frosted white cake he'd ordered before Stan destroyed his appetite. What the governor and Blankenship proposed meant at a minimum a bitter endless war, even a full-blown insurrection west of the mountains. The Ichneumon emperor must have dreamed up this madness.

"The governor can count on your cooperation in this?" Stan asked. Joe needed to stall the implementation until he could wreck their insane scheme. Refusing outright to help would just cut him out of the loop. He figured the sheriff would be willing to help Stan. Joe also figured those two politicians were too wily to give him their foolish deputize-the-slavers order in writing.

"Have the attorney general issue a finding that court fines can be collected through an indenture labor contract. I'll need that legal ruling to get Donnelly and a judge on board," Joe said. Knowing the cautious nature of the attorney general and the bureaucratic inertia of his office, Joe reckoned that order would be a while in arriving at the IRS Roanoke office.

"That's a great suggestion, Joe. We knew we could count on you. I'll get that out next week." Stan looked relieved. He then picked up a small package that had been on the chair beside him and placed it on the table.

"General Guderian sent a gift for his niece, Fräulein Weidman. Can you make sure she receives it? It's one of those new 9mm revolvers. Doesn't seems the type of gift a young woman would like, but it's from General Guderian, and who are we to question his choice?"

"How is the war going?" Joe asked while accepting the heavy package. The Mongol invasion across the Volga River the previous winter had thrown the Prussian army under the emperor's brother into a disastrous retreat.

"Emperor Schnabel promoted his brother and put General Guderian in charge. The last news I received said that Guderian had closed a huge encirclement between the Don and Volga Rivers, trapping the Mongol army and killing their leader, Khan Temujin, along with a large number of enemy soldiers. I heard a number, like 50,000, though that sounds high. I figure the war will be over if the Prussians manage to cross the Volga with a large force."

"I guess your reasoning is the Mongols will fear another encirclement and head back behind the Ural Mountains?" Joe asked.

Stan nodded and added, "If that happens, the emperor will reward Guderian by making him the Prussian field marshal in charge of the army, and maybe even the imperial fleet. Whatever you do, Joe, keep his niece happy and safe."

The lead slug had ripped the leather vest button off and bruised Clem's belly. One or two millimeters to the left and the sniper's bullet would have sliced open his belly. He hadn't hesitated in throwing himself behind the sycamore for protection. He had been lucky.

Four of his men had vanished two days earlier while investigating where Zack and those Wapiti children had disappeared to, then the five guards shot down at the salt furnace stockade, and now last night and today several more of his men were dead. He'd lost more men in the last couple of days than he had in the twelve years of working for Herr Donnelly. His boss would go crazy when he learned how many of his men were dead. Clem believed that when fate dealt you a bad hand, the only proper action was to fold.

Never before had the Wapitis chosen to stand and fight, instead they had specialized in a quick ambush of several shots or arrows followed by a swift disappearance into the forest. These murderous bastards seemed to relish a blazing firefight. Hell, he didn't even know how many there were or even for sure who they were. They seemed too disciplined to be Cinnabar's warriors.

According to the saline workers, the large Prussian had returned and murdered the fools guarding the Wapiti prisoners. Why, no one knew. Clem did know the Prussians had paid for the two women at Hinton, so it wasn't to avoid paying. Besides, he couldn't imagine any Prussian worrying about the Wapiti prisoners or freeing them. They would be foolish to free the Wapiti warriors who might then turn around and try to free those women the Prussians had paid serious money for.

One thing Clem was certain of; those horse tracks up the ridge behind him had to be from those two Prussians working for Ruffner. Well, if those killers across the river didn't get the Prussians, his men would catch them at Hinton or Rainelle. Only four horses remained. If he was going to make a break for reinforcements, he needed to go. Waiting any longer would result in only more shot horses and men. The riders he sent up river wouldn't return from blocking the north trail at Rainelle until he sent word. Clem motioned for his man, Rat, to come over.

"Are you game to hide here and ambush these bastards after we leave? I'll give you a hundred D-marks for each one you get."

"Do you have a pistol I can have?" Rat asked. "How long should I wait?"

He had two muzzle-loaded percussion-cap-single-shot pistols. He handed the pistols to Rat, who already had a Krupp rolling block rifle. Clem added a small bottle of schnapps.

"We'll ride to Rainelle and get help. I'll be back tomorrow by mid-day. Kill them all if you can. And Rat, I won't forget this. Thanks."

The remaining Donnelly men and their horses were hiding out of reach in a shallow depression about 100 meters from the edge of the riverbank where he and Scott had forded the river the previous night. Several large boulders and a grove of huge sycamores helped protect Clem's crew from Scott and Rex's bullets. The sun had passed its zenith when three riders with an extra horse suddenly galloped up the river trail. Rex made a quick shot at the last rider, who raced on out of sight.

"Damn, I shouldn't have done that."

"Don't feel bad. It was an impossible shot," Scott said.

"It's not that. If I hadn't shot, any potential ambushers might be lulled into believing no one remained across the river and get careless."

The Wapiti warrior shrugged, and they sit about working their way around to the ravine with their horses. There, they settled back to wait for darkness or the Prussians to make a move. The solid brown horse Rex had taken from the dead slaver nickered on seeing him. Though the previous owner of the horse, Zack, had been a murderous sociopath, Scott and Indira had started calling the horse, Zack. Rex figured that name was as good as any name for the friendly animal. He spent a minute rubbing the animal's muzzle and ears while considering their next move.

Friedrich Burgdorf shared Rex's concern that Donnelly's man had left ambushers as he studied the rocks below. He believed the gang across the river would prove to be allies, probably several young Wapiti bucks after the girls. Fräulein Weidman slipped into his observation post.

"Clem would have left men to ambush us," she said.

"Probably one or two, but he's lost a number of men. I figure most of Donnelly's remaining men not tied up with guarding the stockade at the salt furnace just fled up the river," Burgdorf said.

"You're suggesting the way down the river to the Wapiti's camp is open?" He nodded and she asked, "You think we could sneak past the saline works at night?"

"Getting off this hill without being ambushed is my current concern. We'll wait for night."

"Tara has a good idea. She offered to go down and pretend she'd escaped. If any of Donnelly's men are down there, they'll grab her. If we wait until it's dark, Clem's bushwhacker might not see her first but later hear the horses and shoot one of us."

"It is a decent idea, but damn dangerous," Burgdorf said. "For it to work, you're right, we'd need daylight and clear shots at whoever grabbed her. We're not dealing with trained solders, but scum, rapists. Do you see that double-stacked rock pillar across the river? Look through this and tell me if you see anything." Burgdorf handed Franciscka the small telescope he had been using.

"Can't say for sure, but I think there's a scope, a piece of glass, on the log at the base of the rock, maybe someone looking at us?"

"I figure it's the mystery shooter," Burgdorf said. "Let's talk with Tara."

"That's Tara! She's escaped!" Scott shouted. He'd been watching the hillside with the Topcon while Rex rested behind the rock.

"Let me look," Rex said, standing to approach the telescope.

"I'm going to rescue her." The Wapiti warrior grabbed his rifle and started toward the horses.

"Don't, you know there's at least one Donnelly rider hidden over there just waiting for you to show yourself. Crossing the river will make you an easy target," Rex said while blocking him.

Scott punched him in the gut without warning, knocking the wind out of him. Before he could recover, Scott was on the horse, thundering down the ravine and into the river.

Franciscka was still high enough up the hill to see across the trees to the opposite shore. The appearance of a lone horseman emerging from the forest startled her. He shouted and waved, "Tara! I'm over here! Wait!"

The rider plunged into the swift current, intent on intercepting Tara. A shot rang out and knocked the rider back in his saddle, but he still managed to stay on the struggling horse.

His shout had stopped Tara. Franciscka threw caution to the wind and raced down the hillside toward where she thought the shooter was. A puff of smoke from the windrow of driftwood and debris jammed against two large sycamores growing on a sandy ridge near the riverbank gave away the sniper's location. She realized the bastard hadn't even seen Tara. Instead, he had been waiting on the men across the river.

A small, thin man materialized on the riverside of the debris pile and shot again at the horse rider now a couple of hundred meters down the river. A shot boomed across the river from that rock pillar, and the thin man stumbled behind the larger of the sycamores, holding his right arm. The driftwood entangled against the sycamores shelter him from the shooter across the river.

Clem's ambusher hadn't seen Franciscka standing sixty meters away just off the river trail. She shot him in the back. Since the person or persons across the river wouldn't know her from that sniper guy, she didn't walk over to verify the sniper was dead. Instead, she shot the bastard again in the head and ran back to the trail in time to meet Burgdorf and Lily crashing down the hillside. She grabbed her horse and followed them down the trail.

Tara had waded out to the dead horse to help the Wapiti rider tangled in the saddle stirrups. Another rider came crashing out the forest, plunged into the river, and headed toward the dead horse and Tara holding the rider's head above the water.

"Franciscka, stand guard while I help. There may be other snipers," Burgdorf said. He waded out to help the second Wapiti, and the two men lifted the rider clear of the saddle and carried him to shore. The wounded rider was a Wapiti warrior whom Tara knew. What wasn't clear was whether he was alive.

The other rider was a mammoth Prussian man, bigger than Burgdorf. Though he didn't point his rifle at Burgdorf and Franciscka, she had no doubt he could in an instant if he felt threatened. The man's lack of concern that they'd shoot him was without a doubt due to having any number of Wapitis across the river backing him up, ready to blow her away at the first sign of hostile action.

"Is one of you Indira's sister, Lily?" the blond-haired, blue-eyed monster demanded. The question froze the two Wapiti women for a moment; then Lily nodded yes. The women clearly didn't know the monster, who then asked, "Is he a slaver, an enemy?" He pointed at Burgdorf with his rifle while watching Franciscka.

The Hopkins woman came alive. "No, they're not. They're helping us escape. Who are you?"

"Indira hired me to find you. How bad is Scott hit?"

Scott Belcher died an hour after Rex and Burgdorf rescued him from the river and the dead horse. Tara Smith was grief-stricken and refused to leave Scott's body.

"Scott deserves a proper Wapiti burial. I want him to go with us," Tara said.

"I'll ride with Tara, and Scott can have my horse," Lily said.

Rex thought Lily's idea workable as he warily studied the two Prussians. The older Prussian's no-nonsense demeanor reminded Rex of a sergeant major. Burgdorf might be a dozen years older than Rex and an inch or two shorter, but he'd be a tough opponent in a fight. The younger Prussian, he was surprised to discover, was an attractive female, though a grimy and guarded one. She held a Krupp rolling block rifle at the ready and kept a suspicious watch on him. He knew she wasn't afraid to use the rifle. The dead sniper testified to that.

Scott's death was a blow to Rex. The young man, during their brief acquaintance, had become a friend. His death was so avoidable, if Scott had just waited. The lost made Rex sad, but he had tried to stop him. Having met Tara, he could understand his friend's interest.

The two young Wapiti women, even filthy and scratched up, were among the most beautiful women Rex had ever seen. That insight caused him to take a second look at the Prussian woman. He decided she could hold her own in a beauty contest with the Wapitis, if she ever smiled. What a bewildering world, one moment it's murder and mayhem, then suddenly, beautiful women.

Don't get too interested in the local women, Rex reminded himself. He knew nothing of their expectations and values. Look, but don't touch would be his rule until he better understood the culture.

The sun was low in the west by the time Rex and the Prussian had finished securing Scott to Lily's horse, and the women were ready to travel. Knowing Clem would had an ambush waiting up the river trail, the Prussians decided to travel with Rex and their former prisoners.

Rex Knight's claim that he and Lily's sister, Indira, had freed all the Wapiti prisoners at the stockade a few hours after they had bought Tara and Lily found a skeptical audience in Franciscka. That there were no other Wapitis with Scott and him amazed her.

The stranger had favorably impressed the feldwebel. He told Franciscka in a private moment, "I think our mystery man is one of those special force officers that Berlin sent on some secret mission, probably to evaluate the Donnelly-Wapiti conflict for the Prussian General Staff."

"There were half-dozen armed guards inside a four-meter-high stockade with a locked gate. How did he and a thirteen-year-old girl manage to overpower them?" The feldwebel just shrugged as they rode through the dark forest.

"Why don't you ask the man?" Burgdorf said.

She wasn't about to do that. Still she couldn't decide what to make of the colossal blond. Cleaned up, he'd be nice looking, but if he was claiming credit for the work of a dozen brave Wapitis, she wanted nothing to do with the braggart.

"You heard the Smith and Hopkins women. Scott Belcher was one of the prisoners inside the stockade when we left, so someone released him," Bergdorf said. To Franciscka's embarrassment, she learned the stranger had overheard them talking about him.

"Fräulein, you appear dubious of my tale. Just wait until you meet Indira," Rex said. He didn't appear overly concerned if they believed him or not.

"How did my sister and you meet?" Lily asked.

Franciscka thought that was an excellent question and waited to hear what new wild tale the man would tell. He told Lily and her about witnessing the murder of an elderly woman and encountering Zack with four captured children. The one who had survived was Indira.

"Oh God, they murdered Bobby," Tara said. Tara and Lily were shocked to learn the slavers had captured and killed Chief Hopkins's youngest son and Lily's brother, Bobby.

"I thought they had escaped," Lily said. After crying over the loss of Bobby and Grammy, they verified Rex's story of the elderly woman's murder on the trail.

An exhausted group arrived at the burned-out Wapiti fish camp a couple of hours after sunrise. Fifteen angry Wapiti warriors ambushed them. The recognition of Tara Smith and Lily Hopkins by several of the warriors lying in ambush prevented a tragic confrontation from occurring. The Wapiti men might not have much of a reputation for fighting, but their camouflage skills were impressive. Franciscka hadn't had a clue there were a dozen warriors within twenty meters of their column, and she'd bet the feldwebel hadn't seen them either.

Indira's rescuer had hung back at the river crossing, whether from worries about the eels or an ambush, he hadn't said, but as a result, the Wapiti trap didn't catch him. As Franciscka waited for the giant to cross over, Sam Wilson erupted in anger at seeing Scott's body.

“Those bastards will pay. Scott was my friend,” Sam said. “I’m going to destroy Donnelly’s furnace, plug his brine wells, and kill that bastard, Clem.” The young hot-tempered Wapiti leader looked around to see if anyone in his group disagreed, before adding, “I’ll even slaughter their horses. They will pay for this.”

“Instead of razing the salt works and Donnelly’s stockade, why not seize and operate it?” Rex said. “Call the salt Belcher Red or some such name to honor Scott, and kick that bastard Donnelly out of the valley.”

The Prussian stranger’s suggestion didn’t set well with Sam, but it did precipitate an intense private discussion between Sam and several of the Wapiti warriors. From the bits of conversation Franciscka overheard, they were debating Chief Smith’s likely opinion on the Wapitis operating Donnelly’s salt furnace.

The warriors appeared to be a fit, tough group of men, with many of them quite handsome. Franciscka wondered if they were sensible and waited by the riverbank to learn how Sam and his warriors would react to the blond monster’s rational idea.

“Who are you? Are you the American who helped Indira rescue our people?” Sam asked. The question caused the monster to momentary look concern, before smiling along with several of the warriors as they waited for his response. Sam still appeared unfriendly. *Who is this Indira? American? Where have I heard that term, or was it America?* Franciscka wondered.

“I couldn’t have done it without Indira. Is she okay?” Rex asked.

The Wapiti warriors received the American’s response with good humor. Franciscka sensed that even Sam had settled down. After several more minutes of discussion, Sam put several men to work burying the scattered remains left by the scavengers of the Wapiti corpses from the earlier raid.

"Tara, tell your father we've gone to secure the furnace and stockade," Sam said. In response to Tara's direct question about his intention, he added, "I'll wait for Chief Smith's opinion on the salt furnace and stockade."

Along with ten warriors, Sam plunged into the Hopkins River and crossed to the river trail. As they disappeared up the river trail, the remaining warriors escorted the teachers and Prussians to the main Wapiti settlement at the mouth of the Jarrell River.

Chapter 4

The several neat farms that their little column passed reminded Rex of the Amish farms in Pennsylvania. The Wapitis had planted numerous corn, oat, and wheat fields along the river bottomlands. The corn, recently planted, was only a few centimeters high. The wheat and oats looked like bumper crops coming on. Sawed wood boards instead of whole logs were the principal building material. Rex wondered how they powered the sawmill, steam or water wheel, and if they used iron nails as fasteners.

Their arrival at the area across from Chief Smith's settlement brought out a crowd of Wapitis, and Rex saw his first black man since he had arrived on this world. The town looked to contain thirty to forty wood buildings, a mix of one and two-story structures and not all that different from a town in the early American West. On their side of the river, the east side, were a half-dozen large wood-framed barns and warehouses with a dozen smaller buildings scattered among them. The area appeared to be more commercial than residential.

Several corrals held a large number of horses and dark brown goats with horns. The Wapiti community had the appearance and ambiance of a prosperous enterprise. The workers, both men and women, appeared healthy, welcoming, and busy. Gardens populated most of the spaces between and behind the buildings. The roads were gravel and dry mud.

"Rex, your horse's left rear shoe appears loose," Lilly said. "Ask Imus to check all the shoes."

"Thanks. I hadn't noticed," Rex said, looking around the yard. "Where's the blacksmith?"

"Blacksmith? I'm a farrier, and I see the problem. Herr Knight, leave your horse and I'll fix the shoe," Imus said. He dismounted and handed the reins to a smiling short muscular man. "I see it has the 'D' brand. One of Donnelly's horses I gather?" Rex nodded in agreement, he doubt the Wapiti care he had taken one of warlord's horses.

"We need to cross the river and pay our respects to Chief Smith first," Lilly said to Rex, Franciscka, and Burgdorf. "Then I'll show you where you can clean up." The other Prussians asked Imus to have their horses looked after. Tara Smith had left to deal with Scott Belcher's corpse.

Two sober men rowed them across the river in a long, flat-bottomed wood boat while they asked Lily how Scott had died. Rex told them that Franciscka had killed the sniper who murdered Scott. Rex saw a waterwheel sawmill operation located near the Jarrell River and decided to visit it after he finished with Chief Smith and had a chance to clean up.

The chief's office was a two-story, whitewashed wood building with pine-shake roofing. The building was about thirty-five meters by twenty meters, with several offices in which clerks were busy entering information in journals and files using quills. A young, handsome man rushed out of the chief's office and swept up Lily. Then Indira blasted through the rear door and ran to Lily to hug her. Lily told her younger sister that Scott had died.

"Not Scott. How . . ." Indira said, looking at Rex and her sister with tearful eyes. "Who did it, the Prussians?"

"No, one of Donnelly's men, he ambushed Scott as he crossed the river to help Tara. The Prussian woman shot him before he could kill anyone else," Rex said. He pointed to Franciscka. Work in the office had stopped. The several women working in the clerk's office watched and listened. Indira ran to Rex to hug him. He waited for Indira's sobs and tears over Scott's death to subside before introducing her to Franciscka and Burgdorf.

The several clerks and a number of passersby came in the room to meet the Prussians and Rex. He learned Chief Smith was still down the river completing the sale of last fall's winter-sloe nut crop to Ichneumon traders. Rex noticed that mention of Ichneumon traders had caught the young Prussian's interest. The chief would return in two days.

"Lily, I'll show Rex and the Prussians their rooms," Indira said.

Rex quickly realized he'd fallen into a nest of budding capitalists. Indira had waved to an attractive woman in the kitchen as she raced up stairs to the second floor and opened a door.

"Helen's rooms are clean. It's only three D-marks a day," Indira said as they climbed the narrow stairs. Looking in he, had to agree; the room was a clean cozy second-floor bedroom with a tub.

"How much to fill the tub," he asked.

"Hot water," Indira asked. Rex nodded. "It's three D-marks, but you have to carry the buckets," she said. He hoped the hot water included soap and a towel. "Laundry service is extra, one D-mark." Probably per sock, he figured.

Miss Indira Hopkins, ever solicitous of his needs, said, "Just throw your dirty clothes into the hallway after you fill the tub. There's hot water in the kitchen. Since you smell bad, you might want to beat the Prussians to the hot water." Indira left with a promise to find him something clean to wear while the laundry attended to his clothes.

After the wonderful bath, Rex laid on the bed for a moment. He woke in the dark. Lacking a clock, he walked to the room's leather-covered wall opening, a glassless window, and pulled it open to look east. Rex could detect a lightening of the night sky and knew he'd slept for twelve hours. His clothes were on the chair with his cleaned and dry boots and a small roll of D-marks with a note. Indira had sold one of their captured horses and left him a third of the sale proceeds. Why only a third, the young trader hadn't said. The middle-aged woman, Helen, who ran the boarding house, was a thin, attractive green-eyed Wapiti who offered to fix him breakfast for three D-marks when he entered the kitchen.

"The Prussian lady asked me to ask you to knock on her door when you got up. Indira said to remind you that you owe her a rifle lesson. Did that girl really help you rescue our captives from those terrible Donnelly people?" the housekeeper asked.

"Yes, I couldn't have pulled it off without her help. Indira Hopkins will probably be your chief in a few years," Rex said. He found the saltshaker, noticed the reddish color, and decided it tasted like other salt as he ate the four over-easy eggs.

"Well, she does come from a long line of bossy women. Her mother runs the schools, and her grandmother was sheriff a while back. We're all proud of Indira and want her to attend the Jesuit College in Roanoke like her sister Lily did."

"Is that college expensive?" Rex asked. *Someone in this world needs to discover coffee*, he thought, while trying another sip of the awful grassy green tea. He learned from Helen that the Jesuit College provided scholarships for gifted students that covered the 3,000-D-mark annual tuition.

"Is Indira a good student?"

"She'd never admit it, but she is, and she helps with teaching the young children to read. The Jesuits already have their eye on her."

The Prussian woman wandered into the kitchen, yawning. Rex did a double take. He'd been correct. Franciscka was a beautiful woman in her own right with that elliptically shaped face, vertical forehead, small straight nose, angular cheekbones, and dark blue eyes. She had cut her light brown hair short.

"Is that girl your daughter or niece?" Franciscka asked. "The cute one who brought your clothes back last night." She ordered three eggs, a venison steak, and fried potatoes; the price, four D-marks.

"Indira, she's my assistant," Rex said, half teasing.

"He got that backwards; he's her assistant," the house keeper-cook said, laughing. She left to fix Franciscka's breakfast order.

Rex told Franciscka Indira's story and that he had promised her a rifle shooting lesson. After that, he wanted to check out the camp and see a winter-sloe tree. He invited her along.

"She's a bit small to handle a rifle. I have a pistol. How about I show her how to use it?"

"Let's show her both. This business with Donnelly isn't over," Rex said.

"No, it isn't. Where are you from, the land of giants?"

"Ah, a distant place, up north. What kind of pistol do you have?" Rex asked. He needed an answer for that damn where-are-you-from question. "Let's find a place to set up a target." He walked around behind the rooming house to check the rear yard. Franciscka trailed along behind him holding her cup of tea.

"In the empire, which even the wilderness is part of, the Jesuits are charged with being on the watch for false prophets. Ninety-nine percent of the Jesuits are good people, but a few are dangerous fanatics. Richard Wilhelm is one of them. If you encounter him, don't joke about being an American."

That bastard's name again, Rex had hopped Scott had exaggerated the danger, apparently not. "I don't understand," Rex said, stalling to learn how great this Prussian woman's interest in his background was.

"The priest patrols the various western territories, though I haven't seen him around here yet," Franciscka said. "He looks friendly, but any false prophets he finds are whisked off to the Holy Prussian Church administration center south of Berlin." Franciscka took a sip of tea before adding, "The poor souls are never heard from again."

She made a slicing motion across her lovely throat. Rex found the intense scrutiny of those dark blue eyes perturbing. He realized she was not joking.

"What exactly is a false prophet?" Rex asked. He was undecided on whether to tell her his story. He wanted to verify Scott's information.

"A person supposedly not from our world, and I can tell you're wondering why the church would care. Think about it; our first emperor claims to have descended from God to lead the world to greatness. That's why much of the world considers the emperor's family royalty. If every few years strangers keep arriving from other worlds, the citizens might start thinking that members of the royal family weren't gods."

"You believe such alien nonsense?" Rex asked. They had stepped outside on the porch for privacy. The sun was warm, but her news cast a chill over him. Franciscka Weidman was a beautiful young woman, sounded intelligent, acted concerned for his well-being, but she had been involved with those slavers. He couldn't decide if she was friend or foe.

"It's not nonsense, just extremely rare. My day job is working for the Imperial Revenue Service. Trust me, I hear a lot, and there's no place called America."

Rex wasn't sure how to reply to that and changed the subject. "So how did a respectable bureaucrat end up in the wilderness? Were the slavers not paying their taxes? Wait, I know; you grabbed Lily and Tara for Donnelly's back taxes."

"How can you joke about such cruelty?" She appeared upset.

"Okay, I'll be serious. Until you explain your presence with Donnelly's thugs and helping them transport slaves, why shouldn't everyone think you're a slaver?"

"I'm an engineer who came along-forget why. I had my reasons. I hate slavery, but believe what you want." She was mad, and Rex didn't want that.

"Actually, I kind of believe you," Rex said. "I figure the IRS sent you on some hare-brained scheme to do with taxes. Probably didn't expect a war."

"No one anticipated you. It's over cocaine."

"Ah, the winter-sloe nut . . ." Rex said.

"Anyway, on this, trust me," Franciscka said. "If asked where you're from, you're an unemployed cod fisherman from the northern ice sheet who got tired of the cold and wanted to live in a warmer area. You hope to make some quick money in the winter-sloe nut trade."

"A cod fisherman . . ." Rex said. Was the woman serious? How common was whatever had happened to him?

"Sure. It's believable. Many of the icemen are big, dumb blonds. And it's far away. Just a helpful suggestion, I'd hate for you to end in one of the holy fire pits." Franciscka had a hint of a smile after delivering that dire counsel.

"Fire pits?" Rex asked. "For a Prussian tax collector or engineer or whatever, you don't sound too enthralled with the emperor or church."

Rex was already convinced that his experience wasn't unique in this strange world. And he didn't like hearing that there were religious issues connected with his misfortune. But how had this attractive woman deduced the truth of his situation? What was her motivation for helping him? Would she attempt to blackmail him? A day ago, they had been enemies.

Franciscka must have sensed his tentativeness. She added, "Please, I'm an accountant and deal with tax cheats, fraud, and illegal contraband, the dark side of the empire, but understand, I'm a loyal citizen of Prussia. So where are you from, Rex Knight?"

"You guessed right. I'm a nomad from the ice sheets." He felt a bit foolish, but decided after this second warning, he had better formulate a response. "I'm an unemployed cod fisherman. I got tired of freezing, wanted warm weather, heard about the winter-sloe trade, and wanted a chance to make a few D-marks." He looked at Franciscka, waited for her response.

"That's about what I guessed. No need to be secret about it, being a fisherman is nothing to be a shame of," Franciscka said. Rex had no idea if she believed his nonsense. She added, "Where are we meeting Indira?"

The rifle lesson with Indira and the large fisherman had been an education for Franciscka. The Krupp rifle had a nasty kick. She had plenty of bruised shoulders from past sessions with the rifle.

"It kicks like a mule," she told the girl. "Put this cotton towel between your shoulder and the rifle butt, after you plug your ears with waxed cotton."

For a target, Rex had set a broken wood shingle against an earthen-berm at the forest edge. The distance was thirty meters.

The shot set the girl down. "Wow, what a kick," Indira said, a bit embarrassed. She was sitting on the ground, still holding the rifle toward the unharmed target.

"Are you okay?" Rex asked, helping the girl to her feet.

"Of course, it just caught me off guard," Indira said as she dusted off her seat, injected the spend cartridge, and loaded a new one. The Wapiti girl spent a long time sighting on the target. Franciscka wondered if she was having second thoughts.

The second shot rocked Indira back, but she kept her grip on the rifle. The target flew up in the air. "There, I did it," the girl said. The target fluttered to the ground against the bank.

"Pure luck, you couldn't do that again," Rex said. The tease wiped the smile from the girl's face. "Don't reload," he added. "I'll go reset your target."

"Your shoulder's going to be bruised," Franciscka cautioned. She had the job of handing out the 11.6 x 65mm cartridges and collecting the fired ones.

"Men, they think we can't fight or hunt. They're wrong," Indira said. Rex trotted back and joined them. Franciscka handed the Wapiti girl another cartridge. Another long aiming, then the shot, and the target shattered. The girl, beaming, looked toward Rex.

"I'm impressed, Indira. With practice, you'll be a fine marksman, ah, markswoman," Rex said while hugging the girl.

"Good recovery," Franciscka said, taking the hot spent brass from Indira. The reality, not widely appreciated in her opinion, was that the new Krupp rifle enabled people like this young girl, with minor training, to provide effective assistance to warriors in defense of their homeland.

"Lily's cooking pancakes. Let's stop and have breakfast," Indira said. Franciscka figured the girl had had enough kicks for one day. Rex took the rifle, promising to clean it.

Franciscka and Rex walked with Indira to Chief Smith's home where the Hopkins girls were staying until their parents returned from down the river. Lily and the chief's oldest son were cooking pancakes and invited them in for a late breakfast.

An elderly woman working in the kitchen and Indira ran to her.

"Rex, Franciscka, this is Mazie Keeney," Lily said. "She's our maternal grandmother." The bent gray haired woman nodded to Franciscka and Rex who was standing behind her.

"You're the man that saved my granddaughters?" The grandmother asked. Rex nodded yes, and the woman crossed the room and hugged the big Prussian. "Words are inadequate to express my gratitude for what you did Herr Knight. If ever I can help you, please ask. Thank you for saving them." Rex appeared much moved by the grandmother's words. Indira beamed.

Franciscka had a meeting with Friedrich Burgdorf, but the pancakes smelled delicious, and though she'd already had a big breakfast, she took time to wolf down two pancakes.

"Lily, those were great. I apologize for eating and running, but I need to catch Herr Burgdorf," Franciscka said, before hurrying to the dock. She found an empty canoe that she rowed across the river to the dock by the blacksmith's barn.

The chief's reaction when he learned the details of Donnell's raid and their involvement worried Franciscka. She hoped Lily and Tara didn't turn on her and Burgdorf. If they did, she'd be in a precarious position and far from help. Burgdorf, who worked for Len Ruffner, might be especially vulnerable to Wapiti vengeance since he had handled the actual purchase of those two Wapiti women.

As far as she knew, the man still believed her to be an engineer sent to evaluate the feasibility of a river valley toll road by the Prussian IRS. Now she was glad she had kept silent about the women.

The blacksmith barn was a noisy and busy place. Two muscular Wapiti men were working the forge and shaping red-hot iron horseshoes. Rex's horse, Zack, was getting a new set of iron shoes. She spotted Burgdorf in a dark corner stall with two men who looked suspiciously like blue bloods, Ichneumons traders. That causal thought of linking blood color and Ichneumons gave her pause.

Franciscka had recently read that Prussian scientists had determined that Ichneumon blood's blue color was due to a copper molecule, hemocyania, instead of the red iron hemoglobin molecule being the blood's oxygen carrier. That discovery had upended the Jesuit's contention that all people regardless of color shared a common ancestor. The Ichneumon people, though superficially the same in appearance, were definitely a different species from the rest of humanity. It probably accounted for Ichneumon-human unions being sterile.

It might even explain why those chauvinistic bastards never willingly dealt with women. That was a shame, because if anyone knew the source of illegal cocaine, it would be those two Ichneumon traders talking with Burgdorf. Unfortunately, Ichneumon traders were most unlikely to divulge any useful information to a woman, let alone one who worked for the Prussian IRS. She'd have to hope Burgdorf passed on what he learned.

Cheering from the river area alerted everyone in the blacksmith's barn that travelers had returned. Franciscka walked to the riverbank to watch eight large, fully loaded canoes arrive. Chief Smith and the Hopkinses had returned, along with a number of Wapiti warriors from their trading trip down the river. The canoe crews' cheerful racket died off as they noticed the somber mood of the crowd waiting along the banks. Burgdorf slipped up to her left side as she waited in the crowd on the riverbank.

"I wonder who's going to tell Chief Hopkins that Donnelly's men murdered his son and any number of his tribe." Franciscka asked.

"Not me," Burgdorf said. "I'm leaving now before the chief decides someone needs to hang for his son's murder. If you're smart, you'll leave with me. You saw those blue bloods?" Franciscka nodded yes. "They're upset with the chief. The Wapitis are converting the winter-sloe into cocaine, instead of selling the nuts to them."

"Did they provided any names?" she asked. Without specifics, it was no better than tavern gossip. Burgdorf shook his head, as he studied the riverbank crowd.

"I doubt the chief's too concerned about the Ichneumons' feelings, but he should be concerned the IRS might issue an arrest warrant for him," Franciscka said. "Besides, we had no part in the Hopkins boy's death." The feldwebel seemed more concerned about the Wapitis turning on him than bootleg cocaine; probably a guilty conscience, she figured.

"As if that fact will matter if they start looking for someone to blame. Did you get the information needed for the toll road survey?" Burgdorf asked. Franciscka wondered why he cared.

"Yes, and I've had enough excitement on this trip," Franciscka said. She watched Rex and Lily approach her father and mother at the dock across the river. Lily then said something to Chief Smith, who, along with her parents, turned to look direct at her and Burgdorf. Franciscka feared things might get dicey. It was time for her to distance herself from Ruffner and his henchman.

"I'm not interested in getting involved with illegal drugs. Are you going to tell IRS about the Ichneumon's claim?" Franciscka asked, curious as to whether his response might help her resolve the question of for whom the feldwebel actually worked.

"Well, yeah. I mean, don't you think I should?"

"If you're working for the IRS you'd better, but keep me out of it," Franciscka said. "I'm thinking about staying here until the Jesuits leave for Roanoke in July."

Burgdorf looked pleased to learn he might be free of her. It decided the issue for Franciscka.

"I also heard the Wapitis told Donnelly's men at the furnace that we killed the stockade guards," Burgdorf said. "That's why old Clem and his men were after us. He thought Ruffner had double-crossed him. If I were you, I'd be sure to stick close to the Jesuits when you're near Hinton."

"If I were you, I wouldn't go near Hinton," Franciscka said. Herr Burgdorf laughed at that suggestion and left a few minutes later that morning for Narrows.

Franciscka Weidman had no luck scheduling an appointment with Chief Smith. The no-nonsense grandmother who served as the chief's office manager refused to commit to a time and date until the chief had time to clean up the business that had accumulated during his absence.

Franciscka suspected the real issue was that the Wapitis viewed Burgdorf as an employee of a Prussian slave broker who had lost his nerve and switched sides though everyone was too polite to say so. To the feldwebel and her good fortune, no Wapiti had suggested they had been involved in Donnelly's raid and the Hopkins boy's death. The Wapitis probably viewed her as Burgdorf's patsy.

In contrast, the Wapitis revered Rex Knight. Indira Hopkins could give lessons to the Prussian emperor's PR team. Franciscka still had difficulty accepting the girl's story of Rex leading her with a slave collar around her neck to that stockade with several of Donnelly's armed guards watching and in a flash killing all of them and freeing the prisoners. Their audacity had amazed her and the Wapiti warriors, and she knew now it was all true. She needed Herr Knight as her friend and ally.

Rex Knight waited on the riverbank by the dock as Lily Hopkins told her parents and Chief Smith about the raid. Her information that Donnelly's men had raided the Hopkins River fishing camp and murdered their grandmother, Chief Hopkins's mother, her brother, and another dozen Wapitis had stunned the chiefs. A sobbing Indira held her sister's hand as Lily turned and pointed at Rex. The other Wapitis seemed to back off leaving him waiting on the now-empty riverbank as Chief Hopkins with his wife and daughters walked across the dock to his location.

Rex related his encounter with Zack and the other Donnelly raiders. Indira's mother then gathered Indira up, and after a brief thanks, the woman left with her two daughters.

"Herr Knight, please don't take this wrong, for I acknowledge my debt to you for saving my two daughters and neighbors. Thank you. You're a brave man. However, I'm not clear on who you are or how you happened to be there," the Wapiti father said.

Chief Hopkins was middle-aged and about a head shorter than Rex. He had a muscular physique, the Wapiti coloration, and their angular face structure. Rex thought the chief a handsome man with an intense demeanor, but sensed they could be good friends. The question for Rex, remembering Franciscka's caution, was whether the chief could be trusted with knowing his origin.

He hedged. "I'm from the ice sheets. I got tired of the cold and fishing. My mother was a Wapiti," Rex said. Where'd that come from? "My father, who was a cod fisherman, bought her from some Greek traders thirty years ago." Is this story believable? The chief looked skeptical.

Rex needed a name for his Wapiti mother. "Her name was Betty." He hadn't a clue as to the names of missing Wapiti women from twenty-seven years ago and impulsively decided to use his real mother's name. He added, "I was hoping to find some winter-sloe trees to harvest, make a few dollars, and learn more about my mother, who died shortly after my birth."

"Are you in trouble with the law, an army deserter?" The chief asked. He shook his head no, as the chief studied him. "I suspect there's much more to your story, but my daughters vouch for your character. The council could use a man with your talents if you're willing to work for room and board. Later I figure the council would grant a grove of winter-sloe trees and some land as a bonus when you complete a special task for the tribe."

"What's the task?" Rex asked. The chief motioned for him to walk along the riverbank for privacy from the men unloading the canoes. Several new-looking flintlock muskets made up part of the cargo.

"Chief Smith and I want you to go to Roanoke and buy us modern weapons, Krupp rolling block rifles, good powder, and bullets. Territorial laws prevent the sale of modern rifles to us savages. No one will question you buying the rifles. Then help me bring James Donnelly to justice."

"I'm willing. In return, I want you to help me find my mother's family," Rex said. "Prove I'm a Wapiti." They shook hands. Chief Hopkins told him the council needed to resolve a number of items before putting the plan into effect. The chief then invited Rex to go with him on a trip the next day. The condition of that year's winter-sloe crop needed checked.

John Hopkins and Pete Chin, the man Rex freed from the slavers, acted as Rex's guide to the winter-sloe trees. The nearest trees were in the upper end of the Jarrell River which, on Earth, Rex knew as the Coal River. The Wapitis had a camp up the Jarrell River about twenty kilometers from the mouth, an easy day's trip on horses. The round trip and time to inspect the new crop would require three days. Franciscka had wanted to see the winter-sloe trees, but Pete Chin said no, she couldn't travel until Chief Smith decided her status. Rex thought that harsh.

The Wapitis' winter-sloe business intrigued Rex, and he was keen to understand it.

"Those are winter-sloe trees," John said. He pointed to several trees on the steep hillside they were crossing. To Rex, the trees looked similar to the hawthorn and crabapple trees. "Those tiny, green nuts are what we harvest in the fall."

"The tree has some wicked thorns," Rex said, studying one of the winter-sloe trees. It had rich dark green leaves and a short, thigh-size trunk that supported a bushy top about five meters high and similar in diameter. "How does the harvesting work?"

"The nut is collected in the fall. By then, it's dark purple or blue and the size of a walnut," John said. "Inside the shell are two kernels." They were standing on a steep hillside among a grove of winter-sloe trees and massive oaks giving the horses a break. *A timber man's heaven,* Rex thought. Squirrels chattered crossly at them from the safety of the oaks.

"Want squirrel for dinner?" John asked.

"Too much work skinning them," Pete said. "Jerky is okay with me. Those nuts are what we harvest. If a person eats the nut after roasting it, he feels a boost of energy. That's our market. In its raw state, it's possible to convert the nut to cocaine."

Examining one of the gleaming finger-long sharp thorns, Rex asked, "What kind of nut yield do the trees produce?"

"A mature winter-sloe can yield five kilograms of shelled nuts," Pete said. "The trick is beating the squirrels, turkeys, and deer to the nuts. The trees grow best in this area under the big oaks and chestnuts, about halfway up the north side of the ridge. They like partial shade and don't grow well in full sunlight. The other advantage of growing under an oak is that the acorn falls about the same time as the blue-nut, and the wildlife much prefers acorns and chestnuts to the winter-sloe."

"How involved is the process for converting the nut into cocaine?" Rex asked. Pete and John exchanged looks.

"Cocaine is a delicate topic," John said. "We stick to selling the nuts, which are nutritional and non-addictive, unlike cocaine, which is addictive and devastates people. Few Wapitis have an interest in encouraging drug abuse."

Rex knew a taboo subject when he heard one and switched directions. "Who owns the trees?" he asked while taking another bite off the piece of leftover venison jerky from dinner. *Squirrel might be worth the effort*, he thought as he chewed on the tough, leather-like jerky.

"Good question," Pete said. "On unclaimed land, we treat the trees like hunting wildlife; whoever finds the tree first gets to claim the nuts. Otherwise, the property owner owns the trees."

That evening around the campfire, the three men, Rex, John, and Pete, discussed the slave raid threat and the salt furnace. James Donnelly had been running the salt operation for years. Then several years ago, he started kidnapping people, using them as slaves at his various plantations and selling or murdering those he couldn't use.

"If you hadn't arrived and saved those Wapitis," John said. "It would have been a serious blow to the Hopkins tribe and cost us two teachers. It was the most brutal attack to date. James Donnelly needs stopped."

"Violence just leads to ever-escalating violence with a foe we can't beat," Pete said. "Not that I didn't appreciate being rescued." Rex thought Pete's added remark about his appreciation sounded insincere, though why the chief wouldn't have wanted rescued escaped him.

"I fail to see where the Wapitis have any other choice but to resist Donnelly's marauding. The council needs to form a well-armed police force to go after outlaws and slavers," John said. Rex realized that Pete was unaware of the council's plan to send him to buy rifles in Roanoke, which meant dissension existed among the Wapiti chiefs.

"Our few muskets and bows are no match for modern rifles," Pete said. "Who will control the police? We need to ask the

Ichneumon for help. Let them fight with people like Donnelly and the Prussians. They have the weapons and money."

"Why would they do that without demanding something in return? They'll want something, gold, the blue-nuts, more slaves." John said, poking the fire to stir the hot coals.

"Why should we care if they use the winter-sloe to make cocaine and sell it to the Prussians?" Pete said. He refilled his metal mug with more of the grassy tea, and then offered to refill their mugs. One mug full was all the grassy tea he could stand, and shook his head no. John held out his mug. Rex wondered if he'd ever taste coffee again.

"No one, the Ichneumon included, will fight our battles for free," John said. "We need our own soldiers armed with modern weapons. We need to fight our own battles if the Wapitis are to control this land."

Rex agreed with John but kept quiet. The Wapitis needed to resolve among themselves the self-defense issue versus pacts with foreign parties and drugs.

"Was anything decided on the saline operation?" Pete asked.

"Chief Smith's concern regarding the salt furnace is whose law will apply in the future," John said. "Currently, Prussian rule and laws end at the mountain divide. Our Wapiti traditional common sense and few poorly written laws won't suffice when an influx of strangers swarms in. I fear that we'll end up lawless except for the gun if we don't act. Chief Smith expects the Prussians to claim the area within the next few years, and the Wapitis need to be united if they hope to have a say in how the new territory is run." John then, using a stick, pushed into the bed of hot coals the charred log ends Rex couldn't reach from his side of the fire.

"I hope you're wrong," Pete said. "Those Prussians will just take everything."

"That's a concern," John said. "Depending on how property rights are resolved, it could be a beneficial event for the Wapitis or a disaster. Past emperors tended to give the new land and property to their pals. We don't know what to expect from Emperor Schnabel. We're endeavoring to find out."

"I had heard the Chief Smith is trying to open a dialog with Berlin, but the Guderian territorial governor refuses to cooperate," Pete said. "New Hamburg politicians are claiming the Wapitis run the illegal cocaine business. Manuel Prado told me the emperor needs money for his war and isn't favorably disposed toward the Wapitis because our bootleg cocaine reduces his excise tax income. We need to ally with the Ichneumon."

"That's disingenuous gossip spread by the Ichneumon traders," John said. "You know the Wapitis don't allow bootlegging of cocaine. Ask Manuel to name one Wapiti who's making cocaine. He can't."

"Your chief needs to talk with that IRS agent, Fraulein Weidman," Rex said.

"She's an agent," John asked. "I thought she was some slaver pretending to be an engineer looking at toll road routes."

"With Burgdorf, I have no doubt that he saw he was trapped and switched sides. Agent Weidman is a more complex story. Your chief needs to talk to her."

"Yeah, right," Pete said. "She's a beautiful woman. That's your complexity. You didn't see her in the stockade looking at us like we were animals."

"I have reason to believe you're wrong on her character, but your feelings are understandable," Rex said. "Hell you might be right and I might be wrong; still no reason for Chief Smith not to hear her out."

Sam Wilson, the lanky Wapiti warrior Franciscka Weidman had met on the trail, was waiting in the rooming house kitchen with a summons to the chief's office. Neither Sam nor the lady running the kitchen was friendly. Franciscka's usual robust breakfast appetite abandoned her, and she told Sam she was ready.

"Helen, would you frisk our guest for weapons?" Sam asked. Franciscka cooperated with the search, handing over her pistol to Helen. When Franciscka was relieved of her boot knife and weaponless, Sam escorted her to the Smiths' home.

Chief Smith was a middle age, long-limbed man about her height of 1.65 meters. He was sitting at his kitchen table drinking tea. The chief wasn't a handsome man, his daughter must have taken after her mother, and he didn't look friendly.

"Thank you, Sam," the chief said, taking her single-shot derringer, a small pocket pistol, from the warrior and placing it on the table beside his cup. "You can go. Fräulein Weidman and I have several items to cover. Would you care for some tea?"

"No, but thank you for asking."

"Contrary to nonsense you may have heard, we're not savages. Saving my daughter from rape earns you a free pass to Narrows. However, she wouldn't have been there if you and those bastard goons of Ruffner hadn't brought her as a slave." The chief's red face alarmed her but didn't stop her temper.

"What a fine select memory," Franciscka said. "No one expected a rescue attempt. We thought we were saving her from slavery. Whoever told Donnelly we killed his guards is what damn near got your daughter killed."

The chief looked thoughtful. "Who told Donnelly what?"

"I don't know who; probably one of the free captives. Someone told the workers at the salt furnace that we killed those guards. Whoever it was knew they would send a pigeon to Hinton.

They probably didn't realize that in trying to block our escape up the river, they put the girls at risk."

"They're women! Well-educated women, not girls!" the Chief roared. After a moment, in a more normal voice, he added, "I'll follow up on that, but that doesn't explain your part. I know those bastards Ruffner and Donnelly . . ." The chief glared at Franciscka for a moment before taking a sip of his tea. His hand was rock steady. "Let's try a different tack. What did you want to see me about?"

"The Roanoke IRS wants to stop the contraband cocaine. My instructions were to befriend the teachers and help rescue them from Ruffner's buyer. My boss had the foolish idea that in gratitude, the Wapitis would tell me who was making the illegal cocaine."

She wished she had gotten a cup of tea. Chief Smith was turning red again. To avoid a scathing lecture, she hastily added, "I know, I know. It was a juvenile scheme, but here's something for you to ponder. Ruffner knew those two women would be among the captives at least three days before the raid occurred."

The information stopped whatever remark the chief was about to say. "Tara, come here!" Chief Smith yelled. His daughter stuck her head through the door from the kitchen into the rest of the house. "Why were you at the Hopkins fish camp?"

"Pete asked me," Tara said. She was holding a rolling pin and had flour dusted across the front of her blue apron. "He told me that the Johnson tribe wasn't happy with the quality of some of the salted eel they bought last year. Pete thought the Hopkins workers were skimping on the proper amount of salt required to preserve the eels through the summer. He knew Lily was in charge and wanted my opinion. I rode with him to the camp. Anything else?"

"No, thanks, daughter, I was just curious," Chief Smith said. Tara left, closing the door, but her attitude suggested she thought her being at the Hopkins fish camp had been an unlucky coincidence. The chief appeared to agree.

Franciscka was skeptical that chance had placed the two women that Ruffner wanted at the site of Donnelly's raid. She believed there was a traitor among the Wapitis. Her candidate was Chief Chin, but he had been among the prisoners captured by the raiders, so Franciscka didn't know what to make of it.

The rolling pin had her curious about what the chief's daughter was baking. Franciscka couldn't smell any delicious aromas and wondered if Tara was making dough for a piecrust. Then realized she'd better get to why she had requested a meeting, for the chief now appeared irked.

"So are you converting the blue-nut into cocaine?" Franciscka asked.

"No. The Wapitis are not converting the winter-sloe into cocaine," the chief said. "It makes some financial sense to convert it, but the roasted nut business is also good. If I were to start making cocaine, I would want Emperor Schnabel's approval first."

Franciscka decided he must read minds after he suddenly yelled for an extra cup and more hot tea. Tara brought her a cup and refilled the chief's cup.

"So who's using the nuts to make it?" Franciscka asked. She'd forgotten the Wapitis drank green tea, not the black tea that she liked.

"I don't know, but I suspect the Ichneumons, or at least their front man, that Southern broker Benjamin Purnell. He brought a lot of the raw nuts along with Len Ruffner," Chief Smith said. "Plus, I've heard the tree grows in the Erie Territory. So the nuts are widely available. I'm sure there are a few rogue Wapitis, even Ichneumon gangsters, who are not averse to cooking up some cocaine on the sly. Tell your boss to take his pick. There's no shortage of scoundrels. Why can't your boss ask the seller who's supplying them?"

"It's being sold through a network of illegal dealers who supply small neighborhood peddlers," Franciscka said. 'The few dealers caught claim they bought it from Wapitis." She added several drops of honey to her tea. Maybe the sweetener would make it fit to drink.

"How big a problem is it?" Chief Smith asked. He had fieldstripped Franciscka's pistol and was examining the barrel as he waited for her answer. She knew it was spotless.

"Here's the other thing Herr Hansen wonders about. My boss has heard that with winter-sole nuts, the cost to make a dose of cocaine is much cheaper than the Ichneumons' cocaine. So his question is why does anyone use the Ichneumon cocaine instead of the Wapitis'?"

"No one realized cocaine could be made from the blue nut until about four years ago," said the chief. "The shame is that they ever did. Now you can convert a benign stimulant that helps prevent drug addiction into an addictive drug, cocaine. But your boss is way off on the conversion cost. The Ichneumon coca-leaf cocaine cost is about a third of the winter-sloe and it's not competitive as a legal cocaine supplier."

"I didn't realize the conversion process was so ineffective," Franciscka said. "How strong of stimulant is the nut?"

"Chewing on or simply eating a couple of the kernels gives a boost similar to a cup of strong black tea with lots of sugar," the chief said. "I've been trying for two years to interest the Atlantic Tobacco Trust in a deal to sell the roasted nut."

"I'd thought they'd be interested in new business," Franciscka said.

"They're not interested. They're worried it might cut into their cocaine sales and can't chance pissing off the Ichneumon, etc., etc. Purnell was a big buyer of this year's crop, but Manuel told me the boat carrying the Orleans trader's nut purchases sank in a storm, so I'm not sure what's going on. A boat sinking would be a convenient explanation if Purnell were undercutting the Ichneumon

Empire using the Wapiti winter-sloe as a cocaine source while not paying any of your boss's taxes. For sure, I haven't seen anyone new selling the roasted salted nuts."

Chief Smith had completed the reassembly of her pistol and was studying the 9 x 19mm cartridge. "Does this round pack a punch?"

"Yes, it's quite effective-on people. Any message for my boss," Franciscka asked, returning to the illegal cocaine issue.

"First, tell him that the Wapitis aren't the source," the chief said. "Second, I agree the nut could be a source, but because of the cost, only bootleggers who bypass the tobacco company and tax collectors and who sell directly to the street dealers could make a profit. Regardless, the Wapiti tribes aren't the converters."

The chief had a sip of tea and then added, "Third, give the Wapitis a license to sell the roasted nuts throughout the empire. We'll pay the emperor's excise tax and not sell the raw nuts to outsiders. Or even better, outlaw cocaine sales."

"Nice in theory, but drug users will keep buying, and the emperor doesn't need more criminal gangs getting rich selling illegal cocaine," Franciscka said. "And he'll still want to know who's supplying it."

"Ah, you're correct. The addicts will still demand cocaine and someone will provide it. Emperor Schnabel and your boss need to kick the Guderian territorial police in their butts and tell them to find out who is selling the cocaine, for it's not the Wapitis."

The Ichneumon traders wore a comfortable and practical-appearing outfit similar to the Prussian fatigues set of a blouse and cargo pants tucked into combat boots. Unlike the solid WW1 gray-green Prussian color, the Ichneumon outfit looked surprisingly modern to Rex Knight with its light universal camouflage pattern. Helen had promised to modify the two sets of fatigues he'd bought from Burgdorf to fit his 6'-4" frame. The outfit he'd arrived in didn't look alien, but after Franciscka's warning, he feared the clothes might still attract Jesuit attention. His height and size would attract attention, but offer nothing to prove he wasn't born on the ice sheets.

Rex went into the blacksmith's barn to check on Zack the morning after returning from the Jarrell River and give him a carrot. His left arm still itched from the smallpox vaccination Tara insisted he have. He had learned the Ichneumons were carriers of smallpox. To prevent outbreaks of the disease, Wapitis vaccinated every tribal member. Rex paused to watch the blacksmith hammer on a glowing red piece of iron before turning his attention to the two Ichneumon traders who approached.

They were similar in size, about 5'-8" or, Rex *thought, 1.7 meters using the metric system*. Their brawny build suggested they would be powerful foes in hand-to-hand combat. If their blood was blue, as Franciscka claimed, it wasn't obvious. The Ichneumons' large, alert eyes were golden brown with a vertical slit for the pupil, not a round opening. They had small pointed noses and vaguely feline faces.

"Imus, my man, be reasonable. Those three nags aren't worth 2,000 D-marks," the older Ichneumon trader said. The blacksmith-farrier tossed the piece of iron he had been working into the bed of red coals before answering.

"Listen to you, insulting those fine horses. I have several with the 'D' brand I'll sell cheap, if you prefer," Imus said.

Negotiations for three packhorses went on for several minutes, before the younger Ichneumon trader addressed Rex. "I'm Bret Paget, and we're hiring guards for a trip to the Roanoke. Job pays one-hundred D-marks a day, figure we'll be gone thirty-days," the young Ichneumon said. "We heard you know how to shoot. What do you say? Nothing is going on here. Give you a chance for some city life." The Ichneumon offered Rex a cigarette, a machine-paper-wrapped cigarette from a pack with a blue eagle embossed on a green background. He declined the smoke.

"Thanks, Herr Paget, but I have some family business that I need to handle," Rex said.

"No need to be formal, Rex. Call me Bret. This is my partner, Manuel Prado."

Manuel, who appeared to be a few years older than Bret was, wore a boonies hat crammed over his tangle of dark curly hair. "May I ask where your family's from? I've been dealing with the Wapitis for a number of years and don't recall any Knights." Rex figured Manuel was too perceptive a haggler to feel the need to bring up his blond hair, blue eyes, and extra foot of height.

"My father was a charmer from the ice sheets who charmed my mother, a Wapiti slave. I'm the result. Has the raid affected your business?" Rex asked. He couldn't read the Ichneumon, wasn't sure if this interest in his background was normal curiosity among strangers or malice driven.

"The amount of winter-sloe nuts available has never been affected by past raids," Manuel said. "I figure business will be good."

"How do the prices for the nut look this winter?"

"That'll depend on the crop. How are the trees looking?"

"Those I saw are loaded with berries, so I figure a decent crop, though the acorn crop looks sparse. Hopefully it'll be similar to this year," Rex said.

"Ah yes, those thieving squirrels; you'd think by now they'd know to leave the blue nuts alone. Well, in that case, I'd figure around forty D-marks a kilo for clean nuts. Some of the Wapitis are shipping too many shell fragments in the nuts. Not the Smiths or Hopkins, but with Johnson we docked them fifteen percent for trashy nuts," Manuel said.

A gray wolf-sized dog followed the younger blacksmith into the stables, the first dog Rex had seen. It gave a growl on seeing them, and the blacksmith told it to hush. Bret had grabbed the pitchfork resting against the stable wall. The Ichneumon's reaction was quick.

"You don't like dogs?" Rex asked.

Manual and Bret traded looks. "You mean wolves. We think they're filthy creatures. I don't like them, though our police use a few for guard animals," Bret said.

Sam Wilson joined them and after greetings said, "Rex, Chief Smith asked me to find you and request you come to his office."

On that note, the group parted company. Sam and the Ichneumon traders went up the riverbank to another large barn while Rex sauntered over to greet the pet wolf. The animal licked his hand, seemed to enjoy having its head scratched, and was friendly. The dog-wolf must have been growling at the Ichneumon. Sam saw him from the other barn petting the wolf and yelled, "Rex, Chief Smith is waiting." Rex hurried across the river in a small canoe after giving Zack his carrot.

"Rex, we followed your advice and talked with Fräulein Weidman," Chief Smith said. "She actually works for the IRS. Emperor Schnabel wants his excise tax paid and the illegal cocaine business shut down. I don't want the emperor sending a Prussian army over those mountains. To have a chance of avoiding that, I need her safely returned to Roanoke. Will you help her?"

"Yes, I'll help her. I would also like to find my mother's family." Rex figured reminding the other chief wouldn't hurt.

"John told me. I'm checking on a young Wapiti woman who disappeared about twenty-five to thirty years ago. She was rumored to have been taken in one of the early slave raids," the chief said. "I heard those cheerful Ichneumon traders offered you a job. Being, ah, from those nomad settlements on the ice sheets, were you aware that the Ichneumon believe cutting a beating heart out of a living person each day will assure the sunrise?" He laughed at Rex's expression.

"Of course, they don't here, at least not every day, but keep that fact in mind if you decide to accept their offer."

"The Ichneumons believe in human sacrifices--those traders I was just talking with seemed so normal," Rex said while passing on an offer of green tea by the chief's daughter.

"Benjamin Purnell, one of the nastiest creatures God ever cursed the world with, is a trader in Orleans. He deals often with the Ichneumons, so he probably knows of what he speaks. He told me the Ichneumon Empire bought over a thousand slaves last year just for sunrise sacrifices. Between Ratakonda's wars and their insane religion, I wonder at times if their plan is to depopulate the world of non-Ichneumon people."

He must have looked perplexed for Chief Smith added, "Ratakonda is the Ichneumon emperor. Also be aware the Ichneumons are big on cutting off hands and feet."

"What? Like punishment for a crime?"

"Yes, things like robbery, embezzlement, and other non-capital crimes. For those unfortunate souls, the punishment is usually to lose a foot or a hand. For capital crimes, they use the four-step punishment where each year the prisoner gets to choose what they amputate. After three years, if you survive, they release you. Of course, you don't have any hands or feet."

"That's incredibly cruel."

"Keep that in mind when dealing with those friendly Ichneumon traders. So where was your father from?"

Chief Smith's query caught Rex's mind engaged in comparing the Ichneumon viciousness to tales of brutality and murder he had read about in history. He almost answered Charleston. "He was a cod fisherman, lived on the ice sheets. Ah, Chief Hopkins mentioned another project."

"I'll have a name for you in the morning. Now go find Sam Wilson and Fräulein Weidman. I want to meet the three of you in my office in an hour. I want her back in Roanoke before those Ichneumon traders. After I finish with them, we have a private talk with John."

The party escorting Franciscka Weidman had finally left the Kanawha, or Southern River, valley after crossing the North River. Rex, on hearing what Sam Wilson called the fast-flowing stream, thought it worked as well as Gauley for the river's name. They had reached an agreement on the route and size of the escort party during an evening meeting in Chief Smith's kitchen two days prior.

The Wapitis favored the north route through Rainelle, Lewisburg, and on east to the Prussian outpost at the Guderian Territory border. Hinton on the river was James Donnelly's main stronghold, but he also had small stockades at Rainelle and Lewisburg. The Wapiti route would take them through Donnelly's territory. Hence, the reason for twenty Wapiti warriors in the escort armed with the Wapiti's few Krupp rolling block rifles. Rex and Indira's rifles made seven modern rifles. The rest of the party had bows and flintlock muzzleloaders along with a dozen cap and ball pistols.

After the meeting to decide on the path east, Chief Smith asked Rex to remain and sent the others off. "As John explained, the council wants to set up a small, well-armed police force to deal with people such as Donnelly."

"I'm a bit surprised you don't have one," Rex said. Thirsty, he considered asking Tara for a cup of the tea she was refilling her father's cup with; then, remembering its gagging taste, he asked for boiled water.

"The Prussian ban on selling modern firearms to the indigenous people, which includes the Wapitis, has prevented us from accomplishing that goal. The Ichneumon traders have promised to sell us the Krupp rifles, but there always seems to be some reason the sale has to be postponed," Chief Smith said. His skeptical look implied he thought the Ichneumons' excuse for not selling Krupp rifles nonsense.

Rex considered the chief's excuse for not having a formal police force rather lame, but he was in no position to criticize his host.

"Their reluctance to deal surprises me. I'd thought the Ichneumon would be happy to trade guns for winter-sloe nuts. Being a separate empire, I wouldn't have thought them much concerned about Prussian sale bans."

"Tara, enough tea. Bring that bottle of Schnapps. You'd think so, but so far, no guns. However, you could pass for a Prussian, and I want you to handle the purchase. That's part of your task. The other part is delivering Franciscka safely to Roanoke," the chief said. "You want this instead of water?"

"Sure," Rex said. He poured a shot from the chief's liter bottle of schnapps sitting on the kitchen table while waiting for the chief to explain.

"Tribal politics require a Wapiti be in charge of the column. John and I consider you a Wapiti, but Pete kicked up a fuss. You're still a stranger to most of the men, so we made Sam the leader. However, we're giving you the money to purchase Krupp rifles and ammo."

"I'm not overly impressed with Sam's leadership," Rex said.

"I know it's not a clean command structure," said the chief, "but if you're willing to accept the task, I'll get the money."

"It could get violent. People-Wapitis-could die, even Prussians."

"The council knows that."

Though Rex wasn't clear on the risks, or what the entire task might entail, he needed the council's support and figured he'd better help. Might as well be positive and he said, "Then with that understanding I'm agreeable. I'll make it happen," Rex said. Chief

Smith asked his daughter to bring in the large duffel bag from her bedroom and give it to Rex.

"That's all the tribe's ready cash. Try not to lose it."

Chapter 5

The recently completed six-month tour as captain of an infantry company on the Prussian Empire eastern front had eliminated any illusions Hauptmann Frederick “Fritz” Caprivi had that savages couldn’t fight effectively. His father, General Caprivi, who commanded Marshall Guderian’s southern army, had yanked his oldest son from his cozy position with the Prussian General Staff in Berlin. His new assignment: command of an infantry company attached to the Royal 77th Division. Their orders: to establish, then hold, the bitterly contested Volga River crossing and bridgehead.

Hauptmann Caprivi’s company had crossed the Volga on the third day of the attack and taken a position near the center of the front line. They arrived just as the enemy launched a massive counterattack against the Prussian bridgehead, later estimated to have involved over 30,000 Mongol soldiers and cavalrymen. Four thousand Prussian infantrymen stopped the Mongol attack that day.

The determined and fearless Mongol horsemen killed half the Prussian soldiers and wounded most of the rest along the bridgehead line, but the line held. Hauptmann Caprivi received several minor wounds, but rallied his and the neighboring companies’ leaderless soldiers to throw back the Mongols’ three times. By the third assault on that endless day, dead horses and their riders had formed a wall that broke up Mongols charges and prevented the riders from leaping the Prussian trench. The added distance rendered the Mongols’ preferred weapon, a breech-loading double barrel shotgun ineffective.

After two more days of exchanging harassing sniping, the Mongol army withdrew from the area of the Volga. Hauptmann Caprivi gave up trying to count the dead horses in front of their position. He later learned from his father that over 8,000 horses and presumably a similar number of Mongols had died that day. Fritz Caprivi knew the Prussians had been fortunate. Twice that day fewer than five hundred infantrymen held the four-kilometer front of the bridgehead. The Prussian infantryman's new Mauser bolt-action rifle had saved the day.

After the Prussian army's reinforcements had successfully crossed the Volga River, the Mongol army faded away to their mountain homeland several hundred kilometers to the east and the conflict dwindled into occasional minor frontier raids. Hauptmann Frederick "Fritz" Caprivi received the Iron Cross for his bravery and performance on the Volga bridgehead and a coveted transfer to Military Intelligence.

The Prussian General Staff had received conflicting reports on the intentions of the Ichneumon Empire and reports of armed rebellion in areas west of the new territories. Military intelligence decided to send Hauptmann Fritz Caprivi to Guderian Territory. His cover story was that the trip was a vacation reward for his heroic conduct on the Volga River. Fritz's real orders were to travel west of the mountains, determine what the savages and Ichneumon were doing, and if whatever the various parties were doing, it should be a concern of the emperor.

So far, Rex's trip east had been uneventful, even enlightening. The area the Wapiti column had traveled through was sparsely settled and brimming with unexploited natural resources. The land would offer many opportunities for him to use the knowledge he'd brought from Earth, perhaps even a chance to make a fortune. He should have been elated; instead, his mood was bittersweet. The magnificent and pristine environment surrounding him would never survive the coming timbering and mining.

The stockade at River Falls was abandoned and empty. After fording the North River, Sam followed a steep trail that left the river valley floor and emerged on the north rim area of the main river valley. Their party had five packhorses with supplies, one of the items being a wood cage with six pigeons trained to return to Chief Smith's home. The pigeons would serve as Franciscka's messengers back to the chief on the status of her negotiations with the Prussian IRS. The column stopped after reaching the valley rim and made camp. Their first night on the trail passed without incident.

Rex Knight found an ally in Franciscka when dealing with the haughty column leader, Sam Wilson, and the several overconfident Wapiti warriors who were itching for a fight. On the first day, they had traveled as a tight column that would have suffered high losses in the event of an ambush.

"I'm worry about being ambushed," Rex said. "If you put a couple of riders out ahead of the column, they could warn us."

Sam and his pals were sitting on logs around a large fire and had been speculating on how many Krupp rifles they'll recover from Donnelly's men and how to share the battle spoils. That the blazing fire silhouetted them as perfect targets seemed lost on Sam's warriors.

"You mean scouts?" The Wapiti sub-chief asked. "I plan to start using them tomorrow."

"Good. Then will you split the column into two groups far enough separated so an ambush can't pin both groups down?" Rex asked.

"Why do that? It'd just weaken us."

"The unengaged warriors could form a maneuvering force to flank and rout the ambushers," Rex said.

Franciscka had joined them at the fire. She apparently realized that he had exhausted Sam's willingness to accept advice on protecting the convoy.

"If you have two groups, it'll allow you the turn the table on the attackers," she said. "You can hit the ambushers from several directions. Think of the rifles and horses you'll capture." Her effort helped. Between them, they convinced the proud Wapiti warrior to reorganize the column. The country was too rough to put flanking riders on each side of the column, and Rex didn't raise the issue.

The third day put the Wapiti party on the high ground west of Rainelle. Rex and Sam found an overlook and set up the Topcon to study the stockade.

"Not much to the place," Rex said.

"At least there're two taverns," Sam said.

Rainelle consisted of a dozen wood-frame stores and taverns in the shadow of a wood stockade. The builders had used rough-cut lumber to construct the buildings that they could see along the dirt road. The two-story buildings had peaked roofs with wood shakes. The single-story buildings were shed types. None of the owners had painted their buildings, but they all had glass windows and painted signs. The windows used wood frames and multiple small panes of glass.

The abundance of windows in Rainelle had Rex curious. The manufacturing of glass required furnaces and factories. Glass was heavy and fragile, not easy to transport. Rex wondered where it had come from, as he studied the fort. The stockade was similar in size to the one at the salt furnace, a thirty-meter-diameter ring of sharpened logs sticking out of the ground about four meters.

"Those six horses in front of the Blue Star Tavern look like Donnelly's nags," Sam said. "I'll bet their riders are in the bar drinking."

"Probably are. That'll make slipping by easier," Rex said. Another several horses were inside the stockade ring. Were those riders also in the tavern, he wondered. "Can you get us through there tonight without alerting those men?"

"I might be able, if we take that side hollow to the south of the stockade, not the main trail," Sam said. "But why not kill them and take their horses and rifles?"

Two Wapiti warriors, cousins to Scott Belcher, had crept up to the overlook and grunted their agreement with the idea. The glaring weakness in Sam's plan was thinking Donnelly's force hadn't learned from their salt furnace defeat.

"We have no information on the number or location of the enemy," Rex said. "You'd be attacking blind. Chief Smith wants us to deliver Franciscka to Roanoke. If we engage the garrison and don't wipe them out, the survivors will alert Donnelly, who'll then know which way we're travelling. He'll alert Lewisburg to block the trail. As it is, until those Ichneumon traders arrive in Hinton, Donnelly probably is unaware of us, and not expecting any Wapitis. I say we keep him unaware."

"Ah, you're just worried we'll kill more bluecoats than you have. We need those rifles and horses," Sam said. The Belcher cousins nodded agreement. "We'll do both, kill those bastards and sneak by to the south. They'll think a few Wapitis made a raid for vengeance over Clem's slave raid."

"It's a foolish risk; don't do it." Rex realized too late that telling a narcissistic young buck to be cautious guaranteed reckless behavior.

"Don't say anymore, friend. I'm in charge and I've decided. Now get ready to move out. You will go with the packhorses and women. I'll handle the bluecoats." Sam left an exasperated Rex at the overlook with the Topcon.

He found Franciscka and Rex a half hour later. He had an older Wapiti warrior, Steve Johnson, with him. "Steve's been through the south trail. He'll lead your party around Rainelle and we'll catch up after we deal with the bluecoats."

"You know my thoughts, Sam," Rex said. "So how many warriors are you leaving with the escort party?" Franciscka looked curious.

"What are you doing, Sam?" she asked while rerolling her bedding to tie behind the saddle.

"I'm going to raid the stockade and kill some Donnelly men. We need the rifles and horses."

"That's idiotic," Franciscka said. "Your raid will just alert him to our presence in his territory."

So much for her diplomatic skills, Rex thought as Sam stormed off, after pausing to tell Steve to be ready to move out.

"You raised a valid point fräulein, but the young bucks want blood. Let's get moving," Steve said.

The Wapiti group took an hour to reach the valley floor where the trail turned north toward Rainelle. Sam and the six warriors split off and waited for the remainder of the column led by Steve to disappear up a rocky side hollow. Rex waited with them until then. He wished Sam success and then followed the column east.

The clear night sky and bright quarter moon made seeing and following Steve Johnson's trail easy. Rex Knight and Franciscka Weidman formed the column's rear guard and had just reached the ridge-top east of Rainelle about two hours after leaving Sam when distant gunfire erupted in the valley they had left. Rex counted at least twenty quick shots, then single shots every few minutes or so until he dropped into a ravine a few hundred meters from the mountain crest. After that, he heard no more shots.

"I didn't care to hear those single shots," Franciscka said.

Rex didn't either; it sounded like a running pursuit. He hoped it was Sam chasing fleeing Donnelly's men, not the opposite, but regardless, for whatever reason, Sam's initial ambush hadn't been decisive.

Around midnight, Steve rode back and asked Rex's opinion on stopping for the remainder of the night. The animals and the men could have all used a rest, and it would give Sam a chance to rejoin the column. They stopped.

Rex woke as the dark eastern horizon lightened and learned Sam hadn't returned. He found Steve with several of the Wapiti warriors by the packs. Franciscka was on the other side of the packs caring for the pigeons. The area where they had stopped was at the forest edge before a lush meadow. The trail ahead snaked around several beaver ponds in the clearing.

"We're near the intersection with the main trail, about a hard day's travel to Lewisburg," Steve said. Rex figured the party was in the area of Sam Black Church, and he wished I-64 existed. "Should we wait for Sam or keep heading toward Lewisburg?"

"How long will Donnelly's men need to cover the distance between Hinton and Lewisburg?" Rex asked.

"A long day," was his answer.

"Then let's go. We need to get through Lewisburg before he can close the trail."

"What about Sam? He had all the good rifles," Steve said.

Rex ran a quick verbal check. The party had his, Franciscka's, and one other Krupp rolling block rifle.

"We're not looking for a fight. Once past Lewisburg and across the Greenbrier, we'll be fine." The Wapitis scattered and mounted up.

"What's the Greenbrier?" Steve asked. "You mean the Sulfur River?"

Franciscka smile; she had caught his slip.

"Get the column moving, Steve. I want two riders out ahead. I'll watch the tail."

The day went without encountering another person, though the column passed several homesteads in the distance. More troubling was that Sam hadn't showed, which meant the attack had gone haywire. His secret worry was turning around and seeing Sam riding into view on a lathering horse with fifty angry men on his tail. If Sam had to flee, Rex hoped he had enough sense to flee west as a Wapiti raiding party would.

Two hours before sunset Steve stopped the column and rode back to Rex. "The Lewisburg stockade will be visible from the next ridge. Should we stop?"

"Have the riders find a spot out of sight of the trail on the north side," Rex said. The wind was coming out of the southwest, and it would help carry noise and smoke away from the trail. "Fix a fire and tell everyone to have a hot meal. Then we're going through Lewisburg, tonight."

All afternoon, Rex had considered the best way to accomplish his task of getting Franciscka safely to Roanoke. That no one from Sam's group had caught up with the column meant the Wapiti raiders had encountered a much larger group of Donnelly men in Rainelle than the horses indicated to be present. It also meant hostile riders were as likely to arrive from the west as Sam's surviving Wapitis.

Rex had an advantage, if this place was a twin of Earth, and so far, it appeared to be. Two summers during college, Rex and several friends had climbed all the marked high peaks in the Peters, John Creek, Potts, and Sinking Creek Mountains of the Jefferson National Forest. He was confident he knew that wilderness as well as anyone, and he could find a way through those mountains to Roanoke. Rex needed to ask Steve a question and went to find him. He found the Wapiti beside two fires with iron pots suspended from small, simple iron tripods where the men were cooking some stew, which smelled delicious.

"When we arrive in the mountains, could you keep the column together for several weeks?" Rex asked. Steve went to consult with Maria Belcher. Franciscka had told him the previous day that two of the Wapiti warriors were women. One was Sue Sweetwater, Scott Belcher's oldest sister. The other woman, Maria, was Scott's younger sister. They were both short, dark-eyed, brown-skinned women who looked like their Clovis ancestors, not Wapitis. Maria returned to the fires with Steve.

"We'd be fine all summer. Why do you ask?" Steve said.

"I need a safe place to leave the column while Franciscka and I go to Roanoke. The chief wants me to buy a dozen new Krupp rifles and as much ammo as I can with the D-marks left after paying for the rifles. I'll need help taking them back to the chief." Steve and the warriors loved that news. "Have everyone rest until dark; then we're sneaking through Lewisburg and head for the mountains."

"I know the teacher in Lewisburg, Sally Atman," Maria said. "She's a Prussian who married a Clovis from the Moyer tribe and lives in Lewisburg. She hates slavery and the attacks on the Wapitis. Donnelly's men, if they even noticed me, would just figure I'm part of her husband's family visiting. I could ride ahead and talk with Sally. She would know of any alerts." Steve nodded in agreement with her suggestion.

Rex liked that suggestion, but then the west guard ran up to their small group by the fire. "Two riders are coming from the west. They have a couple of prisoners," the young Wapiti warrior said. "What should we do?"

The combat fatigue set he had bought from Burgdorf and was wearing gave Rex an idea. "I look like a Prussian. Tom, saddle Zack for me."

If he rushed, he and Zack could slip down the ravine the column had stopped in and circle the ridge to rejoin the trail where it came up from Lewisburg. The riders would think he had ridden out of Lewisburg.

"I'll time it to meet them on the trail across from here," Rex said. "Cover me. If I start shooting, you're free to shoot the riders." He'd pull his Ruger pistol from the backpack after he was away from Franciscka, who appeared alarmed about his dangerous plan, but said nothing.

Zack had slipped among the large trees and over the moss-covered fallen logs and rocks on the ravine slope to the Rainelle-Lewisburg trail with no difficulty. They had reconnected with the trail below the crest of the ridge and out of sight from the riders. Trotting his horse back west, Rex soon met the two riders.

The rear rider was leading two Wapiti prisoners chained together. Rex stopped his horse and waited across from the column's hiding spot for the lead rider to approach. The blue coat man had a Krupp rifle pointed at Rex and yelled for him to keep his hands in sight. As before, Rex had the cocked and loaded pistol jammed between his left thigh and the saddle, out of sight but handy.

The unresolved issue troubling Rex was whether to take prisoners. From a practical consideration, how could the Wapiti column expect to pass through Lewisburg masquerading as a Donnelly operation with Donnelly men as prisoners? On the other hand, the warlord's men had taken prisoners; proof currently blocked his passage.

For peace to have a chance, the inhabitants needed to stop killing each other. Rex reckoned this was a good opportunity to demonstrate mercy. They could leave the Donnelly riders alive and tied to a tree along the trail. The chance of the prisoners being discovered or escaping before morning was remote, and by then the column would have cleared Lewisburg and be in the mountains.

The lead rider was nervous and stopped about twenty meters away. "Who are you?"

Rex started to lower his hands.

"Keep those hands up, pal. Why are you out here by yourself?"

The rear rider closed the gap and stopped beside the rider demanding Rex's information. Both had their rifles pointed at him. Their prisoners were in sorry shape and collapsed on the trail when the rider leading them halted.

"I'm Herr Hansen," Rex said, picking a name he'd heard Franciscka mention. "Headed to Rainelle to find Clem Hubbard, and quit pointing those rifles at me. Who are your prisoners?"

The rider with the prisoners, an older potbellied man with the red-vein covered face of a heavy drinker, seemed satisfied Rex wasn't a threat, and turned his attention to prodding the two captives back onto their feet. The front rider, a young, lanky hillbilly type with a missing upper-front tooth, looked relieved and lowered his rifle.

"He's Stan. I'm Jake," the young rider said. "You're wasting your time. Clem's not there. He's chasing their pals."

"Well, hell. Clem said to meet him at the Rainelle stockade. Where'd he go? What happened?"

Zack started fussing and turned toward the Wapiti ambushers. Rex needed to learn what had happened in Rainelle. He gave Zack's reins a gentle pull to keep the horse's head facing away from the Wapitis waiting for his signal.

"A bunch of savages attacked us in the Blue Star Inn," Jake said. He turned and pointed toward the woebegone prisoners who were casting imploring looks toward Rex.

Looking please, Jake turned back to Rex and added. "We showed them not to mess with their betters; killed a couple and caught these two. The rest fled toward the falls." He paused to cram several blue-nut kernels into his mouth.

"Where are you taking them, to Lewisburg?" Rex wondered why Clem wouldn't have held the prisoners in the Rainelle stockade.

Jake placed his rifle across his knees and edged closer to Rex. In a soft voice, he said. "Clem doesn't like to mess with prisoners. He told me to find a spot where no one would find the bodies."

Jake's statement left Rex cold. The thug's next bit of information infuriated him.

"I bet Stan that the wounded Wapiti could walk to Lewisburg. Looks like I'm going to win."

"Then what?" The cruel treatment of the wounded prisoner disgusted him, though what left Rex at a lost was the suspicion that they would have already shot the prisoners, except for the bet.

"Shoot them, Clem's order," Jake said. He laughed, clearly enjoying his power over the prisoners. Rex's revulsion must have shown, for he added. "Don't look so concerned, they're vermin that no one wants. Hey, Stan, you agree I won?"

Stan looked argumentative.

"If you agree," Jake said, "We'll do the deed and leave them in the woods, not have to dig a grave in Lewisburg." The unwounded prisoner had heard him and started pleading for mercy.

"You shouldn't have attacked us," Jake said. He picked up the rifle and aimed it at the prisoner who had started begging and crying. "You agree Stan, I won?"

Stan never got a chance to answer. Rex had pulled his pistol and shot Jake in the head. Almost simultaneously two rifle shots rang out, and both riders fell to the ground. Rex had to grab the fat man's horse to stop it from galloping off with the prisoners. Jake's horse seemed stunned and nudged the rider's body with its nose.

The wounded prisoner, beyond caring, collapsed to the ground, dragging the crying prisoner with him. Rex didn't recognize either prisoner as he picked up the two Krupp rifles while waiting for

Steve, Maria, and Franciscka to cover the couple of hundred meters from the column's hiding spot.

"Was killing them necessary?" Franciscka asked. She looked worried as she studied him. Rex nodded.

Steve Johnson and Maria Belcher knew both prisoners and soon had them free and their story. Sam had made the mistake of dividing his forces before knowing the enemy's strength. He had sent three men to the stockade and had the other three with him. Sam successfully surprised the six Donnelly men in the tavern next to the stockade and killed four in the first moments. Unfortunately, the two surviving bluecoats had revolvers and returned fire, killed Sam, and wounded the prisoner relating the tale. The other two Wapitis with Sam's group had panicked and bolted.

The other prisoner, the unwounded one, was Eddy. He'd been with the group that raided the stockade. They had encountered several Donnelly men in the stockade. After a short, ferocious exchange of gunfire, the bluecoats' boss, a man called Clem, captured him. Gunfire had killed the two Wapitis with Eddy. He'd heard Clem say that two of Sam's raiders at the tavern had escaped toward the west. Eddy then told Steve, Franciscka, and Maria what he had heard Jake tell Rex about the bet and planned execution.

Rex was thankful that the surviving Wapitis fled west, but still, Sam's affair had cost them five men, dead or missing, and seven rifles, though two had just been recovered.

"At least Clem is off to the west chasing the remains of Sam's group," Rex said. "Not waiting in Lewisburg. I need two volunteers to dress in Donnelly outfits. Steve, have the men strip those bodies before burying them."

The Wapitis stripped and buried the two Donnelly men in the forest. Two of the warriors whom Sam hadn't like and had told to go with the column, the Jarrell brothers, Tom and Lou, volunteered to wear the riders' blue coats and campaign hats. While the brothers switched outfits, Rex and Steve found Maria.

"Maria, stay with the column tonight," Rex said. "On our return trip, I want you to visit your friend Sally Atman the day before the column needs to pass back through Lewisburg. That way we'll know if Clem has ambush plans. Tom, Lou, take the lead. Wave to people in town; look friendly. After all, we're Donnelly's supply convoy."

That evening, the column passed through Lewisburg. Several residents waved to the two Jarrell brothers dressed in blue coats, who tipped their black campaign hats in greeting. Rex and Franciscka followed the column and stopped at the Cross Road Tavern. The popular inn was located where the trail along the Sulfur River crossed the northern east-west trail out of the Southern River valley.

The tavern was located in a poorly constructed wood-frame building built around an earlier log cabin whose front porch now served as the inn's bar. Several men, two dressed in blue coats, sat along the heavy wood plank that functioned as the bar. They were drinking a brown, foamy liquid that might have been beer. The bar and table surfaces Rex could see looked filthy. The floor was unspeakable. He'd fear to eat or drink anything fixed in the establishment.

"Where are you going?" the gray-haired man wearing one of Donnelly's blue coats asked. "Damn late for being on the trail." He stood up to get a better look at the convoy passing the tavern.

"We're headed to Waynesboro for supplies. Clem wants us to push hard," Rex said.

"What supplies?"

"Hey pal, you know James and Clem don't like us talking about their business." Rex said. Franciscka gave the man and the other bar patrons a friendly wave, and then they rode off into the night, leaving the man holding his mug of beer and a peaceful Lewisburg.

Eight days had lapsed since Rex Knight and Franciscka left Chief Smith's village at the mouth of the Jarrell River. The Wapiti column had stopped in the high meadow area between Potts Mountain and Nutter's Mountain, a day's ride away from Roanoke. The Wapitis had set up a camp there to wait.

Rex and Franciscka rode on to Roanoke where he had found a rooming house with stables in the northwestern section of the town. He rented a room for a week, left the packhorse with the pigeon cage, and then followed Franciscka to her place, a rented small cabin. The cabin was a couple of blocks north of the IRS office. She boarded her horse at the large stable near the IRS office.

After a quick check of her place, Rex returned to his rooming house to have Zack pampered, then verified that the stable worker had fed and put the packhorse in a clean stall and the worker had housed the pigeon cage in a place out of the weather and safe from cats and foxes. Satisfied, Rex had a steaming bath and a good night's sleep. In the morning, he would visit hardware dealers and learn what weapons were available for sale.

Checking her body in the mirror for contusions and discolorations, Franciscka decided the adventure, forgetting the terrifying moments, had been good for her body. She had her hard body back and wondered what Rex would think of it. She would like to see that massive blond warrior naked, but alas, so far he had conducted himself as a perfect gentleman with all the women. She suspected the chief's daughter, Tara Smith, was interested in Rex, and that Wapiti woman was serious competition. Enough dreaming, Franciscka knew tomorrow's return to the IRS office, after being absent almost a month, would be a tough readjustment for her.

"Franciscka Weidman, what a pleasant surprise and you're in one piece," her boss said. A relieved Joe Hansen hurried around his desk to hug her. "Herr Ruffner told me last week that he feared the Wapitis had killed you and his man Burgdorf." He yelled for his secretary to bring a fresh pot of tea.

"It wasn't the Wapitis," Franciscka said. "It was that animal Donnelly, or at least his man Clem Hubbard who tried to kill us." She waited for the secretary, an old male veteran of the Prussian and Greek War, to leave and close the office door. "I did manage to meet with the Wapiti chief and discuss our problem."

"Did you find the source of the illegal cocaine?" Joe asked. Franciscka spent fifteen minutes recounting her discussion with Chief Smith. "He'll agree to pay the excise tax and limit sales of the raw winter-sloe nut to other parties? Is he capable of enforcing such an agreement?"

"Yes, I believe he can. The slaver predation has united the Wapitis and I sense the chief would be open to joining the Prussian Empire as another territory." She knew her boss was the enthusiastic sort and her report should have thrilled him. It didn't; in fact, Joe appeared a bit subdued. "Okay, what happened while I was gone?"

Joe Hansen told her about Stan Blankenship's visit. The tale made her fear for the Prussian Empire. Franciscka's professors at Heidelberg University had beat into her class the belief that empires usually fall from the rot of moral corruption and greed.

"Why would the Guderian governor risk a revolt to help the cotton trust?"

"Why do you think?" Joe rubbed his fingers and thumb together in the universal hand motion for money. "Before you get mad, listen. We're meeting with James Donnelly in an hour, along with lawyers from the attorney general's office. I want you there thinking clearly and listening, not arguing."

A month ago, Franciscka would have felt in her legs the effort required to climb the steep stairs from her first-floor office to the third floor. Not today, she could have run up the steps and not been winded. Her boss, on the other hand, had gone red in the face.

"Are you okay?" Franciscka asked. "Let me have that attaché case."

"I've got to lose some weight," Joe said handing off the heavy bag. "What was I thinking to put the damn conference room on the third floor?"

Holding his bag, she followed him as he slowly plodded up the stairs. Still, his wheezing was alarming by the time they gained the third floor. Rudolf Hoess, the assistant attorney general in Roanoke, represented the Guderian Territory attorney general office, was waiting in the conference room with an attractive, fit middle-aged man. The man was James Donnelly.

The lawyer wasn't fit. He was a young, flabby wastrel, the only son of Baron Hoess. Though he was a close friend of Heinz William, Franciscka didn't think the assistant attorney general was quite as despicable as William was. However, in James Donnelly, she feared she was about to meet pure evil.

"Fanny, I'm so glad you're okay. I heard those savages had attacked you," Rudolf said. He had jumped up when they entered the room, rushed to grab her hand, and planted a chaste kiss on her cheek. "Have you meet Herr Donnelly?" His garlic breath made her wince.

The businessman stood and held out his hand. He was about 1.8 meters tall, was well groomed, and smelled clean. His smile never reached his cold blue eyes studying her and served to remind her to be careful. The man was a dangerous predator.

"Herr Hansen, while we wait on His Honor, Judge Hey to arrive, I'd like to hear how Fräulein Weidman escaped the savages," Donnelly said. "You may not be aware, but Herr Burgdorf stopped at Hinton and we had a long talk." His tone gave Franciscka the shivers as she thought, *the feldwebel should have known better than to stop at Hinton.*

"No, I didn't know. Where is the man?" Joe asked.

"No idea. Perhaps the Wapitis murdered him, or he drowned in the river. He was working for Ruffner, so he was likely heading to Narrows for his pay, but I have no other information. I had hoped to hire him, but he wasn't interested."

The man acted so normal, Franciscka had to remind herself not to forget the terrible treatment that his men had inflicted on their hapless prisoners at the salt furnace. "So, Fräulein, how did you escape and survive the perilous trip when an experienced feldwebel might not have?"

"Well, first, I'm an excellent swimmer. Perhaps the feldwebel wasn't."

"Herr Hansen we're entitled to hear how your assistant escaped, or is she a traitor who sold out to the savages?"

Rudolf Hoess looked startled by that idea and set up. Her flippant remark had plainly angered Donnelly.

"Unless you have proof to support such an outrageous claim, I suggest you remember that she is the niece of Field Marshall Guderian and listen to her story," Joe Hansen said. Her boss was again an alarming shade of red.

"Herr Donnelly is worried over his involvement in slavery being exposed." Her statement had the man shaking his head no. She continued, "My main purpose was to examine the river valley for a future toll road. Herr Burgdorf's reason for the trip, I learned involved the transportation of two female slaves whom Herr Ruffner had purchased from Herr Donnelly's men. An illegal transaction, I might remind everyone."

"Was it illegal? Where did the exchange take place?" Rudolf Hoess asked. Franciscka described the salt furnace, the horrific abuse of the captives at the stockade, the return trip to the river falls where

Donnelly's men pinned them down, and after a day of sporadic gunfire exchanges, the Wapitis capturing them.

"Well you certainly had a harrowing experience, but it occurred outside Prussian territories," Rudolf said. "No Prussian laws were broken."

"Why were your men shooting at Ruffner's men?" Joe asked.

"A couple of my guards claimed Burgdorf tried to steal two horses," Donnelly said. "I had nothing to do with it. The feldwebel later claimed the Wapitis had stolen the animals, not him. The foolishness did allow the savages to catch them and carry off Ruffner's property. That's his problem. What I'm interested in hearing about is how she escaped," he said, addressing Joe.

"Are we to understand you're claiming not to have been involved with the slave purchase?" Joe asked. Franciscka looked to see if the assistant attorney general was listening. He was.

Donnelly laughed. "I can't believe you, Joe. I thought you knew the score. There's no law against slavery in the borderlands. Hell, there's no law west of the mountains. In Ichneumon territories, slavery is legal. You both know that, so I'm in no mood for lectures from your pampered princess on subjects she can't comprehend. I just want to hear how your agent escaped."

What a lying bastard, Franciscka thought before answering, "Burgdorf convinced the Wapitis he was trying to save the women after they captured and hauled us to their camp at the mouth of the Jarrell River."

"I'll be damned. That's what Burgdorf claimed," the warlord said. "He told me he had waited until the savages settled down, then slipped off. Are the savages that simple minded?"

"That's what he did. He abandoned me. The Wapitis dragged me before their chief, who to my good luck proved to be a gentleman."

"More likely he was a man responding to a wanton female's sexual charms."

Franciscka put a hand on Joe's arm to stop her boss from reaching across the table.

"If you're done interrupting . . .," she said. After a short silence with no additional remarks from the smiling businessman, she continued, "After listening to Chief Smith complaining about your slave raids, he asked me to convey a message to Mr. Hansen. He even offered to let me hitch a ride with their supply convoy headed to Waynesboro." Her ability to distort what actually occurred without lying amazed Franciscka. Perhaps she should have taken her uncle's advice and studied for the law.

James Donnelly was on his feet, smile gone and his face red. "What lies; those savages never sent a convoy to Waynesboro. How'd you get back?"

"I'm not going to argue, but five days ago, we passed through Lewisburg. I even talked with some of your men at the Cross Road Tavern. Dozens of people saw us. Two days ago, we emerged from the mountains. The Wapitis went north, and I went south. I just got home last night. It was an uneventful but tiring trip."

"You lying bitch, no way would Clem's men have allowed those thieving animals to pass through Lewisburg. He'd have shot or put them in irons. How did you get here? Did the Ichneumons help?"

"Your language is unacceptable and I don't understand your belligerence, Herr Donnelly," Joe Hansen said. "What's the big deal about the Wapitis going to Waynesboro? They range all over the mountains. Hell, you know they trade as far away as Port Delta. Your conduct today causes me to have serious reservations about empowering you to arrest Wapitis dealing in cocaine."

"I'd have to agree with Herr Hansen," Rudolf Hoess said. "I don't think you're the man for this project. The purpose is to stop illegal drugs, not start a war." Franciscka gave Rudolf a big smile while thinking the governor's man, Blankenship, must not have clued the baron's prodigal in on the cotton trust plans. Donnelly looked murderous.

Franciscka's boss delivered the bureaucratic coup de grace to Blankenship's scheme. "This project clearly needs additional study. I wish to thank everyone for attending. I'll fill the judge in when he arrives. Franciscka, have the guard escort Herr Donnelly out of the building."

Joe Hansen invited Rudolf Hoess into his office for a glass of Schnapps and to make him aware the Wapitis were willing to cooperate with their efforts to stop the illegal cocaine trade. After asking the guard to show the flabbergasted warlord out of the building, Franciscka found one of the IRS messengers. She wrote a quick note, and the messenger rushed it to Judge Hay's office. The note advised the judge that the meeting had concluded and Herr Hansen would send a report.

Franciscka arrived back at her boss's office in time to hear Rudolf express delight that the IRS was addressing the lost excise tax revenue problem. Finishing his second glass of schnapps, he repeated the liturgy that their duty as loyal Prussians was to help Emperor Schnabel find all the revenue the empire required. She escorted the assistant attorney general out of the building while pleading prior commitments to avoid a dinner date with the licentious jerk. When she returned to her office from escorting Hoess out, there was a message that her boss wanted a meeting.

"If we're going to nip Blankenship and Donnelly's war in the bud, the Atlantic Tobacco Trust needs to be willing to sell the Wapitis' winter-sloe nuts," Joe said. He pulled a gift-wrapped package out of his lower desk drawer and handed it to her. "It's from the general."

"Two Ichneumon traders were waiting to meet with Chief Smith when I left. Their plans were then to visit Donnelly and

Ruffner's operations and Roanoke. I suspect they're involved in the illegal cocaine. Maybe you could have them detained and questioned," Franciscka said, as she opened her uncle's gift.

The box contained one of the new five-shot revolvers Walters Arms had recently invented. The revolver had a 12cm barrel and a dark blued finish, a beautiful weapon that fired the 9 x 19mm cartridge. Her uncle's gift delighted Franciscka.

"A neat gun your uncle sent," Joe said. "As to riling up the Ichneumon traders by arresting them, I'll think on that. I already requested a meeting with the tobacco trust and expect their representative tomorrow around mid-day. I want you there."

Jacobs and Jacobs Warehouse was a large redbrick building with several loading docks along the rear wall. The ground floor at the front of the building served as a display room for their merchandise. Farm implements, such as walk-behind iron plows, rakes, grain sickles, and many different styles and sizes of shovels, picks, axes, and hammers were on display. Another area had dozens of wooden barrels full of different-sized iron nails, ropes, and chains. The room's air had a pleasant hint of molasses and pinewood.

Business was brisk. Busy clerks sat at a long wood counter discussing orders with customers leaning on the other side. Other clerks and laborers carried items from the rear area of the store to show customers or to fill orders. Other than his height, Rex blended in with the men. A few women worked behind the counter and several women were among the customers. Bib overalls made from a bluish denim like material were popular, though many of the men wore fatigues similar to Rex's outfit.

Firearms and shooting supplies were in a separate room with iron-barred windows and door. The room looked like a jail cell converted for merchandise display. Most of the rifles were new muzzle-loaders that used a percussion cap ignition system, though a few flintlocks were available. Four Krupp rolling block rifles were on display with 1000-D-mark price tags. The muzzleloader price was 298 D-marks. The store sold five-kilo wood kegs of gunpowder in different grades, FFg for muskets and reloading cartridges, and FFFFg for pistols and priming flintlocks. A keg of powder was 112 D-marks for either grade.

"How much are primers for the 11.6 x 65mm Krupp cartridge?" Rex asked the elderly clerk. Unlike the gunpowder, the chalkboard didn't list the primer prices.

"They're sold by the box. A box of one hundred primers cost ten D-marks, same price as the percussion caps for the muskets."

"I'm from up north; are these Krupp rifles and cartridges available?" Rex asked the elderly male clerk leaning on the firearm counter.

"The rifle is new and popular with hunters," the clerk said. "It's been difficult to get this year because of the war. However, Herr Donnelly's order for fifty rifles was filled, so maybe the factory has increased production."

"How quick could you fill an order for ten of the rifles?" Rex asked. Damn, the clerk looked skeptical instead of pleased by the question. Surely, he passed as a Prussian.

"Ten? That's quite a large order," the suspicious clerk said. "Who are they for? Sales to the savages are not allowed."

"Spare me the obvious," Rex said, stalling for an inspiration. Then he thought of Lily and Tara's buyer. "The supplies are for Herr Ruffner from Narrows. So how long is it going to take to find the rifles?"

"Odd," the clerk said, studying Rex. "I haven't seen a request or bank draft. Herr Ruffner always arranges firearm orders ahead of sending a man to pick up the order." The clerk's mistrustful attitude irritated Rex. If not stopped, it might endanger the Wapitis' rifle purchase.

"Maybe he didn't trust those men with cash," Rex said. "I've had enough of your dilly-dallying. My boss, Herr Ruffner, wants those rifles and powder, now, not next year." He looked around the room and then added, "Where's your boss, Herr Jacobs?"

"Why didn't you say it was a cash deal? Wait here. I'll check on rifle availably." The arthritic clerk limped into the back room to check while Rex pulled up a stool and sat at the counter to recheck and add up the other supplies he needed.

The store-supplied pencil he used was a heavy, flat, wood affair with a hole drilled through one end for attaching a string anchored to the counter. The heavy string was short and interfered with using it. Rex assumed the string's purpose was to discourage people from carrying it off. Pencils must be costly or Jacobs was a miser, Rex reasoned as he awkwardly slid the scrap paper to compensate for lack of movement allowed by the short string. Aggravated, he yanked on the pencil to snap the string. Instead, the pencil snapped.

With the now-free stub of pencil, Rex checked his initial calculation on the amount of gunpowder required to reload the 11.6 x 65mm Krupp cartridge. A five-kilo keg of powder would reload a thousand rounds of ammo. To make bullets for a thousand reloaded rounds, he'd need twenty-seven kilos of lead. Chief Smith had entrusted twenty-five thousand D-marks to Rex for buying supplies to equip an eighteen-man police force. Ten rifles and two thousand rounds of ammo would put a serious dent in his funds. The Wapitis also needed powder, primers, and lead for reloading empty 11.6 x 65mm brass and the tribe's existing muzzle-loaders.

"Herr Knight, for Herr Ruffner, we'll sell ten of the rifles with cleaning kits for eleven thousand D-marks." The Jacobs' clerk noticed the broken pencil and added, "How'd my pencil get broken?"

"It just snapped," Rex said. "Why is the price higher?"

"We had to pull six rifles from Donnelly's large order," the clerk said while examining the piece of the broken pencil still attached to the string. "It's for the extra shipping cost to replace those rifles. You'll need several bullet molds for the Krupp. Should I add those?"

Rex and the clerk worked up the order. The order included primers, caps, eight kegs of coarse gunpowder, and two kegs of fine gunpowder, along with twenty of the eight-kg ingots of lead. The order would provide sufficient material for the Wapitis to reload 5,000 rounds, plus have supplies for the muskets. He made a 10,000-D-mark deposit to secure the order and arranged to pick up the order in two days.

Rex left for the Wapiti camp at Nutter's Mountain. He hoped, on return, he'd be picking up his order, not the local sheriff picking him up.

Tom and Lou Jarrell, for whatever mysterious genetic reasons, didn't look like typical Wapitis. To Rex, they looked like a couple of lanky, young, blue-eyed redneck hicks. Maria Belcher had told him the Jarrell brothers were two of the more sensible and intelligent of the students she'd taught, and they would listen to and follow orders.

He also learned Donnelly's men had captured the brothers' two teenage nieces in a raid the previous month. Maria figured they would be willing precipitants in any of his plans to bring Donnelly to justice. The brothers had handled the column's lead-guard duties well when they had passed through Lewisburg the other night. Tom and Lou had the bystanders, mostly Donnelly employees, trading jokes with them and even waving to the Wapiti column. Hate of Donnelly and their understandable desire for vengeance wasn't interfering with the brothers' ability to think.

"Lou, Tom, I want your help with the pack-horses and supplies. You two look like a couple of Clem's thugs," Rex said.

The Jarrell brothers laughed and agreed. Steve looked disappointed not to be included. As part of the Jarrell brothers' camouflage, Rex had bought two pairs of those blue bib overalls that many of Jacobs and Jacobs's customers wore. He handed Tom the bundle. "Wear these overalls tomorrow. With the coats and hats you stripped from the late Jake and his buddy, you'll pass for a couple of Clem's thugs, or in this case, two of Ruffner's."

At the campfire that evening, Rex explained to the group that he needed to return to Roanoke in the morning to coordinate certain matters with their Prussian friends. Maria Belcher agreed to enter Lewisburg the next night to scout the town. Rex asked Steve to assist Maria.

"Maria, plan on staying two days in Lewisburg. On the evening of the third day, Steve will meet you on the east side of the Sulfur River and escort you back to the column. Depending on your findings, I'll decide on when and where to cross," Rex said. He cautioned her to be careful.

Before sunrise the following morning, Rex and the Jarrell brothers left for Roanoke. Tom had stuck several large feathers into his hat, which Rex considered a bit too much. "No feathers for now."

The meeting was in Joe's IRS office. The representative from the Atlantic Tobacco Trust, Rahul Malhotra, a lawyer, was a small, bald man with a large hooked nose. His dark glasses prevented seeing his pupils. Franciscka wondered if his blood might be blue; he had that vague feline appearance of the Ichneumon except for his nose. After perfunctory greetings, her boss started the meeting.

"Rahul, before I lay out our thoughts, I wanted to reemphasize that the emperor is not pleased with the results of our efforts to eliminate illegal, non-taxed cocaine sales in the territories. Berlin is looking for someone to make an example of."

"Well, the tobacco company isn't happy either with the lost sales," the tobacco man said. "However, it's a matter for the police. Why aren't they arresting the dealers and hanging a few?"

"Why indeed," Joe said. "The sheriffs claim that new dealers replace the arrested dealers, often within a day. The supplier is the mystery. I figure, let the police continue to chase the dealers. It has to help some."

"If it does, it's not discernible," the lawyer said.

"Instead, the IRS wants to try another approach," continued Joe. "I have reason to believe the Wapitis would agree to stop all winter-sloe nuts sales to independent traders and instead roast and package the nuts for individual retail sales, not unlike the way the tobacco trust packs its cigarettes."

"Those savages aren't capable of that!" Rahul said. "They can't even manage to shell, clean, and bag the raw unshelled nuts in large burlap bags on a consistent basis. Now you want me to believe they can bag clean, roasted, salted nuts in individual-size paper bags. You can't be serious."

Franciscka's boss scrutinized the tobacco lawyer for a moment, and then continued. "However, the only feasible way for the Wapitis to sell large amounts of the roasted nuts would be to market through Atlantic's dealer network. Acceptance of the Wapitis' proposal by the tobacco trust would help eliminate a growing criminal problem plaguing the Prussian Empire. My question, Herr Malhotra, is, why hasn't the trust agreed to this sensible and financially attractive proposal?"

Joe's secretary, the elderly Prussian-Greek War veteran, served everyone hot black tea. The tobacco representative seemed embarrassed by his prior disparaging remarks. The man spent an inordinate amount of time fussing with the sugar and cream and tasting the tea before responding to Joe's question. Franciscka wondered if it was a ploy by the attorney to gain time to think. Then again, her boss's tea was so bad that maybe the lawyer was simply trying to assure he'd added sufficient sugar and milk to render the poisonous brew drinkable.

"It's true the trust has received similar proposals, the most recent one from a savage who claims to be chief of those tribes living in the area where the blue winter-sloe grows," Herr Malhotra said. "And maybe he is the head man, and maybe they do want to sell nuts to the trust, but we believe they would prove undependable partners, being illiterate savages. And you are aware those roasted nuts eliminate the desire for cocaine? I know the Ichneumons are aware of that fact."

Franciscka exchanged looks with her boss, who was probably wondering the same thing. The tobacco trust and Ichneumon Empire feared the roasted nuts might adversely affect the population's demand for cocaine.

"The trust's other concern is that the Ichneumon emperor has threatened to cancel the current arrangement in which all Ichneumon cocaine is sold through the tobacco trust," said Herr Malhotra. "Many independent dealers want to buy cocaine direct from the Ichneumons. The Ichneumons claim they're losing business to the winter-sloe cocaine, cocaine that is competitive with Ichneumon cocaine only because the bootleggers don't pay those outrageous Prussian taxes. Yet Emperor Schnabel does nothing to stop the illegal sales."

"What do you think we're discussing? And the Ichneumon emperor and the tobacco company shouldn't forget the reason that agreement exists is that Emperor Schnabel chose to allow cocaine sales in return for tax revenue. If the Ichneumons start supplying dealers with cocaine who don't pay the taxes, I expect the emperor will stop all cocaine sales."

“That imprudent action would just ensnare the Prussian Empire and territories in an expensive drug war,” Rahul said.

“I don’t disagree, but it’ll cost the tobacco trust a lucrative business. Ratakonda is a fool if he thinks the Prussians will passively accept cocaine sales to unlicensed dealers. It’ll make the Ichneumons enemies of the Prussians, and if Berlin thinks the Atlantic Tobacco Trust has been less than candid in this illegal cocaine business, your company might be barred from operating in the empire.”

Franciscka thought the lawyer looked off balance. His hand shook as he put his tea down. For sure, her boss’s remarks had the tobacco lawyer bristling.

“Please refrain from threats and derogatory remarks regarding Emperor Ratakonda. As for the current illegal drug problem, our understanding is that Governor Bullard has decided on a solution. He plans to eliminate the savages. In fact, I wondered why you even requested this meeting, knowing that.”

“New information,” Joe Hansen said. “There’s reason to believe rogue traders based in Orleans control the nontaxed cocaine network. They buy the winter-sloe from the Wapitis, and then convert them to cocaine. If the Wapitis stop all raw nut sales, those bootleggers are out of the cocaine business. It’s a simple solution to a complex problem and doesn’t require starting a war, just your cooperation.”

“Is the governor aware of your proposal for the tobacco trust to deal with those savages?” Herr Malhotra asked.

“I’m curious; why do you keep referring to the Wapitis as savages?” Franciscka asked. She’s had heard enough disparaging remarks about the Wapitis from this Ichneumon partisan. “They send their children to Jesuit schools, they don’t worship idols, many follow the Reformed Prussian Church rites, and they marry; whereas the Ichneumons worship demons, treat their females as chattel, and make a sport out of cutting the hearts from living and hapless captives. It would seem to me that the Ichneumons are whom you should call savage."

Franciscka willed her hand steady as she took a sip of her boss's wretched tea. To her delight, the bigoted tobacco lawyer turned crimson. Her boss nodded in agreement with her comment.

"The Ichneumons are a proud and powerful race with great gods who demand blood," replied Rahul.

"Oh, spare us, they're barbarians," Franciscka said. Her boss gave her a look that meant she might have gone too far.

"They don't expect lesser people to understand," the haughty lawyer snapped back and then paused to study her, before adding, "Especially women. And I'm in no mood to explain their ancient rituals."

Franciscka decided that nonsense didn't merit a reply.

"Back to the purpose of this meeting, I'll pass on your request," Rahul said. "In the meantime I suggest you make the Guderian territorial governor aware of what you're asking of the tobacco trust."

"I'm not finished, Herr Malhotra," said Joe. "A common misperception is that the IRS answers to the territorial governor. That's not the case. Emperor Schnabel is our boss. My instructions are to end the illegal cocaine traffic and collect the excise tax due. If you wish, I'll inform Emperor Schnabel that the Atlantic Tobacco Trust fears the displeasure of the Ichneumon emperor more than his."

"You're twisting my meaning," said Rahul Malhotra. "Both the company and I hold Emperor Schnabel in the highest regard. Instead, I have been attempting to explain why I believe your ill-conceived proposal has the potential to disrupt an important business and cost the empire tax revenue. However, I may have been a bit bleak as to the Ichneumon and board of directors' response. I need a week to discuss your proposal with the trust's management. Perhaps accommodations are possible. I'd like a chance to explore potential resolutions before you bother the emperor."

"Certainly, Herr Malhotra," Joe said. "May I suggest we meet again in two weeks, here?"

Franciscka Weidman watched her boss escort the tobacco lawyer to the front door. Anyone viewing the backslapping and laughing would think the two men were friends. Joe returned in a few minutes to his office and told her he wanted to send the Wapiti chief a warning using one of her pigeons. They worked on the note together.

"How's this sound?" Joe asked. 'Tobacco trust is indifferent to Wapiti winter-sloe proposal, not clear on reason. T-Trust has questions on Chief Smith's authority. Fear possible assassination attempt on Chief Smith. Follow up meeting in two weeks.'

The IRS had special rice paper and fine-tipped glass pens to write the message. Franciscka printed Joe's words on the rice paper. He verified she had it correct and then she left for Rex Knight's rooming house to find her pigeons. Instead, she found Rex and the Jarrell brothers with three packhorses. They had arrived before her, dusty and tired from the trip back. She let Rex read the note before attaching the tiny ivory cylinder with the note sealed in it to the pigeon's leg. After Franciscka launched the pigeon, she told Rex about the meeting between the Prussian IRS and the Atlantic Tobacco Trust.

Jacobs and Jacobs opened at sunrise. The owner, Herr Jacobs, greeted Rex as he rode up to the rear loading dock with the Jarrell brothers. The enterprising merchant appeared of Semitic ancestry and caused him to wonder if one of Herr Jacobs' ancestors had been a Phoenician trader snatched off Earth or if he shared Clovis heritage. Regardless, the storeowner was a cheerful, energetic man about Rex's age and a third of a meter shorter.

"Herr Knight, I'm pleased to make your acquaintance. Is Herr Burgdorf no longer handling Len Ruffner's orders?"

"My boss has him busy on projects across the mountains. He told me not to dally, but then you're familiar with Herr Ruffner- all business."

Jacobs, smiling, nodded and yelled, "Snap to it, these men don't have all day." The two dockworkers and Jarrell brothers got busy loading the packhorses.

Rex knew the balance owed and handed over a bundle of D-marks to Herr Jacobs. The action brought a smile to the storeowner's face.

"Loading will take time. Would you care for a cup of tea or coffee while the men finish?" He motioned for Rex to follow him into his office. Bookshelves lined the small office walls from the floor to the ceiling, predominantly ledgers and parts catalogs.

"I'd love a cup of coffee. Where did you buy the beans?"

"The Ichneumon trader had some. Have you had coffee before?" Jacobs's question made Rex suddenly cautious; then he thought of his supposed background of being from the northern ice sheets.

"Yes, before I started working for Ruffner, I was a fisherman, and traders came from everywhere for the salted cod." He madly racked his brain for where else coffee grew besides the Ichneumon territory in South and Central America. Coffee grew in Ethiopia, Africa, but he didn't know what people on this version of Earth called the continent. He decided not to chance a misstep and invented a trader. "One of the items the Greeks traded for the cod was coffee."

"I'd never had dealings with them. Well, you'll have to tell me how the Ichneumon coffee compares. How'd you get so far from home?" the storeowner asked as he handed Rex a metal cup of steaming rich, black coffee.

He considered the wisdom of suggesting a connection to the Wapitis for he needed to get that story circulating in Roanoke to nip any interest in the Jesuit circle about rumors of a false prophet among the Wapitis. Jacobs appeared to be a man who traded in rumors and news. The problem for Rex was his alleged employer being a dealer in slaves. Jacobs might wonder why a man with a mother who was a slave would work for a slaver. Rex decided not to worry about it.

"My mother was a Wapiti slave traded to cod fishermen. I returned to handle some old family business. Needed a job, and Ruffner offered this one, at least until Burgdorf is freed up. This coffee is excellent. Do you by chance have any extra beans I can buy?"

"I can spare a kilo bag," the storeowner said. "You'll need a small mortar and pestle to grind the beans, which I have. Herr Ruffner must know you well to entrust all the cash to you. He never allowed Burgdorf to pay in cash."

Having met Burgdorf, Rex wouldn't trust the man either. Rex was tempted to ask about the banking system, but decided to play safe and offered no comment.

After a moment, Jacobs said, "I'm sorry to hear of your mother's misfortune. Slavery is a plague on the Guderian Territory. The emperor wants to end the practice, but certain short-sighted business interests promote it."

"My father was a kind owner," Rex said. "It could have been worse."

"It's still slavery. I have a good friend, heads the IRS office, Joe Hansen. He told me the cotton boys have hired slavers to round up Wapitis for workers in Myrtle Territory. Since Donnelly bought fifty new rifles, I figure Joe has the right of it. Now Ruffner buys rifles. I hope he's not planning to be involved, or you, in that nasty business."

Rex disliked having the friendly storeowner think him in league with a slaver, but staying in character was essential, and he emptied his cup. "Herr Jacobs, I need to check on my men."

Jacobs and his elderly clerk were most helpful in instructing them on how to load the packhorses and in the process sold Rex several rolls of hemp one-centimeter-diameter rope. At the suggestion of Lou Jarrell, he bought two 25-kilo bags of corn meal and a bag of oats for the horses, along with two sides of bacon. He would have bought more, but the six horses were loaded down. Each rider carried four of the 8-kg lead bars in his saddlebag.

By mid-morning, the Jarrell brothers were packed and they were waiting for Franciscka at the rooming house to hand over the pigeons. She rode up with an older man as Rex finished reading the receipt Jacobs had given him at the dock for Ruffner's accountant. There was a one-D-mark charge for a pencil included in the total.

"Rex, Tom, Lou, this is my boss, Joe Hansen. He wanted to meet you." They must have looked worried, for she added, "He knows."

Rex wasn't sure just what the gorgeous Prussian woman meant by that. Her boss even smiled on hearing that cryptic remark. He was an older man and projected gravitas despite the belly and rumpled clothes, a man whom Rex speculated would be more comfortable behind a desk than on a horse.

"I wanted a face to go with a name and asked Fräulein Weidman to introduce us. I understand you're in a hurry and won't delay you. However, I wanted to thank you for returning my assistant in good health and to advise you that James Donnelly and Myrtle Territory's attorney general have a plan to arrest Wapitis, fine them large amounts for sham illegal drug dealing, then rent them to the Southern Textile Trust as slaves to collect the fine monies."

"Donnelly won't encounter passive victims this time," Tom Jarrell said.

Rex hoped the young Wapiti had enough sense to say no more as the IRS manager gave their packhorse loads a meaningful glance.

"So I understand, though I thought territorial law prohibits the sale of firearms to indigenous people such as the Wapitis and Clovis. Hard to have a fair fight when one side has Krupp rifles and the other side is armed with atlatls and darts."

"I agree. Perhaps the Ichneumon traders will help the Wapitis. I really must be going. Herr Ruffner can be impatient."

"Those are Ruffner's supplies?" Joe, startled, looked toward Franciscka for verification. He got a shrug for an answer.

Steve Johnson and Maria Belcher arrived back in camp riding one horse. Maria's right leg was a bloody mess. Rex learned a large bear had ambushed them near the trail's crest across Peters Mountain. After several questions, he decided Steve was describing a short-face bear, the largest carnivorous mammal ever to bless North America. On Earth, the bear had gone extinct at the end of the Pleistocene era. *What a strange world, could mastodons existed*, Rex wondered?

"It burst out of the thicket and grabbed Maria's horse, throwing her into the ravine. My rifle had no effect on the monster."

"Because you missed and shot my horse instead of the bear," Maria said. "It was awful. My leg is a mess. Can I have some whiskey first?"

Rex ran to his saddle, got his flask of corn whiskey, and returned in time to hear Steve arguing.

"Maria, I couldn't miss at that distance. Since it seemed satisfied with the horse and ignored you, I decided not to chance enraging it by shooting it again. Instead, I grabbed you," Steve said before addressing Rex, "We galloped about a kilometer before I stopped and put the tourniquet on her leg."

He gave Maria the flask. Her loss of blood had been severe and Sue's efforts to clean the dirt out of the ripped muscle would cause more, but infection was even more dangerous. He urged Maria to drink all the whiskey, knowing the pain had to be bad. She would be out of action for a couple of weeks.

As Sue cleaned the dirt out of her sister's ripped flesh with cooled boiled water, Maria related her information between moans. Her news was unfavorable.

"Donnelly sent Clem with eighteen men on horses to Lewisburg with orders to intercept our supply convoy and enslave any survivors," Maria said. "My friend, Sally, said they all believe we went to Waynesboro for their supplies."

"Well, that helps some," he said, wondering why Clem would think that. Franciscka?

"Is this hurting too much?" Sue asked. "Should I stop?" Steve had found a clean cotton towel for a bandage. "Go boil the towel first. Then use a clean stick to bring it here. Don't let anyone touch it."

"No, get it finished. Also, Clem apparently thinks the terrain around Lewisburg offered too many trails for us savages to sneak by the town. Instead, he's set the ambush at the mountain pass a couple of kilometers east of the Sulfur River bridge, according to Porky, the guy who cares for the pigeon coop in Lewisburg."

"I know that area," Rex said. "Clem has picked the best spot to block the column if we were in Waynesboro. I assume Porky's pigeons are those Clem and Donnelly use to carry messages."

"Yes, there's a pigeon coop above the stables at the Lewisburg stockade."

"Who and how do they keep track of the pigeons?" asked Rex. "For example, do the birds have leg rings?"

"Porky, a one-leg veteran, cares for the birds," Maria said. "Damn, Sue, don't dig so deep." Her sister muttered something about needing to get all the dirt. After a moment to settle her breathing, Maria said.

"They're two types of pigeons. Gray ones trained to home on Lewisburg, and the brown pigeons that home on Hinton. Porky collects those on the open roost each day and, after removing the messenger tube, puts the birds in the coop. Later, someone collects the gray pigeons and takes them back to Hinton. Often the same person will bring back the brown pigeons at Hinton on his return trip. Porky is not an organized man, and I don't believe the pigeons are otherwise identified."

"Who sends Clem messages? Donnelly?" Rex asked. She didn't know. Between the whiskey and her wounds, she was drifting off and needed her rest. Sue finished up by wrapping the wound in the clean boiled towel.

The Wapiti column made excellent progress down the mountain and then south through the beautiful valley along the west face of Peters Mountain. They followed a game trail and crossed a small, clear stream several times and a saddle between watersheds that offered an easy path west toward what on Earth was Gap Mills and on toward the Sulfur River.

Chapter 6

James Donnelly poured a generous measure of corn whiskey into his battered tin mug, leaned back in the wobbly wooden chair, and told Gene Peters to bring in the new hires. The chair was on a temporary wood plank stage supported by several barrels of salted pork in the large rear room of his Hinton warehouse. Gene, his Hinton commander, had been busy hiring eighty new fighting men. Now he would meet his newly hired crew and learn if Gene still knew how to find capable fighters.

While waiting for the new hires to enter, he thought again of the cost. The tobacco crop had exceeded his expectations, two-hundred metric tons of the finest burley leaf. The money from that crop plus the half million D-marks he hoped to net from the Ichneumons' campaign against the Wapitis would allow him to join Purnell's railroad syndicate as an equal partner. Then his family and those Berlin aristocrats would regret their shabby treatment of him.

But enough dreaming he needed to stay focused on the new hires. Wars were expensive undertakings, and could go haywire in a moment. Keeping tight reins on the cost of the new campaign was vital, or it would spiral out of control before the first shot. James had been shocked to learn a man with his own horse now demanded 150 D-marks a day, plus fodder for his horse. That damn eastern war with the Mongols was causing all kinds of shortages.

Gene could still hire horseless men for 50 D-marks a day. However, James preferred to avoid those individuals. Almost to a man, they had serious drug and alcohol issues. The eighty mostly unwashed bodies quickly fouled the room air. Thinking of the twelve thousand D-mark daily payroll the group in front of him represented, James wasted no time on preambles and stood up.

"In a few days, we'll march down the river and teach the savages who their betters are." The group loudly cheered James's comment. That response surprised him. Apparently, the new hires were unaware of Clem's difficulties at Salt Furnace. Or if they were aware, they agreed with James' opinion that Clem, despite his denials, had been drunk. No one believed a gang of those Wapitis' half-breeds and savages could beat trained and armed white men in a fair fight. It just didn't happen, and he planned to replace Clem as soon as this campaign ended.

"All spoils are split fifty-fifty," James said. "Captured weapons belong to the company." The group was quiet on those conditions. Their lack of appreciation for his generous offer to split the spoils irritated James. Not that he intended to spit everything of value with this motley gang.

"Captured women are yours to have fun with. When you're done, they become company property."

That got a roaring enthusiastic response, as everyone knew he was talking about Wapiti women.

"Commander Peters will assign you to a squad. The sergeant in charge of your assigned squad will be your leader. Obey him, and all will be fine. Insubordination will result in facing a firing squad."

No surprise; no cheer greeted that pronouncement. Having had a chance to study his audience, James feared the crew had a disproportionate number of obvious alcoholics to healthy ex-soldiers.

"I want results. I'm paying you well. Clean out those worthless savages, and as a bonus, I'll let you keep the new Krupp rifle." Cheering greeted his pronouncement. With that promise, James turned the eighty mercenaries over to Gene and his five former Prussian sergeants to organize into a fighting force. Gene and the sergeants had three days to achieve that miracle.

Before leaving the warehouse, James spent several minutes renewing old acquaintances with mercenaries he recognized from prior campaigns and greeting some of the new men. He then walked next door to his office in the nearby stockade. The fresh air was a relief after the warehouse. He knew it would be short lived; the Ichneumons usually smoked those disgusting island cigars.

Manuel Prado and Bret Paget, cigars a going, waited in James' office. A layer of gray smoke had already accumulated against the ceiling. The Ichneumon trader and his partner Bret Paget sat at the conference table. A large canvas duffel bag was on the floor between their chairs.

"They're not much," Manuel said. James knew the Ichneumon trader was referring to the group of men in the warehouse he was hiring as mercenaries. The blue-blooded jerks enjoyed speaking disparagingly of his men and efforts, but in the end, the Ichneumons always hired them.

"Gene Peters and his Prussian sergeants will whip them into fighting shape. Besides, the Wapitis are docile folks. Did you bring the money?"

"Docile?" Manuel said. "The main subject of conversation at Chief Smith's village was over their warriors wiping out your garrison at the salt furnace and freeing the captives. The Wapitis even caught the Prussians and freed their captives."

"The Wapitis and their chief take credit, but the Prussians ambushed my men at the stockade," James said. He knew that wasn't true, but he didn't believe the Wapitis had been the gang either. Even Clem, whose men had been involved, couldn't identify the attackers. Though due to the attackers discipline under fire, Clem didn't believe they were any of the local savages. Burgdorf's claim that it was one rogue Prussian wasn't credible and James didn't mention it.

"I talked with Ruffner's man," Manuel said. "He claimed he knew nothing about any massacre at the furnace until your men turned on him at the falls' crossing."

Burgdorf had told James the same tale. Neither of them knew who had sent the original pigeon message, but Manuel didn't need to know that either.

"Burgdorf stopped on his way to the salt furnace and settled Ruffner's debt," James said. "I haven't seen him since, though I'd heard he did pass through on his return trip to Narrows. I'd also heard the other Prussian was a girl. Burgdorf probably used her to distract my men. For sure, I'm not worried about a bunch of aborigines armed with spears."

James walked to the bar and poured each of them a small amount of the corn whiskey that he had Simpson making near Lewisburg. The Ichneumons didn't need to know Burgdorf was now in his employment.

"I did hear a rumor that Burgdorf had drowned in the river near Narrows," James said. Drowning was his favorite explanation for answering inquiries about people who had disappeared after a visit to the Hinton stockade. He hoped the Ichneumon traders would think James had murdered Burgdorf over the salt furnace fiasco and drop the matter.

"To the successful enslavement of the Wapiti tribes," James said. Neither Ichneumon responded to his whiskey salute.

"Spare us your placating drivel. Emperor Ratakonda is not satisfied with the results of your efforts to eliminate Wapitis. You have lost control of the salt furnace stockade. That defeat has emboldened the tribes who are now talking about forming a territory under Prussian rule."

“That’s not happening. Emperor Schnabel would never trust these savages.”

He knew Purnell’s railroad syndicate planned to control the coal and timber. They would never tolerate the emperor allowing those savages to control the rich territory. The syndicate members would join forces with the Ichneumons, if necessary, to block the Wapitis.

“The Wapitis are even discussing a deal with the tobacco trust to sell roasted nuts,” Manuel continued.

“Now I know that’s nonsense. Why would anyone think the tobacco interest would sell a product that eliminated the craving for cocaine?”

“Is it? You do grasp that Emperor Ratakonda wants to sell more cocaine, not less,” Manuel said. “Having those roasted nuts available in the same outlet with the cocaine will not help our emperor accomplish that goal. We’re wondering if we should be dealing with Cinnabar.”

The criticism infuriated him. It wasn’t fair, but he needed that payment. Hell, after what he’d just learned, it was in his interest to help eliminate the Wapitis. He held back that response. Manuel might try to pay him less, if the Ichneumon thought he was worried about the Wapitis acquiring their own territory. Then for an insane moment, he considered killing the two Ichneumon traders at the table and simply taking their money.

After another moment to assure his temper was under control, James said, “What the problem, Manuel? Ratakonda threatening to make you a Sun God sacrifice. Cinnabar would be more likely to eat you than deal.” He did not want the Ichneumons talking with Chief Cinnabar.

“Don’t joke; we’re discussing serious matters,” Manuel said. His partner, Bret, must have agreed, for his normal contemptuous look was now menacing.

"The salt furnace was a fluke. I have the men and equipment here, ready to go and deal with the Wapitis. My force can and will kill and scatter those savages. In a week, the Wapitis will be more concerned about staying alive than forming a territory. Should I proceed or tell the men to go home?" He needed the money, but he'd had his fill of Manuel's judgmental attitude.

James finished his whiskey and poured himself another from the bottle on the table. If the Ichneumon bastards wanted more whiskey, they could serve themselves. He waited for Manuel's answer.

"The bag contains one million D-marks. Half as low denomination paper bills and half, as you requested, in Prussian 500 D-mark gold coins. Those four leather pouches each contain 250 coins," Manuel said while placing the heavy bag on the desk.

James reached in and pulled one of the leather pouches from the bag. He felt the pouch's heft before opening it and relaxed. Only gold was that heavy. The Ichneumons were going for his deal.

"There's a little over one kilograms of pure gold in each pouch. I figure you could buy Cinnabar's entire force with two bags," Manuel said before adding, "If your drunks can't handle the Wapitis."

"Probably, but who wants to deal with that insane animal? He'd be more likely to eat the captives, than turn them over as slaves," James said, ignoring the slur. He now wondered if the Ichneumons knew of Burgdorf's mission.

"Slaves? I'm glad you reminded me of that issue," Manuel said. "Ichneumon interests are financing this campaign, and we don't want your efforts spent on collecting Wapitis alive to sell to the cotton growers. Dead Wapitis are what we're paying for; is that clear? If a few survive and you want to sell them, fine, but Emperor Ratakonda wants the Wapitis eliminated as a potential ally in the Prussian western expansion. Not slaves that can escape from the cotton fields and return here. Are we clear on that point?"

"But Blankenship told me the cotton plantations needed thousands of slaves and this payment was from them. They expect five hundred slaves in payment," James said. Kill the captives, what a harebrained plan. These bloody Ichneumons always manage to complicate a deal.

"Well, I'm pleased to learn Stan Blankenship believed my nonsense about the cotton growers paying for slaves; helps to hold down talk about genocide. Who wants those troublesome Jesuits involved," Manuel said.

"But … they will pay two thousand D-marks for each healthy male Wapiti. Why waste them? Selling them as slaves still ends the nut harvest," James said.

"Bret will remain as the Emperor Ratakonda's observer to verify you've killed sufficient Wapitis that this year's nut crop rots on the ground. It's especially critical that your crew eliminate Chief Smith and his ally John Hopkins. That needs to be your main priority, followed by destroying the Wapiti villages up the Hopkins River and at the mouth of the Jarrell River."

"I understand," James said, dropping his objection. The fool didn't need to know he planned to sell the captives as slaves. If Bret became a problem, well Burgdorf could eliminate him.

"Have you ever met an Ichneumon woman?" the trader asked.

James, confused by the sudden change of subject, admitted that he hadn't.

"The reason you haven't, they're precious and protected from all threats. However, the emperor is considering establishing breeding colonies at Port Delta, Hickory Ridge, and River Point."

"Breeding colonies?" James asked. He started to add a sarcastic response about insects, then realized he might be about to hear the real reason for the Ichneumons' murderous campaign, "I don't understand."

"Currently," Manuel said, "all our wives and children live in Cusco. Emperor Ratakonda is in the process of deciding if our three Erie River forts are secure enough to assure the safety of our women. He is waiting on the army's report. If General Bezdek guarantees the river forts security, the emperor will allow a limited number of the wives to leave the protection of Cusco, my wife, for example."

The Ichneumons were murdering the Wapitis so they could bring their wives across the ocean. Manuel must think him an idiot.

"The main issue holding up General Bezdek's final report is the security of the River Point fort, should the Prussian army invade the Southern River valley," Manuel said. "The general's concern is that the Wapitis' yammering for a new territory will provide the Prussians with a pretext for an invasion."

"No Wapitis, no territorial request makes a certain sense," James said. More sense than Ichneumons longing for their wives. "Is the fear the Prussians would kill your wives?"

The Ichneumons were protective of their women folk, but this seemed extreme. He finished his cup of whiskey, reached for the bottle, then realized he'd had two cups already and stopped.

"In battles, cannonballs don't discriminate on who they kill. An Ichneumon man who loses a wife before she gives birth to a healthy daughter becomes a pariah, even denied entrance to the Cusco temple. Of course the same high priests demand your wife have at least five children, which can be difficult to accomplish when the emperor's demands keep your beds three thousand kilometers apart."

Manuel tasted his whiskey, and then added, "None of that is your concern. Your job is to rid the valley of Wapitis. The problem with selling them as slaves is they can still breed and return."

Could those rumors be true? He had heard most Ichneumon births were males. Only one out of five live births resulted in a female, which could explain the other rumor that their population was in decline. You'd think Manuel's neighbors would keep the wife warm, but he was correct, it wasn't his concern; keeping the Ichneumons' payment was.

"I understand. We're to kill Wapitis. We'll march in three days," James hoped Burgdorf was being successful with Cinnabar.

"With Chief Smith, we may be able to help," Manuel said. "Good whiskey. Might I have another taste?"

James asked how the Ichneumon might help as he refilled the metal cups. Manuel told him about the army's plan before adding a new complication.

"Prince Cherukuru is at River Point's stone fort," Manuel said. "He wants to see your force. I've invited him to the salt furnace, told him he'd get first pick of the captives. Try not to disappoint the emperor's favorite nephew."

"So some slaves are okay?" James asked.

"Who said anything about slaves?" Manuel asked. "The prince will amuse himself with some of the young Wapiti women before you kill them."

As Rex had expected, there was no settlement in the area where on Earth the town of Alderson existed. A trail did snake off north on the other side of the Sulfur River, so there was a ford. The main river valley trail from Hinton to Lewisburg was also visible on the opposite shore. Rex knew the column had to cross that ford before Donnelly located them. The knowledge that a few men on the opposite riverbank could block the crossing spurred Rex to action.

"Tom, let's live dangerously. We're going across the river and find a place that will allow us to ambush anyone who shows up to block the ford." He hadn't forgotten yesterday's narrow escape. Those few Donnelly men at Gap Mill could have stopped the caravan if Larry hadn't spotted them. Instead, the Wapitis managed to ambush them.

"Marvelous idea," Tom said. "I like ambushing ambushers."

The river flow was low and other than for a narrow channel of fast-flowing water that came to the horses' knees, an easy crossing. They left the horses out of sight behind the low ridge, then walked back to a cluster of several boulders about fifty meters up the slope from the river trail and across from the ford. They settled down to wait for darkness and the column. About an hour later, Rex heard horses. Six riders were trotting up the river trail. The group stopped below their hiding spot.

"You want this crossing or the one up the river?" the lead rider asked the older man beside him. The lead rider appeared to study the riverbank by the ford, and after a moment, he added, "Two horses crossed here today. Probably tracks from a couple of the tobacco boys making their rounds. I'll take this crossing. You three cover the one up the river."

The other rider hesitated as if he wanted to dispute that decision but said, "Hell, it's another five kilometers. How long should I watch it? Donnelly worries too much. You know Clem's going to handle those savages."

"Save your bitching for Gene. Wait two days, then we'll meet back here," the lead rider said. Seeing the indecision in the older rider, he added, "Just remember this is easier work than hauling Anders Breuer's supplies to the salt furnace."

The man dismounted from his horse, walked to the water's edge, and pissed in the river. Two of the other riders dismounted and found logs to rest against while the other three riders, after a moment, rode off up river.

Rex figured nightfall was about two hours away. He expected Lou Jarrell and the column's lead riders to arrive soon on the far bluff, which meant he needed to decide on how to eliminate the three guards without alerting the other three up the river. Faint gunfire, about an hour before sunset, from the direction where Rex expected the Wapiti supply column broke the valley peacefulness. They heard a half-dozen shots, then stillness. The guards had too and were on their feet looking off toward the bluff.

"Was that gunfire?" the rider who had been on the log asked.

"Sure sounded like it," their leader said, "We'd best go investigate."

The guards' move toward the horses made Rex's decision. Before he could reload his rifle, Tom had shot the third guard. The horses milled about nervously, but soon settled back to munching on grass.

"Tom, round up their horses, then hide the bodies," Rex said. "I'm going back to check on the column. I want you to guard the crossing. Let's hope the other guards didn't hear the shots."

Rex found the stopped column of Wapitis about two kilometers from the bluff on a dirt lane between two cornfields. Maria lay sprawled in the corn with Steve bent over her, crying. The prisoner they had captured at Gap Mill when they killed Donnelly's guards lay several meters away in the ditch. Larry Hopkins, on a horse, and four emaciated strangers on foot, were talking excitedly and pointing across the south field. Looking, Rex spotted Jerry Jones, the leader of the Owl squad, and a couple of his men leading three rider-less horses back from the woods bordering the field.

"A work column of slaves and three mounted guards surprised us. They had emerged from that path in the woods," Larry said, pointing across the field toward Jerry. "We were strung out on this lane between the open corn fields with no place to hide."

Rex could see there was over hundred meters between the column and where Donnelly's men had emerged from the woods.

"They hesitated, probably confused as to who we were. I feared the guards would bolt and sound the alarm. I told the men to fire."

The leader of Eagle squad was nervous, as if he wasn't quite sure if he'd done the right thing. "Larry, you made the correct call," Rex said.

Sadly, Maria's luck had run out. During the ensuing exchange of gunfire, the guards' bullets had killed her, Amos, and one of the Wapitis' horses. None of the Donnelly men guarding the slaves had survived.

Rex was in a quandary. He had learned from the rescued slaves that there were six more Wapiti slaves in the barn near the river. The plantation's entire tobacco crop from the previous year was in the same barn. The loss of that tobacco would be a serious financial blow to the Hinton slaver. According to the rescued slaves, two guards remained at the tobacco barn and slave pen.

The bad news, the guards would have sent pigeons to Hinton warning of the unknown gunfire. Their Gap Mill prisoner hadn't known what he was talking about, or he'd cleverly given them false information. Rex needed to decide whether to take the time to free the Wapitis and burn the crop while knowing that Donnelly's men could be there within a few hours of hard riding, or to push on. He compromised.

"Larry, take two of the Eagle men and check out the tobacco barn. If you can, without being bogged down in a gunfight, free the slaves and set fire to the tobacco. I'm counting on your good sense to walk away if it's not practical to free the slaves. Delivering the supplies is more important to the Wapitis than freeing those men. Our trail will be across and up the river about three kilometers. Don't dally; Hinton riders could be here in a few hours."

Rex sent Lou and Larry's remaining squad member ahead to support Tom at the crossing. He put Jerry Jones and Owl squad of warriors behind the column as the rear guard while Steve got the column under way. The men had tied Maria's body to her horse, hastily buried the dead, and helped the freed slaves find spare horses to ride. Rex left the free slaves unarmed until he had an opportunity to assess their knowledge of firearms.

It had already been a long day, but the column needed to reach Sam Black Church ahead of Clem's crew out of Lewisburg. An hour after sunset, the column was across the river and headed north. Rex knew the trail would take them through what on Earth was the Blue Sulfur Spring valley. The burning tobacco barn lit the evening sky red, a memorable sight, Rex thought, to remember the night he started a war.

The Wapiti caravan was moving almost soundlessly, and at a fast walk, through the silent dark forest. Rex was actually starting to like horses. He had to agree, in a road-less wilderness horses worked well. Good thing, because gasoline powered cars didn't exist and he probably wouldn't live to see them invented on Erden. That gloomy reflection resulted in a more depressing thought. He would never see his parents again, and they would never learn what happened to him.

What Rex had encountered in Roanoke and saw in Jacobs' store gave him hope. He'd never again enjoy all the wonderful conveniences of the twenty-first century America. But creating a pleasant and productive life was possible. He just had to survive Donnelly's killers, whom he reckoned, looking back at the red night sky, would soon be in hot pursue.

Larry Hopkins arrived two hours later with six thin Wapiti males doubled up on three more 'D' branded horses that he had liberated from the plantation's corral.

"Did the guards give you much trouble?" Rex asked.

"No, they were a couple of old men who threw down their muskets when we arrived. In fact, the guards asked to go with us, but the men we freed warned us the guards were evil bastards. They wanted the guards locked in the barn and burned along with the tobacco."

"Please tell me you didn't," Rex said. The red glow had faded and the night was moonless. Larry, on a horse trotting beside him on the narrow trail, suddenly vanished with a grunt. Startled, Rex grabbed Larry's horse by its reins to stop it from running off. Larry dangled from a broken oak limb that had caught his leather vest. Steve, who had been following them, helped the embarrassed warrior get untangled from the wayward limb and reach the ground.

"Damn, kid, you're lucky you didn't lose an eye," Steve said.

Larry just shook his head and walking to his horse. Back on his horse, he resumed their conversation as if nothing had happened.

"No, I didn't burn the guards. I left them free by the river. The good news is they claimed to have been out of pigeons. The barn guards sent no warning to Hinton or Lewisburg."

"If true, that is good news. Of course, what else would they say?" Rex said. He was relieved to learn the young man wasn't heartless and had left the guards alive by the river.

The Wapiti column stopped near midnight. Rex permitted no fires and had the column moving again an hour before sunrise. By early afternoon, the column had climbed the steep trail out of Blue Sulfur Spring and passed west of the area that on Earth was Sam Black Church.

The goal was to reach the less-traveled trail that went south and bypassed Rainelle. An hour later, the Wapitis passed the spot where they had camped on the night of Sam Wilson's failed attack on Rainelle. Rex stopped the column in the late afternoon at the headwater of the small stream the south trail followed. They were about six kilometers east of Rainelle. As had become the column's practice, it located its campsite down wind and out of sight of the trail in a defensive position. He allowed fires, and the weary travelers soon fixed themselves a hot meal as they waited for night.

In preparation for the Wapiti campaign, James Donnelly and Gene Peters had split the new mercenaries into two groups, one under Anders Breuer with eight-five men and one group of fifteen men under Bill Keegan, who would join Clem Hubbard's group. Both groups had supplies for two weeks and ten thousand rounds of Krupp rifle ammo between them.

Bert Paget, the Ichneumon, would travel with Anders Breuer and had his own supplies. Anders understood the Ichneumon observer was an important person whom he and Bill Keegan were to show every consideration and respect.

The two commands had just started down the river valley when three guards galloped into the stockade with alarming news. Someone had torched the tobacco plantation.

The three hapless guards from the six-man force that James sent to guard the river crossings had no explanation for the disaster. They had seen no strangers in the area, had heard no gunfire, and hadn't a clue as to where the other guards or slaves had gone or why.

Their news caused Donnelly to send word for Bill to wait with his group, but for Anders to go on as planned. James had difficulty accepting that a fire had destroyed his tobacco crop and storage barn.

"There was over two hundred metric tons of high-grade burley tobacco in the barn. It can't all be gone. Bill, get your crew and follow me."

If it was, it was a disaster. The Atlantic Tobacco Trust had advanced him seven hundred and eighty thousand D-marks for the tobacco. His crew had been waiting on Simpson's new barrels to pack the tobacco leaf in. Had the barrels arrived when promised, he would have shipped the tobacco two weeks before. For that failure to deliver, the cooper can help repay the trust's advance. Even so, returning that sum of money would be painful and put at risk his full partnership in the railroad consortium.

It was true. By late morning, a smoldering James and a nervous Bill Keegan, along with his mercenaries, sat on lathered horses looking at the still-smoking mounds of tobacco and wood timbers. The mercenaries had discovered the two elderly guards hiding in the springhouse and dragged them before Donnelly for questioning.

"Who did this?" He asked the trembling elderly guard.

"Three Wapitis surprised us. We couldn't reach our rifles," the younger guard said.

"Where are the other guards and slaves?" James asked. The two terrorized guards didn't know. "How do you know they were Wapitis?" James couldn't quit thinking of the seven hundred and eighty thousand D-marks lost.

"I, I don't know. Who else could it have been?" The elderly guard asked.

"Ruffner, Ichneumon raiders, Prussians," he said. "Five guards, and you let three savages burn my crop, with my barn, and you did nothing? Didn't even kill a couple of the bastards?" Beside himself with rage, James told Keegan to tie up the two guards.

"Hang them. No throw them into the bed of coals."

The Prussian army trained their feldwebels to obey orders, not question them. Bill Keegan, the middle-aged leader of the mercenary group, with help from one of the other mercenaries, easy tossed the pleading guards into the basement of the barn. Bill thought himself harden to cruelty. But the screams and struggles of the elderly guard went on and on as the man crawled blindly about the pit of burning embers. It nauseated him. He wasn't alone judging from the looks on the mercenaries with him. Not their boss, who just smiled as he sat on his horse watching the guards die in the coals.

"Bill, take your men and find those three savages. Try to keep them alive for me," James said. Bill Keegan saluted and rode off to pursue the raiders.

Hauptman Frederick "Fritz" Caprivi had known Franciscka Weidman since they were small children and knew that she now worked for the Prussian IRS in Roanoke. Even better, Franciscka had been west of the mountains and would have current information on the people inhabiting the borderlands. He planned to meet her at the IRS office in Roanoke after his visit to the William plantation.

Fritz had met Baron William's only son, Heinz, at Heidelberg University. They had shared a number of classes until Heinz's poor grades caused him to drop out and return to Guderian Territory. Military Intelligence knew of their past acquaintance, and the department had arranged for Fritz to stay at the plantation.

Baron William had been thrilled to learn the hero of the Volga River would be his guest. In honor of the visit, the baron had planned a large party and invited many of his neighboring plantation owners.

Fritz looked forward to the trip across the Atlantic to New Hamburg. He was a passenger on one of the new steam-powered dual paddlewheel freighters. It carried a heavy cargo of new steel rails for a railroad track under construction across Guderian Territory. Fritz had once traveled on a steam-powered train from Berlin to Hamburg. He hadn't been enthralled with that method of travel. Unlike the steamboat, the train had been slow, unreliable, and dirty, spewing burning embers over the passengers and cargo.

In New Hamburg, the buzz at the hotel dining room the evening Fritz arrived ranged from the new railroad project to the rising ocean levels.

"Those docks are about useless. You need to replace them with higher ones and move the warehouse section before cargo is ruined by flooding," the paddlewheel captain, who shared the table with Fritz, told the businessmen who owned the steel rail cargo. "You need to act. The ocean has risen over two meters in the past thirty years I've been coming to the New Hamburg docks. It used to be I'd wait for high tide to unload to avoid having to lift cargo. Now I have to wait for low tide and for the dock to reemerge from the water to unload. It's no way to operate a dock."

Fritz gathered the businessmen weren't concerned, as the younger one said, "They're steel rails. They wouldn't float off during high tide." His friends at the table, along with even the captain, laughed. The businessmen ordered another bottle of schnapps to share.

"Well, you're right about that. My crew will start unloading this evening before low tide. They will be finished before high tide, so have your man there to verify the count before the rails are under water. I plan to embark at first light for the coal dock to load the bunkers."

Fritz knew the oceans were rising but thought the rate was more like thirty centimeters over a century. He figured more likely the docks had settled into the harbor muck, not that the ocean had risen that much, but with the northern ice fields in retreat, who knew?

"Where are you headed next?" Fritz asked. He knew coal was expensive in New Hamburg. Guderian Territory had no coalmines. Most of the coal came from Wales. Normally the steamships carried enough fuel to make the return trip to Wales.

"Port Delta," the captain said. "The owner has a load of cotton he wants me to pick up."

"I'm surprised there's any available. Cotton has been scarce in Prussia since the war," Fritz said. The table conversation turned to the war and shortages as he finished his plate of pork ribs with the delicious sweet, tangy pepper sauce.

"What is this sauce?" Fritz asked the captain. A local concoction called barbecue sauce, he learned.

The next morning, Fritz acquired for his trip west two horses, a saddle horse, and a pack animal. He had three of the new Mauser bolt-action rifles chambered for the Bismarck 11.6 x 65 mm ammo that was common in the territories and several of the new 9 x 19 mm revolvers. He had told the department that a savage living in a wilderness would be more impressed with firearms then gold D-marks. Fritz's boss, General von Moltke, had cautioned him not be the savage's first target.

Rex Knight knew Steve Johnson was correct. The column needed to rest, especially the horses. The column had covered over ninety kilometers across mountains and through rugged wilderness in three long days, had fought and killed several men, had lost Maria Belcher, and had rescued ten Wapitis being held as slaves or captives. Since he landed on this violent world twenty-two days ago, a large number of Donnelly's men and seven Wapitis had died around him. The bloodletting had been fearsome.

So far, their enemy had seemed shocked that anyone, especially their traditional prey, the Wapitis, would dare attack them. Rex suspected the advantage he'd enjoyed from their enemy misjudging the Wapitis' willingness to use deceitfulness and violence had ended at the tobacco barn. Still, old habits do tend to linger. He called the Jarrell brothers over to the log he was using as a chair. Earlier he'd unsaddled his horse, and Zack munched on grass nearby.

"I need to know if anyone's on our trail. That tobacco fire had to stir up Donnelly, and I don't want him ambushing the column. Tom, Lou, do you have any suggestions on how to answer my concern?" Rex paused in cleaning his rifle barrel to hear their answer.

"Well, sir, we could ride back our trail and look, but there's no good way to get word back to you if we meet the enemy. They're as likely to spot us as we are to spot them, then it's a chase. We'll all arrive back at the column more or less simultaneously. Not much of a warning in that method. Besides, you know a blind man could follow our trail, what with thirty horses chewing up the ground and pooping."

"You're right, Tom. Besides, surely by now Donnelly has figured out the Wapitis burned his tobacco barn and he has sent warnings to Rainelle and Lewisburg. We should plan that the Rainelle garrison expects us. Even our old pal, Clem, will finally realize we slipped by him again. He's probably moving west, aggressively searching for us. It's his only way to redeem himself. I hope in the rush he gets careless."

"You have a plan?" Tom asked. Rex nodded yes and took a moment to finish wiping an oily rag across the rifle.

"The best spot on this trail to ambush a column rushing west is on the bluff above Rainelle near Myles Knob. So I want you two to check out Rainelle and the bluff, and then hurry back. But please be careful. Don't take any unnecessary risks. I can't afford to lose you."

The Jarrell brothers smiled. "Mom wouldn't want that either. Come on, Lou. More adventure awaits," Tom said. The brothers hurried off to saddle their horses.

Rex walked over to where Jerry Jones, Steve Johnson, and Larry Hopkins were consoling each other by the fire. "We're going through Rainelle this evening. I want to be west of the town by midnight; then we'll stop to rest. Are you ready to bury Maria?"

Bill Keegan, a retired Prussian sergeant, had thought murdering those two old men a disgusting act. He'd heard that his new boss was a heartless bastard, but roasting those guards alive was an action he would have expected from an Ichneumon, not a Prussian. When this campaign of chasing ignorant savages through wilderness was over, he would find a saner outfit, such as the cotton trust, to work for as a crew leader.

Sending fifteen men to hunt three Wapiti raiders seemed excessive, but it was Donnelly's money. Well, the quicker they found the savages, the quicker they could rejoin Anders and start rounding up slaves, maybe find one of those green-eyed women he'd heard so much about for his own slave.

One pleasant surprise the raiders' trail was easy to follow. About three kilometers above the barn, the Wapitis had left the main road and headed northwest following a game trail. They weren't alone. About two dozen other riders, or at least horses, had taken the same trail.

"Nat, what do you make of the tracks? Are the six horses we're after following the larger group?" Bill asked. "Or is that group pursuing our six horses, or have they joined the group?" Bill had dismounted to better study the chewed-up ground. As disorganized, as Donnelly seemed at times, Bill wondered if Clem's group out of Lewisburg might also be chasing those raiders.

"Many horses, the ground . . ." Nat paused for a loud belch, and then said, "What's your question, Captain?" Bill had told Donnelly that his former Prussian rank had been captain.

"Are the bastards we're following, being followed by the larger group, or are they behind the larger group?"

He was aware the Haggards were alcoholics, but his boss had insisted Bill use the trackers.

"Ah, well, I think . . . Luke can you tell?" Nat asked his brother. The two Clovis trackers, on foot, studied the torn-up trail.

Luke had a stick that he occasionally to poke the tracks with, for what purpose escaped Bill. After several pokes, Luke looked up at him and, waving the stick toward the northwest, said, "Many horses went that way, Captain Bill."

"No shit, Luke. You figured that out?" Disgusted with the Haggard brothers, Bill yelled for his sergeant. "Take a couple of men and our gifted trackers a couple hundred meters ahead to serve as point guard for the group."

Since little tracker effort was required to follow the torn-up trail, Bill pushed his horse to a trot that ate up the distance. Darkness forced them to stop near Sam Black Church. Based on signs, the interior of the horse droppings were slightly warmer than the ground; the gang they were pursuing wasn't all that far ahead of them. He expected to catch the raiders by mid-morning, unless the Rainelle garrison caught them first.

James spent an hour checking the plantation for damage and trying to locate the other guards. He found no one. The corn crop looked fine. In fact, other than the burned barn, the place was untouched by raiders. The mash house and distillery located two kilometers down-river from the ill-fated tobacco barn was undisturbed. James knew the master distiller, Herr Simpson, and his two helpers were in Rainelle organizing a cooperage to supply white-oak whiskey and tobacco barrels. Again, as at the tobacco barn, there was no sign of the slaves. If the raiders had killed his men, where were their bodies?

Burgdorf rode up and joined him by the still-smoking barn remains. "Are those charred bodies?" he asked. The fire had reduced the guards to bones with some blackened flesh. "Who did it?"

"If I knew, I wouldn't be sitting here. They thought the raiders were Wapitis," James said, pointing at the smoldering skeletons. "I sent Bill after them."

"Hard to believe they'd have the balls . . . unless it's the Prussian," Burgdorf said. He pulled out a clay pipe and banged it on the saddle-horn to empty the old tobacco ash from its bowl. "Or Ruffner was mad at you for some insult."

"I've wondered the same thing. Earlier, I'd approached him on being the exclusive distributor of the Simpson whiskey in Guderian Territory, but I later chose Manuel. He has better connections in the territories. If Ruffner's heard of the switch, that might piss him off enough to get reckless."

"You're right about Manuel's connections, but he's a slippery creature with secret agendas too. Maybe he told Ruffner," the ex-feldwebel said. "The tobacco farm raiders might have been Ruffner men dressed like Wapitis. His way of embarrassing and hurting you financially for pulling the whiskey distributor deal." He paused to pack more tobacco in his pipe. "Damn crime to waste all that fine burley leaf."

"You think that Prussian who caught you is still around?"

"Well, we both have been scrimmaging with Wapiti and Clovis raiders for years. Now the savages are trouncing your men. Seems to me something has changed. As to Ruffner, did you spread the rumor that I drowned?"

"Yeah, no one is looking for you. I even told those IRS bastards. Have you heard of mysterious supply columns across the mountains?" James asked. Burgdorf shook his head no after exhaling an impressive puff of tobacco smoke. "I know some Wapitis slipped by Clem at Rainelle. Did you know Ruffner's engineer was an IRS agent?"

"No, hadn't a clue," Burgdorf said. "Wonder if she knew her boss had paid me to deliver those women to him instead of Ruffner."

"I met her at the Roanoke IRS office," James said. "She's an opinionated bitch. Claims she was with a Wapiti column that passed through Lewisburg while Clem was chasing ghosts west of Rainelle. Said the Wapitis went north to Waynesboro. She never answered my question on how many Wapitis had slipped by at Rainelle. I figured a half-dozen men probably made up the fugitive supply convoy since Clem killed several Wapitis during the Rainelle raid. You agree most Wapiti raiding parties rarely exceed a dozen warriors?"

"Yeah, at least that was so in the old days. Now I wouldn't count on it, and with the Wapitis obtaining modern rifles and ammo, it'll complicate our plans," Burgdorf said, remembering the Wapitis' lethal rifle fire at River Falls.

Two of the riders who had been searching for the missing slaves and guards rode up to report. They had found three dead guards in the woods near the upper cornfields.

"Leave them to rot. I have another job," James said.

He'd been wondered where the Wapiti supply convoy was. Clem had the Lewisburg road blocked, Scarface had the Gap Mill trail blocked, and nothing moved on the river without his approval. The Wapiti convoy should be east of the mountains. Still, a nagging doubt lingered. It wouldn't hurt to check. James called two of the riders over and sent one to Gap Mill and one to Lewisburg to verify that no Wapiti supply column had tried to pass.

"Now tell me about Cinnabar."

The returning Jarrell brothers meet Rex and Larry Hopkins two kilometers east of Rainelle. "Rainelle isn't on alert," Tom said. "Everyone's talking about the whiskey barrel factory that Donnelly's hiring men for. The stockade is manned. However, five guards are in the Blue Star getting drunk on raw corn whiskey. And no hostile forces are waiting on the bluff, so the trail is clear."

"The other thing we learned is that Donnelly has hired an army to attack the Wapitis. Hundreds of men left from Hinton two days ago," Lou said, adding, "at least according to the Blue Star's bartender." He handed Rex a small glass bottle filled with a clear liquid. "This is what they're drinking."

Rex sniffed the liquid and thought it smelled okay, but whiskey before breakfast didn't appeal. He re-corked the bottle and was about to nudge Zack to start the column moving again when Jerry Jones rode up all excited.

"Rex, I saw several fires started near the camp we just left. There's a large force behind us. Is it Clem's gang?"

Larry said, "It's not the Lewisburg group. Clem would have stayed on the main trail to Rainelle; it's shorter, faster. The tobacco guards probably lied and did send a pigeon. I figure it's some of the Hinton men following our trail from the tobacco plantation."

"I suspect you have the right of it," Rex said. "But regardless of who they are, we have to assume it's a large enemy group about five kilometers behind us. More important, the pursuing group will catch us in the morning since our horses are exhausted and need a break."

Chapter 7

During their ride back from the destroyed tobacco barn to Hinton, the Prussian ex-feldwebel, Friedrich Burgdorf, told his employer about the meeting with Chief Cinnabar.

"The chief has a hundred and fifty warriors with horses," Burgdorf said. "The chief is willing to send a hundred mounted men for a month, but he wants hundred thousand D-marks . . . in gold."

"Gold, paper bills, why would the lunatic care?" James asked.

"Maybe he fears the Prussian Empire is going bankrupt," Burgdorf said. Both men laughed at the absurdity. "He also wants five Wapiti women, young ones."

"For slaves?"

"I'd hate to think what for . . . to abuse, rape, eat, all of the above." Burgdorf said. A Clovis boy herding about a dozen goats had the trail blocked. They slipped around the milling goats by going through the trees.

Cinnabar's request for Wapiti women, as part of his payment, confirmed that James's original reason for approaching the psychopath was sound. He needed men who would carry out the Ichneumon genocide. The depravity of those tattooed devils had no limits, whereas the Prussian mercenaries were a mixed bag. Many claimed mercilessness until faced with crying children and wailing women. Cinnabar's warriors didn't have that weakness.

"I want you to leave for the salt furnace and find Anders," James said. "He's raiding the Hopkins River area. Tell him you get the first six women captured. Get an extra one just in case. Bring them back here. I'll send word to Cinnabar we have a deal. However, the deal requires he come to Hinton for payment."

The hung-over slob who served as Donnelly's guard commander at Rainelle, Captain Drake, claimed no group of Wapitis, nor anyone else, had passed by the stockade the previous night. Bill thought, *what an idiot.* They were standing on the trail and looking at the evidence that many horses had passed since yesterday's afternoon shower.

"Did it rain here yesterday, Captain Drake?" Bill asked.

"Well, yeah it rained here . . . hard in fact. So what?" the captain answered. Sweat beaded his flushed forehead. A disgusting odor oozed from the Rainelle commander.

"Look at the tracks. They're fresh, so the horses that made those tracks passed through here since the rain. If it had been Clem's crew, he would have stopped to check in, at the very least alert you about the Wapitis. So who else do you think would have snuck by, except the raiders who burned Donnelly's tobacco plantation?"

The logic of Bill's explanation seemed to be beyond the ability of the alcoholic captain to grasp. Bill seriously considered drafting Drake and his guards for point duty. If there was an ambush waiting, let these worthless bums trigger it.

One thing was now clear. The numerous horses weren't from Clem's group chasing the three Wapiti raiders. He would have alerted the stockade. Only the fugitive Wapiti supply column could account for all the horse traffic, and the six raiders he'd been chasing must be part of the group. Still, having seen a disappointed Herr Donnelly in action with those old guards, Bill wanted to verify the group's identity. Then he would send word that they had found and captured the Wapiti supplies.

"Who's been over the trail from here to the main river?" Bill asked the group. None of the mercenaries had been over the trail ahead, though the consensus between the men was that the distance to where the trail rejoined the river and the start of Wapiti territory was about sixty kilometers.

Bill looked for the Haggards in the group gathered around him. Not seeing the trackers, he asked about them.

"They were in the tavern earlier," one of the cashiered Prussian ex-feldwebels said. Bill couldn't remember the man's name, but did recall the man's transgression, rape.

"Well, go see if they're still there. Tell them they're needed." The man went to find the Haggard brothers. Bill planned to use the useless trackers as bait for triggering any Wapiti ambush that might be ahead on the trail.

"You're wasting time," the opinionated mercenary said. "We don't need trackers. A blind man could follow their trail," "Those savages can't be far. We need to ride hard. Catch them before they become aware we're on their tail."

The rapist returned to report that the Clovis trackers had told the bartender they didn't like their boss and were going home. Bill thought, *good riddance to the drunks*, while he listened to several of his outspoken men, all former feldwebels. They agreed with the mercenaries, Bill should allow them to rush and catch the Wapiti column.

The feldwebels had collected around Bill to argue that his worry of an ambush wasn't a realistic concern. Sure, they argued, a trained military force might use an ambush for a delaying action but not a bunch of frightened savages fleeing with their plunder.

The opinionated mercenary added, "You know they'll freak out when we burst upon their camp. Untrained in Prussian military tactics, they'll run, even abandon the pack horses, to reach other Wapitis and help below the North River."

Bill was by nature a cautious man but agreed with his men's contention that being untrained, the Wapitis should panic on learning a heavily armed force was closing on their column's rear and they would become easy targets.

"Mount up, men," Bill said. "The chase is on."

The Hopkins River had a number of Wapiti communities along the river valley. Indira's village had contained around thirty families farming the wide river bottomland before the disaster at the fish camp the previous month. Now, after that deadly raid, a third of the houses remained empty.

During the workday, the mothers left the babies in the conference room between feedings where the village's older girls took turns watching over them and doing the endless laundry. Today was Indira's turn. The group Indira cared for consisted of five children too young for school and three infants. The job wasn't difficult. Indira rather enjoyed caring for the babies but not cleaning their soiled diapers.

"Make sure the water is boiling," her mother said. "Peggy didn't yesterday, and the mothers were complaining the diapers smelled. I don't want them griping that my daughter cut corners."

"I know. I'll boil the water if there's enough fire wood." Indira said. "When's Dad coming back?" Her mother had fixed Indira's favorite breakfast of over-easy eggs, greens, and grits. Well the greens she could do without, but her mother insisted she eat them.

"I figure tomorrow, depending how far east the men went to check the blue-nut crop. I'd feel better if he'd left a few men to guard the village instead of sending most of them to Smithtown for training."

"Maybe he'll find that bear. I wish he'd let me go on those hunts."

"Girls don't go on hunts, silly," her mother said while cleaning the cast iron skillet. Indira was ready to break her last egg yolk. "I swear, daughter, you have the strangest way of eating fried eggs. Why do you eat the white part first instead of eating both together?"

"Mom, times are changing. Women will be hunters, even soldiers. Uncle Rex promised to teach me how to be a markswoman," Indira said, then became suddenly quiet. "Was that a scream?"

Anders Breuer knew his Ichneumon watchdog, Bert Paget, was skeptical of his men and their willingness to slaughter every Wapiti encountered. In turn, Anders thought the Ichneumons' goal stupid. Where would the future Wapiti slaves come from if they didn't leave some alive after each raid? Next, he learned Bert wanted several Wapiti women for Prince Cherukuru to entertain himself with during his inspection tour of the salt furnace. Anders found Gene Peters handing out fifty rounds of ammo to each mercenary riding past.

"Any suggestions on where I might find Wapiti women for His Majesty?" Anders asked Gene. Neither of them liked the Ichneumons, especially their prince.

"Clem always liked raiding villages up the Hopkins River. Claimed they had the best-looking women. Our boss is in an evil mood, so keep those Ichneumons happy. I don't want Paget complaining to him."

That was yesterday. After arriving at the salt furnace, Anders had picked twenty of his best men to go with him on the raid. Setting up camps, latrines, and defense berms was boring work, so he had plenty of volunteers. Anders told the men he didn't need on the raid to finish setting up the tents and camp in preparation for the

Ichneumon prince visit. Before he could leave the salt furnace, James's assassin, Feldwebel Burgdorf, arrived on a lathering horse.

"James wants six young Wapiti women," Burgdorf said. The ex-feldwebel looked disdainfully at the camp's organization. Before Anders could complain about the extra work, the feldwebel surprised him. "Make you a deal. I get first pick of the women before the Ichneumons. In trade I'll get your inept boys and the camp organized while you raid the Hopkins River."

"Hey, I didn't hire them," Anders said. "If Bert doesn't kick up a fuss, you have a deal." For once, he was glad to see the killer. The Prussian knew his business. "I just hope there're enough women to go around."

"Teenagers, younger girls will work for James's needs," the feldwebel said. "Give the Ichneumon perverts the older women; there'll be enough." They shook hands. Burgdorf then rode off toward the furnace.

The other issue weighing on Anders's mind was Tyler Reed. The pimp was making threats. Reed wanted his 20,000 D-marks back, or those four promised Wapiti women, or Anders's head. The Reed brothers were nasty thugs and only fools ignored their threats. He needed a successful raid, at least a dozen prime women.

"Herr Paget, are you ready to hunt?" Anders asked. The Ichneumon watchdog nodded in agreement. The group mounted up and Paget joined him at the head of the column. "I told the men that I want all the attractive women and girls captured alive. They're too valuable to waste. You have any problem with those orders?" Anders asked.

"No, it's your operation. I'm just an observer."

"I told them to kill everyone else. Let's ride."

Rex and the Wapitis waited five kilometers west of Rainelle on the crest of a flat open area between two densely forested ridges.

The area formed a saddle between two watersheds. The sun wasn't yet visible, but the horizon was blood red when three riders quietly entered the open area of the saddle. Rex figured the riders were part of the Donnelly's group pursing them. The riders stopped. He reckoned they had seen the two tiny yellow dots from the Owl's campfires at the west end of the open area.

After a moment, one of the riders galloped back toward Rainelle. The other two waited. The top of the sun's rim, a bright red edge, had emerged on the horizon when a dozen riders returned. During the wait, the two riders who had first shown up had by the time the other riders returned drifted about half the distance toward the campfires. Then the fires went out. There was now enough light to see all the riders wore blue coats.

Rex could hear Jerry Jones screaming. "Get up! Donnelly's riders are here!" The blue coat riders also heard Jerry's panic act. It sure sounded real. *The man should have been an actor*, Rex thought.

More riders arrived at the bluff. Someone in the group made the decision to charge, and a dozen riders galloped toward the camp. Four shots rang out from the camp. The main body slowed to return fire from their horses. They were by then in front of Rex, and he fired. A moment later, the Wapitis hidden beside him on the densely forested ridge started firing into horsemen. The smoke and long, dark shadows made it difficult for Rex to determine the effectiveness of his men's gunfire, but every horse was now rider-less.

Bullets slamming into the trees and hillside around Rex offered explicit evidence that the gang still had some fight left in them. Nonetheless, his men were giving the raiders hell. Over the next few minutes, the gunfire from Donnelly's men dwindled to nothing as Wapiti marksmen located and finished off the survivors of the ambushers' initial devastating volley.

Then another intense burst of gunfire in the area where the Jarrell brothers were hiding told Rex some reinforcements must have attempted to come up the trail from Rainelle. After another few minutes of quiet, Larry and Steve joined him.

"Should we go down and finish off the wounded?" Steve asked. The ambush appeared to have been far more effective than Rex had dared hope and that gave him an idea.

"Steve, take three men and disarm the survivors," Rex said. "Tell the rest of your men to stay hidden. Yours too, Larry, until Steve has all the Donnelly men that are still alive disarmed, tied up, and blindfolded."

"That's crazy, they'd kill us," Steve said.

"You're probably right, Steve, but do as I say," Rex said. "And be careful, some of the bastards may still have some fight remaining in them."

"Any who resist I'll kill," Steve said.

"You will not. I need some live prisoners," Rex said. "Now go. Larry, I want you . . ."

The Wapitis cautiously approached the downed Donnelly riders and Steve's men disarmed and secured the few survivors. By then, the sun was clear of the horizon and the smoke had dissipated. Rex jogged to the crest of the trail to learn what the Jarrell brothers had shot at.

Tom met him at the trail's crest. "That fat stockade commander and several of his men tried to join the fight. Lou and the boys are down collecting their rifles and horses."

"No one was hit?" Rex asked. Tom assured him none of his team had suffered wounds. "Great. Finish here and help Jerry quietly reform the column. Keep everyone out of sight of the prisoners."

Three of Donnelly's men were alive but seriously wounded. The Donnelly men had killed two of Jerry Jones's team in the initial gunfire, the Wapitis' only casualties in the brief raging fight. Actually, it had been a slaughter. Twelve of the fifteen Donnelly men who had charged Jerry Jones' camp were dead along with several more of Donnelly's men from the Rainelle stockade. The twenty-two Wapitis had given a good account of themselves and become a disciplined fighting force.

Rex hastened over to where Steve crouched beside a badly wounded stout, middle-aged man who reminded him of Friedrich Burgdorf. Steve, despite Rex's orders, appeared about to cut the man's throat while the older Wapiti who had been searching enemy corpses nearby for valuables waited.

"I'd better not find other cut throats," Rex said. "I need to talk with him." Steve let go of the man's head, relieved him of his wallet, and backed away.

"Your leg's a mess, but you might survive if I stop them from cutting your throat," Rex said. "Tell me Donnelly's plans, and I'll leave you here alive."

"If things were reversed, the bastard would cut your throat," Steve said. "Another surprise-we've collected over seven thousand D-marks from these animals. What should I do with it?" Apparently, Donnelly had paid the mercenaries recently and they hadn't had a chance to blow their wages.

"Divide it evenly with the men," Rex said.

The wounded man's name was Bill Keegan and some persuasion was required to convince him to talk. In the end, he told about Anders Breuer's group and their mission to destroy the Hopkins and Smith settlements and kill the chiefs before raiding the other Wapiti settlements. He also claimed that a large force was waiting east of Lewisburg.

Rex was standing beside the prisoners, considering if Keegan might know more about Clem's present location when Larry Hopkins rushed up.

"Herr Knight, I can't take our dead, I don't have enough horses for all the wounded," Larry said. "There are only five of us left."

"Be quiet you fool," Rex snapped. Steve looked surprise and about to speak. "Steve, Larry, not another damn word. Steve, go and show this kid what to do. We're wasting time."

The immediate danger for Rex and the Wapitis was Clem's force. Maybe he was still east of Lewisburg, but when word of Keegan's defeat reached him, the man would rush west and try to catch the Wapiti's supplies. Rex also figured the man would interrogate the Rainelle garrison and Keegan on how the Wapitis escaped.

A pensive group of men followed Rex west on the river trail. He ignored the grumbling about leaving the three wounded raiders behind and alive.

Early the following afternoon Rex, with Larry Hopkins's Eagle squad leading the column, arrived at the North River. The Jarrell and Balers brothers, dressed as Donnelly men, had left before sunrise to recon the river ford area ahead of the Wapiti supply column arrival. Their luck still held. Three of Anders' guards escorting seven captured Wapiti warriors had arrived at the North River ford just after Jarrell's group had crossed to the west bank. They soon learned the Jarrell brothers weren't part of Bill Keegan's group.

The captured Wapitis had been working at the salt furnace when Anders's mercenaries had stormed out of the woods without warning two days before and captured them.

"It could have been worse," Bow, the older freed Wapiti prisoner, said. "I heard from these assholes, that a warning from the Prussian woman to Chief Smith saved the Smithtown residents." He indicated to Rex with a point of his hand that the captured guards were the referred-to assholes. "The Hopkins families didn't get a warning, because I saw a number of Hopkins women, even Indira, chained together."

"Indira, you know her?" Rex asked. "Did you get to talk with them?" He feared the evil bastards were going to destroy the girl's soul.

"Everyone knows Indira. These jerks made us leave before I got a chance, but she was in terrible shape."

"What do you mean?"

"She'd been beaten, her face slashed, maybe blinded. Lee, you were by Anders' tent. Did you hear anything?" Bow asked the thin, young pox marked Clovis man with him. Rex said a prayer for Indira's recovery.

"Not much, though I heard their leader telling the Ichneumon big shot about killing every Hopkins but those women," Lee said. "One of the men had refused to kill a baby and they were harassing him."

"They killed everyone?" Larry asked.

"He didn't say killed, it was oh-liver-ate, or something like that."

"Obliterated?" Larry asked. Lee nodded yes.

The Wapitis, shocked, looked at the captured guards, who now appeared terrified and answered all of Rex's questions. One fact was clear-Donnelly forces had reestablished their stronghold at the salt furnace. More ominous, they were busy building several boats large enough to transport half-dozen horses across, and/or down the river. The reason for the boat project was clear. Anders' forces planned to bypass the Hopkins River ford defenses, and land on the south side of the river above the Jarrell River to attack the Smith settlement.

Anders had also established a small stockade force at River Falls to control that crossing area. The only encouraging news was that none of Donnelly's men suspected a strong Wapiti force of thirty-eight horses, twenty-one men, and one woman, Sue, was behind them just a few kilometers from the river falls.

Rex held a war council after the Wapiti supply convoy finished crossing the North River. The Owl squad had the task of established a defensive perimeter.

"Steve, divide the freed prisoners among the two squads." Rex said. Then he remembered there were seven new men, and making decisions wasn't Steve's strong point. "No, on second thought, give the Owls four of them and Larry's squad three."

The seven men were a welcome boost to their numbers. Learning they'd receive a Krupp rolling block rifle delighted the new members of Rex's force.

"Larry, find Lou. I have an idea on how to capture the River Falls stockade."

The voice of the young man behind the River Falls stockade gate was cautious. "Only if you have the password can I allow you in."

"It's dark," Lou said. "What am I supposed to do with these prisoners? No one said anything about a damn password. Nope, the sergeant just told me to get off my lazy ass and deliver these prisoners to the stockade. In the morning, I'm to go to Rainelle and join Bill's crew. I can't be dragging them to Rainelle. What am I supposed to feed them?"

The wood planks on the gate blocking Lou had several holes from bullets. He wondered if they were from Scott and Rex's earlier attack.

"Bill? Do you mean Captain Keegan?"

"Yeah, what's your name? Do you know the captain?" Lou said.

"I'm Art Walker. That's my brother Pete who'll blow you away, if you keep lying. Captain Keegan is following us down the river. He's due here in the morning."

"You haven't heard? Wapiti raiders burned Donnelly's tobacco barn. Bill caught the bastards in Rainelle."

"Burned the tobacco, the entire crop? There were tons of fine burley leaves. I helped bundled the leaves. That's terrible, you can't be serious."

"I'm serious . . . the entire crop. James is crazy mad," Lou said. He could see Larry was too close to the gate and motioned for him to back up a bit to better hide in the darkness from Pete.

"All that work, what a waste," Art said. Lou heard someone in the stockade ask a question. "There are Wapitis above us? Did Captain Keegan wipe them out?"

"What'd you think happened? He did lose a few men, though, and that's why I'm to join them. I also heard old man Simpson is going to start making whiskey barrels in Rainelle."

"A cooperage, I love working with wood. Maybe the old man will hire me."

"Look, maybe he will, Art, but for tonight, let me in, or at least take these prisoners off my hands," Lou said. "And I'll just leave. I can't believe how afraid you are."

"Yeah, well, after hearing what happened at the salt furnace, I like to be careful. Pete, come on down and help with the prisoners."

The Walker brothers opened the gate, and Lou Jarrell rode in with the prisoners in tow. Only one other guard was in the little stockade, an older man who came over to help with the prisoners. After dismounting, he grabbed Art's hand to shake as his brother walked up to check the prisoners. Suddenly Lou was sick of killing, but this was war and he had a duty. He pulled his pistol and grabbed Art in an arm-lock.

"Pete, be sensible and your brother will live to one day make whiskey barrels," Lou said as Larry's crew slipped in through the open gate to point four rifles at Pete, who still had his rifle pointed at Lou. The prisoners seized the other unarmed guard, and, along with everyone else in the stockade, waited for Pete Walker, a scared, skinny kid, to make his decision, life or death.

"Come on, brother, put the rifle down. We'll hope they're better people than us," Art said.

Rex was pleased that Lou Jarrell and Larry Hopkins, two of his best and most aggressive lieutenants, had managed to seize the River Falls stockade without killing anyone. It gave him hope the Wapitis weren't a vengeful people and a lasting peace might be possible. He was sick of the killing, but knew the bloodletting wasn't finished. If he could believe the rumors, Anders' men were acting like the ISIS terrorists had in northern Iraq.

The Wapitis desperately needed the column supplies, especially the Krupp rifles. But Rex now knew the river trail at the salt furnace was blocked. The only timely way to reach the beleaguered Wapitis at Hopkins River would be to rout those mercenaries at the salt furnace. That would not be an easy task.

"Donnelly and Clem have to know by now that we wiped out Keegan's crew," Rex said. "He'll send Clem rushing west to find us and send a pigeon with a warning to Anders. Of course, fear of another ambush will slow them."

"Unless Captain Keegan believed Larry's tale of woe and told Clem," Steve said. "You think that bastard believes there are only five Wapitis?"

"We can hope," Rex said. "I figure we have a couple of days before Clem shows up and we need to be ready because the trail is blocked at Salt Furnace."

"Should I dig in and fortify the stockade," Larry asked.

"No. The place is a death trap. Go burn it so Donnelly's men can't use it," Rex said. The order surprised the men, but after a moment, Larry left to attend to the destruction of the stockade.

Anders Breuer's force, at least according to the freed Wapitis, consisted of around ninety, mostly Prussian mercenaries and several dozen of Donnelly's men. The Wapitis were outnumbered six to one not good odds even with surprise. One option was try to punch through the salt furnace camp and run for the Wapiti line. Another option was to send word to Chief Smith for twenty of his best warriors to beef up Rex's group.

"Steve, are you good with a canoe?" Rex asked.

"Sure, one of the best. I know the river. Why?"

"I want you to pick three men and put two of them with Krupp rifles on the river shore across from the salt furnace's wharf. The other man will help you. I want those two men to snipe at Donnelly's forces around the salt furnace. They need to be marksmen, men who don't scare easily and can survive in the woods. It'll be like kicking a hornet's nest with their first shots. They need to understand that Anders will send men across the river to hunt them."

"I know just the pair; two of the freed slaves from the tobacco barn, the Baler brothers," Steve said. "They were hunters before being captured, and they used to win the fall turkey shoots." Rex waited for Steve to locate and tell Kyle and John Balers.

"Steve tells me you're marksmen."

Kyle, the older brother assured him they were both excellent marksmen.

"I want you to stop or at least delay work on the boats until I deal with Clem." Rex explained his plan, and the Baler brothers thought it workable. They especially liked the freedom to kill as many of the Donnelly's men as possible.

"Steve, give Chief Smith this letter. He needs to send at least twenty-five men." The snipers and Steve departed soon afterward to time their arrival at the salt furnace area just after sunset.

Keeping Clem's men from joining Anders was the next goal. Rex found a flat rock and smashed a handful of his precious coffee beans to boil in the teapot he was heating on the stockade's embers. While waiting for the coffee to boil, he considered Clem's likely response. The thug, after learning about the disastrous ambush of Keegan's men, would be as cautious as a rat eyeing the corncrib and not knowing where the farmer's rat terrier lurked.

The man would be leery at the North River crossing, but after not encountering opposition, then he'd expect opposition at the River Falls stockade, not a burned out and abandon stockade. Would that suggest to Clem that the Wapitis lacked sufficient men to man both the stockade and guard the supply convoy?

Rex hoped the empty stockade persuaded him that Bill Keegan's information was correct about five Wapitis guarding the supplies. If those were Clem's thoughts, then when his men encountered resistance, Rex figured the man would assume he'd made found the poorly guarded Wapiti supply column. After letting the caravan slip by him twice, he would be desperate for a success to report to James Donnelly. He also believed the thug wouldn't want to share the glory of capturing the Wapiti's supplies with Anders Breuer, especially, if Clem believed only five exhausted Wapiti warriors guarded it.

Rex finished his coffee, made his decision, and went to organize Clem's welcoming party.

Franciscka Weidman wondered how the handsome cod fisherman, Rex Knight, was faring at delivering Chief Smith's supplies as she closed the door to the IRS third-floor conference room. Joe Hansen, her boss, had asked her to attend the meeting with Manuel Prado, who had recently traveled the western wilderness. Instead of his usual black coveralls, the Ichneumon trader wore a gold colored cotton jacket with dark blue dress pants and polished black leather knee boots. Franciscka liked the jacket, though she thought the style and color more appropriate for a woman.

"Fräulein Weidman, I'm pleased to see you returned safely from the Wapiti territory. Your partner and my friend, Friedrich Burgdorf, never reached Narrows and Herr Ruffner. He probably had an accident on the river."

She just shrugged and said, "He a restless sort, probably changed his mind after their scheme fell apart."

Their visitor looked around the bare room as if searching for the refreshment bar. After a moment, the trader must have realized they weren't in the mood to socialize and said.

"The main reason I requested this meeting is that James Donnelly is now making a delicious corn whiskey and seeking outlets for the product. I'm thinking of becoming his distributor in the Guderian Territory. Before deciding whether to pursue this opportunity, I need to know what the IRS taxes are on alcohol."

"The same excise tax as on schnapps, thirty D-marks per liter of pure alcohol," Joe Hansen said. "Herr Donnelly was here two weeks ago and never mentioned his whiskey project. He also mentioned Herr Burgdorf's failure to return. Did you bring any samples of the corn whiskey?" Franciscka's boss liked whiskey.

"Certainly," the trader said. "I'm having third-liter glass bottles prepared to hold the samples. They should be ready in the morning and I'll send you a dozen."

"Will you market through Baron Hoess's National Distillery?" Franciscka asked. "As I'm sure you know the baron controls the schnapps, vodka, and gin wholesale business in the Erie and Guderian territories."

"No, I'm thinking of developing a separate distribution channel through the Atlantic Tobacco Trust. Herr Donnelly already supplies them raw tobacco."

"Does this mean he's giving up the slave business?" Franciscka asked.

"I wouldn't think he'd wish to violate Prussian laws, though he did speak of working with Myrtle Territory in arresting illegal cocaine dealers. The Myrtle attorney general gave him police power to arrest, convict, and sentence drug dealers. Instead of throwing lawless aborigines into prisons, Donnelly told me that he plans to rent the convicts to cotton plantations to pay off their fines."

"That hasn't been agreed to by the Guderian attorney general or the Wapitis," Joe said. "How are things across the mountains? Peaceful?"

"I was just in Hinton. Everything seemed peaceful. Herr Donnelly was focused on shipping his tobacco crop east and, of course, establishing his whiskey business in the territories."

Two days later, Franciscka's boss, Joe Hansen, told her that Jacobs, owner of the large hardware wholesaler in Roanoke, feared territorial laws might have been broken. He wanted the Prussian IRS's assistance. Joe had thought Jacobs's request smelled of a territory versus empire rule dispute. He didn't want to attend such a meeting without first understanding the issue, so he did the time-honored boss thing and sent his assistant instead.

"The issue is simple," Len Ruffner, a thin, intense man about her height said. "Some savage told this fool he represented me and bought a bunch of illegal weapons, tens of thousands of D-marks worth! Now there's a damn war on west of the mountains. I don't want the IRS or the governor thinking I instigated it."

"Please, Herr Ruffner," Jacobs said. "The west territory is always in turmoil with those slavers and Wapitis fighting. How was I to know the man didn't take Herr Burgdorf's place? Herr Knight was a Prussian. How do you know he worked for the Wapitis? I've never heard of such a thing, and he paid cash."

People knew Franciscka had traveled with the Wapiti column to get back over the mountains after Burgdorf had abandoned her.

"If you're talking about Rex Knight, I know him." Jacobs looked pleased by her admission. "He's the trader who saved me after your man had cruelly abandoned me in the wilderness." She decided to ladle on the female helplessness. "Herr Hansen is most upset with your man's irresponsible conduct."

"Irresponsible conduct, those animals murdered my man. He didn't abandon you," Ruffner said. Jacobs looked satisfied with the direction the conversation had veered.

"You are sadly misinformed," she said. "Manuel Prado and James Donnelly both told my boss and me they hadn't seen Burgdorf for a while, though there was a rumor the man might have drowned. Who told you otherwise?"

"Donnelly sent a pigeon, or at least the message was supposedly from him," Herr Ruffner said. The Narrows businessman took a moment to relight his appalling cigar. Jacobs asked if they'd like tea, coffee, or something stronger. "Coffee with sugar would be great," he answered, releasing a noxious cloud of smoke.

Fresh air would be better, Franciscka thought. She made a mental note to get serious about having that window installed in the IRS conference room after watching Herr Jacobs simply raise his office window to allow the cigar smoke to escape.

"Fräulein, when will your report on the feasibility of a toll road be available?"

Toll road report, she'd forgotten people thought she was an engineer. "Berlin has to review my report, before releasing it," Franciscka said, using a favorite bureaucratic excuse.

"James has other problems," Ruffner said. "Has the IRS heard about his loss of last year's tobacco crop or the massacre at River Falls?"

That was news to Jacobs and Franciscka. She asked for details.

"Well, again, this is pigeon news, so I can't claim it's accurate. Someone raided Donnelly's tobacco plantation and set fire to a couple of hundred tons of tobacco a week ago."

"Two hundred tons burned?" Jacobs asked. "That's a hell of a financial blow." Ruffner nodded. Franciscka thought tobacco a public health hazard and wished similar disasters would befall all tobacco warehouses.

"Donnelly sent his Lewisburg garrison and Clem Hubbard in pursuit of the marauders," Ruffner continued. "Yesterday I got another pigeon message that said Hubbard had caught the Wapitis at River Falls and killed them. Donnelly probably has your rifles now."

The news made Franciscka ill. Surely, her wily iceman wouldn't have dropped his guard. The meeting needed to end, but first she decided to sow some dissension. "Herr Ruffner, have you heard Donnelly is making whiskey?"

"Yes, that's one of the things I wanted to discuss with Herr Hansen," Ruffner said. "Donnelly asked me to be his partner and distribute the whiskey."

"Manuel Prado was in the IRS office asking about the tax rate on whiskey. He told us that Donnelly had offered him the exclusive right to sell his whiskey in Guderian Territory."

Her news stunned Ruffner and prompted Jacobs to say, "That makes sense. I had wondered why Manuel bought all my small glass bottles and ordered fifty cases of half-liter bottles. He's planning on bottling whiskey."

"That can't be," Ruffner said. "Donnelly wouldn't do business with the Ichneumon. You two have misunderstood." He appeared dismayed. Jacobs shrugged and gathered his papers to clear the table.

"I don't profess to know Donnelly's plans, only that the Ichneumon trader did ask about the excise tax on alcohol," Franciscka said while finishing her black coffee, a beverage for which she was acquiring a taste. Remembering the official purpose of the meeting, she added, "Herr Jacobs, I would suggest you be more careful about whom you sell weapons to in the future. Perhaps you and Herr Ruffner could agree on an authenticity code for use in future weapons dealings. If there's nothing else, I must return to the office. Berlin wants that toll road report."

The Wapiti squads deployed into the woods and about fifty meters up the hill from the edge of the river trail after Rex finished explain his plan. The Jarrell brothers were dubious.

"Let's hope you're right. What should I do?" Tom asked.

"I would like for you to help Jerry position the eight two-man teams centered along that area," Rex said, pointing at a large black oak above the river trail. They had stopped at a point several kilometers west of the burned stockade.

"Lou, help with the horses. Take them up that small ravine about a kilometer down river. After securing our horses, get with your brother and pick a location where you both have clear shots at this spot. Tom and you need to shoot the first riders who arrive at this spot. I want to cause most of Donnelly's men to stop on the trail in front of the ambushers' location. If we shoot first, Clem will just race on down the river before I can spring the ambush. The men will do much better shooting at stationary targets than at galloping targets."

"When should we shoot?" Jerry asked.

"When I shoot," Rex said. Wasn't easy coordinating action in a world that lacked radios and cellphones.

"When I hear that shot, then we're free to shoot?" Larry asked.

"Yes. Tom and Lou's shots will be in the distance. You and Jerry should have no trouble telling my first shot from theirs," Rex said. "Remember, not a sound until my shot, and then your job is to block their retreat. If Clem puts a few men in the empty burned-out stockade, let him. We'll deal with them afterward."

At daybreak, the first of Donnelly's riders came into view. One of them was an older man with a large red feather in his hat. When the man was about fifty meters past the last pair of ambushers on the west end of the ambush, the Jarrell brothers fired. Rex recognized Clem Hubbard, who was on his horse pointing down the trail and gesturing wildly toward were the Jarrell brothers were. The lead rider of Clem's force, with the red feather, was on the ground. Excited men and nervous horses collected on the trail below Rex's position as they waited for Clem to move.

Rex drew a careful bead on Clem's head and fired. The hillside exploded, and the trail was jammed with downed horses and screaming men. Several of the Donnelly men escaped on foot, seeking shelter along the riverbank. Stray shots rang out for the next half hour as the Wapitis spotted survivors among the carnage on the trail. Rex could hear gunfire down-river, which he hoped were the Jarrell brothers killing the few riders who managed to bolt out of the ambush zone and escape down the river trail. Rex's shot had knocked Clem Hubbard off his saddle. The Donnelly leader lay face down on the ground and appeared dead.

Tom rode up. "We couldn't get a clear shot on Clem, but no one escaped down the river."

Rex could hear steady rifle fire from up river, which was disconcerting. "Who could Larry's team still be engaging? Jerry, use the Owl squad to sort the living from the dead and secure the area and weapons. Don't forget, the men hiding over the riverbank. Tom, bring up our horses. I'll jog back with a couple of men to learn what Larry was shooting at."

The gunfire from Larry's squad on the hillside above the River Falls stockade area had ended when Rex arrived at the clearing. Out on the river, the remains of two swamped canoes were wedged in the rocks above the falls. He spotted Larry by the stockade rubble and jogged to him.

"Five canoes with twenty men came down the river," Larry said. "Three of the boats sank like a rock, and several of the men managed to swim to the opposite shore." Black grime from the gunpowder residue smeared his face, causing his teeth to appear very white when he smiled.

"Are they armed? Are Sue and the supplies at risk?" Rex asked.

"Those men ran up river, so not from them, but there are numerous wounded and unhorsed stragglers around."

"You're right. Leave two men to cover the river, and organize a search party to round up and disarm the survivors. Where are your prisoners, the Walkers?"

Larry pointed toward the hillside and said, "They're not mercenaries; haven't caused any trouble."

"Don't worry," Rex said before walking over to the young prisoners. The violence of the last half-hour had clearly stunned the Walker brothers. They looked to be in shock, huddled and trembling on the ground behind the large sycamore tree Larry's men had tied them. "Can you swim?" Rex asked.

After a moment, Art asked, "You're not here to . . .?" Rex shook his head no. "Yes, we're both strong swimmers."

"I'll make you two a deal. Swim out to those sunken boats and retrieve their cargo, and I'll free you."

Steve had returned along with fifteen Wapiti warriors, including the chief's son, Andy Smith. The reinforcements had arrived mid-morning as Rex was returning from putting the Walker brothers to work. Matt Brewer, a hunter from upper Hopkins River area, had led the warriors on a roundabout trip through the mountains to reach the supply caravan. The newly arrived men were sorry to have missed the fight. Rex was thankful they hadn't arrive earlier. They might have spooked Clem and blown the Wapiti ambush.

"Tell your men to trade their muzzle-loaded muskets for a new rifle," Rex told Matt. The group had plenty of news.

"No one is certain how many men Donnelly has at the salt furnace," Andy said. "Our best guess is around two hundred men, half mercenaries, the rest his usual collection of guards and laborers. All of them are well armed."

"It's still a large force for us to confront," Rex said. He could tell Andy hadn't shared all the bad news.

"Anders sent at least thirty mercenaries on a deep raid up the Hopkins River, passed Claytown," Andy said. "It was a murderous rampage that captured an unknown number of women and destroyed several settlements, including Indira's village. Unlike past raids, they murdered every Wapiti they encountered except for those women they hauled to the salt furnace stockade. And no, I don't know her fate."

"Son of a bitch, those bastards," Rex said. He understood that Andy meant Indira's fate. Anger surged through him, then hate. The desire to kill the Donnelly prisoners was fierce, but he knew that wouldn't help Indira or the Wapiti cause. He gestured for Andy to continue.

"There's a rumor that Ichneumon traders from the stone fort at River Point were at the salt furnace buying the young girls and women," Andy said. "Even reports of a steamboat. Everyone has heard the rumors, but no one knows who started them. I have no idea if any of it is true."

"We all know the purpose of these raids-to obtain slaves. This outrage is going to stop."

Andy had other distressing news. "A group of masked men attacked Smithtown and my home at some point after I had left for the Hopkins River line. The raiders put the village to torch. Burned everything and killed all they encountered. No one knows if my father survived," Andy Smith said, before adding, "The most worrisome rumor, which Steve believes to be likely, concerns Chief Pete Chin."

"The word is Pete has asked James Donnelly for a truce," Steve said.

Rex realized the problem. With the two recognized Wapiti leaders, Chief Smith and John Hopkins missing no other chiefs of sufficient stature were available to countermand the truce.

"He was one of the slaves I freed," Rex said. "After that experience, how could Pete Chin think Donnelly would honor any truce? We're winning this war. Look around. Well, I'm not stopping."

"I don't claim to understand the man. He didn't want to send warriors to help you. We ignored him and came anyway," Andy said.

"He even allowed the Ichneumon traders to build that fort where the river joins the Erie River," Steve said. Rex at least knew about that from the winter-sloe tour.

"It's almost a shame he left before the raid," Andy said. "I wonder what Pete would have said to the raiders. Dad was expecting trouble. I'm sure he escaped."

Rex put the men to work gathering the dead men and horses. The men used other horses to drag the several dead horses over to a small deep ravine near the river. They then rolled the animals into the ravine to hide them from travelers on the trail. They buried Clem and his men in a pit not visible from the trail. Rex's goal was to hide Clem's fate from Anders Breuer and James Donnelly for at least a few days. Unlike Keegan's men, Clem's men had little in the way of money. Still they collected 2,800 D-marks from the dead soldiers to add to Steve's bag.

During the hasty cleanup, Rex learned Sue Sweetwater had shot dead the four Donnelly men who had sought protection under the riverbank. She claimed to have feared they'd swim the river and try to seize the supply column. Rex figured it was her payback to Donnelly's men for killing her brother, Scott, and sister, Maria.

Rex wasn't sure how he'd avoid a cycle of revenge killings and feuds. Now, he didn't much give a damn. Still, he knew if he allowed it to start, the Wapitis would never know peace. But this wasn't the time nor place to challenge Sue's action. At least she had the supplies and packhorses back across the river and ready to head west. It was time for him to tell the Wapitis his plans.

Clem Hubbard's packhorse had three blood-spattered gray pigeons with glossy black wing feathers cooing nervously in a wooden cage. In the small leather pouch attached to the birds' cage, Rex found folded pieces of rice paper with Clem's authenticity code, 88HUB, written on one. He figured the code was the result of his earlier false messages to Clem and James Donnelly. Rex had used several of those Donnelly's pigeons they had capture at Gap Mills to convince Clem that the Wapiti column was east of Lewisburg.

Rex figured the birds' home was Hinton and decided to engage in some more misleading mischief. He wrote a message from Clem to Donnelly bragging about catching the Wapiti supply column at River Falls and slaughtering the dozen Wapiti guards.

"Larry, take the pigeon over by the river and release it."

Rex was gathering up the message supplies to put them away when Larry rushed back. "The bird went down the river toward the salt furnace," Larry said.

"Must be an Ichneumon bird and it went to River Point. Get one of the brown pigeons. I know they go to Hinton," Rex said. He painstakingly printed another message to Donnelly. After attaching the carrier tube to the pigeon, he went with Larry to the riverbank to watch the release. The bird went up the river. Hopefully the pigeons would avoid being dinner for hungry hawks and arrived safely. Satisfied the pigeon was gone, the signs of the battle hidden, Rex told Larry and Lou to get the caravan moving.

A few months before his abrupt change in worlds, he'd done extensive survey work in the Witcher Creek watershed for a coal surface mine application. The roads and trails he'd used on Earth wouldn't exist, but he had been over those Witcher Creek ridges numerous times during the survey. He felt confident that the column could pass through the wilderness to the west ridge of Simmons Creek. That location would put the column on the ridge above the salt furnace and Donnelly forces' camp. The Wapitis left the river trail near where Cedar Grove existed on Earth, about dozen kilometers up-river from the salt furnace.

The frontier life had whipped Rex into superb physical condition. Since crossing into the Witcher Creek watershed, he'd turned Zack over to Sue Sweetwater and had started traveling on foot with the four hunters. He would have put guards along the ridge top above the salt furnace, and he figured Anders Breuer would also. The packhorses with the precious supplies made noises at inopportune times. To avoid alerting the expected guards, he told Steve to have the column trail the trackers by a couple of kilometers. Rex wanted complete surprise when they attacked the salt furnace garrison.

Matt Brewer, an elderly but extremely fit and tattooed Wapiti warrior, was the hunters' leader. Sunset was about an hour away when Rex smelled the campfire smoke. It gave the guards' presence away. Matt then quickly located the two bored Donnelly men stretched out on a sunny rock overlook of the river valley. They had built a small wood fire within a ring of stone fragments. The guards were leisurely cooking two squirrels on a simple spit arrangement.

The time of day presented a problem. It was that quiet period near sunset. Sounds and voices tended to carry a long way in these mountain valleys. Rex could hear people talking in the camp below them even though it was over a kilometer away and a couple hundred meters below their position.

Matt whispered, "I'm going to use arrows, okay?"

Rex nodded. On a hand signal from Matt, the two hunters notched arrows and aimed. A moment later, each guard had an arrow in his brain stem. One of the guards thrashed about a bit, knocking the spit apart and causing the squirrels to drop into the hot coals. Matt snatched them out of the hot coals before they flared up and caused smoke that might attract attention from below.

Rex helped drag the bodies back into the woods before setting up the Topcon to study the camp below. Matt went back to stop the column and ask the various lieutenants to come quietly, but quickly ahead to the overlook.

There was a substantial armed force camped below them, over a hundred men and as many horses. The salt furnace was in use but not for evaporating brine. Instead, Anders had commandeered it and the salt drying shed to serve as the kitchen-mess operation for his army. Rex could see several large wood-plank boats in various stages of completion scattered along the riverbank. The Balers brothers had accomplished their mission of delaying the boat building.

"It looks and sounds like a celebration," Tom said. A group of boisterous men had a large fire going by a clump of trees near the riverbank. The men with Rex could hear the laughing and shouts. A party was occurring about hundred meters up the river from the small dock in front of the stockade.

"Any idea why," Tom asked.

"Not a clue, but I hope they have a large keg of Donnelly's corn whiskey," Rex said. "You see that boat?"

Tom nodded. Partially hidden by the trees where the men were partying was a small paddle-wheel boat. Rex estimated it to be twenty-five meters in length with a single smoke stack, though the fading light made it hard to tell. It had to be the rumored steam-powered boat, and it had to have come up the river.

"I want you and Lou to seize that boat without damaging it when we attack," Rex said. "Don't let it escape."

"It's going to storm early tonight," Matt said. They all looked down the river at the heat lightning and dark clouds. "A storm would be most helpful in masking the noise of our approach," the tracker said.

Several banners and a large flag with the Ichneumons' double-headed snake emblem flapped in front of a wide green tent. The tent, located beside the Salt Furnace stockade, appeared to be Anders Breuer's headquarters. A dozen pup tents were in a double row between the stockade and the riverbank. Another cluster of pup tents was located between the furnace and the stockade where some of Donnelly's men had erected their tents in four rows of ten pup tents each. The orderliness of the camp suggested tight discipline and experienced military men.

The horse corrals were between that large group of tents and the drinking party by the trees. Rex had forty men to take out a force three times that number; doable with surprise, but if Anders was expecting an attack and the partying was an act, then it was a toss-up. Rex couldn't resolve in his mind if the apparent carelessness of Donnelly's men was real and asked his trusted lieutenants their opinion. To a man, they believed the incautious behavior was real. They wanted to attack tonight and free the captives.

"Then we'll move out at midnight," Rex said. "Chain the prisoners to trees and leave the wounded man to guard them. Leave the packhorses. The first concern tonight is killing or capturing Donnelly's men. The stockade and its captives we'll deal with after destroying Anders' force." Everyone nodded in agreement.

Rex knew an old-fashioned steamboat when he saw one, but wondered how common they were in this strange world. "Has anyone ever seen such a thing?"

"I saw a similar boat on the last trip down the river to sell winter-sloe," Andy said. "Never been on one, but I heard they burn wood and use steam to move the paddles. Everyone says the things are dangerous, can blow up,"

"Maybe so, but a steamboat can travel against the current," Rex said. "Lou, Tom, you know your assignment; capture that boat intact." He then proceeded to assign each team its target and allowed the team leader a few minutes to study the target through the Topcon scope before total darkness prevented seeing the valley floor.

Anders's raid had captured ten prime Wapiti women and four younger teenagers and girls. Now the haggling over who got them. Burgdorf had just completed two aggravating days organizing the salt furnace encampment.

"We had a deal, Anders. I'm not waiting on your moron of a prince to arrive."

"You'll wait like everyone else until Prince Cherukuru has his pick," Anders's Ichneumon watchdog, Bert Paget said. "Our deal with your boss stipulated Prince Cherukuru had first choice of the women." The fool reached for his revolver.

"If you have a lick of sense," Burgdorf said, "you'll leave the revolver alone. Donnelly told me six, but since pickings are slim, I'll take the four youngest."

Paget jerked his hand away from the gun. Which four Wapiti women didn't matter to Burgdorf; he figured Chief Cinnabar would be happy with any of the captives.

"Anders, I'll take these four," Burgdorf said. "Cheer up, Paget. Your Prince Charming will have ten women to abuse. I know you Ichneumons think you're studs, but no one needs ten women. However, if I'm wrong, go catch more."

"Not so fast, feldwebel. It's not your call, besides the prince requested two young girls," Paget said. He looked to Anders for support.

Burgdorf wondered what the Wapiti women thought. The captives were sitting two to a horse, connected together by a short chain between the iron collars. He held two of the horses' reins. Paget had two horses, Anders had one, and a mercenary held the other two horses. All the women had their hands tied and black cotton sacks over their heads, so they could hear the bickering.

"Paget's right," Anders said. "What's your rush, we're going to celebrate Clem's victory tonight after Prince Cherukuru arrives." Now the reason why Anders's sergeant had rolled the barrel of whiskey over to the riverbank, where other men were constructing a large fire, made sense.

"You're celebrating Clem's victory, over what? Killing a few Wapiti warriors?" Burgdorf asked. "Or is it over his capture of a half-dozen muskets?" The two horses Burgdorf held had all the young female captives. He walked over to the mercenary and traded a set of reins. "There folks, you now have a couple of young girls. Tell the prince to enjoy."

"If you do get lonely on the trail, you might want to pass on the tall, skinny one," Anders said. The mercenaries' commander smirked. "The bitch stabbed two men."

"I suspect she had good cause," Burgdorf said. He motioned for the two guards assigned to travel back to Hinton with him and the captives to mount up. The guards would helped with the feeding and watering of the group of prisoners and their horses.

It would be dark in two hours, but Burgdorf wanted clear of the camp before the mercenaries started drinking. He'd always heard Anders was a fool; giving that armed gang of murderous alcoholics a full barrel of whiskey confirmed it. A small steamboat was out on the river, maneuvering to dock, and blew its horn as Burgdorf led his group out of the camp. They made good time up the river trail and arrived at the North River ford around midnight.

The Donnelly party by the paddle wheeler was still going strong when Rex's group broke camp and started down the mountain. Sue Sweetwater and two of Matt's hunters headed up the river trail to locate and kill Anders's guards. They would then prevent other Anders men from escaping up the trail. Larry Hopkins and the Eagle squad would deal with the men in the forty-pup-tent cluster, using knives at the start to delay alarming the rest of the Donnelly men.

Jerry Jones and Owl squad would attack the large tents near the stockade and the ten pup tents between the stockade and the riverbank. Steve Johnson, Lou Jarrell, and several of the new men from Chief Smith would deal with the party stragglers and the paddle-wheel steamboat. Matt Brewer and two of the hunters would investigate the stockade defenses and do what they thought best to protect the captives from vengeance attacks by the guards.

Riding past the furnace, Rex Knight and Andy Smith, with Jerry Jones and Owl squad following, encountered two Donnelly men. They demanded their identity.

"Clem sent us ahead to check the road and report to Anders," Rex said. "He promised us good corn whiskey."

"Who promised?" the clearly intoxicated guard asked while his equally drunk partner haphazardly held his rifle by the barrel with the rifle's stock resting across his right shoulder, smiling as if the joke was on Clem's men.

"Clem said if we went tonight, there'd be a keg of Donnelly's best waiting for us."

"You'd better hurry; that keg's about empty," the inebriated guard said. A voice from the salt-drying shed yelled for them to be quiet or breakfast would be late.

"It better not be empty," Rex said. "Where's Anders hiding? He'll get us a keg."

More of the Wapiti raiding force piled up around Rex and Jerry and beside the drying shed. The guard, oblivious to the danger collecting around him, told them Anders was in the big tent entertaining the Ichneumon chief.

"They've got that cute Wapiti woman and her daughter to play with. He's not going to be happy over being interrupted; probably tell you no whiskey," the guard said. The man staggered off toward the drying shed laughing, and weaving between several of the Wapiti warriors on horses behind Rex. The closest Wapiti warrior made a slicing motion with his hand across his throat. Rex shook his head, meaning not yet to the warrior.

Not many of Donnelly's men were about as Rex and his men crossed the camp. They were probably sleeping, or he hoped, passed out from too much whiskey. The only sound from the Wapitis trailing behind Rex was the creak of saddles and the soft clop of hoofs. Laughing and shouts from the Donnelly men around the bonfire by the river further masked the sounds of the Wapiti warriors infiltration throughout the Donnelly camp. Rex knew the next few minutes would determine his future on this strange world.

Rex stopped in front of the big green tent with the Ichneumon flag. Andy, Tom Jarrell, and Slim, one of Matt's trackers, remained with him as other Wapitis split off to their assigned points.

The Ichneumon trooper guarding the green tent wasn't drunk, and he was alert. He had his rifle at the ready as he said. "The captain's busy. Come back in the morning."

"I have business with Breuer that won't wait," Rex said as he dismounted from Zack. A woman cried out from in the tent, and the Wapiti party could hear a young girl sob and ask them to stop hurting her mother.

"As you can hear, the man's busy," the trooper said. He seemed hesitate and studied the men behind Rex still on their horses. "What's with the feathers?" the Ichneumon asked.

"The feathers are Clem's dumb idea of celebrating our kicking of the Wapitis' ass," Rex said. He pointed at the silent Slim and added. "The bow he's holding is a gift for Anders from Clem. We're after our whiskey. Where is it?"

The woman screamed in pain again. Rex knew the Wapiti warriors were having difficulty acting unconcerned and not charging into the tent to kill Anders.

"Wait here and I'll check," the guard said. He turned to open the tent flap. Earlier Rex had asked Slim, if a chance to kill the tent guard silently presented itself, the hunter was to take it. An arrow snapped by Rex and embedded in the guard's brain stem.

Rex helped the fatally wounded guard stagger into the tent, shoved him toward the sofa, and pointed his rifle at the surprised muscular man holding a long reed switch. In front of the man, a bleeding and nude Wapiti woman slowly twisted from a rope tied around her wrists and suspended from the tent's center frame. A girl no older than Indira was on her knees in front of a sleek man about Rex's age. The lithe, fit male body spun toward the tent entrance, his angry expression at being disturbed fading along with his erection as Andy, Tom, and Slim crowded into the tent with their rifles. An Ichneumon, Rex decided, judging by the golden eyes and feline face. He was otherwise a handsome young man.

The shot guard proceeded to twitch and bleed out at the foot of the sofa beside the man holding the switch. A fusillade of gunfire erupted throughout the camp. Neither of the surprised men said a word. The one who had to be Anders Breuer dropped the switch and, along with the Ichneumon, raised his hands. Rex figured the raging gunfight occurring outside the tent explained what had occurred.

"Tom, chain them together. Use those slave collars," Rex ordered the tracker. "Andy, help Tom, then find something for her to wear." He cut the woman's bindings. Slim helped him assisted her to a chair where her daughter hugged her. Lacerations from the reed switch, many seeping blood, covered the woman. Though her pain had to be considerable, she stood and pointed at Anders.

"He's a monster. Shoot him now. Don't let him escape."

"Please calm down. He'll not hurt you anymore."

"It's not that. He killed our babies. Him . . . he made us watch. Let me have your rifle."

Anders looked at her and laughed. Tom stopped his laugh with a brutal jerk on the collar chain and dragged the gasping prisoners out of the tent.

"Anders and his men will face justice," Rex said. "But first he'll answer who was paying him and why."

Rex had heard about the Ichneumons having blue blood but had discounted it, figuring it for bigoted nonsense. It was true, he discovered on seeing the pool of bright blue liquid under the dead guard who had attempted to stop them from entering the tent. Lou found him outside the green tent with his brother Tom. They were discussion where to hold the prisoners.

"Boss, you need to see what we found in the boat," Lou said. Then he glanced through the open tent flap and noticed the woman and daughter. "Then again it may not surprise you."

"Abused women?" Rex asked.

Tom nodded yes, and they jogged to the steamboat. A number of the pup tents were burning, and shots still rang out across the camp. Clearly, though, the Wapitis had the upper hand and the short run to the river went without having to fight any mercenaries.

"Look at this boss," Lou said while motioning Rex to enter the forward hole in the boat. Six frightened Clovis women and girls huddled in the forward cabin. Open slave collars and chains littered the room's floor. "We didn't know where it'd be safe to send them. They need more clothes."

"Where did they grab you?" Rex asked the women.

"We were fishing by River Point and the Ichneumon troopers just grabbed us," the older Clovis woman said. "The Ichneumon had never cared before. Where are we?" she asked, and then added, "I'm Chief Redfox's oldest daughter, Jan."

Kyle entered with an armload of Ichneumon coveralls from the boat's supply closet. "Here, ladies, try these on. At least they're dry and clean."

The Balers brothers had heard the gunfire in their hideout across the river and had returned, swimming the river, to help the Wapitis finish their assault on the paddle wheeler.

The steamboat presented a quandary for Rex and the Wapitis. The Ichneumon's spooky gold two-headed snake emblem on a blue flag flapping from the boat's mast made clear it was an Ichneumon vessel.

"Confiscating the vessel could precipitate a war with the Ichneumon Empire," Tom said. Rex and Tom had stepped back outside to give the women some privacy.

"With the Ichneumon and Donnelly interests in cahoots, as far as I'm concerned, the war has already started," Rex said. He decided to commandeer the vessel. "Put the captain in chains and with the other prisoners."

Chapter 8

The early-morning shower had finally extinguished the remaining smoldering tent fires as Rex surveyed the scene. The Wapitis had surprised Anders's forces, but the mercenaries had recovered quickly. A fearsome and brief, point-blank gunfight had raged among the pup tents, but the more motivated and sober Wapiti fighters quickly smashed the mercenaries' resistance and routed the guards. In a few short weeks, the amiable and peaceful Wapitis had become a ferocious fighting machine.

Tom suggestion that the Wapiti raiders all spike large turkey feathers in their hatbands had helped to limit the confusion between who was friend and who was foe. Still, the assault cost five Wapiti wounded; two of the men wouldn't live to see sunset. A rifle shot had wounded Larry Hopkins in the attack. Rex would miss that young man's counsel.

The surviving Wapiti captives told of the heartless campaign conducted by Anders Breuer and his raiding parties. The raiders killed all Wapitis encountered, including babies. The only Wapitis spared were young women and older girls.

The men wanted vengeance. Hell, Rex wanted to kill all the evil bastards, but there were issues far more important than satisfying their urge for revenge, such as having hostages to trade for Wapiti prisoners. He needed time to think, but right now, he needed to put the men to work.

"Steve, use part of the Donnelly prisoners to dig a trench along the west side of the clearing to serve as a grave for all Anders Breuer's dead men," Rex said. "Jerry, after your men have collected all the loose weapons, have them strip the enemy corpses of all weapons, money, and valuables. Give Steve everything collected. Later, we'll divide it evenly among the Wapitis who took part in the actual attack. Put the prisoners not digging to dragging their dead and stripped comrades over to the trench."

Rex added, "Steve, I want you to deal with the Wapiti dead. Have our men carry them to the salt storage shed, no dragging. See that their property and share of the spoils get to their families."

Andy found Rex and told him the woman and her daughter from Anders' tent had gone to help Sue at the kitchen.

"Good. Now, Andy, I want you to pick a couple of our more literate men and have them record the names of the Wapitis who helped in the attack, then the names of all the prisoners, dead mercenaries, and freed captives. Tell them to ask the freed captives to remain in camp until the chiefs or I have an opportunity to interview them."

Rex had the Ichneumon boat captain brought to Anders's tent for questioning. The excavation of a large burial trench had shredded the Ichneumon captain's earlier belligerence. Two of the bigger Wapiti warriors helped Rex hang the boat captain from a rope tied around his hands and suspended from the same hook that had held the woman. He then had the man's pants dropped. That action shattered the last of the captain's composure.

"Do I need to have the Wapiti cut something off to convince you to answer my questions?" Rex asked. He sipped his mug of coffee while studying the middle-aged man. The Ichneumon physique, excepting the blood color, appeared human as far as he could tell. Ichneumon psychology, Rex suspected, would prove quite alien. "Where were you taking the women?"

"I just follow orders," the sweating captain said.

"That wasn't my question."

"Those Clovis women, here," the Ichneumon said. "An earlier group of eight Wapitis were taken to the fort."

"Here? Why?" Rex asked. Kyle Balers had found a knife steel in Anders's tent and started honing his hunting knife while eyeing the captain's penis.

"I wasn't told," the captain said. "Speculating, the women were easy pickings, being in the middle of the river by themselves. It was a simple matter to grab them. Jai wanted them for the priest who will need a couple of women over the next two days. Please, I just follow orders. Ask Bret Paget. He works for Manuel Prado who handles those details."

"I will," Rex said. "Now, how big is the River Point fort garrison and is anyone, other than Ichneumon manning it? Wait, you said a priest. What's he want the women for?"

"For the usual reason men want women, but also for the sacrifice."

"Where they cut the person's heart out?" Rex asked. He'd heard of the evil Ichneumon practice, but had hoped it was just a rumor. "Do they use the Wapiti women? Have they . . . how often are the sacrifices made*?"*

"Wapitis, Clovis, men, women, the priests aren't fussy. How often? Once or twice, a month is required when we're outside the empire capital. However, the Prince Cherukuru wanted one each day he's in Wapiti territory."

Christ, the captain acts as if the priest is sacrificing goats, not humans, Rex thought. He felt rage building toward the evil Ichneumons, their revolting creed, and all their enablers who allowed the depraved practice to function and exist. He struggled to hide his revulsion for the Ichneumon captain and finish learning all he could about the stone fort. "Tell me about the fort."

"The fort is three times the size of this ring fort and made of stone; a real fort, not a log pile," said the captain. "It has six cannons and a minimum of twenty soldiers guarding the walls."

Rex yelled for Steve, who stepped in the tent to ask what he wanted. "Check and see if Bert Paget is among the prisoners or the dead," Rex said. "If he's alive, I need to talk with him." Turning back to the captain, he asked. "Cannons of what type, brass or iron?"

"I'm not sure. Brass, I think. They're Prussian guns."

"Where was the boat built? What's its fuel?"

"Wood, though coal works better. It's a copy of a Prussian river tug, but much improved on." Even with his life hanging in question, the captain's pride in the boat emerged. "It's a river boat, tough. Those drive paddles could move the boat across dry ground. Orleans Boatyard built it with a new high-pressure Focke-Wulf compound engine. Its boiler is the best in the world, the new-style boiler called a Caroom. It flies. I need only about three hours to reach the fort from here. Of course the return trip, coming back against the current, takes a bit longer."

"What's your name?" Rex asked. His name was Harsh Malik. "Who is Jai?"

"Prince Cherukuru, he's Emperor Ratakonda's nephew and representative, a powerful man. He tells everyone what to do." Rex wondered how the prince liked digging graves. He told Kyle to free the captain.

"All right, Captain Malik, I'm going to assume that you're smart enough to realize your life depends on being useful to the Wapitis. Go with these two gentlemen and show them how to run that boat. Betray us and Kyle will kill you."

Rex was living on blue nut kernels and needed a real meal. *If only there were a Tudor's Biscuit World*, he thought while walking to the salt-drying shed to see what Sue's crew had wiped up for the men's breakfast.

The woman from Anders's tent greeted him. She was resting and waiting for Sue to look at her wrists. Her name was Silva Johnson. Jerry Jones joined him at the shed. Rex told him to build a scaffold for hanging after he finished setting up the tents for the freed Wapitis. Silva smiled on hearing that order.

"Locate it between the stockade and the headquarters tent," Rex said. The guard at the headquarters tent sent a message that a pigeon had just arrived, and Rex returned to the tent while his breakfast was cooked.

It looked like one of those gray pigeons with the shiny black wings that Anders had in a coop behind the tent. Rex removed the message and placed the bird into the coop.

The message read, "Keegan's force attacked by unknown party, survivors claimed by a Wapiti force. Be on guard for a surprise attack. Protect the Ichneumon prince, Manuel will return to escort prince to safer location. JD"

Rex was thankful the pigeon hadn't arrived last evening.

After breakfast, he had the bedraggled and dirty Ichneumon prince brought from the trench-digging site to the headquarters tent and hung him from the rope harness used on Silva Johnson.

The man, Jai Cherukuru, had recovered from his earlier fright. "You're making a serious mistake treating me in such a fashion," he said. "I'm an Ichneumon diplomat, and I have diplomatic immunity. I demand my clothes and my immediate release."

"I know who you are, Prince Cherukuru. I'm also tired and busy, so I'll be brief. I want all the Wapiti women and girls you had shipped down the river returned." The problem was that he didn't know how many women the slavers had captured and shipped.

"Returned all the women? That's ridiculous, it's an impossible demand," the prince said. "Let me down. These ropes are cutting my hands."

"Yes, I noticed the Johnson woman's wrists looked terrible, even gangrenous. But then again, if you don't agree to have those women and girls returned, you will not leave this tent alive. So maybe you wouldn't need your hands after all. I have to check on the scaffold. Be back in an hour."

Rex left a screaming, kicking prince dangling from the hook and went to the smaller tent next door. It had been Anders Breuer's tent, and he lay down on the bed to rest.

Art Walker and his brother, Pete, still wet from the earlier salvage work at River Falls, had decided to cross the North River first, before making camp. A hot fire and warm June night soon had their clothes dry and nerves settled.

"What do you think happened to Clem?" Pete asked.

"After all that gunfire, I figure he's dead," Art said. "I thought we were dead when that big Prussian arrived, instead we're free. I don't know what to think." He was hungry and figured his brother was too. "Pete, cook some corn mush."

"We're out of salt. Plain boiled cornmeal isn't much. You have any beans left?" his brother asked. Art didn't. When the Prussian had said to leave, they had left. Fearful the monster might change his mind, they didn't stop to worry about food. Later, Art found a hefty stick for walking and using as a club, in case a rabbit or woodchuck crossed their path. None had.

"We'll get an early start. We should reach Rainelle by late tomorrow evening."

"I hear horses," Pete said. He started to put out the fire, and Art stopped him.

"Too late," Art said. "Listen brother, if it's Donnelly's men, Captain Keegan sent us to help Clem. We don't know nothing." Pete looked worried but nodded in agreement.

Five horses splashed across the river and rode to their location. Art recognized the lead rider, Feldwebel Burgdorf, from seeing him in Rainelle with Herr Simpson. The three riders had their rifles pointed at them. Burgdorf's reputation for violence motivated Art to throw up his hands. Pete followed a moment later with his hands in the air.

"Herr Burgdorf, we're part of Captain Keegan's men," Art said. "He sent us to help Clem. Is he far?" Art had no idea how to handle this. Where had the Wapitis gone? Burgdorf had to have come from Anders force at the salt furnace. How'd he miss running into the Wapitis?

"Clem? Last I heard, he'd killed some Wapitis at River Falls, but the place is abandoned," the large mercenary said. He rode around the camp area checking the woods, before adding. "A few Wapitis must have escaped across the river, and Clem's off chasing them in the wilderness. He wasn't on the river trail. Don't worry about finding him. I need your help."

Burgdorf pointed at Pete. "What's that swill you're cooking, corn mush?" Pete nodded. "That rear pack horse has some split peas. Fix some of them, enough for everyone."

Art realized the hooded prisoners were Wapiti women, and he wanted nothing to do with slaves. It wasn't his decision. Burgdorf dismounted and, after stretching, told Art, "Help those prisoners dismount and untie their hands."

The first horse had what appeared to be a mother-daughter pair chained together. Art untied their hands to make dismounting easier. The woman removed her hood, and then the girl's hood. The girl's age appeared around twelve to fourteen years old, on the edge of womanhood. Someone had severely beaten her. One eye was swollen shut. A wicked gash ran diagonally across her right cheek.

The short chain length between the neck collars and the girl's injuries made walking difficult. The mother helped her to the river. The second horse had two girls that Art guessed might be ten to twelve years old. They appeared terrified. *They weren't the only ones,* Art thought, realizing who had descended on their peaceful camp. He feared for his brother and his life. Mercenaries didn't like leaving witnesses to their evil activities.

The prisoners all had that lanky build common to certain Wapiti tribes. The two guards ogled the prisoners as they half-heartedly cleaned themselves at the river's edge. Pete had a good fire blazing that provided some light for the women.

"Where're you taking them?" Art asked. Was there anything he could do to help those abused Wapitis? The guards ignored him.

Lou Jarrell shook Rex awake. It was evening. "The chiefs are waiting in the main tent," Lou said. Seeing Rex's confusion, he added, "They found us below the Hopkins River. Come on, wake up, man. That weasel Ichneumon trader is in the other tent. He's convincing them to free that bastard hanging in there."

Rex's mouth tasted terrible, and he took a few minutes to wash and brush his teeth with the brush and powder he had bought at Jacobs' store. Collecting his pistol, he went next door to find Manuel Prado with two large Ichneumon guards, the three main Wapiti chiefs, Smith, Hopkins, and Chin, with Andy Smith, the Jarrell brothers, and several Wapiti warriors. The argument stopped when Rex entered the tent.

Manuel was beside the prince, helping him stand on the three-legged wooden stool to take the weight off his arms. Manuel was too short to reach the knots and free the prince. Ichneumon guards and Wapiti warriors were too busy watching each other and waiting for the first person to pull their weapon to bother with the prince. On realizing everyone was armed, Rex wondered what Tom and the Wapiti guards had been thinking to allow armed Ichneumons among the chiefs.

"Your barbaric treatment of Prince Cherukuru is outrageous," Pete Chin said. "You have no authority to hold a diplomat. I want him released immediately to Herr Prado's care along with their boat."

"Tom, escort Herr Prado from the tent, and hold him at the stockade until I send word. Lou, cut that asshole down and escort him to the furnace, and guard him until I send word," Rex said.

"This is outrageous. I'm not leaving my prince," Manuel said. The Ichneumon guards had revolvers in hip holsters. They moved to intercept Tom. Rex pulled his pistol while ordering the guards to stop. They wheeled toward him, pulling their revolvers, and he shot both guards in the head before they could fire. The Wapiti guards by then had reacted and shot the Ichneumon guards.

The docile behavior of the Wapiti chiefs had disheartened Rex. After all the horrors perpetrated by Donnelly and the Ichneumons against the Wapitis, the chiefs should have summarily executed those bastards and not be worried about their feelings. He'd expected better of Chief Smith and Chief Hopkins. Chief Chin was just another conniving fool from who Rex expected nothing good.

"Tom, need I repeat my order?" Rex said. After a moment to be sure he hadn't overlooked any immediate threats, he shoved the Ruger pistol into his cargo pants pocket, hoping no one had noticed it was an alien pistol.

The older Jarrell brother, Tom, recovered quickly and punched the stunned Ichneumon trader in the gut, slung the gasping man over his shoulder, and walked out of the tent. Lou pulled a knife and cut loose the prince, who promptly collapsed to the floor with a moan. A jerk on the prince's long hair got the naked, moaning man on his feet, and with a bit of prodding, Lou had him out of the tent. The Wapiti chiefs appeared dazed by the sudden violence.

"Andy, take everyone outside except the chiefs and post two guards around the tent," Rex said. "First, have your men drag these blue-blood freaks to the grave trench. The chiefs and I have some private business to sort out."

"Yes sir. I'll round up the other Ichneumon guard at the canoe and send more of Owl team warriors to, ah, protect the prince," Andy Smith said.

"That was cold-blooded murder," Chief Chin said. "You'll start a war. We'll never be safe."

"We're already at war. We're just not sure who with," Chief Smith said, while looking at the dead Ichneumons being drag out of the tent.

"Chief Chin, have you spoken with your cousin, Frau Johnson, and her daughter today?" Rex asked. The trembling man shook his head. "No? Well, she was hanging naked from those ropes this morning. Andres was whipping her to motivate her daughter to perform fellatio on the prince. You should make a point to visit with her after we're finished. Now, before we start, am I still in charge of the Wapiti force or not?"

"You're not even a Wapiti. We need Brian Orcel in charge, not this hothead." Chief Chin, recovering his nerve, looked to the other chiefs for support.

"No, he's just what we need," Chief Smith said. "Herr Knight has taken a dozen of our men and women with a few rifles, crossed mountains, dodged much bigger enemy forces, won several battles, and in the process developed the best fighting group the Wapitis have ever had. Frankly, your conduct, Pete, is shameful."

"Haven't you listened, Pete?" John asked. "Heard what these bastards did to my village and family?" John waited, and after receiving no response from Pete Chin, he added, "Rex, you have the Hopkins tribe vote to be our military commander."

"I can't believe I allowed that Ichneumon bastard, Manuel Prado, to mesmerize me with his duplicitous proposals," Chief Smith said. "Especially after learning what those animals did to your family, John. I also agree with your vote on who should be the military commander. Rex, I located your mother's family. You're definitely a Wapiti. The Smith tribe votes for you as the commander of our warriors. Now, what about the Johnson tribe vote?"

"I spoke with your uncle, Steve Johnson, and he said if you proved difficult, he would put the vote on Rex to the entire Johnson tribe," Chief Hopkins said to a startled Chief Chin. "Steve said that when the people learned about their warriors' accomplishments and your Ichneumon buddies' involvement, they'd vote you out and appoint him as their new chief. And Steve's vote is for Rex Knight. Do you doubt your uncle's word, Chief Chin?"

"He just shot those men with no warning," Pete Chin said. "I need to talk with my cousin. The Ichneumon can't be that cruel. He's just justifying his violent conduct."

"She's over at the salt-drying building helping with the wounded. We'll wait on you," John said.

Rex dragged the wooden stool over by the other chairs for a seat. "We need a strategy to recover the missing women and girls. Bert Paget was involved, and he works for that Orleans trader, Benjamin Purnell, so they probably all went to the fort at River Point."

"Have you questioned the man?" Chief Hopkins asked.

"Haven't located him, yet," said Rex. "He may be dead. I have Steve checking. We also need a strategy for dealing with James Donnelly at Hinton. These killers were hired by him."

John Hopkins had a troubled look. "I know one person's personal matters shouldn't be allowed to control strategy, but my wife and youngest daughter were in that group sold to the Ichneumon. I can't help but dread the horror they're suffering as we set here discussing tactics and campaigns."

"I agree," Chief Smith said. "First we need to save our people, then deal with Donnelly."

Rex realized it was getting dark outside, and it would soon be night, which gave him an idea. "The best we've been able to determine is that all the missing women went to River Point. If a rescue of the women is to be attempted, it needs to be tonight. Before tomorrow's human sacrifices at River Point or Benjamin Purnell's agents ship them on to Orleans."

"That moron Chin had no business or authority to grant the Ichneumon permission to build that fort at the mouth of the river," Chief Smith said. "You have a suggestion on how to rescue the woman?"

"It hasn't been a day, and I doubt the Ichneumon garrison is aware of our force or the loss of their boat. I can be there by midnight with twenty picked men and storm the place. I doubt they're on alert. With surprise, we'd have an excellent chance. If not, we can blockade the river so the women can't be moved until we have a chance to trade the prince for them."

"I've been there, and it's a strong position with cannons," Chief Smith said. "With those Krupp rifles and shot-loaded cannons, it would be suicide to rush the rock walls with ladders. I don't want to lose the cream of our new force."

"I understand, but the Ichneumon hubris, like Donnelly's, is a weakness the Wapitis can still exploit if we strike now," Rex said. "The Ichneumons are wily characters, unlike James Donnelly. When they learn of the boat hijacking and their prince's troubles, the opportunity will be lost."

Harsh Malik proved amazingly disloyal and remarkably accommodating. The amoral Ichneumon boat captain and Kyle Balers had quickly established a working partnership. The steam engine fascinated Kyle, and he wanted to learn all about the marvelous boat.

"Kyle, the understanding I have with Captain Malik is that at the first sign of treachery, death. Is that right, captain?" The Ichneumon officer nodded and appeared unworried. "Otherwise, the captain will continue to operate the boat and educate the Wapitis. Now you had a suggestion, captain?"

"They're expecting Anders's cargo of Wapiti girls and women tonight," he said. "That'll bring them out of the fort."

"Is arriving in the middle of the night going to raise alarm?" Rex asked. The Jarrell and Balers brothers, along with Andy Smith, were crowded into the pilot's cab to listen. "Would they open the fort's gate at night?"

"The arrival time won't be a concern," the captain said. "A middle-of-the-night arrival isn't unusual. On rivers, all kinds of things can delay a boat. Normally, they'd wait until daylight to open the gate, but a new load of women will bring them out. They haven't had a new batch of Wapiti women for a couple of months. They'll be anxious to sample the merchandise first."

"We'll give them something to sample," Tom Jarrell said. Nods and oaths confirmed agreement among the Wapitis crowded in the pilothouse with Tom's aside.

"Wait, what happened to the eight women you hauled down there a few days ago?" Rex asked.

"The prince was here and claimed them," Captain Malik said. "The men could only look. Don't get side tracked. Listen, I know our beliefs are alien to yours, but I'd like to live to operate my boat, so pay attention to what I'm saying." He gave Tom a contemptuous look, and then finished his instructions. "The guards' foolish rush to get first pick of the women will present your only opportunity to get through those gates. When I arrive at the dock, I'm to hit the steam whistle."

"For your sake, it best not be a warning," Rex said, earning a sour look from their prisoner.

"If I don't blow the whistle they will be suspicious and on guard. The Ichneumons are not stupid like those Donnelly guards. So what do you want me to do?"

Rex wasn't sure what to make of the cantankerous ass, other than to agree with him that Ichneumon beliefs were alien to his. The boat was nearly to the stone fort, forcing him focused on the mission.

"Are the eels gone from this section of the river?" Rex asked. What a dumb question to ask your enemy, he realized. The captain just shrugged as he studied the river ahead while making a minor adjustment to the steam valve. He didn't seem overly concerned about eels, probably because eels wouldn't eat Ichneumon flesh.

"They're gone," Kyle answered.

Rex decided to chance the swim and asked the captain to pass close to the north shore a couple hundred meters before the dock area. Kyle and Andy, with three other Wapitis, would stay on the boat.

The lack of electricity on the strange world meant they didn't have the worry of searchlights illuminating the clear area around the rock fort. A short swim had Rex, the Jarrell brothers, and a dozen warriors on shore. They then sprinted to the shadows by fort walls. It was a repeat of the River Falls stratagem, only this time the boat with the expected load of female captives would be the bait. Rex hoped his luck held.

The River Point fort walls, about six meters high, were made of smooth sandstone blocks. The place was nothing like the elaborate European castles with towers, steeples, and multiple parapet levels and walls that Rex had visited. The rectangular shape of the Ichneumon fort located on a low ridge at the confluence of the

Southern and Erie Rivers was a pedestrian design, a stone box. It lacked proper bastions to allow flanking fire along the entire face of the fort's walls, but the fort was still a formidable barrier.

The approach area around the fort would be a killing field in daylight. At a bit past midnight, the fort was dark, silent, and ominous as the band of wet Wapiti warriors arrived near the main gate. To Rex, the main wooden gate looked weak compared to the solid stonewalls surrounding it. No guards were visible on the fort's wall or by the closed gate.

The Prussian gray-green fatigues that Rex favored had become popular with the Wapiti warriors. As a result, all the men in the gate assault force wore Prussian fatigues. For added camouflage, Rex had the men stuff weeds and grass in their mesh vests to break up their body outlines. The mesh vests were bands cut grudgingly by Kyle from his prize large fishing net.

A quick check by Rex showed everyone in position. The grass and weed clumps had helped the men blend into the grass as they lay on each side of the gate. Their goal was to slip into the fort and lock the gate after the men going to meet the boat had passed their hiding spot.

Rex had asked the Jarrell brothers to take positions away from the fort's gate area. "Get far enough back, that no light from the Ichneumon soldiers' torches can possibly illuminate you to the guards on the wall. But that you still have a clear view of any guards who might appear on the wall above the gate. Your job is to kill any guard who attempts to lean over the fort wall and shoot at the assault team."

Captain Malik tooted the steam whistle briefly several times out on the river as he maneuvered the boat toward the dock. Rex could hear the guards above the gate shouting that the boat and women were there. They must have led a tedious life based on the shouts of excitement coming from in the fort. More worrisome, it sounded like more than twenty men inside the fort.

The whistle sounded again as the gate opened. Several guards exited carrying surprisingly bright torches. Rex was thankful he had the men stay twenty meters away from the road. Otherwise, those torches would have illuminated them to the two guards who had suddenly appeared on the wall above the gate. He hoped the Jarrell brothers were paying attention.

One of the two guards with a torch standing just outside the gate said, "Notify the commander that the boat is docking."

"Why? He'd have to be deaf not to know the boat's here," the other torch-carrying guard said. "I want to see what's aboard. You go tell him if you're worried." He then walked toward the dock. Unfortunately the guard who had worried about notifying the commander, remained by the gate with his torch.

Two long minutes later, several men walked out the gate, still buttoning their blouses. The older Ichneumon in the group collecting in front of the open gate said, "The priest's clerk just reminded me, the church gets first choice of the women, then the prince. We're not to touch them until then."

The Ichneumon soldiers gathered by the gate laughed. "Too lazy to get out of bed, I'll bet," one of the other solider said. "Well, I'm not waiting on the fat bastard." They meant the priest, Rex gathered, who apparently had first choice of the women.

"Yeah, brave talk," the older Ichneumon said. "What are you going to tell Prince Cherukuru if he's on board?" Rex wondered why the fort commander wasn't present.

"You think our commander would still be in bed if there was any chance the prince was on board?" the same opinionated soldier said. The group's laughter indicated general agreement with that observation as all the soldiers left the gate and walked toward the dock and boat.

The boat had docked. Captain Malik gave a long final blast on the whistle. Rex rushed the open gate and smashed his fist in the startled guard's face. The guard had been watching the boat, not the shadowy area at the base of the fort's wall. Two shots rang out behind him. The Jarrell brothers, he figured. Several more Ichneumon men, dressed in pants only, stood in the open area inside the fort and stared dumbfounded at the Wapitis pouring through the gate.

Ichneumon guards on the wall started shouting they needed help. "We're shot! Close the gate," one of them yelled several times. The Wapitis obliged them, slamming the gate closed after the last of Rex's men had entered the fort.

By then, shooting was occurring both inside and outside the fort. Rex and two Wapitis beside him shot three of the four thunderstruck Ichneumon soldiers standing in the interior parade ground. One man, screaming warnings, escaped around the wood-frame building across from the gate. The Wapiti marksmen with Rex killed the several guards on the wall while racing up the stairs to reach the walkway behind the fort's parapet. They then joined the men on the boat in making short work of the Ichneumons trapped outside the fort.

The surviving Ichneumons who had holed up in the large stone building built into the southeast corner of the fort's wall managed to shoot two of the Wapitis trying to cross the fort's open parade ground. A square stone block sat on top of the wall at the building's rear. An altar, Rex wondered. That building was likely the Ichneumon temple and the priest's residence.

Examining the interior of the fort, Rex wondered if the Ichneumons had the earlier captive Wapitis stashed in one of the buildings. The fort had a number of slate-roof, wood-frame buildings built against the inside of the rock outer wall. Any of those buildings could be holding Wapiti slaves and needed searched. Unfortunately, armed Ichneumon soldiers could also be in the buildings.

Rex turned over the job of flushing out the priest and remaining enemy soldiers to the ever-willing Jarrell brothers who joined him after he reopened the fort's gate. He then jogged to the dock where Andy was finishing-up verifying the status, wounded or dead, of the Ichneumon soldiers lying about outside the fort.

"Herr Knight, the boat is nearly out of firewood," Captain Malik said. "I need a crew to haul firewood to the boat." The man showed no remorse over the six dead Ichneumon soldiers scattered about the dock area.

"Harsh, let Andy handle that," Rex said. "I need to know where the Wapiti women are being held."

"The priest had only two. The others, they'll be on the second floor of the center warehouse, the building along the north wall," the captain said pointing toward the fort. "But the wood bin is nearly empty. Look, I know your focus is rescuing your women, but we need to be able to escape if Purnell's stern-wheeler arrives. I can't do that without steam."

"Larry, help Andy find enough firewood to get us to Smithtown," Rex said.

The captain and Rex had started to walk back into the fort when a young barefoot girl, maybe about eight years old and wearing a raggedly leather vest and pants, burst through the gate and ran to them.

"Help my mother!" she cried latching onto Rex's leg. He didn't recognize her.

"Where's your mother? The rest of the women" The girl's neck had sores from the iron slave collar that looked infected.

"That bad man has her. You got to save her." The girl, suddenly recognizing the Ichneumon captain, backed away. "Please don't let him take me." She started crying.

The captain, alarmed, asked, "Is that your daughter?"

Rex figured the captain was starting to fear their deal wouldn't survive exposure of the horrors the Ichneumons had inflicted on the Wapiti women. He shook his head while whispering assurances to the clinging girl she was safe.

The captain, anxious to be helpful and away from the girl's fearful stare, said, "Kyle, I'll show you the small boiler used to supply hot water to the bathroom in the barracks."

The Ichneumon captain and Kyle had just disappeared into the stone building beside the gate when a loud explosion occurred. A moment later, wall mounted torches by the temple door illuminated a cloud of dust beside the temple. The Jarrell brothers had fired one of the fort's cannons to try blowing in the front door. Their first shot had hit the ground to the side of the temple. The iron ball had bounded down a walkway between the temple and a warehouse. It hit the outer wall with a bang and rebounded back into the parade ground, where it rolled to a stop. If it were not so serious, Rex would have laughed, until he realized the danger.

"Tom, don't," he shouted.

A second cannon blast drowned out Rex's shout. The Jarrell brothers' second iron ball didn't miss. It ripped open the temple door. The little girl tightened her grip on his hand as she watched bits of the door and frame debris land in front of the temple.

The two younger hunters were through the hole before all the fragments had stopped landing in the assembly yard. Rifle fire rang out an instant later, then silence. Two more Wapitis ran into the temple and about a minute later emerged with a portly Ichneumon in a dust-covered robe. Then a woman emerged with one of the Wapiti warriors helping her.

The woman was the girl's mother, and she ran to her, shouting, "Mom, Mom!" Rex was thankful that in their haste to free her, they hadn't killed the woman.

Rex learned from the little girl's mother that she was the only Wapiti woman at River Point, had been there for three days. She thought a paddle wheeler might have loaded other women two days earlier.

The news that the Wapiti women weren't there, though feared, wasn't unexpected, and the news left Rex sad. His little friend, Indira, was likely doomed. Standing by the dock, he considered his next move.

A chase down the river after the paddle wheeler and Wapiti women would quickly put them in Ichneumon territory. It seemed pointless without first understanding the people involved and the dynamics that drove the human slave trade. Plus, protection from arrest or attack by the Ichneumon army would be required. The fort at Hickory Ridge controlled river traffic on the Erie. Chief Smith had told him the Ichneumon garrison there could sink a boat on the Erie River with ease. After news of this Wapiti attack reached them, the Ichneumon garrison wouldn't hesitate to sink a Wapiti boat. More gunfire interrupted Rex's thoughts, and he went to investigate.

A number of Wapitis stood outside the two-story stone building across from the temple with the shattered door. They were inspecting a dead Ichneumon man lying in the doorway.

"I think he's the garrison commander," Kyle said. "He charged us with his revolver blazing. Damn poor marksman, but I can't fault his bravery." The men with him still were inspecting themselves for bullet holes in their clothing and hats.

"He knew he had no future," Captain Malik said. "The emperor would have beheaded him over the loss of the fort. You did him a favor."

The stone fort was a priceless asset to anchor the western boundary of the proposed Wapiti Territory and to control river traffic. It needed garrisoned, and Rex weighed whom in his raiding party he should put in charge. Tom Jarrell had some experience managing a group of men from running his small sawmill and coal mine. Even better, he was clever and aggressive. An Ichneumon force trying to recapture the fort would find a worthy foe in the older Jarrell brother. Tom would do until the chiefs chose a more senior person.

"Tom, you're in charge until I return. Have the men clean up the place, and let them share whatever they find on the bodies, but the commander's and priest's offices are to remain locked until an inventory can be made."

"Okay if I make an inventory of the warehouse and powder magazine while you're gone?" Tom asked.

"Yes," Rex said. "Don't drop your guard. No whiskey. Remind the men of what happened to Anders's men after their celebration of Clem's victory. Oh, and take care of the pigeons."

The Ichneumons had provisioned the fort well. Food wouldn't be an issue, but having enough men to man the walls was a problem. "I'll leave everyone except the Balers brothers and Andy Smith. And learn how to use those cannons while I'm gone."

The farms and villages Hauptmann Fritz Caprivi passed after leaving the Guderian Territory capital of New Hamburg appeared prosperous. The inns he stayed in at night on the trail were clean, bug free, and pleasant, the people were friendly, and the countryside was peaceful until the previous day.

Near the intersection of the road to Roanoke and the western toll road from New Hamburg, Fritz passed a group of twenty men chained together. Three unsociable riders armed with shotguns and whips and dressed in blue coats and dark wide-brimmed hats were guarding the group. *Slaves*, he wondered, *or criminals?* The unmistakable misery of the chained men spoiled Fritz's mood for the rest of the day.

The William's plantation location in the front foothills of the Appalachian Mountains was lovely. Apple orchards were everywhere Fritz looked during the last few kilometers of his 300-kilometer, six-day trip across Guderian Territory. The sun had nearly set when Fritz entered the William estate's white-stoned lane. Massive oak trees lined both sides of the plantation's entrance that curved up to a white mansion. Baron William and Heinz were waiting on the front veranda with several servants to welcome him, and they appeared delighted over his visit.

The bedroom assigned to him was on the north wing's second-floor of the enormous residence. The room was larger than his Berlin apartment. Two male servants had helped him secure his bags in the bedroom and then they had seen to the care of the horses. Fritz had then cleaned up and changed, before joining the Baron and his son in the library. Since it was late, they then went straight to the dining room.

The baron's only son, Heinz, was similar in height to Fritz but carried an extra twenty kilos of fat and had that pale, swollen appearance of a young man with too many unhealthy habits and too few outdoor activities. Heinz asked about Franciscka Weidman.

"She's practically your neighbor. She's in Roanoke working for the IRS," Fritz said. The news surprised Heinz, who then asked if she'd married.

"No. Probably won't until her tour is up in the territories."

"How's the emperor's health?" The baron asked as he expertly sliced a large ham.

"Please appreciate that the only time I've ever meet him in person was at the ceremony for the Volga River survivors. I thought he looked well and spoke well."

"What an honor . . . the Iron Cross," Baron William said. "From what I read, you deserved one for your courageous resistance at the Volga bridgehead. It forced the Mongols to leave Prussian territory."

"The Prussian soldiers deserve the credit, not me. I was one rifle among hundreds," Fritz said. He didn't like talking about that day. That he had lived was pure chance.

"Were you scared?" Heinz asked. He had a slight smirk on his face.

"Terrorized might better describe my state of mind that day," Fritz said.

"I had no idea the emperor bestowed Iron Crosses on terrified soldiers. No wonder that war dragged on so long," Heinz said.

Fritz was tired and not in the mood to explain the difference between apprehension, a healthy fear, and intimidation with a loser like Heinz. He ignored the insult and focused on the ham and sweet potatoes while the son polished off two glasses of a red wine. All the food he'd tried so far on the trip had been delicious. After months of living on the army's dark rye bread, Fritz especially liked the biscuits and local corn bread with butter and honey.

"I'm an investor in the new railroad being constructed in Guderian Territory. Rails are the future," the baron said as the butler cleared the plates and supplied brandy.

Fritz spared his host a recital of his negative impression of Berlin-Hamburg rail travel. "Then you'll be pleased to learn a large shipment of rails were on the steamer."

"That is good news. I seem to recall Benjamin telling me he expected our second and third shipments this month. Any idea how many rails there were?" Fritz's news on the rail shipment had revitalized the baron's flagging attention.

"I heard a figure of three thousand tons. For sure, the rails were the bulk of the ship's cargo. Who is Benjamin?" Fritz asked. He was tempted to have another glass of the brandy the plantation made from their excess apple juice. It was surprisingly tasty. He made a mental note to ask why the plantation didn't market it in the territory.

The Baron glanced at his nodding off son before answering, "He's the main investor in the trans-Guderian rail line. Benjamin Purnell, a wealthy trader from Orleans in Myrtle Territory. Three thousand tons of rails will allow us to start laying rails on the Roanoke section next week. See any sign of a locomotive?"

Did the baron know Purnell was an agent for Ichneumon interests? Fritz knew Berlin wasn't aware Ichneumon money might be financing the territory's railroads, though it was always possible the man was using his own funds. Rumor had him extremely wealthy. General von Moltke and the Prussian General Staff needed informed of that fact when he arrived in Roanoke. The IRS office there had a secure messaging service.

"No sir, no locomotive, just piles of rails. Will the fuel be coal?" he asked.

"When will the army drive those Mongols back across the Volga? Will you be sent to the east?" the baron asked. Fritz realized age was catching up with his host when he repeated his question from earlier. Heinz's snoring finally ended the conversation between Fritz and the baron.

The next morning they rode around the plantation in a four-in-hand carriage on a sightseeing tour. The driver was a retired feldwebel of advanced age who had heard of Fritz's exploits along the Volga. He congratulated him for his bravery and for upholding the proud Prussian soldier tradition of never yielding a line.

The driver's fulsome comments made Fritz a bit uncomfortable and caused the baron to comment that he wished his son showed similar dedication to his duties. Heinz, Fritz learned from his father, never rose before noon and had no interest in the plantation business. The William plantation's main cash crop was apples. The facility canned enormous amounts of juice and applesauce for shipment throughout the territories.

"The business suffers from the lack of cheap labor," Baron William said. "I worry if enough laborers will be available for this coming harvest season." They were relaxing in the carriage between two rows of large, beautiful trees loaded with young green apples.

"Does the plantation use many migrant workers in the fall?"

"There are few of them available. We used to rent slaves and criminals from James Donnelly, but lately he's been unreliable. Now the cotton growers are expanding and buying up all the slaves. I'm getting the transportation problem solved with the railroad, but now we have a labor problem. I'm not sure how we'll get the crop picked this fall."

"I thought slavery had been outlawed."

"Only in name, it still goes on. What happens is the police arrest the person for violating some law, usually drug possession. Since it's the savage's word against the policeman's word, he's always found guilty and fined. The judge gives him the option of serving a five-year prison sentence or working for a year or two to pay the fine."

The baron reached up and picked an apple. As he cut it to examine its quality, he added, "The prison time is a death sentence due to the lack of food because of the thieving guards. However, the supervised work is probably good for the man. Drugs and alcohol abuse are terrible problems among the aboriginals. At least we're keeping him away from the drugs and whiskey. Give him a chance to sober up."

"That's a rotten system. Who's behind it?" Fritz asked. He hadn't been aware drug abuse was such a serious problem in the borderlands. Could that explain the bootleg cocaine?

"Yeah, you're right," the baron said. "Slavery was better; none of the corruption that's going on today. All the plantations are having problems with labor shortages. The emperor needs to stop this foolishness and allow slavery. Let's head back for lunch."

Baron William had misinterpreted Fritz's comment. The indifference that his host expressed to the corrupted enslavement scheme, the perversion of the emperor's judicial system, and his host's support of slavery had been a shock to him. More depressing was his discovery that evening at the ball. All of Baron William's fellow plantation owners shared his host's sentiments on the need for slavery to ensure cheap labor costs. However, the ball wasn't a completely depressing. Several of the plantation owners' daughters were pretty, charming, and a delight to dance with.

The domestic staff at the William plantation seemed of a cheerful temperament and contented with their lot. Fritz figured they were regular employees, not slaves. He wondered who controlled the outside work force of disgruntled slaves and criminals that his host thought so critical to plantation prosperity. Heinz William couldn't control himself, and Baron William's age precluded him from cracking the whip.

Fritz found out the next morning. While in the stables checking on his horses, he met Jake Hatfield, a robust older Prussian about his size. A guard with a shotgun was watching five men busily cleaning out the stalls. He heard Hatfield tell the guard to have his crew at the corral at noon.

"Hauptmann Caprivi, my pleasure to meet you," Jake said. "You dealt those animals on the Volga a lesson they won't quickly forget. I was a feldwebel in the Twelfth Royal Mountaineers during the Iberian campaign and at the bridgehead across the Ebro River. We're all proud of you." Fritz figured that didn't include their audience of slaves and criminals shoveling manure.

"We all do our duty for Emperor Schnabel. What's happening at the corral?"

"One of those Wapitis refused to work. I'll give him a dozen lashes to adjust his attitude. If that doesn't work, we'll hang him next time. It helps keep the scum in line. Hey, get that stall cleaned!" One of the younger slaves, a Clovis by his appearance, had stopped shoveling the manure to stare at Fritz.

"Guard, give that lazy bastard a taste of the whip," Jake said.

The guard flicked the whip, and all the slaves started shoveling faster. *This plantation society is despicable*, Fritz thought, as the man motioned for him to step out of the stable.

"Has Heinz shared those two Wapiti slaves?" The burly foreman's leer made Fritz wary.

"I don't understand. What slaves?"

"He bought two Wapiti girls last week. He has his way with them for a while, and then gives them to us before putting them out in the orchard. They looked choice. Ask him to share them with you. He won't mind."

Is he talking about rape? How wide spread is this evil. Fritz wondered. The Prussian army had few taboos for their officers' conduct, but violating the prohibition against rape guaranteed the end of any Prussian officer's career and, depending on the woman's social standing, his life.

"Where are these girls?" Fritz asked. "I haven't seen any in the mansion."

He was curious about the girls but didn't want Jake to know. Instead, looking around the stable area, he added, "Your crew does a good job. The grounds are clear of horse manure, the corral fence is in good repair, and the buildings freshly whitewashed with lime. The baron's fortunate to have you."

It was true; by all visual clues, the William plantation was a prosperous operation. The moral rot didn't show.

"Thank you," Jake said. "We work hard to keep it that way. I don't think he'll mind me showing you. They're in the cell block under the north wing."

Two young girls shared an old wool army blanket for warmth and modesty. The best Fritz could tell they were naked under the blanket. They did appear reasonably clean but had bruises on their arms clenching the blanket. Someone had hacked off most of their beautiful raven hair. Their faces were heart shaped, with sharp, angular cheekbones and a neat, small nose. He had heard tales in Berlin about beautiful savages who lived west of the mountains. If these two girls were any example, the rumor was correct. Two sets of hostile green eyes studied him in return. The girls looked more angry than terrorized.

"They need a good beating," Jake said. "Heinz says he can handle them; I'm not so sure. I told the boy I'd be happy to help break them in." The man chuckled, clearly enjoying the concerned look on the older girl's face his offer had caused.

Fritz felt unclean just standing there. He needed to vacate this evil place, but how in good conscience could he just leave knowing what awaited those girls.

They were in a stone floor hallway with three jail cells on each side. The other cells were empty, the Wapiti girls in the west row center cell. The builder had constructed the cells using mortared stones and no windows. The ceiling was wood. Hammered square iron rods formed the cell doors and gave them a homemade aspect. Still, it was an effective cell. The girls wouldn't escape without help.

"What are your names?" Fritz asked. The girls exchanged looks.

"Will you feed us?" the older one asked. Her clear English surprised him. Just how educated were these supposed savages?

"You animals will get fed when you agree to behave. Now answer the captain's question," Jake said.

Two defiant mute faces glared at the foreman. Fritz feared the man might rip into the defenseless girls and beat them. The foreman seemed to have an ugly temper.

"I've seen enough," Fritz said. "Let Heinz discipline them." He noticed the cell door key hanging from a peg at the entrance into the cellblock on their way out.

Chapter 9

Rex's thoughts were on what action to recommend to the chief's council. The Ichneumon army had to respond to the loss of their fort and the Wapitis needed to be ready. The unknown was how much time the enemy needed to organize their counterstrike, not whether they would.

"We're almost out of firewood," Captain Malik said.

"You mean we have to stop and cut some damn trees, then split them? That'll take hours," Rex said. He then received a lecture on their commandeered boat's prodigious appetite for wood when certain people demanded it travel fast up river against the current.

"The quickest place to obtain firewood is at Smithtown," the captain said, "Strip a couple of the burned-out buildings and burn the planks in the Mischief's firebox. It should be enough firewood for us to reach the salt furnace."

Rex nodded okay while wondering where that name, Mischief, came from. He suspected Kyle Balers. The firewood issue reminded him that since he was stuck on this strange world, he'd have to find a paying occupation when the war was over. Maybe, if he couldn't obtain a grove of winter-sloe trees, he could make a living brokering coal to steamboats.

The mysterious raiders had burned the stables to the ground along with the town. The wolf dog that Rex had seen on his earlier visit to the stables across the river was living in the ruins of Chief Smith's office. The dog had taken a beating judging from the missing patches of fur and a slight limp as it kept a careful distance from the Wapitis collecting scraps of the burned buildings to fuel the boiler.

Rex whistled. The dog started wagging its tail and ran to him. Petting the fearsome-looking gray dog, he discovered a bullet had grazed its skin, resulting in a missing strip of fur. The mutt was lucky to be alive.

The Wapitis soon had the boiler room piled high with wood plank scraps, and everyone boarded the boat, including Rex's new gray friend. Then the wolf saw Captain Malik, snarled, and lunged at his throat. Fortunately, for the captain, Rex had a firm grip on the wolf's collar. The terrorized captain fled into the pilot room, slamming the door. Which of the raiders had burned Smithtown, or at least how they had arrived, was now clearer. The wolf looked confused by Rex's reprimand, but settled down on the stern of the boat by his backpack. The wolf had ignored the trembling Ichneumon priest. Kyle told him the wolf's name was Hokee.

The Mischief arrived back at the salt furnace dock near dark, out of wood, and to a happy reunion with Chief Smith, who knew the woman and her daughter. Indira's father stoically accepted the news that his wife and daughter weren't among the rescued. Indira's sister, Lily, burst into tears and left with her father.

Later that evening the chief's council decided to name the growing Wapiti community Salt Furnace. Next, the chiefs appointed the wounded Matt Brewer as the stone fort commander with Andy Smith as the assistant commander. They even allowed the men's family to live in the fort.

When he asked why, Chief Smith explained, "The men will fight harder and behave better in the garrison. Plus it will allow the husbands to train their wives and older children to use the Krupp rifle, and provide more people to help with the fort's defense. There are so few Wapitis that every able-bodied person needs to help with the defense of the homeland."

"I didn't have a problem with it. Just curious," Rex said.

"Take a break, get cleaned up and eat, then John and I want to discuss the Ichneumon prisoners first thing in the morning," Chief Smith said.

That evening Fritz told Baron William that he would be leaving early for Roanoke. Their dinner conversation focused on the trans-Guderian railroad project until Heinz expressed disappointment that his friend would miss the fun. His father, Fritz suspected, also understood that his son was referring to raping those girls locked in the basement.

"Heinz, you need to stop messing with savages and get a wife. They'll give you some terrible disease or attack and harm you."

"I'm curious . . . what do girls like that cost?" Fritz asked. Might not be polite to ask, but he was curious. Heinz told them that he had paid fifteen thousand D-marks for the two girls.

"Man, you could buy a dozen horses for that amount," Fritz said. Not hard to understand why trade in young women continued to flourish despite the emperor's edicts against the practice.

No way was he leaving those girl prisoners to Heinz and Jake Hatfield's tender mercies. An hour before dawn, he found the stairs to the cell block. His appearance in the dark cellblock made the girls nervous, and as he fitted the key into the door lock, they awkwardly backed into the far corner of the cell while using the single dirty wool blanket to shield their nudity.

"Listen carefully. I'm leaving for Roanoke in two hours. If I see you along the road, I'll give you a ride and protection. I have no idea where you can find clothes, but those stairs go to the guest section, and you might find something. Good luck." He left two mute sisters huddled in the corner of an open cell.

Baron William had risen early to have breakfast with Fritz and wish him a safe journey. Heinz had stayed in bed and Fritz hoped that would delay the discovery of the open cell. Though anxious to get on the road, he didn't rush his departure to avoid raising suspicions he was involved in the escape. Also, the sisters would need time to clear the plantation and meet him along the road.

Last night Fritz had bought a spare horse from the baron for 1,000 D-marks. By then, he knew he wouldn't leave those Wapiti girls, and if they chose to travel with him, they would need a horse. If instead, they fled into the western wilderness, he could always use another packhorse. He had told Jake to pick one out for him from the half-dozen horses in the stable.

The big bay that the foreman had picked was an even-tempered gelding with new iron shoes. Fritz was pleased with the choice, and while they waited for the stable man to finish, the former feldwebel had examined Fritz's five-shot revolver.

About a kilometer south of the plantation entrance, the two Wapiti girls stepped from an autumn olive hedge growing beside the road. They appeared ready to bolt back into the brush until Fritz smiled. The oldest one held a dull dinner knife. Clothes must have eluded them, for they had ripped the brown wool blanket in half, and then managed a ragged slot for their head. The half blanket with the rope belt made a crude dress of sorts, but on the busy road between Lexington and Roanoke, the scarcely clad girls would attract too much unwanted attention.

"Heinz will send Jake to look for you," Fritz said. "Take that horse and leave the road. Wait, can you ride horses?"

"Yes, but why are you helping us?" the older girl asked. The younger girl had already approached the bay. The horse and girl examined each other while Fritz answered her older sister.

"That's a good question. I must have lost my mind. Now, take that horse and get off the road before someone sees you. At the next village, I'll try to find some clothes for you two. Hunt me up on the other side of the village. Now go."

"What's your name?" The wapiti girl asked. She didn't appear overly worried about pursuers. "My name is Jenny Jarrell, and that's my sister, Sue."

He told her, "Fritz Caprivi."

Instead of jumping onto the big bay, the Jarrell sisters spent another minute greeting the animal, whispering into the horse's ear while petting it. Then the girls helped each other crawl onto its back, and after a moment for everyone to get used to each other, Jenny galloped out of sight over the ridge with her younger sister holding on. Fritz wondered if he'd ever see that horse again.

The first town Fritz encountered was about ten kilometers south of the William plantation. It had a respectable size general store called Keeney and Sons where he placed an order for two sets of blue bib coveralls and matching blouses along with straw hats, two razor-sharp hunting knives with ten-centimeter steel blades, and a bar of soap.

Fritz hoped neither girl was about to start their menses before he could involve Franciscka Weidman in his scheme. He had worn his Prussian army fatigues with his rank and name sewed on them. His uniform attracted the rural store manager who wasn't about to pass up a chance for news on the Mongol war progress. He was in no rush to fill Fritz's order. Instead, the cheerful man had invited him into his office for a cup of coffee.

Jake Hatfield stormed into the store as the manager was refilling Fritz's mug.

"Listen up. Has anyone seen two escaped girl slaves?" the William plantation foreman demanded. "Do you have them?" He asked Fritz.

"Me? Heinz probably got careless and they escaped," Fritz said. He hoped the store clerk didn't have his order laid out on the counter. The items would be a bit hard to explain. "Would you like some coffee?" Fritz asked Jake. "The store's coffee is great."

"He claims he hasn't been in the cell block and accused you of stealing them."

"You know as well as I that boy drinks too much. You see any girls around here. Those wild creatures are halfway across the mountains by now."

"Why'd you stop here? What are you after?" Jake asked.

Fritz knew the plantation foreman was a suspicious bastard and no fool. He hoped Herr Keeney, the storeowner, likewise wasn't a fool.

"First, I don't have to answer your questions. Second, I have no use for creeps who rape women, so I'm glad to learn they escaped. But they're not with me."

The store manager, a middle-aged robust fellow, gave Fritz a wary look before turning to Jake. "No one like that has been through town or in my store. Besides, everyone knows Wapiti escapees run west into the mountains. It's your business, Herr Hatfield, but why'd you waste time coming south?"

"He listened to that drunk he works for. I left this morning. The slaves escaped last night, and Heinz figured the events were connected. His drugged confusion I can accept, but Jake, you waved me off this morning. Why would you waste your time chasing me?"

The angry foreman had no response, and after a moment stormed out of the store. They watched Hatfield's posse thunder off back north, clods of mud flying from the horses' hooves.

"Is the Baron's son still up to his old tricks of brutalizing young girls?" Herr Keeney asked.

"I was a guest at the William plantation for several days. I shouldn't comment on their private matters."

"Fair enough, so how old are they?" the owner asked.

"Just guessing, they're maybe fourteen, fifteen."

"That disgusting animal, the sheriff needs to stop it. Do they have underclothes, toothbrushes?"

"They have nothing, only a wool blanket," Fritz said. "They're probably hungry, so add some Beckman bars, crackers and cheese, and jerky to my order."

An hour later and three hundred D-marks poorer, Fritz left Keeney and Sons with a bag of girls' underthings and the coverall outfits. The Jarrell sisters were watching for him about two kilometers south of the little town and rode out of the trees to stop him.

"Here are some clothes, but first go wash in the creek. You stink."

Jenny was sorting through the bags and found the bar of soap, which she sniffed before examining the buffalo jerky. Sue found the hunting knives.

"Are these our knives?" Sue asked.

"Girls shouldn't travel unarmed, don't you think?" Fritz said. Sue flashed him a smile.

"No, nor be hungry, and you thought of food. Thank you," Jenny said. The two sisters scampered to the creek, trailing cracker crumbs. Fritz gathered the bay gelding's reins and moved a couple of hundred meters down the trail to wait for the girls.

As he waited, he loaded his Mauser rifle and one of the spare revolvers. He shoved the loaded revolver down his right boot; not the most comfortable carrying place, but handy. Another revolver was in his army-issued shoulder holster. After waiting a half hour, he rode back to remind the Jarrell sisters they were supposed to be fleeing, not having a picnic.

The girls had cleaned up well. In the coveralls and hats with their cropped hair, they had acquired an androgynous appearance. The Jarrell sisters would definitely be attractive women if they survived.

"Listen, if anyone asks, you're going to the Jesuit school in Roanoke. I'll tell them that you're boys the army is evaluating for page positions with the Prussian frontier troops. Now, let's get to Roanoke."

The girls thought the idea diverting and started addressing each other in deep voices as they rode toward Roanoke.

The past days had been hectic but productive for Rex. The stone fort magazines had contained a treasure in ordnance. Ammo for the Krupp rifle and black powder supplies wouldn't be a problem for a long time. There was sufficient black powder to allow Matt's men to start a cannon-firing program to train crews on loading and aiming the fort's six cannons. The item in short supply was the solid iron ball.

"Well, they're solid iron balls. Any reason they can't be cleaned up and used again?" Rex asked.

"One way to find out, okay if I fire one at the far bank?" Andy asked.

"First I'll warn everyone," Matt said. "Use that section of the far riverbank for your target." He pointed across the Erie at the high riverbank. "That way, the ball will slam into a sandy-gravel bank, instead of the river, or into the farm field. A crew can then dig the ball out of the riverbank."

"Don't miss, Andy, or you'll never hear the end of it," Rex said and left them to search the magazine. He found two small brass cannons in a dusty corner beside a stack of orange-sized steel balls. Earlier, Rex had discovered wooden boxes full of tin canisters containing one-centimeter diameter iron balls. At the time, he had wondered what the canisters were for since they were far too small to work in the fort's cannons. The small, brass cannon looked similar to the M1841 mountain howitzer of Civil War fame that Rex had seen at Fort Still near Lawton, Oklahoma.

While Matt and the garrison organized the cannon practice, Rex supervised the loading of the supplies needed for the Hinton campaign. Until that operation was completed and Donnelly routed, he couldn't go after Indira. Two small cannons were loaded onto the Mischief along with fifty of the iron balls, twenty canisters of shot, and ten kegs of coarse-grain cannon black powder. The powder kegs made Captain Malik nervous. He worried about the shower of sparks that on occasion spewed out of the boiler stack. Rex had a wetted tent canvas placed over the powder kegs as protection from burning embers during the trip up-river.

Feldwebel Burgdorf knew a battlefield pyre site when he saw one. The charred skull in the trail had alerted him. The bone pile was located in the center of a clearing, just a few kilometers west of Rainelle. The two stragglers he had commandeered at the North River appeared as surprised and worried as he was on seeing the charred bone pile. They claimed to have heard nothing about a battle, which he didn't believe, but Burgdorf figured he'd learn the truth at Rainelle.

Two Donnelly men appeared to guard the main gate of the Rainelle stockade, though lately, Burgdorf didn't trust appearances. He called the older Walker boy to him.

"Ride over and ask those guards if the commander is receiving visitors. Remember, your bother Pete is with me."

The commander was in, and Burgdorf's little convoy rode into the stockade. The women prisoners waited on horses with their guards while he went to the office, where he found a badly wounded Bill Keegan.

"Bill what happened?" Burgdorf asked. "Where are your men?" He didn't like the room's smell. The man had gangrene.

"You saw the pyre? Most of my men are in it," Bill said. "The Wapitis ambushed us. Tell me Anders and Clem caught the bastards."

"I came straight from the salt furnace, never encountered a soul except the two Walker brothers who said you told them to join Clem's force."

"I didn't have anyone to send; they're not my men."

Burgdorf rushed out the office into the yard, yelling for the Walkers. The older mercenary guarding the women prisoners told him they had gone looking for food and whiskey.

"You believed them? Damn, they're deserters from Anders or Clem's force. Go check the two bars. If you find them, bring them here. Then feed the women." He went back to Bill's office to learn about the battle.

"Clem was here five days ago, the day after the ambush. His men help build the pyre. The thing is they found no dead Wapitis." The wounded commander pointed to a liter-size green glass bottle on the table by the door. "Simpson dropped off a bottle of his rotgut whiskey. Open it and we'll try it."

"That's not surprising, the Wapitis like to bury their dead," Burgdorf said. "How big was the Wapiti force?" He poured both of them a small shot of the liquor. "Was there a big Prussian with them?"

"Yeah, he saved me from a cut throat," Bill said. He told about the battle's aftermath, the Wapitis stripping the dead of weapons and valuables, and overhearing that only five Wapiti warriors escaped uninjured.

"Then Clem with his two dozen men should have had no trouble dealing with the Wapiti convoy," Burgdorf said. "This is good whiskey." Then after pouring them both another shot added. "So where'd Clem go, neither party was on the river trail." Bill had no answers.

First, no Wapitis or Clem encountered; second, Bill Keegan's veteran force wiped out; now, two mystery men who had just vanished. Events were in motion that Burgdorf didn't understand. He needed to ride for Hinton, deliver his prisoners, for he suspected James Donnelly was going to need Cinnabar's warriors.

Hauptmann Fritz Caprivi wondered if all Wapitis were as chatty as the Jarrell sisters were. The girls were voluble and cheerful company. He'd made the mistake of idly commenting that longer hair would look attractive on them and had asked if their hacked-off hair was a Wapiti custom.

"Nope, you might say it's the slaver's cut," Jenny said. "It's to control lice. Most of the older women have long hair, especially those cute Smith and Hopkins girls. Jarrell women are the plain-looking Wapitis." Fritz gave the girl a skeptical look while her sister nodded in apparent agreement with Jenny's claim.

"That's okay," Sue said. "We're the smart ones. I can do fractions. Are Prussian women pretty? I've heard they start looking like sacks of potatoes after they get married."

"That is nonsense," Fritz said. "My mother is attractive, and she had four kids. Prussian women are like all women, some are beautiful, and a few are homely. Are you claiming there are no ugly Wapiti women?"

The sisters had their usual exchange of looks before responding.

"Of course not, but wait until you see our teacher, Tara Smith," Jenny said. "Who are those riders?"

Hauptmann Caprivi reckoned they were about a dozen kilometers from Roanoke, and several hours of daylight remained on the beautiful July day. Four men who looked threatening sat on horses and blocked the trail. They wore the same types of light blue coats and campaign hats the slave column guards had worn. On closer inspection, the four riders had distinct feline faces. Ichneumons, Fritz realized, not the usual Prussian thugs he would have expected William to employ.

"Hauptmann Caprivi, I see you managed to capture Herr William's chattel," the thinner, older man in the center said. The girls were stunned quiet by the sudden danger. Two of the riders rode over and blocked the big bay gelding.

"And who might you be?" Fritz asked while cursing his carelessness. He'd forgotten those damn pigeons.

"My name isn't important. Whom I work for is, and that's Herr Purnell. He asked us to help Herr William recover his property." The rider beside the speaker had his rifle aimed at Fritz, a Krupp rolling block with the hammer back. The other two riders were trying to pull the resisting Wapiti girls from the bay.

"Tell those bitches to behave or I'll have them clubbed to the ground," the speaker said. Jenny had bitten the rider's hand pulling on her arm.

Fritz's best hope was the pistol in his boot if the rider covering him with the rifle gave him a moment. More cursing, then a scream from the rider trying to drag Jenny off the bay distracted everyone but Fritz. He had the revolver out and fired his first shot into the rifleman's face, then one shot into the center of the speaker's chest, before swinging to aim at the riders grabbing the girls. The one rider was holding his arm while the other one stared open mouthed at the knife sticking out of his partner's arm. Fritz shot both men. The blue blood leaking onto the ground told him they had been Ichneumon men.

Little Sue had stabbed the rider. He told Jenny to follow him. They galloped south on the trail for a kilometer to clear a small ridge that blocked the rider-less horses and downed men from view.

The road had traffic, but their luck held. They encountered no one in the kilometer they galloped. Fritz forced the horses to slow to a normal pace before they encountered another traveler. They needed to avoid attracting more attention. The Jarrell sisters were quiet for the remaining kilometers into Roanoke, though Fritz heard Sue softly complaining to her sister that she hadn't allowed her enough time to recover her knife.

The head of the Guderian Territory branch of the Prussian IRS asked Fräulein Weidman if she had received any messages from Chief Smith.

"I've been working on the winter-sloe agreement," she said. "I sent the chief a request to attend our meeting with Rahul Malhotra next week on reaching a deal with the Atlantic Tobacco Trust. I haven't heard back from him."

"My friend Herr Jacob told me two ginseng traders just in from the southern wilderness had talked with several Clovis who said Donnelly had a large force at the salt furnace with many Wapiti prisoners. There might no longer be a Chief Smith to deal with," Joe said.

"Sounds as if Donnelly getting his vengeance for the tobacco, if it's true," Franciscka said. "Is Manuel Prado still in town? He usually knows what's going on along the river."

"I'd hate to have that prick tobacco lawyer show up for the meeting and have to tell him the Wapitis never responded. It'd make me look weak."

"Blame your flighty female assistant," she said. "Or better I'll get a couple of border guards and make a quick trip to the salt furnace and find out what's going on."

"Your uncle would have my head if I sent you into a war zone. It would be nice to know what's happening on the other side of the mountains. Hauptmann Caprivi is staying at the William' plantation and I know he'd like to visit the area west of the mountains."

"Fritz staying with that snake Heinz, I'd thought better of him."

"Actually," Joe said. "I believe part of his mission is to check on the loyalty of the territory plutocrats toward the emperor."

"Well, until we hear otherwise, I'd like to finish this agreement between the Wapitis and tobacco trust. You need to review the agreement." Franciscka handed her boss the five-page document.

The commander of all Ichneumon forces, General Bezdek, had ordered General Meringa and Colonel Paget to report immediately to the military headquarter at Port Delta's fort. He waved off their salutes.

"Have you read the dispatch? The Wapitis seized the fort at River Point six days ago. The day before, the savages captured Prince Cherukuru and his steamboat during James Donnelly's salt furnace fiasco. The savages have the emperor's nephew!"

Colonel Paget had read the dispatch. *What lousy timing,* he thought. For years, the younger Ichneumon army officers had requested Emperor Ratakonda's permission to allow their wives to live in the three Erie River forts. The emperor had recently accepted the army's assurances of the forts' invulnerability and had agreed to allow a few Ichneumon females into the Erie valley.

"I'll keep it simple," General Bezdek said. "The forces assigned to you for staffing the forts in preparation for the arrival of the wives, along with what extra soldiers Delta can spare, you will use to boot those savages out of our fort."

"How did it happen? A traitor," General Meringa asked.

"What difference does the how make? The garrison probably got careless, believed the nonsense of backward savages who knew nothing of military tactics. Our concern is to retake the fort before Emperor Ratakonda receives the news."

Colonel Paget knew speaking up would piss General Meringa off, but all their heads were in danger. "I've been to the fort. Several hundred troops will be needed, along with heavy cannons to breach the wall."

"Breach the wall?" General Meringa said. "Destroying the fort won't accomplish our goal of assuring the Emperor our temporary loss of the fort was a subterfuge to lure the troublesome savages into a killing field. Plus a bombardment would endanger the prisoners."

To the colonel's surprise, the commander liked Meringa's ruse idea.

"The loss of the fort was a planned deception? The emperor might believe it, if you move fast. How many men do you have?" General Bezdek asked. Meringa thought around hundred and fifty soldiers and sixty sailors on two of Purnell's stern-wheelers.

"That's a bit short," The commander said. "I agree with the colonel, around three hundred infantry would be better. I have fifty troublesome Aztecs I want out of Delta. Can you handle those animals, Colonel Paget?"

The colonel's nod of agreement to commanding the Aztecs earned him another scowl from General Meringa. Those western warriors were a bit tough to control, but they were fearless. And they gave him his own command so he didn't have to be the general's lackey.

"Is that cannon platform available?" General Meringa said. "A breach of the fort's wall might be required and I'd like to have the equipment, just in case."

"The monitor is too slow," General Bezdek said. "I don't want the assault delayed. Instead, load three of the large siege cannons on one of Purnell's sternwheelers. They're fast boats and speed is critical. I want your task force under way by noon tomorrow. Sooner would be better. Remember, the loss of the prince shouldn't cost our heads, but the fort's loss could. Go recover the fort and slaughter anyone who interferes."

The Wapitis had switched the cannons and their supplies to thirty packhorses at River Falls. The river wasn't passible to steamboats above the falls. To reach Hinton, the Wapiti force would travel the trail by way of Rainelle and the Sulfur River valley. The first evening, Rex stopped on the overlook above Rainelle near where he'd ambushed Keegan's mercenaries a month earlier. Today, he had over fifty mounted and well-armed men along with thirty pack horses and a new Wapiti flag, a white rectangular banner with a gold border and a five-point solid green star in the center.

Rex had never viewed the Rainelle stockade force as much of a threat. Still, he couldn't leave an enemy force in a position to cut the Wapiti supply line.

"Tom, take your brother and several riders, scout the stockade," he said. "I'll have the main force set up the night's camp and a defensive perimeter."

The Jarrell force returned at dark with a jovial gray-haired man whom Tom introduced as Herr Simpson, and a young skinny man whom Rex recognized was Art Walker.

"Art, how's your brother Pete?" Rex asked, figuring this was a parley of sorts for Rainelle.

"He's fine, Colonel Knight. Thanks for asking."

"What's your part in this Herr Simpson?" Rex asked, smiling over his sudden rank of colonel. The name of the Santa Claus looking man sounded familiar.

"I'm currently setting up Donnelly's cooperage operation in Rainelle and running his distillery," the businessman answered. "The stockade commander fears you'll burn the stockade. He asked me to offer his surrender. I asked Art to help. Bill's not aware of Art's history with you, and I'd like to keep it that way, if you're agreeable. We won't fight the Wapitis and hope you'll spare our town."

"I gather Bill's leg is still bothering him?" Rex said. "Why didn't he just abandon the stockade and flee?"

"The quack who serves as the town doctor wants to amputate his leg," Herr Simpson said. "I'm sure you can understand the captain doesn't want that, but it's infected, and he's in no position to ride nor defend the fort. However, his main concern is the three Ichneumon mercenaries whom Donnelly sent a week ago. He doesn't trust or control them. They also know you're here and on guard. Bill suggested you send several of your men to the stockade and, ah, arrest those Ichneumon men. I've already sent a keg of whiskey to the stockade. My other purpose is to serve as a hostage for Bill's behavior."

For sure, Rex liked the man and thought the plan workable, but the involvement of Ichneumon mercenaries made him cautious. "Are there many Ichneumon in the area?"

"These are the first Ichneumons I've ever seen in Rainelle. The rumor is that Donnelly has a small number of Ichneumon soldiers at Hinton and is expecting the stone fort to send him more. Also, the other rumor is that Cinnabar has a hundred warriors on the way to Hinton."

"You should be aware that the Ichneumon brought their own pigeons," Art said. "Well, I call them pigeons, but I'm not sure what they are. The birds are black . . . actually look more crow than pigeon and they eat mice."

"So you figure they've sent word of our arrival to whoever their commander is?" Rex asked. The young man nodded and then after walking away, turned, and returned.

"One more thing, the night you freed us, we were camped on the North River when some of Donnelly's mercenaries crossed with four Wapiti women. They went on to Hinton after talking with Bill."

One frustration had been putting a number to the captured Wapiti women. The destruction, murdering, and burning of settlements along the Hopkins River had resulted in entire families disappearing. Rex knew Indira and her mother had been at the salt furnace the afternoon of the Wapiti attack, but they weren't among the freed prisoners or at River Point.

"Did you get a name?" Rex asked.

"No sir," Art answered. "One pair was a mother and daughter. The other pair was two young girls. Burgdorf's men guarded them all the time and permitted no talking. The teenage daughter had been badly beaten."

Rex tried not to get his hopes up, but that mother-daughter pair was the best clue to date on Indira's fate. He needed to speak with Keegan.

The Jarrell brothers had organized a ten-man assault force to secure the Rainelle garrison. They were just leaving when a rider galloped into camp. "Tom, go ahead," Rex said. "I need to speak with the rider." Tom's group rode off with Art Walker and Rex walked over to the rider, one of Matt's hunters.

"This message came on a gray pigeon to River Point," the hunter said. "Matt said to tell you he believes it's from Hickory Ridge." The rider and horse looked exhausted.

"Get something to eat while I read this," Rex said. The pigeon note read, "Two stern-wheelers with 300 soldiers headed to River Point." The note from Matt read, "I suspect the Hickory Ridge coal yard manager sent the pigeon. Magazine work is finished, but River Point is short on men to defend the walls. Please return. Hinton will wait."

"I gather the Wapitis have woken up to the need of forming an army and a territorial government," Simpson said, interrupting his thoughts. The cooper-distiller had rolled a piece of log over close to the fire and sat down after the Jarrell brothers and Art rode off. "I never understood why the Wapitis were so passive in the face of the cruel predation. Now they're acting like the Prussians."

"Is that so?" Rex asked. The notes certainly upset his plans for Donnelly. Curious what a businessman would suggest, he handed the notes to Herr Simpson. "Read this. What would a Prussian do?"

Rex inspected the piece of goat jerky that would be their supper while Simpson read the pigeon note, then Matt's note. Hokee slipped in to lie beside Rex, eyeing the jerky. The wolf liked all types of jerky. It ignored the distiller.

"What a beautiful gray wolf. I've been trying to find one for years. If you find one in your travels, I'll pay well for a puppy. As to the notes, I agree with the writer; Hinton will wait."

"The complication is the fate of those Wapiti women that Burgdorf dragged to Hinton," Rex said. Goat jerky wasn't nearly as tasty as venison jerky. He gave half of it to Hokee.

"I'm no expert, but generals who don't concentrate their forces often get in trouble," the distiller said. "I'd think the Ichneumon army would pose a greater danger to the Wapitis, than Donnelly's mercenaries. He's just a land-based pirate. The man needs to go, but he'll wait. The Ichneumon army won't and more women will be endangered."

"After he's gone, will the valley accept the Wapiti council?" Rex asked. He knew the distiller was right.

"If the Wapitis bring fair laws and respect for women and property, I think the valley will welcome them. Most of the residents are mutts like us, a mix of Prussian fugitives, York deportees, and Clovis. The Ichneumon mentality, I don't understand."

"I'm beginning to fear I do," Rex said. "The blue blooded bastards want the place all to themselves."

"I hope you're wrong. Otherwise endless war will be our future," Herr Simpson said. "If the Wapitis envision a peaceful future melting pot of the empire's rejects, which is what this area has been, tell the chiefs to consider a neutral name like Sylvania for their homeland instead of the some pretentious name like the Greater Imperial Wapiti Empire." He smiled to show he intended no insult.

Chapter 10

Franciscka Weidman was considering what to have for dinner when someone knocked on her cabin door. The Prussian IRS expected Fritz Caprivi to arrive from William Plantation the day after tomorrow. It had been over a year since Franciscka had talked with her friend, and she wondered if the war and Heinz William had corrupted him.

It was Fritz, along with two cute young Wapitis, girls dressed like boys. *Lord, not more Indiras; are there any ugly Wapiti females?* Franciscka wondered while hugging her friend. Fritz introduced the girls, and she invited everyone into her cramped cabin. The Wapiti girls and the neighborhood tabby cat that had adopted her were instant pals. Fritz was his usual polite self and apologized for his unannounced arrival, but he needed her help. He gave her a brief explanation on how he came to be traveling with the Jarrell sisters.

Jenny Jarrell, deciding Fritz's account lacked sufficient heroic details, described his opening of their cell door, buying them a horse and clothes, and the amazing shootout with the Ichneumon slavers. Her sister, Sue, supplied additional adjectives to assist her sister's portrayal of their daring rescue.

"Well, you young ladies have had some day," Franciscka said. "They can stay here until we can deliver them back to their family. Meet us at the IRS office in the morning."

Fritz and Franciscka stepped into the kitchen while the girls used the bathroom.

"Crazy rumors of bloody battles between the Wapitis and Donnelly have been arriving all week," said Franciscka, "and my boss wants us to find out what's happening on the other side of the mountains."

"Is the place all wilderness, with no roads and inns?" Fritz asked.

"It's pretty sparsely settled. The river is the quickest way to travel, though James Donnelly's stronghold at Hinton makes that a bit risky."

She explained he was a warlord with several stockades scattered across the western wilderness. Slaves were an important part of his business and his men would have been the ones who captured the Jarrell sisters. She also passed on the latest rumors that the Ichneumon forces had allied with Donnelly to annihilate the Wapiti tribes.

"The IRS is operating blind," Franciscka said. "A few days prior the rumor was Donnelly had captured a large number of Wapitis and the salt furnace. Today a couple of Clovis trappers have been telling around the bars that the Wapitis had kicked the Donnelly and Ichneumon forces out of the salt furnace. Joe talked with the main Ichneumon trader, Manuel Prado, who said that was nonsense. However, he cut short a trip to inspect the new railroad construction west of New Hamburg, which makes me suspect something unexpected did occur."

"These stories of the Wapitis' military feats against Donnelly's larger, experienced forces don't match the tales of Wapiti passivity I heard at the William plantation and in New Hamburg. Aren't they still using muskets and bows?"

"When I was there a couple of months ago some of the Wapitis had rolling block rifles and knew how to use them," Franciscka said.

The Jarrell sisters, hands washed, had been wandering around the rooms, Jenny holding the purring cat while Sue casually opened and looked into drawers and books. After a quick inspection and exchange of glances between themselves, the girls would carefully replace the book or close the drawer. Franciscka grabbed the sisters' full attention with her tale to Fritz about the rescue of the two Wapiti teachers.

"Tara Smith's our teacher," Jenny said. "She's the one you need to see. She's beautiful." Realizing her comment might have offended their hostess, she added, "You're beautiful, too, Fräulein Weidman."

"She'd heard Prussian women look like sacks of potatoes," Fritz said. The sisters looked mortified by that exposé of their bigotry and ignorance.

"Young girls . . . well, you're correct about Tara Smith. She is a beauty. Now let's eat and get a bath. Tomorrow may prove to be long, depending on my boss's orders."

The meeting with Franciscka's boss, Joe Hansen, was brief. The last few days had brought new rumors of bloody battles and Ichneumon forts west of the mountains that had the Prussian IRS and government of Guderian Territory alarmed. Joe wanted them to take fast boats to Hinton and the salt furnace and learn first-hand what was fact and what was nonsense. Joe would even supply twenty pigeons and a person to care for the birds to accompany them.

Her boss, after some private persuasion from Fritz that Franciscka wasn't party to, finally agreed to support her request that the Guderian Territory attorney general arrest Heinz William for violation of the anti-slavery act. The Jarrell sisters had offered to provide depositions on their enslavement at the William plantation. Hauptmann Caprivi offered to testify in support of the girls' story.

General von Moltke had given Hauptmann Caprivi names and letters of introduction for several retired Prussian feldwebels living in the Roanoke area to call on if he needed experienced and trustworthy guards. He left the IRS office to find two feldwebels willing to travel west of the mountains on empire business while Franciscka arranged for the necessary supplies and boats at Narrows.

The Ichneumon mercenaries proved to be cunning opponents, but not quite cunning enough to handle the sly Jarrell brothers. Before entering the Rainelle stockade, Lou Jarrell sent Art Walker into the Blue Star Tavern with a message for the guards.

"Captain Keegan wants you in the stockade," Art said. He knew the three Donnelly men had been drinking and playing poker and as expected, they kicked up a fuss.

"Piss on the sorry cripple," the fat guard said. "It's our night off. If he needs something, tell him to use those asshole Ichneumons. I'm not leaving; it's my night off." His pals joined in the whining; they didn't appreciate being bothered on their night off.

"Suit yourself. Burgdorf said you'd regret making him come and fetch you."

"You mean the outlaw feldwebel?" the fat guard asked. Art nodded. "Well, hell, why didn't you say so?" The guards left for the stockade after draining their mugs.

Lou had told Art to let the men enter the stockade gate first. The mercenaries ambushed the three hapless men without warning as they crossed the yard to enter the commander's office. Lou clamped a strong hand on Art's shoulder to prevent him from running to the downed men.

One of the Ichneumon mercenaries led three horses out into the stockade's dark interior yard from the small stockade stable. Tom

Jarrell and the other two Wapitis materialized out of the dark alley behind the stockade to wait by the gate.

They could hear the Ichneumon checking the bodies, "Damn it these aren't Wapitis, nor is Simpson here. It's a trap!" The Ichneumon bolted for their horses, thundered through the stockade gate, and died.

The Rainelle commander, Bill Keegan was dead, murdered by the Ichneumons who had cut his throat. The gunfire rousted the rest of the pitiful garrison of a half-dozen men and a number of residents. Rex Knight, Herr Simpson, and several Wapiti soldiers arrived around mid-night, just after the Jarrell brothers had finished disarming the spectators and surviving garrison troopers.

The senseless murder of the crippled garrison commander by the Ichneumon mercenaries had shocked the residents. They were equally concerned about the Wapiti force's intentions toward Rainelle. The residents knew what had happened to Donnelly's tobacco barn. The crowd gathered around the three dead Ichneumons consisted of about a dozen Wapitis, the surviving Donnelly men, and about two dozen town residents including the owner of the Blue Star tavern. Rex decided he needed to tell the crowd what to expect going forward.

"Lou, improvise a flag pole and put up one of the Wapiti flags." Rex then turned to the crowd. "The Wapiti tribes have united to end slavery and bring the rule of law and justice to their homeland. After today, if the Wapitis catch you with slaves, we will hang you. Effective immediately, Herr Simpson is the mayor of Rainelle, and Art Walker is commander of the stockade. If anyone has a problem with those arrangements, you'd best be gone by sunrise."

Hauptmann Fritz Caprivi agreed with Franciscka Weidman that the river wilderness was scenic, but he would have enjoyed it better from horseback. Instead, he'd spent the day in a wet flat-bottomed boat dodging and scraping by boulders and whirlpools in the fast-flowing river, never quite confident that the next rock wouldn't dump him and his equipment into the river. He wanted to ditch the boat, buy horses, and travel overland. Hinton would offer that opportunity. Franciscka, not trusting James Donnelly, wanted to sneak by Hinton and continue on the river to the salt furnace or even Chief Smith's village on the Jarrell River.

Their departure at Narrows from the Ruffner trading dock had reminded Fritz of a tense battlefield parley to exchange prisoners. The slender, middle-aged proprietor, Len Ruffner, quivered with barely restrained hostility toward him and the Jarrell sisters. Jenny and her sister, Sue, kept mute as ordered by Franciscka, but Fritz still watched them closely. Sue had her hand on the new knife he'd bought to replace the one she had left in the Ichneumon highwayman's arm. Ruffner intimidated neither girl.

Only Franciscka Weidman's presence kept the violence from exploding between the three Ruffner men, who looked suspiciously like Ichneumons, and the three Prussian men. Fritz had no doubt that Ruffner would send his partner at Hinton a pigeon alerting him to their plans.

If Donnelly intended them harm, the river offered no protection from rifle fire, another reason Fritz didn't like traveling by river. The only chance they would have to pass the stockade safely would be at night. Unfortunately, they were nearly to Hinton, and several hours of daylight remained. They beached the three boats at the last bend before Hinton. Fritz had just asked the two retired feldwebels, Hans Melas and Ednard Schnitger, to check the wooded riverbank when a dozen mounted tattooed warriors emerged from the woods, demanding they drop their firearms. The three Prussians and Franciscka had pulled their revolvers.

"Not going to happen, Chief. Take us to Herr Donnelly," Fritz said.

Be thankful for small favors, James Donnelly thought. At least Cinnabar's brother, Chief Qua, was sober. Regrettably, he also appeared irresolute. The savage had arrived across the river from the Hinton stockade a few hours earlier with fifty mounted warriors and had promptly seized a local fisherman's canoe, then paddled across the river to demanded payment.

"The deal was a hundred mounted men armed with rifles," James said. "Burgdorf tells me there's half that number across the river." He was desperate. The Wapitis had destroyed Anders's force at the salt furnace, hung Anders, and apparently, Wapitis were now in Rainelle.

"There's a hundred riders," Chief Qua said. "Some are up the river, some haven't arrived." Several of the chief's warriors with their fearsome red jagged-edge facial tattoos had crowed into his office. They stunk. "I want the promised women and gold."

"That's not the agreement with your brother. First, go with Burgdorf and run the Wapitis out of the salt furnace. Then I'll pay."

Qua shook his head and looked ready to quarrel. Anxious as he was, James knew from his experience in dealing with Chief Cinnabar, you never permitted a savage to renegotiate the deal in the field. Qua had already invested a lot of effort just to reach Hinton. He won't want to leave with nothing for his troubles.

"A deal's a deal," James said. "And don't give me that dumb, savage look, Qua. You know damn well that was our agreement. And tell those freaks with you to wash off in the river. They reek." He reached under his desk for the hidden five-shot revolver as Qua wavered between being rational and violence.

A guard delivered a message to Burgdorf, who was standing by the office door.

"Herr Donnelly, you have Prussian visitors," Burgdorf said. Qua looked as surprised as James felt.

"Qua, ask your men to leave, and we'll learn what the Prussians want," James said, standing up and laying the revolver on the desk for all to see. A couple of minutes after Cinnabar's odorous warriors exited his office, the IRS agent, Franciscka Weidman, a Prussian Army captain, and the two female slaves he'd sold to Ruffner crowded into the room.

Fräulein Weidman sniffed the air and looked around the room, before she made the introductions.

"Herr Donnelly," Captain Caprivi said. "Berlin asked I tour the western territory and talk with the various parties involved in the fighting. But looking around, Hinton seems peaceful."

"The only fighting in the valley are some Wapiti bandits terrorizing settlements down the river. They know better than to bother my property," James said. He hoped the Prussians didn't scare off Qua.

"Odd," Franciscka said. "One of the rumors in Roanoke was raiders burned you entire tobacco crop. I'm glad to hear that wasn't the case." The IRS agent attention turned to Chief Qua. "Are you Chief Cinnabar's brother?" Qua looked away from studying the girls and nodded.

"Regrettably, that loss isn't a rumor. Careless guards smoking caused the fire," James said. The girls were glaring daggers at chief. "It's considerate of you to return my property." His comment got a momentary gasp from the younger slave. The other girl hugged the young one. Qua licked his lips.

"The Jarrell sisters, they're not slaves. Surely you're aware slavery is illegal," the Prussian captain answered.

"Not outside the Prussian Empire," James said. "In the rest of the world it's a thriving business. Burgdorf, take the girls to the slave quarters." James looked toward the door where he expected the ex-feldwebel to be.

Instead, two other Prussians watched. How many damn Prussians, armed no less, had Burgdorf allowed in the stockade?

The Prussian captain pulling one of those new five-shot Krupp revolver stopped James from repeating his order. Then he noticed Chief Qua, still in the chair, had lowered his antiquated cap and ball revolver to his lap. Some damn ally that savage proved to be. The female IRS agent also had one of those new five-shot revolvers, and she had it pointed at the man's head.

"Did I mention the sisters are under the protection of the Prussian Army?" The captain said. Then he added, "Hans, relieve the chief of his pistol and bring Burgdorf in."

To James' distress, the armed Prussian feldwebels shoved Burgdorf, with his arms tied, into the room.

"Here I thought you were dead," Agent Weidman said. "I've seen enough. Have you, Fritz?"

Chief Qua came alive, leaping to his feet while reaching for the Prussian that had taken his gun and started to yell for help. The feldwebel reacted fast. In a moment, the chief was on the floor, out cold.

The Prussian Captain walked to the office door and looked out. James hoped the tattooed warriors were across the stockade by the horse corral smoking and watching the office, instead of up by the jail ogling the Wapiti women. If the Prussians realized there were Wapiti women here, they'd try to free them, and Cinnabar's warriors would try to seize the women. It'd be a bloody mess. Fortunately, the Prussians seemed unaware of the Wapiti captives.

"Feldwebel Melas, gag Burgdorf," the Prussian officer said, "then lock him in the storeroom. Herr Donnelly, you're coming with us to our boat. If you want to live, keep everyone calm, including the chief." The Prussian captain then nudged Qua with his boot. "Wake up chief. You're coming too."

Rex and his fifty men had pushed hard from Rainelle, crossing the North River late in the evening to reach River Falls, where they had camped to await the Mischief with a barge. Captain Malik and Kyle arrived at sunrise with the former Ichneumon steamboat. Three Wapitis would stay behind and bring the horses to Salt Fork while the rest of the soldiers and Rex's horse, Zack, boarded. Rex had just finished helping secure the two brass cannons aboard the steamboat when Kyle yelled that two of Ruffner's flat-bottomed riverboats were coming.

Several Wapitis recognized the Jarrell sisters sitting between the Prussian soldiers and Franciscka Weidman. Rex rushed the greetings and hugs, telling them they could talk on the boat. A few minutes later, the Mischief was steaming down the river. Rex told Fritz and Franciscka about the warning of a pending attack on the River Point fort.

Three hours later the Mischief stopped at newly named Salt Furnace village. Chief Smith met the steamboat. "Fritz, I wanted to meet you. Franciscka, your boss has been busy. He's sent two pigeons with the same message. The tobacco company wanted to meet in Roanoke in three days to discuss marketing roasted winter-sloe nuts. He wanted you and me to attend the meeting."

"Find some horses. I'm game," Franciscka said. "While you do that, I'll send a message that we'll be there." She went to get a pigeon while Rex assigned six warriors from his group to provide guards for them. "Fritz, take the rest of the IRS pigeons and keep Roanoke informed," she added.

Chief Smith and Franciscka rode from Salt Furnace after turning the Jarrell sisters over to their aunt. The Mischief embarked for River Point at the same time.

Two items caught Rex Knight's attention as the Mischief maneuvered against the river dock. The Wapitis had planted vegetable gardens all around in front of the stone fort's walls, and a large green star flag was flying above the main gate. Andy waited on the dock with several Wapiti warriors. Rex hoped Matt and Andy had succeeded in their efforts to establish a well-trained and organized garrison at the River Point fort.

"People in Berlin are not going to be happy with this development," Fritz Caprivi said. He was standing beside Rex, studying the fort and trying to ignore Hokee's occasional growls. "The Ichneumons have invested considerable money and effort in this fort. And look at the cannons. Manuel Prado is full of it. This place wasn't built for trading goods storage."

"No, it wasn't," Rex said. "The Ichneumon built it to control traffic on the rivers. So how do you think they'll attack?" He hushed the wolf. It didn't like the Prussian.

"I would land a force down-river out of range from the fort and move two or three heavy cannons into position across the river behind us," Fritz said. "It's the highest terrain near the fort, and the height would aid the cannon fire's ability to smash in the fort's walls. While that was going on, I'd land an assault force up the Erie River above the fort, or up the Southern River, doesn't matter which river as long as they're on the same side as the fort. Then when the walls are breached and the fort interior is in flames, I'd have a strong force of men charge over the wall breach."

"You don't think they'll try a sneak attack at night, use an explosive charge to breach the wall or gate?" Rex asked.

"Mining the fort's wall? I wouldn't," Fritz said. "I'd use the heavy cannons. Takes time to set the guns in position, but the bombardment, once started, would produce quick results. These cut stone walls wouldn't resist many twenty kilogram cannonballs slamming into them."

"Do the Ichneumons have such cannons?" Rex asked. Fritz nodded yes. Silly question, he figured the Prussians probably sold them the cannons.

"Setting the big guns up takes time," Fritz said. "You have to build roads. Time that I don't think the general has. River Point's defense was General Meringa's responsibility and his head is on the block. He needs to recover the fort before Emperor Ratakonda learns of the lost. So he won't want to use my slow, but sure approach. Meringa will want fast results, so I think he'll throw a lot of men with ladders and hooks at the fort's wall."

"Have you met General Meringa? Hokee, stop that damn growling at Fritz, he's a friend." The wolf went back to the Mischief pilothouse entrance, probably to snarl at Captain Malik.

"I was in Berlin two months ago and I spent several days with him. The general thinks the indigenous people, the Clovis and Wapitis, are a joke, militarily speaking."

"Well, being underestimated by your opponent is always helpful," Rex said. "I figure you're right that taking one of his forts, along with his prince, has motivated the emperor to demand that General Meringa strike quick and hard. Teach those savages a lesson."

Hokee leaped to the dock as the boat finished docking. Rex introduced the Prussian officer to Matt and Andy. Matt had heard about Fritz rescuing the Jarrell sisters and thanked him.

On the walk to the fort, Fritz added, "Benjamin Purnell is another matter. He's smart and flexible. If possible, he'll try treachery to help the general, pay a traitor to open the gate or blow up the fort's powder magazine to help Meringa's attack. And you should expect no quarter for the Wapitis found in the fort if the Ichneumon's attack is successful,"

"Does that mean we shouldn't take prisoners?" Matt asked.

"No, it means you hadn't better lose the fort," Rex said.

Andy gave Fritz and his Prussian guards a tour of the fort while Rex met with Matt in the commander's office. He had two thin Clovis men about Rex's age in the office who wanted to learn if Wapitis would allow Clovis children to attend the fort's school. The men were from the Beaver tribe. They had odd names, Redfox and Snares.

"Herr Knight, thank you for rescuing my daughter and her friends," Chief Redfox said.

"Actually the Jarrell and Balers brothers freed them," Rex said. "I'm glad we could help. Matt, I'm okay with allowing a dozen of the Clovis children to attend the fort's school in exchange for a fresh whole buffalo every other week. But not until after we have eliminated the Ichneumon threat."

The visitors nodded in understanding and left to pick up a small keg of black powder from the magazine. It was in payment for four choice, live, reddish-brown hogs they had earlier sold to the garrison.

"Where do you figure they found those neat pigs? Are they farmers?" Rex asked. He'd seen the sleek hogs outside the magazine.

"The kitchen wanted several hogs to fatten with food waste," Matt said. "Redfox's tribe has dropped the old tribal property and copied the Wapitis' private land holdings. They're good farmers with farms along the river bottom lands located along the Erie. Like all the Beaver tribes, they grow a lot of corn and hogs, so I figure their hogs are as good as the Johnson's black hogs. The Beavers also trade tobacco, fish, and hunt birds along the river in both directions for a hundred kilometers."

"I'm a bit surprised, farmers? I thought the Clovis were primarily a hunter-gatherer-type society. How do they get along with the Ichneumons?"

"What, you think us hunters can't farm?" Matt said, and after a brief smile at Rex's discomfort, added. "They don't. The

Ichneumons are starting to raid their villages for slaves now that the Wapitis have stopped the raids. As to the schooling for their children, I suspect Jesuit missionaries have convinced the Clovis chiefs on need for literacy. Our new school is their first opportunity to enroll their children. Besides, I thought it was a great opportunity to make friends with our neighbors."

"I agree, but remember, those kids will know all the fort's strengths and weaknesses, which means the Clovis warriors will also."

"True," Matt said, "but I figure we'll learn most of the Beaver tribe's secrets and concerns in turn. By the way, why do you refer to children as young goats?"

"What? Oh, it's a term we use for children on the ice sheets," Rex said.

"How odd, well, you'll be pleased to learn our gun crews are proficient with the cannons. Andy has burned through a lot of powder and about worn the cannonballs out, but we now have several crews who can hit a moving target on the river."

Rex then discussed the Prussian's thoughts on the expected Ichneumon assault on the stone fort.

"Maybe, but I've always leaned toward a surprise night attack, with the assault force using grappling hooks and ropes to scale the walls," Matt said. "How's an Ichneumon general going to find a Wapiti traitor to open the gate-or blow up the magazine?" He opened a small jar on his desk, picked out several blue nut kernels to chew, and then offered Rex the jar. "Of course there is Captain Malik"

"Yeah, my thoughts also, however, Ichneumon traders have been traveling our lands for years and they might know several traitorous Wapitis. I do agree it'll be a night strike. I gather from your note, you corrected that magazine issue?" Rex shook out several nuts.

"Yes," Matt said. "I relocated the main powder inventory to two new deep magazines away from the outer walls and put several smaller and handier powder magazines near the cannons."

"Good. And did you make the decoys?"

"I did," Matt said. "Anyone looking in the old magazine will see what appears to be several thousand kilograms of powder in kegs. There are still a small number of kegs with real gunpowder in the old magazine. I left enough powder to satisfy training needs and avoid questions about where the powder went. Herr Simpson wants his whiskey barrels back before winter ice closes the river."

"In due time," Rex said. "Are you comfortable everyone, like our trusted Ichneumon boat captain and men, thinks the new magazines are vaults for trade whiskey?"

"Only six of our most trusted men were used to make the switch. You still think Captain Malik will be the one to place the slow fuse in the old magazine?"

"I do." Rex had recognized the Ichneumon's error in using a storage room, whose rear wall was the fort's outer wall, as their powder magazine. The explosion of that old magazine would provide the Ichneumon assault force a guaranteed breach of the fort's massive outer wall. The placement of a fuse, by a traitor, in one of the magazine gunpowder barrels would tell them the assault force was outside the walls.

"Andy said a big stern-wheeler went past the fort late yesterday evening. Any idea whose boat it was?" Rex asked.

"It flew no flag, but I figure it was Purnell's," Matt said. "It was new and nearly a hundred meters in length. None of the independent traders could afford that boat. More intriguing, the cargo area was covered, and none of the passengers showed themselves as it steamed by at full power."

"I wonder if Meringa could have responded that fast. Do you think a bunch of Ichneumon soldiers might have been on the boat?"

Rex asked. He needed a cup of coffee. The nuts were okay, but they were not hot coffee.

"Well, Andy and I didn't know what to do, so we let the boat steam by," Matt said. "We can't sink every boat that passes the fort."

"If that stern-wheeler was carrying Meringa's assault force, it wouldn't go far up the Erie before stopping. Do you have any hunters who could check on the boat?"

"Yes, Zoe showed up a few days ago looking for work. I'll send him out. Who's watching down river for the Ichneumon traffic?"

"I dropped two men off across from the fort," Rex said. "They'll send word if the Ichneumons disembark any cannons or troops down river."

The mid-July morning was hot and clear as Rex and Fritz waited on the dock by the Mischief. He studied the river surface and wondered if any of those black eel were lurking near the dock. Several of Tom's cousins had brought two loads of coal from their new mine up the Jarrell River for use in the boat's boiler in place of wood. The cousins had built flat-bottomed barges about six meters long by three meters wide, out of heavy wood planks. They'd used poles to push the barges downriver. The barges had one-meter-high walls and held twenty to twenty-five tons of coal. Rex and the captain had inspected the coal, had found it acceptable, and paid for it.

"That coal looks just like Wale coal," Fritz said. The cousins were busy shoveling the coal into the steamboat's woodbin when Kyle's brother, John, arrived after paddling across the river and asked Rex to follow him off the dock for a private message.

"You were right," John said. "The Ichneumons have docked a large paddle wheeler against the riverbank about two kilometers down the Erie. They're unloading three huge cannons on wheels, along with two ox teams. Should we attack them?"

Rex waved for Fritz to join them and hear John's report.

"They'd had a tough time unloading," John said. "The boat couldn't pull close enough for the ship's derrick to swing the heavy cannons to the dry ground. Instead, the crew had to unload the guns in shallow water, and then use the ox team to drag them ashore."

"Sounds to me like they'll be several days getting those cannons into place," Fritz said. He selected two lumps of coal and banged them together. The lumps fragmented into hard, shiny black cubes with no streaks of dull noncombustible slate.

"Or longer," John said. "They'll have to make a road. It's solid forest to the high ridge, no trails."

"A dozen soldiers would be needed just to guard the guns and supplies. There must be more men on the boat," Rex said. "John, see Matt for several pigeons to take back with you. I want you to keep us posted on their progress. Watch them from a safe distance. Don't engage or let the soldiers know you've discovered them."

Fritz was asking the Jarrell cousins about their coal mine when Matt brought the local Clovis chief, Redfox, over to repeat his story to Rex and Fritz. The chief had investigated the arrival and docking of the Ichneumon stern-wheeler in a section of the Erie River with no docks or settlement. He had been curious why Purnell's newest boat picked that spot to dock. He learned from the recluse fisherman living nearby that a large number of soldiers had disembarked.

"Would that be the stern-wheeler that passed the fort yesterday?" Rex asked.

"I'm confident no other steamboats went by," Matt said. "It has to be the assault force. I'm putting the fort on alert."

"Did Zoe return?" Rex asked. The fort commander had sent the hunter on a reconnaissance of the forest north of the fort and expected him back by evening, if not sooner. He would know where those Ichneumon men were, not that any of them had any doubt of their ultimate destination.

Kyle and Tom had rigged a wooden turntable on the bow of the Mischief to mount one of the brass cannons. They were ready to test their cobbled-together arrangement. Fritz and Rex went with Captain Malik, who piloted the small steamboat out into the river and followed Kyle's directions. The turntable made lining up the cannon on the target across the Erie River easy.

Rex watched the turntable for signs of stress as Kyle fired the cannon. After the smoke cleared and Rex checked the cannon mountings, it was clear the turntable and Mischief had handled the gun's recoil with ease. Even better, the iron ball hit the marked area of the riverbank. After the successful test, the crew covered the cannon with a tarp to hide its presence.

"You have a lethal weapon there," Fritz said. "One of those cannonballs through a boat's boiler would cause a great deal of havoc. Are you thinking of paying one of the steamboats a visit?"

"No, I'm thinking of visiting both boats this evening," Rex said. Holding one of the tie off ropes, he waited for the boat to touch the dock.

Franciscka Weidman, a bit saddle weary from the three-day ride, figured recriminations would soon be flying and tempers flaring in the third-floor IRS conference room. Her boss, Joe Hansen, had just introduced the Atlantic Tobacco Trust lawyer, Rahul Malhotra; Guderian Territory Assistant Attorney General Rudolf Hoess; and the governor's Chief of Commerce Stan Blankenship, to Chief Smith.

"Before we address the winter-sloe issue, I've been instructed by the board to determine Prince Cherukuru's status," Rahul Malhotra asked. "Is the young man safe and in good health?"

"He's in good health and at Salt Furnace awaiting trial for rape and murder," the chief answered. "I expect him to be found guilty and hanged." The tobacco lawyer and Blankenship both appeared shocked by the chief's blunt statement.

"By what right or law are you allowed to try Ichneumon royalty?" Malhotra asked. "Such precipitous action could cause war. The tobacco trust will never do business with the Wapitis if they murder Emperor Ratakonda's nephew."

Franciscka would bet the tobacco lawyer actually believed the Ichneumon prince was above the law, especially Wapiti laws. He was in for an education. The diplomat in Chief Smith answered.

"It wouldn't be murder. Think of it as rightful justice for his victims. However, the Wapitis understand the Ichneumon emperor is an important partner of the tobacco trust. The tribes and I have no desire to cause your employer any difficulty, but I can't allow the rape and murder of our young women. If Emperor Ratakonda wishes to send a defense lawyer to Cherukuru's trail, he would be most welcomed."

"You might want to consider hiring your own defense lawyer," Blankenship said. "I understand Herr Ruffner has filed a complaint that you tried to sell him illegal cocaine and that an arrest warrant will be issued for you. Is that right, Rudolf?"

Chief Smith appeared amused by that information. A sweaty Rudolf looked miserable. Franciscka figured the indolent attorney had allowed Blankenship to maneuver him into agreeing to prosecute a dubious charge by a suspect slaver and likely drug dealer. She decided to help.

"Speaking of arrest warrants," Franciscka said. "Herr Hoess, have you issued that warrant for the arrest of Heinz William and Len Ruffner?"

"What arrest? What the hell is she talking about?" Blankenship asked. She told him.

"Jenny Jarrell and her younger sister, Sue, were kidnapped and sold as slaves by Len Ruffner to Heinz William. The girls escaped and gave depositions and requested the Guderian attorney general have William arrested along with the man who sold them, Len Ruffner. I figured Rudolf would know if they've been arrested."

"Are you crazy, Rudolf? You know Heinz William can't be arrested based on the word of a couple of illiterate savages." Blankenship was on his feet yelling at the assistant AG.

"I had no choice," Rudolf said. His voice growing stronger, he added. "Hauptmann Fritz Caprivi gave a deposition verifying the girls' claim. He'd been at the William plantation as a guest when he saw them locked up in the basement. Hell, that moron, Heinz William, even asked the decorated Prussian officer if he'd like to rape them."

"And in case Caprivi's name hasn't registered," Franciscka said, "He is the army officer that Emperor Schnabel personally decorated for holding the Volga River beachhead against the Mongol counterattack."

"That's right," AAG Hoess said. "So yeah, I had Heinz arrested. And no, I haven't issued an arrest warrant for Chief Smith because of Ruffner's involvement in the William slavery case."

"Those Jarrell sisters, are they Wapitis?" Joe Hansen asked. Franciscka knew he knew that, but nodded. "Chief Smith, as you can witness, we do impartially enforce the laws and that the Wapitis aren't the only ones having problems with rogue Ichneumons and their agents."

Chief Smith wasn't buying Joe's placating words and now appeared quite angry. He was glaring at Blankenship who appeared apprehensive. Her boos sensed the imminent peril and addressed the chief.

"Len Ruffner, whom I figure is conspiring with the bootleggers and Ichneumon criminals, has misled my good friend Herr Blankenship with false accusations. Chief, the emperor's men will not tolerated their lawless behavior. It threatens the territory's peace. And Rahul, their lawlessness even threatens to disrupt Atlantic Tobacco's business."

The governor's man, probably for the first time in his life, Franciscka suspected, was speechless and slowly shaking his head in a negative fashion as her boss added, "We need to allow Chief Smith and Herr Malhotra privacy to discuss their issues. The rest of us will go to my office."

Chief Smith, still appearing a bit suspicious, requested that Herr Hansen have his assistant, Fräulein Weidman, remain to answer tax questions that might arise. After the others had left, the chief addressed the tobacco lawyer.

"Let me be blunt, Herr Malhotra. The Ichneumons are going to lose the western territory. The Wapitis hanged James Donnelly's general, Anders Breuer, at Salt Furnace for raping our women and murder. Prince Cherukuru is a Wapiti captive. His fate depends on Atlantic Tobacco's response to our request for help in marketing the winter-sloe and dealing with their influence peddlers like that bastard who just left, Herr Blankenship."

"Bold talk, chief," the tobacco lawyer said. "But winning a few minor skirmishes with rag-tag traders like Donnelly isn't going to stop the Ichneumon Empire from defending their commercial interests or extracting retribution for the cruel treatment of their prince."

"Well, you're correct. The war isn't over. General Meringa can hardly report to Emperor Ratakonda that a bunch of savages armed with spears ran his army and traders out of the western territories and arrested the emperor's nephew, and he was powerless to stop them. But the larger issue from your company's perspective is whom do you think the Prussian emperor would prefer in control of the western territories, the Wapitis or the Ichneumon Empire?"

"The Prussian and Ichneumon interests get along fine and have many joint arrangements," said the lawyer. "The Ichneumons are just business people, traders, and have no territorial ambitions. The Prussian Emperor's concern is your illegal cocaine sales robbing him of tax revenue."

"The illegal cocaine is coming from Benjamin Purnell in Myrtle Territory, not the Wapitis. Personally, I hope Emperor Schnabel follows through with his plans to stop sales of cocaine. It's a nasty, addictive drug." The chief got up and refilled his mug with Joe's ghastly black tea.

"What nonsense. There's no talk of outlawing cocaine," the lawyer said. He handed Chief Smith his cup to refill.

"Actually there is," Franciscka said. "Berlin is concerned about the toll alcohol and drugs such as cocaine are having on the workers' productivity and health. Your company should consider selling healthy stimulants such as coffee and roasted blue nuts. Hedge your drug business, so to speak, in case the reformers do manage to outlaw cocaine. Besides, having a source of coffee would spare me from having to drink that gruesome black tea to stay awake."

"The Wapitis' proposal is to make Atlantic Tobacco their exclusive distributor for the roasted nut," the chief said. He filled the lawyer's cup and handed it back. "The Wapitis want to market the roasted salted nut as a healthy stimulant. I'm thinking of packaging it in 25-gram sealed paper packs. Price the bag at ten D-marks."

"How would that ten D-mark be split?" the tobacco lawyer asked. The mention of money seemed to dispel the lawyer's gloomy combative disposition.

"I'm thinking twenty-five percent to the nut supplier and processor, twenty-five percent to the distributor-retailer, and fifty percent to the Emperor," the chief said. "The Wapitis could supply five million bags a year to start, which, Herr Malhotra, would allow your company to develop a separate business worth ten to twelve million in addition to your cocaine sales."

"The proposed tax rate would satisfy the IRS, and the emperor would be pleased with the new source of tax revenues," Franciscka said.

"In other words, the Wapitis are offering to not compete with Ichneumon cocaine," Herr Malhotra said.

The chief nodded and reached into his backpack. Franciscka belatedly realized no one had checked the chief's backpack. How many weapons might be in his bag? Fortunately, the chief was just after nut samples. He handed over several small white paper bags with a green star label to the lawyer, who opened one of the bags and dumped its contents onto the table, a dozen roasted and salted blueish kernels.

"I'm impressed," the lawyer said. "Your idea might work. It would help deprive the cocaine bootleggers of the raw nut and limit illegal sales. Of course, on the negative side, I understand the ingestion of the nut diminishes the urge for cocaine. I'll have to inform the board; they make such decisions. However, they'll want to know Prince Cherukuru is safe and will be released."

"The prince is a separate matter," Chief Smith said. "Its resolution will depend on Ichneumon behavior toward the Wapiti people and your board's response to this proposal."

Chapter 11

Matt and Rex were heading to the dock to verify the Mischief's coalbin was full and the two kegs of rock oil were aboard. Fritz was already aboard the Mischief.

"Whose canoe," Matt asked. A large canoe was coming down the Southern River toward the dock.

Pete Chin was in the front of the canoe paddling hard. Rex glanced toward the Mischief's bow. The tarp was still over the cannon.

"Matt, I need to greet the chief before boarding," Rex said. "Tell Fritz and Kyle to keep the tarp over the cannon until they're out of sight from the fort. I don't want Pete noticing we've armed the Mischief." The fort commander gave him an odd look, but did as asked.

"Manuel told me they were only building a trading post with protected storage," Pete said as he climbed out of the canoe. "I decided to take a day off from farming and visit this supposed Ichneumon fort that the council and Chief Smith likes to bitch about. I don't deserve condemnation for promoting trade. It's just a secure trading post."

"Well, it's certainly secure," Rex said. He decided not to tell Pete the Ichneumon army was planning to attack the fort.

"We're quite busy. Perhaps another day would be better for a tour." Pete brushed that polite suggestion aside.

"What are you hiding, making cocaine in there?" Pete asked while studying the fort looming over the dock area. "I don't need a tour. I just want to look around for a bit, unless you fear I might see something the council won't like."

"Please look," Matt said, returning from the Mischief. "But remember, chief, we close the gate at dark, and it'll be dark in an hour. If you don't want to spend the night, best be quick."

Rex had wanted to go with the Mischief to witness the attacks on the Ichneumon steamboats. He agreed with Fritz that the Ichneumon were unlikely to attack until something breached the fort's wall, such as the magazine exploding. With Captain Malik busy piloting the boat out on the Erie River, the fort's magazine should be safe. However, the failure of Zoe and the other hunters to return worried Rex. Until he knew where the Ichneumon soldiers had gone, he didn't want to leave the fort.

With night about on them, the Mischief crew was anxious to depart down the Erie River. Pete had vanished into the fort and that had Rex curious. What was that troublesome man doing?

"Go on," Rex yelled to Captain Malik. As much as he wanted see the cannon in action, the fort's safety came first. Rex and Matt were on the dock watching the Mischief steam down the Erie River in the gathering darkness when Pete and his rowers appeared and walked rapidly to where their canoe lay on the bank about fifty meters upriver from the dock. Pete noticed them on the dock.

"We're going home," Pete shouted. Rex and Matt watched them pile into the canoe and paddle off into the night.

"That was a short visit. They seem in a rush," Matt said.

"Yeah, Pete's an odd guy. I don't trust him," Rex said. It was dark, and the mosquitos were active. "Time to seal the fort," he said, and they walked back into the fort, stopping to verify the guards had added the iron bar to the gate.

"Call me the moment Zoe arrives," he told Matt and the gate-guards.

Matt left to find Jerry Jones and check the guards on the walls were alert and in position. Rex went to check the magazine, after that stop, he planned to find Andy and review his progress on training the wives and older children in the use of a Krupp rifle.

The faint whiff of burning sulfur that Rex detected on entering the dark hallway of the old magazine alarmed him. He yelled for the guard. Only silence answered. Rex needed a light and ran outside to find a torch. The explosion knocked him flat.

The Prussian visit had upended James Donnelly's perception of security. In a moment, he had become a hostage, his guards unable to respond without endangering his life. Even worse, the Prussian military had again taken an interest in his affairs. The principle reason he had lived in this primitive frontier for a decade, besides to acquire the capital needed to return to Berlin a success, was to avoid Prussian laws so he could satisfy his, ah, special cravings.

The first change James had instituted, after that frightful day, was to instruct the gate guards to bar armed visitors from entering the stockade. No exceptions, which explained why he was out in the rain walking to the main gate. Bret Paget was at the gate demanding to see James. The Ichneumon trader had refused to surrender his rifle and revolver. He and his half-dozen men appeared exhausted.

"James, we need to discuss several items that are important to your well-being and future. Now, we can stand in the rain and talk, or you can tell your guard to allow my rifle in the stockade and we'll adjourn to your office." James' curiosity won out over his caution.

Bret wasted no time. "General Meringa is attacking River Point with a large Ichneumon force. I don't have the exact date, but it will be in the next few days. You need to attack Salt Furnace while the Wapitis have their warriors tied down at River Point."

"I hope the general kills all of those bloody savages," James said. "But I'm not sure attacking Salt Furnace is in my best interest. After all, Anders had two hundred men and failed. I don't have another two hundred men."

"You have Cinnabar's warriors," Bret said. "They're camped across the river, bored stiff and terrorizing the local women."

"Chief Qua won't move until he's paid in full," James said. "I don't trust him. Once he has the gold and women, he's more apt to ride back to Panther Creek, than help me fight the Wapitis."

James main fear, which he didn't share with the Ichneumon, was the Prussian captain's parting remark on the riverbank. He'd asked if James had any Wapiti women held as slaves, which he of course had denied.

Fine," the Prussian had said, "but if I find out otherwise, and the Wapiti women are harmed, I'll personally hunt you down and kill you."

Burgdorf arrived. He'd heard the Ichneumon trader was there. "Bret, you and I were damn lucky to escape Anders's fiasco," the retired feldwebel said. "What're your plans?"

James instead explained the Ichneumon's request.

"If that's true, then we're fools not to take Salt Furnace," Burgdorf said. "Besides, the prince is there, think of the ransom he'd bring."

"Reward," Bret Paget corrected, "Probably two million, maybe more."

James Donnelly hadn't thought of that angle. "Two million . . . Let's get the raid organized! Burgdorf, tell that freak, Qua, to get in here," the warlord ordered.

Rex was never completely out, but the blast had briefly disorganized him. It had left him sprawled on the ground in the dust, smoke, and falling debris. The start-up of rifle fire and yelling told him the Ichneumon attack had started. As the smoke and dust cleared, Rex made a quick check of the wall. The blast had collapsed the magazine's sides and front entrance. A section of the outer wall was cracked and displaced, but standing.

Had Matt overlooked some kegs of powder? The surprise was the force those few kegs of black powder had generated on exploding. If the Ichneumons' original inventory of a hundred kegs of powder had been in that magazine, the explosion would have destroyed the fort. As Rex staggered to the stairs that went to the upper-wall walkway, the Wapiti rifle fire had become steady. The fort defenders were returning a constant rate of fire as the wives started appearing on the wall with rifles and adding to the din.

At the top of the stone stairs on the north wall, Tara Smith was leaning far out over the wall, sighting her rifle down the wall. She was taking a terrible chance exposing her body by leaning over the wall. *First chance we need to add several bastions,* Rex thought, as he waited for her to fire. The Ichneumons' black uniforms were difficult to see in the darkness. Finally, she fired, a shadow screamed, and a man fell to the ground about twenty meters from the fort wall.

"You need to stop the men," Tara said. "Most of their shots are wasted. They're shooting shadows." He realized she had just worked a bolt-action rifle, not a rolling block single-shot Krupp rifle.

"Please be careful. Remember, you're silhouetted against the night sky when you lean over the wall." A bullet slammed into the wall below Tara's location causing them to duck. "Where did you get that rifle?"

"Fritz loaned it to me," Tara said. "What was that explosion?" He told her.

Rex, Jerry, and Andy required the best part of an hour to get everyone settled down. Two of the cannon crews had even fired several canister loads into the dark stump-strewn clearing. Rex told those cannon crews to load canister loads again, but not to fire until directed to. He instructed the cannon crews facing the Erie River to watch for the Mischief. Any other boat they spotted on the river, they were to sink it.

"Jerry," Rex said. "Leave your three best marksmen from Owl fire team on the wall to fire at any Ichneumons foolish enough to expose themselves in the moon lit clearing. The rest of your men—and women, I want to stay below the parapet wall. So far, the Ichneumons have injured only two Wapitis. Let's keep it that way."

The most pressing questions Rex needed answered were who the traitor was that tried to blow up the magazine, and were he still in the fort? Had they succeeded in breaching the wall, the Ichneumon would likely now own the fort. Whoever it had been, he was a murderer, having cut the throat of the young Wapiti guarding the magazine. Rex had been wrong about Captain Malik. That error made him cautious. Still, his suspicion had shifted to Pete Chin and his man. Then the men yelled they could see a red glow in the sky down the Erie. He hoped it wasn't the Mischief burning.

The brazenness of Kyle Balers and the Wapitis was an education for Fritz Caprivi. His first lesson, the Wapitis believed in deception. The boat was hardly out of sight of the fort, when Kyle replaced the Wapitis' green star flag with the Ichneumon's double-headed serpent flag. Fritz's second lesson was the Wapitis would accept help and advice from anyone who had earned their trust. The steamboat's captain was an Ichneumon, Harsh Malik, and the first Ichneumon turncoat Fritz had ever heard of. The Wapitis seemed to get on fine with the Ichneumon, who was helpful in other ways, besides piloting the Mischief.

"Go ahead and load the cannon, Kyle. Use extra powder and a solid ball, and then throw the tarp back over it. No need to alarm the guards," Captain Malik said. "Have another charge ready. With a bit of luck, we might have a chance for two shots before rifle fire from the Ichneumon makes things untenable."

As the little steamboat paddled down the Erie River, Fritz was beginning to realize his and the Prussian General Staff's understanding of the conflict developing in the western territories was wrong. It wasn't local savages, outlaw bands, and Ichneumon traders fighting over slaves, illegal drug sales, and cocaine sources; it was an indigenous population of individual tribes and families scattered across what had been a wilderness consolidating into a people and forming their own country. The Prussian Empire would be wise to help them and acquire a future ally in their western expansion, not attack the Wapitis and create an implacable foe as the Ichneumon had managed to generate.

The Mischief's arrival at the Wapitis' target, Purnell's newest steamboat, a large stern-wheeler, ended his contemplation of the conflict's influence on the empire's geopolitical doctrine. Fritz suspected the boat was one of Benjamin Purnell's prized possessions. He listened to the turncoat captain explain the stern-wheeler's vulnerabilities to Kyle and the dozen Wapiti warriors onboard.

"Kyle, try to put a cannonball through the stern-wheeler's boiler," Malik said. "Aim several meters back from the stacks and at the water line. A successful shot will cripple the ship and if there's a fire in the boiler that will likely start the ship burning." To the other Wapitis crowded in the pilothouse, he added, "Keep the Ichneumon soldiers occupied while we maneuver the boat and cannon into proper alignment."

Purnell's stern-wheeler was dark, tied to the south riverbank, and pointed up stream. Several small fires glowed on the riverbank behind the boat where the three massive Ichneumon cannons had been unloaded. Two of the watchmen on the Ichneumon boat waved to them as they made to pass the much larger boat.

Suddenly, Captain Malik reversed one of the paddles and swung the boat ninety degrees. His action pointed the ship's bow and cannon at the middle of the stern-wheeler. Kyle yanked the canvas off. "Remember to aim!" the captain yelled.

The Ichneumon sailors on the stern-wheeler just stared as Kyle turned the cannon barrel down. Fritz handed him the red-hot wire heated in the boiler firebox. The young man jabbed the hot wire in the fuse hole of the little brass cannon. An instant later, it fired the iron ball directly into the boat. The orange-sized projectile punched a neat hole in the wood plank just below the deck. By then the captain had both of Mischief's paddles running at full power in reverse, churning the river. It managed to stop the boat's bow about a meter from hitting the stern-wheeler's side.

Kyle, how the Wapiti managed to keep his footing amazed Fritz, rammed home another powder charge and iron ball as the Wapiti soldiers shot down several stunned Ichneumon sailors. Four other Wapitis dashed past Fritz as he reheated the wire for Kyle, to throw pails of oil and burning torches onto the stern-wheeler's deck. The second cannonball went into the stern-wheeler at a steeper angle, smashing in a jagged section of the side planking and leaving a gaping hole at the boat's water line. The stern-wheeler gave a shudder, and steam shot out of the stack as the oil caught fire.

The Mischief's paddles, still running in reverse, pushed the boat back into the center of the river where the captain threw the paddles into forward spin. The boat turned and started back up the river. Kyle and the Wapitis swung the brass cannon around to fire a parting canister round at the campfires on the riverbanks. By now, the rifle fire from the stern-wheeler and the riverbank had wounded several of the Wapitis. Fritz could see several fires had started on the stern-wheeler by the time a bend in the river blocked his view.

It had been a costly attack. Two Wapitis were dead, three wounded. The Mischief's superstructure had been hit with numerous bullets. Splinters of wood laid about on the deck, as Fritz helped Kyle check the boat and its boiler for damage. To everyone's relief, the little steamboat's engine and boiler were undamaged, and it quickly carried them out of range of the angry Ichneumon riflemen marooned on shore. The heavy wooden side paddles had taken the brunt of the rifle fire aimed at the boat's midsection and boiler.

As the river junction came into view, Kyle and Fritz realized the fort was under attack. Docking would be unwise and dangerous. They decided to head up the river and look for the paddle wheeler that had passed the fort the day before and try to wreck it.

"Do you have more oil?" Fritz asked.

"No. I wish we did. Those pails of oil did more damage than the cannon fire," Kyle said. They watched the riverbank race by. The Mischief was a surprisingly fast boat.

"That last cannonball hit something serious in the stern-wheeler to have caused steam to vent through the stack," Fritz said. "Since you're out of oil, do you have an extra keg of powder that we could put a fuse in and drop onto the next boat?"

Another bend in the river blocked the sounds of gunfire from around the fort. "I have plenty of gunpowder," Kyle said. "I have three kegs, but no fuses. I'll only need part of one keg for all the cannon reloads I'm apt to have a chance to fire."

"I can make a fuse," Fritz said. He noticed the uncovered cannon as he turned to start searching the boat for material to fabricate a short fuse. "You'd better cover the cannon again."

Mischief found the second Ichneumon stern-wheeler tied to the east riverbank with three gangways running to the low riverbank where several fires burned. The boat was several times as long as the Mischief and three stories high. Riflemen in the upper rooms would make short work of the Mischief crew.

At Captain Malik's suggestion, Kyle had left the Ichneumon double-headed serpent flag flying. They also decided to forget using the cannon, the Ichneumon boat was too large to sink with a few hastily fired cannonballs. Instead, the Wapiti captain steamed past the Ichneumon paddle wheeler, turned the boat around to head down the river, and then gently brought the Mischief against the larger boat. Several Ichneumon sailors watched the maneuver, unconcerned. The Ichneumon stern-wheeler reminded Fritz of a fat goose sleeping at a pond's edge.

Kyle and Captain Malik's plan was audacious. Two volunteers each had a 10-kilogram keg of black powder with a one-minute fuse that other Wapitis would help light as the volunteers dashed onto the Ichneumons' boat deck.

"You're about to take a horribly dangerous risk," Kyle said. "Don't waste it by putting the keg in the wrong spot. The goal is to place the kegs at the bottom of the lower stairs inside the hallway. The captain will stop at the right location. You just have to run straight ahead to the center of the boat, turn left, and down the stairs."

One of the Wapiti volunteers said, "A piece of cake."

The Ichneumon watch asked Kyle their business as they bumped against the paddle wheeler.

"The general asked that we deliver these kegs."

On hearing that answer, the five warriors and Fritz hiding on the far side of the cabin wall, stepped around the wall and shot the Ichneumon sailors. At the same moment, the two volunteers lit the fuses and the runners jumped onto the boat, where they sprinted for the hallway between the deck-level cabins.

Time seemed to stand still as Fritz waited for the men to reappear. Suddenly the two volunteers tore out of the hallway door, yelling for them to cast off. As the men leaped to the Mischief's deck the center of the boat exploded, nearly capsizing the Wapitis' vessel. Burning debris rained down on the Mischief, but the tough little tug righted itself, and with the madly spinning paddles finally able to get a purchase in the pitching river surface, it raced off into the dark, leaving flaming chaos behind.

The first light of the day illuminated a catastrophe. Two facts became clear as the sun lit up the clearing in front of the magazine section of the fort. The Ichneumon had assumed the explosion would breach the fort's outer wall and had committed a large force of their soldiers to charge into the breach. The second fact was that the Wapiti defenders weren't wasting ammo shooting at shadows. The bodies of over a hundred Ichneumon soldiers lay scattered across the clearing.

"Man, we kicked ass," Jerry Jones said, looking out over the clearing. Ichneumon still had some fight left in them; a sniper's bullet slamming into the wall near Jerry's head proved that. "Those snipers need to be cleared from the forest. Okay if I take the Owl team and clear them out?"

"Not yet," Rex said. "We need to organize a flanking action. Anyone trying to cross the clearing will be an easy target for those snipers." General Meringa might have soldiers to waste, but the Wapitis had none.

The older hunter, Zoe, had finally returned at sunrise and with a tale of grief. The Ichneumon scouts had ambushed him and his partner as they looped around to enter the forest across from the fort's north wall.

"Apparently, some of the Ichneumon can see in complete darkness," Zoe said. "I only survived because the Ichneumon's pistol misfired. The rest of the night was required to shake off the bastard. Matt, I can't be sure, but I think he dropped his pursuit by the sycamore grove."

"The grove of trees above the dock area," Matt asked. Zoe nodded, and the three of them looked upriver at the distant cluster of large trees on a sandy knoll. "Make a great sniper post," he added. Rex agreed.

Those sniper teams were Rex's conundrum. Though the Wapitis had dealt General Meringa's force a stinging defeat, the Wapitis couldn't safely leave the stone fort or dock boats safely at the wharf. Rex considered how to break the deadlock while using the Topcon scope to study the grove of trees.

The grove consisted of a half-dozen large sycamores on a sand knob located about two hundred meters from both the dock and the fort's southeast corner. He could spot no one in the grove. That was the one fort corner that lacked cannon, a defect Rex set out to correct.

Alvin Crouch was a crotchety Prussian whom Rex figured for an ex-feldwebel with outstanding arrest warrants pending somewhere in the empire. Herr Crouch had showed up several years ago at Smithtown and made himself useful at the horse barn. Questions about his background only earned a basilisk scowl, though clearly the man knew a great deal about field artillery and horses.

"Herr Crouch, move two of the fort's cannons to the southeast corner," Rex ordered. "I want that sycamore grove raked with grape shot.

Crouch grunted, "Alright." His crew quickly moved two of the 12-cm-bore cannons into place and loaded them with nine-kg canister loads. "We're ready," the artillery feldwebel said. "Several canister loads of grape will keep those Ichneumon bastards hunkered down."

While Crouch had been moving the cannons, Rex had Jerry and six riflemen from the Owl squad saddle up and get ready to rush the tree grove. By the time Crouch's crew had fired the second set of canister rounds, the mounted riflemen were out of the gate and charging the grove. Crouch and his crews did a great job of aiming, judging from the debris and sand kicked up by the canister shots. They even managed to fire a third round before Owls blocked their line of fire into the grove.

Zoe's fears were correct. Jerry's squad marched two wounded Ichneumon warriors back and reported the grape shot had killed a third Ichneumon.

"Good work, Jerry. Have the prisoners checked, then locked up," Rex said. While the men locked up the surviving Ichneumons, the men on the wall yelled that the Mischief had just rounded the river bend. That announcement set off a round of cheering. Rex realized that Jerry, in the excitement, had left the sycamore grove unguarded. "Jerry, forget the cheering. I want several men stationed at the grove."

"You're right. Those damn Ichneumons will try to infiltrate more snipers," Jerry said. Within ten minutes the Owls had that accomplished, and Rex felt it was now safe to allow people outside the fort as long as they stayed in front of walls facing the two rivers and didn't wander into the area facing the woods and Ichneumon snipers.

Rex walked down to the dock to greet the returning boat. The Mischief had taken a beating. In response to his concerns, several of the crew yelled, "You should see the other guys!"

"How bad was the butcher's bill?" Rex asked. Kyle told him four dead, four Wapitis wounded. "Christ, we can't stand many more losses like those, but with two steamboats destroyed, neither can our opponent."

"My wound is rather minor," Fritz's added. The Prussian officer had an ugly wooden splinter in his back. Tara Smith didn't agree. She dragged the Prussian, along with four wounded Wapitis, off the boat and into the fort to clean and dress their wounds.

"Is the boat okay? No damage that compromises the boat's ability to function?" Rex asked. Captain Malik assured him the boiler, engine, and hull were undamaged. Rex then told Kyle, "Have the men shovel the rest of Jarrell's coal into the Mischief. I need to get up the river to find more warriors."

Matt Brewer promised to keep everyone in the fort and not attempt to clean out the snipers in the woods. “Andy, please supervise and help with the burial of the Wapitis killed on the Mischief,” Rex said.

“Here, you'll need these more than I will,” Fritz said as he handed Rex his bolt-action rifle and five-shot revolver before leaving to have his wound cleaned.

With the coal bin full and the dead removed, he told the captain to head up the Southern River and asked the spectators to clear off the boat. The captain ate a handful of kernels, splashed water in his face, and shook off the excess water. He yelled, “What's the steam pressure reading?”

“One million, she's good to go,” Kyle answered while adjusting a valve.

Satisfied all was in order, the captain opened the steam valve to start the cylinder stroking and flywheel revolving. After another glance to verify the ropes were unhooked, he engaged the paddle wheel and backed away from the dock. The crew soon had the boiler at full steam pressure. After swinging the bow up river, Malik pulled the steam valve fully open, and the bullet-ridden boat raced up the river.

Rex rested near his animals, Hokee and Zack, in the stall area behind the engine room. His thoughts were on the missing women and Indira. Since talking with Art Walker, he wasn't sure where to search. Down the Erie River was the usual direction captured women went, not up the Southern River. Burgdorf would know their fate, but finding the former feldwebel wouldn't be easy.

The garrison was mounting up. Indira, using a bent nail from a horse, had worried a tiny opening through the lime mortar joint in the wall that allowed her to see a small part of the stockade's inner yard area. She couldn't tell where they were but suspected Hinton.

Those frightening warriors with the gruesome red tattoos were milling around the yard. Waiting for instructions, she figured.

Indira didn't see any of the Prussian mercenaries among the tattooed monsters. The evilness of Donnelly's men had shattered her faith in the Jesuits' God. Forever seared in her memory would be the image of Billy Keeney, a cheerful two-year-old running to the tattooed savage, laughing.

Undoubtedly, Billy had thought the strange-looking man was there to play. Instead, the Cinnabar warrior had used his musket butt to smash in the boy's face. Then he'd grabbed the Keeney baby and stomped the crying infant to death, while two other men, both appearing to be Prussians, crowded into the nursery shouting encouragement. The younger Prussian had shot Jane, a three year old, as she held her rag doll, wailing.

Stunned by the sudden cruelty, Indira hadn't reacted until Billy's murderer grabbed her. She remembered his stunned expression as she buried her boot knife in his throat. Bedlam erupted. She had vague memories of stabbing Jane's killer, but nothing else until her mother helped her wash off in the cold North River. The long gash down her face would assure that Indira would never forget, nor would she ever forgive the men responsible for that heartless butchery of innocent children.

General Meringa needed a victory, or his fate would match that of the dead captain of the gutted Purnell paddle wheeler partly submerged along the Erie River east bank, disgraced and headless. He'd made the unwise choices of believing Emperor Ratakonda court's chatter about backward savages who knew nothing of military tactics, along with trusting that Benjamin Purnell's saboteurs knew how to breach a fort's wall. Both beliefs proved wrong. His one hope of surviving the emperor's wrath would be rescuing the emperor's nephew.

Colonel Paget believed his commander was an idiot. Now, after failing to win the fort, the disgraced general was blindly attacking up the river into the Wapitis' homeland. When Colonel Paget asked what to do with the Wapiti women and children captured at the farm village, General Meringa had surprised him with the kill order.

"Sergeant Kumar, put the prisoners in the barn," Colonel Paget said. "Is the rear door locked?" The sergeant didn't know. "Then I'll check it. You start the fire."

The women started wailing for mercy as Paget walked around the barn to check the rear door while his squad of warriors threw the unwilling and screaming prisoners into the barn. Before nailing the door shut, they had tossed in lit torches. An iron pin through the hasp locked the rear barn door. Satisfied the pin would hold the door, Colonel Paget had turned to round up his men when he heard the kitten. Its tiny paw was trying to pry open the crack at the bottom of the door.

He liked cats and pulled the pin to open the door, but the kitten, frightened of him, disappeared back in the barn. There was no sign of the women, so he dropped the pin onto the ground, and walked over to the corner of the barn to consider his next move. He could always shoot any Wapitis that tried to escape out the rear door.

In a sense, the prince was his cousin, though being the emperor's bastard he could never claim such. He was also confident of two things: Emperor Ratakonda would reward the officer who rescued the prince, and the "passive" Wapitis would make short work of eliminating the General Meringa threat.

A sudden burst of intense rifle fire from up the river snapped Colonel Paget's thoughts back from royal court life. He saw the rear door of the smoking barn creep open. A woman peeked around the edge of the door as a tabby kitten shot across the barnyard to the field of corn.

Seeing him, an Ichneumon colonel, standing at the corner of the barn seemed to paralyze the Wapiti woman. A moment later, a young girl's head appeared beside her leg. White smoke was pouring out of the top of the door opening. He brought his revolver up to shoot, thought of the prince, and knew with sudden clarity that if he shot those women and children down in cold blood and the Wapitis learned his name, they'd never deal with him. He motioned for them to run.

The rifle fire hadn't let up, which meant the general had run into a serious force of Wapitis. The colonel and his men needed to cross the river and vanish. By then all the women and children were running through the corn toward the river. Sergeant Kumar spotted them and brought his rifle up to shoot.

"Don't fire, Sergeant. Tell the men to fall back to the river. We're crossing," the colonel yelled, before jogging through the knee-high corn to the riverbank. Three canoes were on the shore and the two older women were dragging them to the river. "Halt or I'll shoot your children."

If looks could kill Colonel Paget thought, as the two women edged away from the canoes and his men arrived at the riverbank. The gunfire from up the river seemed to be lessening.

"If you wish to live, get out of here," the colonel said. They abandoned trying to launch the canoes. The women, carrying the youngest of the children, instead ran down the river shore. His men looked confused. "Get these canoes into the river. We're crossing." Seeing a couple of his men taking aim at the fleeing women, he added, "Don't waste ammo on anyone not holding a rifle."

Whatever was occurring up the river in the forest around where the side creek discharged, it had kept the Wapitis busy. Their three canoes made it across the river to the tobacco fields without attracting anyone's interest. Colonel Paget had his men drag the canoes into the riverbank weeds to conceal them from anyone looking across the river. Of course, the women would be quick to tell their warriors where his men had gone. The Wapitis would expect them to go down the river. The colonel had other plans.

Colonel Paget had met Chief Chin several times over the last couple of years while traveling with his uncle, Bret Paget, and his uncle's partner, Manuel Prado, on trading expeditions into the Wapiti homeland. Those trips had taken him to the salt furnace and Hinton and had familiarized him with the river and mountain trails.

He needed to locate Chief Chin. Colonel Paget was standing in the dirt farm lane that ran along the river to provide access to the various lush corn, wheat, and tobacco fields that dotted the rich river bottomland. He was waiting for his men to plant a false trail from the canoes in the direction of the stone fort when two men on horses came out of the tree border between two fields. By then, the rifle fire from across the river had stopped.

The sun god was shining on his mission. The riders were Chief Chin and his foolish son-in-law, Brian, who had pulled a rifle from a holster. The chief then recognized him. Even better, Sergeant Kumar had seen the riders and motioned for the men to hide. The colonel doubted these two Wapitis had a clue that six Ichneumon soldiers surrounded them.

"Colonel Paget, what are you doing out here?" Chief Chin asked. "What's burning across the river? Who's shooting?" The chief stopping his horse about ten meters from the colonel.

"That's General Meringa razing farms. He's upset your bomb didn't breach the fort wall as you promised," Colonel Paget said. "And Brian, put that gun down, or my men might get nervous and shoot." That information had both Wapitis looking around. "Sergeant Kumar, show yourself."

The Ichneumon sergeant stood up about thirty meters away with a Krupp rifle aimed at Brian. The sight apparently caused the chief's son-in-law to reconsider the wisdom of threatening the colonel. The man holstered his rifle.

Paget's bomb remark had shattered the chief's composure. "That bomb went off!" Chief Chin said. "I heard and saw it go off. Are you saying the fort didn't fall?" A bewildered Brian stared at his father-in-law.

"It went off," Colonel Paget said. "It just didn't open the wall, and I lost a lot of good men."

"What's he talking about? What bomb?" Brian asked.

"Your father-in-law is smart. He knows who's going to win and works for the Ichneumons," Colonel Paget said. He didn't like Brian's look. "If you have a problem with that, say so."

"You sold out to these sick bastards. How could you? For what, money, Steve needs to know."

Brian started to turn his horse to leave. Colonel Paget looked at Sergeant Kumar, ran his finger across his throat, and pointed at Brian. The sergeant's shot knocked Brian out of the saddle. The chief stared open mouth as his son-in-law gasped and coughed up blood lying in the farm lane. The colonel hoped that one shot didn't alert the Wapitis across the river to their presence.

"Chief, we're out of time," Colonel Paget said. "Find out where they're holding the prince and meet me in two days on the trail below the salt furnace. Tell our pursuers that we shot Brian and ran down the river. And remember, if you're not there with the information, the Wapitis will learn about your involvement with the bomb. Men, fall in behind me."

Colonel Paget trotted off up the river with the men breaking cover and falling in line behind him. He left the chief sitting on his horse in the farm lane beside his dead son-in-law's body sprawled on the ground.

Chapter 12

Rex arrived at Salt Furnace where he found Chief John Hopkins waiting on the dock. “Chief Smith is not back from Roanoke. Did the Ichneumon attack?”

Chief Smith and Franciscka had left to negotiate a sale agreement with Atlantic Tobacco and the Prussian IRS. Rex told the chief about the attack on the fort while walking Zack off the boat to a nearby patch of fresh grass.

“I need men to help Steve defend his village and finish off the Ichneumon force,” Rex said. “Where’s Larry?”

“I agree with your assessment that defenses at the stockade and furnace are strong,” Chief Hopkins said. “There are over a hundred Wapiti men and women, all trained on and supplied with a Krupp rifle, who now live and work here.”

“Then sparing twenty of them shouldn’t endanger the place,” Rex said as Larry arrived.

“Remember we have Ichneumon prisoners in the stockade, still I think we’d be safe in giving you twenty of the Eagle’s mounted riflemen, along with Lou Jarrell. Do you agree Larry?” Chief Hopkins asked. The young Eagle team leader nodded yes.

“That’s what I need. How soon can you round up the men?” Rex asked. He could tell Larry was thrilled to escape garrison-guard duty.

"I can have the men at the Johnson village by tomorrow morning."

While Larry was organizing the Eagle squad's excursion down the river, the chief and Rex paid the chained Manuel Prado inside the salt furnace a brief visit.

"Is the prince alive?" Manuel asked them as they walked up to the front of the furnace's firebox that served as a jail cell. A neck collar and short chain served as the cell's door.

"As far as I know, he's fine. Are you in the mood to be useful to your emperor?" Rex asked while he dragged a piece of log over to serve as a seat. The chief leaned against the brick firebox wall.

"I'm always ready to help. What do you have in mind?" Manuel accepted one of the mugs of hot tea the guard had brought the three of them.

"General Meringa's attack on the stone fort didn't go well for your side. I still have some loose ends to tie up, but the Wapitis have Ichneumon prisoners. They want to exchange those men for Wapitis that the Ichneumons hold as slaves. That sleaze bag, ah, pardon me, your boss, Benjamin Purnell is rumored to have bought Wapiti women before we were able to stop Donnelly. Those women would be part of the exchange. Have any interest in helping?"

"Well, of course," Manuel said. "Despite the Wapiti's famed hospitality, who wouldn't jump at a chance to leave this splendid place? However, there's a weakness in your proposal, the Ichneumon have no shortage of soldiers and Emperor Ratakonda considers a soldier who surrenders a traitor, and not someone to be allowed back in his armies."

"What a charming tyrant, does that mean he considers you a traitor?" Rex asked. The green tea hadn't improved, and he set his cup on the ground.

"I certainly hope not. I didn't surrender. The Wapitis detained me to resolve a trade disagreement. The prince is the only item the Wapitis have that the emperor would be interested in. Now my boss, Herr Purnell, might be interested in a prisoner exchange, he always needs men. Clovis and Wapiti women, he treats as property, so he might do a deal, a trade on the women. I'd be happy to approach him."

"Yes, I suspect you would," Chief Hopkins said. "Perhaps your boss would even know the fate of my brother."

Rex wondered if the trader would be so cavalier if he knew John's wife and daughter were part of the group of missing women. John's brother, Bill, and several Wapitis had vanished on a winter-sloe trading expedition to Hickory Ridge two years earlier.

"I wasn't aware you had a brother, but of course I'll inquire about him when I see Herr Purnell," the Ichneumon trader said.

"Herr Knight has a few items to tidy up, and then the council might take you up on that offer to approach Herr Purnell," Chief Hopkins said.

Rex and Chief Hopkins had just reached the Mischief when gunfire and screams erupted near the upriver trail entrance into the furnace clearing. Horses and tattooed warriors poured out of the woods. A couple of bullets slammed into the Mischief's pilothouse.

"I'll be damn, those madmen are attacking again," the chief said. "Where is Donnelly finding these maniacs?"

"Whoever they are, they're enemy. Kyle, load canister," Rex said, before grabbing Fritz's bolt-action rifle and sprinting to the stockade. The prisoners apparently thought the raid was a rescue attempt and had started yelling. The guards were uncertain about what to do with the prisoners, and welcomed Rex's arrival. He pulled his revolver and fired into the air.

"Anyone not sitting in the center of the yard a minute from now, I will kill," he promised the restless prisoners.

As the prisoners settled down, Rex chanced a glance over the stockade wall. Several homes were burning, and tattooed warriors were shooting or slashing anyone on foot with war-axes. There were five guards on the walkway; only two were shooting at the raiders.

"Start shooting anyone with a tattooed face," he ordered. A moment later, the guard beside him who hadn't fired his rifle collapsed. Rex wondered if the man had fainted until he saw the spreading blood from a head wound. The boat cannon fired as he searched the down-river side of the clearing for Larry and the Eagle fire team. They had to have heard the uproar, and Larry would never avoid a fight.

One break, the tattooed warriors mostly had rifle muskets, which were difficult to reload on a horse and most of them had switched to war-axes and were attacking fleeing women and children. Then a big Prussian and eight to ten mounted mercenaries charged out of the woods straight to the furnace. Rex emptied the rifle's five shot magazine toward the mercenaries, unseating three of the riders. As he reloaded the rifle's magazine, the Eagle squad arrived on the downstream side of Salt Furnace's clearing. Larry, in moments, had his men organized into a sweep across the settlement. The Eagle men soon routed the tattooed warriors.

Within a few minutes, the attack was over. The surviving tattooed warriors had fled back into the woods and disappeared with Larry and his men in hot pursuit. Smoke from all the gunfire and several burning buildings obscured the furnace area. Rex thought he might have hit the big Prussian who appeared to be the raiders' leader as the group disappeared up the river trail. The man was too far away to be certain, but he wondered if the big Prussian was Burgdorf.

Donnelly's latest raid had been costly for both sides. Eight Wapiti men, ten Wapiti women, and three children had died, and another twenty Wapitis had suffered various wounds and injuries. Thirty tattooed devils had died along with five of the mercenaries who attacked the jail.

"This madness must stop," Chief Hopkins said. "I want Donnelly brought to justice. Thankfully, the prince hadn't been there."

Rex and the chief were outside the salt drying warehouse where two nurses attended to the wounded. The chief had earlier sent a pigeon message to the nearest doctor, Freda Hopkins, that they needed her at Salt Furnace. While at the pigeon coop, Chief Hopkins discovered Steve had sent a message about his success and the death of Brian.

Chief Pete Chin rode up to them. "Damn it, I told the council arresting the prince would lead to this. How many died?" Chief Hopkins told him. "Did they free the prince?"

"No, only Manuel," Rex said. He wasn't in the mood for dealing with the suspected traitor and then he had an idea. "We hid the prince across the river in the cave the Balers brothers used. Tom Jarrell's guarding him. Were you aware the Ichneumons attacked Johnson town?"

"Yes, they killed my son-in-law, Brian. Steve said he could block them until I got the Eagle squad and returned," Pete said. He looked around for Larry and his men, before adding. "The prince is across the river?" Rex nodded yes. He hoped the surprised Chief Hopkins didn't correct him.

Instead, Chief Hopkins said, "The Eagle squad isn't available, besides Steve's message said he'd smashed the Ichneumon force and killed their general. When Eagle is free, I'll send them to help hunt down any Ichneumon stragglers." The usually argumentative man seemed satisfied with that offer.

"Well, we all have dead to bury," Chief Chin said, looking toward the smoking row of cabins near the furnace. "I won't take more of your time. Tell Larry not to dally. I need to get back and handle Brain's funeral arrangements." After switching horses and turning down the offer of an escort, Pete galloped down the river trail toward Johnson town.

Colonel Paget only had to wait a short time before Chief Chin and his horse, with no escort, trotted into view.

"They moved the prince across the river . . .," Pete passed on all the information he'd learned while constantly looking back at the trail.

"You best be going before someone shows up and thanks for the information. I'll let the prince know your part in his rescue."

About an hour before sunrise, Colonel Paget smelled wood smoke as he crept along the rock ledge. He held his hand up to halt the four tattooed Aztecs strung out behind him. The colonel was blessed with great night vision and had taken the lead since his men's night vision was just average. Then he spotted a man out on the ridge about eighty meters. Listening carefully, he could hear two men talking. One of the men was complaining about having to guard the royal bastard. The colonel's spirits soared. It wasn't a trap, and the Chief Chin's information was correct.

Motioning for the men to close on him, Colonel Paget heard the guard above the ledge tell the other guard to throw more wood on the fire. Using hand signals, he told the two youngest Aztecs, with those fearsome face tattoos, to slip ahead and kill the upper guards. He then climbed down the rock ledge and approached the fire, which he figured was located near the cave entrance.

It wasn't an actual cave. It was a rock overhang that formed a sheltered space a man could stand under. The dry space was about five meters deep and maybe ten meters wide where the rain didn't reach. Two large rock fragments partly blocked the front of the overhang opening and provided more shelter from the weather. The fire now burned brightly, but no guard or prisoner was visible.

"Throw down your rifle, colonel." An instant later several rifles fired and the two Aztecs with him were down before they reached shelter in the rocks. "A dozen rifles are aimed at you. Be sensible and put down your rifle. You do want to save your prince, right?"

Considering what had just happened to his Aztecs, Colonel Paget figured the Wapitis had several other rifles aimed at him, though damn if he could locate any of them. Then the bodies of his other two Aztecs sent to kill the upper guards rolled off the rock ledge and landed with lifeless thuds about ten meters from where he waited. The sky was lightening. His night vision advantage would be gone, though so far it hadn't helped much. He needed to decide. Make a dash for freedom and die, or surrender. All the while, he wondered what the Prussian had meant by "save the prince."

Two days had lapsed since the capture of the Ichneumon colonel and exposure of Chief Chin's treason, when Rex, Larry, and fifty Wapiti warriors approached Rainelle around mid-day. Had Tom, his prisoner, and Rainelle survived the passage of Donnelly's forces? The raiders would have passed through the village twice during the assault, going to and then retreating from Salt Furnace. Rex, Lou Jarrell, and two warriors rode ahead to check. The town appeared untouched and there was no sign of Donnelly or Ichneumon men. Art Walker greeted them at the stockade.

"Art, how did you survive?" Rex asked as he dismounted in the stockade. He added, "Tom, where's he hiding?" A plain-looking, young, thin, freckle-face, red-haired woman joined Art in the yard as more Wapiti riders crowded into the stockade.

"Linda saved the day," Art said. "The old barn owl that lives in the stable's hay-loft likes to perch on the flagpole. It upchucked on the flag. A smelly mess that Linda didn't think looked respectful. She was washing the flag when Burgdorf rode in with a bunch of tattooed savages. I was off with Herr Simpson."

"He asked me where the Wapitis were," Linda said. "I told them they had run off yesterday. He knew about Bill's murder and asked about the Ichneumons. I told him I worked for Herr Simpson, and that was who he needed to talk with."

"He did," Art said, "but to get a bottle of the aged whiskey before they galloped off." Art hugged Sue.

"Lord, you were brave," Rex said. "Linda, we all thank you for saving this place." He told the other riders to fix lunch. They'd leave in an hour for Hinton. Rex was thankful that Burgdorf's men hadn't discovered Tom and his Ichneumon prisoner, Prince Cherukuru.

"So, who passed through two days ago?" Rex asked.

"Not near as many of the tattooed freaks returned as went, maybe a dozen," Art said. "Burgdorf, who was wounded in his right leg, and three other Prussians, mercenaries, were here. Oh, and one of those Ichneumon nut-buyers was with them. Don't know his name. It was late evening, but after eating, they rode off."

"Think it's safe to put the flag up?" Linda asked.

"No, nothing will be safe until we kill James Donnelly," Rex said. "Art, get word to Tom that it'll be over one way or another in a few days."

The Hinton stockade was located on the flat land below the confluence of the Sulfur River and the Southern River. It was a poor defensive location due to the higher mountains looming over it. However, Hinton residents had cut most of the hillside for firewood, and good cover was scarce. Rex needed another couple of dozen men to invest the fort, as it should be, but figured the two cannons and high ground gave the Wapitis an advantage.

"Larry, put a blocking force above and below the fort," Rex said. "I want no one entering or leaving the stockade by the trail. Put the stronger force on the up-river side, if reinforcements come, they'll come from Narrows, not from down river. For boat traffic, a shot across their bow, yell at them, whatever it takes to get the crew's attention. If they shoot back, kill the bastards. However, any of those tattooed horrors who want to swim across the river to escape, let them, as long as they have no women."

"You think those women who Art saw are here?" Larry asked.

"I wish I knew. My worst fear is Donnelly used them in some deal with Cinnabar for the warriors and they're in Panther Creek."

"Oh God, let that not be," Larry said. He looked as disheartened as Rex was at that thought. "In the past, the stone building was where they used to hold the slaves," Larry added. "It's opposite of the large warehouse and his office. Where should I place the cannon?"

"Keep the canister shot and put the cannon here," Rex said. "Set it to fire down the trail toward the fort. I'll be back after I get the high cannon going. Use your sensible men on those details. Send the men not needed to the high cannon where Lou and I can keep easier control on them. Caution them not to shoot any innocent souls who happen to paddle down the river from Narrows today."

The ledge above the rock face where Rex wanted to place the other cannon was located about eight hundred meters from the upper end of the stockade and about a hundred meters above it. The bench on top of the sandstone outcropping that formed the rock face offered protection from stockade rifle fire. They were outside the effective range of the Krupp rifle, but the spent rifle bullets could still kill.

Looking down on the stockade, Rex thought of the 1777 Fort Ticonderoga battle when the British made quick work of the fort from their battery on Mount Defiance. He hoped to be as successful as the British had been.

The Wapitis' problem was lack of resources for the cannons. Rex had brought fifty iron balls, not many for a fort the size of Hinton. The rectangular layout of the fort's walls ran about a hundred meters along the river and averaged about forty meters wide with four large buildings inside the log walls. A dozen men and horses milled around the stockade's courtyard in front of the large slate-roof building located along the wall closest to the river.

The Wapitis assembled the bronze cannons while Lou and his men found sufficient wood to start a large fire.

"Imus, I'm not sure how you'll accomplish it, but I need several cherry red cannon balls, the hotter, the better."

The blacksmith from Smithtown nodded his understanding. Imus then placed ten of the iron balls into the fire and set up his small bellows.

"Have you ever shot a cannon before?" Lou asked. The younger Jarrell brother had a large bandage wrapped around his head and looked quite fearsome as he sighted down the cannon barrel. Lou was the most experienced Wapiti gunner with the expedition, having fired a cannon twice at the stone fort to knock down the temple door. Rex had considered bring a couple of Herr Crouch's apprentices, but feared weakening the fort's defenses. Besides, the small brass cannons were more like glorified muzzle-loading shotguns.

Rex ignored Lou's question as he considered how to place the gunpowder into the barrel. The larger fort cannons used premeasured linen bags of gunpowder that wouldn't fit in the smaller brass cannons. Rex had to improvise. The brass barrel was too heavy to tip up and pour the powder in as one might load a muzzle-loading musket. Then there was the question of how much powder to use. A bullet pinged off a rock near the cannon reminding him that he needed to decide.

The Wapitis had brought old rags and under clothes for wading. Looking over the collection, Rex decided a somewhat scorched white linen shirt in the basket would work and cut a square piece from it. He then poured two cups of the coarse black powder on the cut piece of shirt. Lou folded the cloth into a bag to contain the powder and placed it in the cannon muzzle while Rex cut several more squares from the shirt.

John Balers shoved the bag of powder home, followed by the iron cannon ball. The ball rolled back out on the ground when he withdrew the ramrod.

"Now what, did you bring the wrong size?" John asked.

"Put an oily strip of rag around the iron ball," Rex said. John had to shove hard to seat the rag wrapped cannonball against the gunpowder and wadding. "Lou, line the barrel up with the fort, and we'll see what happens."

Rex had an L-shaped iron wire with one end heated red hot that he poked down the fuse hole in the back of the cannon barrel. Nothing happened. Rex aggressively wiggled the wire around in the hole. A moment later, the gunpowder ignited with a loud blast that caused the whole cannon to rear violently back in a cloud of white sulfurous-smelling smoke. The iron ball sailed harmlessly into the trees down the slope, falling short of the fort.

"Well, hell . . . John, swab the barrel to remove any embers," Rex said. He scooped out twice the amount of powder on another piece of cloth, paused, and then added another cup of powder. They repeated the gun-loading process.

By now, the Wapiti-cannon crew had the entire valley's attention. Rex reheated the iron wire and jabbed it down the fuse hole; another violent bang, a cloud of smoke, and everyone watched the cannonball sail harmlessly over the fort to splash in the river. The second cannon blast triggered a renewed burst of rifle fire from the fort that proved as harmless as the Wapitis' cannonballs.

"Should we reduce the powder charge or lower the barrel?" Lou asked.

"Lower the barrel," Rex said. "We have more gunpowder than cannonballs. I want to see what damage the ball can inflict. Look at the men. They're taking cover." Rex gave the iron wire to Lou to reheat.

The Wapitis' third shot landed in the fort's open yard, and then caromed into the front of the large slate-roof building in a cloud of dust and flying wood planks. The horses were rearing at their ties and the men had vanished from the yard. Rex checked on the fire. One of the iron balls was glowing dark red.

Donnelly, even considering his loses, had more men that Rex did for the assault, and an assault force that didn't sufficiently outnumber the defenders rarely succeeded. The remaining forty-seven orange-sized iron balls the Wapitis had available to bombard the fort with could make life dangerous for men in the stockade, but Rex doubted it would cause them to abandon the place. But fire would.

Rex was back to the critical question. Where the missing Wapiti women in Hinton? Had they ever been there? Did Donnelly have the missing Wapiti women in his stockade, and if he did, where? Or did Cinnabar have them in Panther Creek? All Rex knew for sure, Burgdorf passed through Rainelle with four Wapiti female prisoners nine days ago. And Franciscka and Fritz had been in Hinton five days later and saw no sign of prisoners. Due to the horrific destruction of villages up Hopkins River, no one had a good number on the Wapiti women and girls captured versus the ones consumed in fires.

Rex hurried back to the cannon crew and told them to load the powder, then a wet rag.

"As soon as John rams that ball home, Lou, fire the gun," Rex said as two Wapitis cautiously carried the faintly glowing iron ball on two smoking tree limbs. The hot ball was a tight fit but went home, and John jumped clear as the cannon roared. The ball went straight into the same building a few meters to the left of the hole from the previous ball. Nothing happened.

"Get a red-hot ball," Rex said. The men brought over a glowing red-hot iron ball. "Looks good, ram it home John." The ball plowed into the roof of the same building the other cannon balls had struck. It scattered slate roofing and the horses.

The Wapiti cannon crew had used ten percent of their cannonballs. Before using more of the precious supply, Rex wanted to know if the hot iron balls were capable of starting fires or if their use a waste of time and effort. Using the Topcon scope, he studied the building that the two heated balls had struck. After a few minutes, he spotted a thin wisp of smoke drifting out of the hole in the building's roof.

The loud boom woke Indira from her fitful sleep. Two days ago, James Donnelly had silently checked on them. The creepy man had said nothing. Afterward, the hateful guard with the half-missing right ear had taunted them.

"Heard Cinnabar's taking you girls to his castle in Panther Creek," the maimed guard said. "You're to be the cannibal's princess, or was it his dinner?" He laughed and walked away.

Well, at least, Indira now knew they were in Hinton. She looked out her tiny spy hole and saw several savages pointing their rifles toward the ridge behind the jail. They fired. Another boom and a couple of the guards pointed toward the sky.

"Mom, could those be cannons? Has Rex arrived?" Indira asked.

Her mother didn't know. It was a childish question, Indira realized. How could her mother know any more than she did? Another boom, and a moment later, a loud nearby crash followed by horses whinnying and people shouting. Indira looked. "It was a cannonball! It hit across from us! It's got to be Dad and Rex!"

The jail door slammed open, and Gene Peters rushed in with two guards. "Chain them to the wall. You'd better hope they stop firing before one of those red-hot balls starts a fire or you'll roast with us."

Another boom sounded. Indira's chain wasn't long enough to reach her spy hole.

"Oh God, our men don't know we're here," Indira's mother said. "They're going to burn the place." The two Keeney sisters started sobbing.

Rex figured that by now, James Donnelly knew the Wapitis had him cornered. For sure, Burgdorf and Manuel would realize their precarious position. The tattooed savages did. Some of them had started swimming across the river. The distance too great for the Krupp rifle to be accurate, but some of the Wapitis still tried to hit the swimmers. Rex figured the splashing bullets would motivate Cinnabar's men to keep moving, might even kill a couple of the devils.

The burning warehouse demonstrated the stockade was defenseless against cannons. However, now that the Wapitis had delivered that message they needed to stop. Rex had gambled that if the Wapiti women seen with Burgdorf were still in the stockade, they were in the stone jail that Larry had pointed out.

"Lou, take over," Rex said. "John and I are going to see Larry. John, load four iron balls on the horse in case Larry needs them to open the up-river gate. Lou, stop the cannon fire until I say to start again, I don't want to risk starting an inferno."

It would be dark in a couple of hours and Rex wanted the assault party ready to go at sunset. Rex met the young Eagle squad leader about half way down the ridge from the upper cannon location.

"Donnelly's men are now using the side gate with Cinnabar's men to reach the river. Should I move men to block their escape?" Larry asked. The black powder residue smeared across his face reminded Rex of the night camo-paint he once used in another life.

"No, let them go, if they're not taking women prisoners," Rex said.

The building Rex had shot those two red-hot cannonballs into was generating a lot of dense dark smoke. Something was burning and that fire would soon spread to the neighboring buildings. Time to find any Wapiti prisoners was running out. Rex and Larry studied the stockade. They saw no men, only dead horses, though they could hear rifle fire coming from the stockade. Someone was still defending the place.

"I don't think anyone is trying to put the fire out," Larry said. Rex agreed.

"If Indira and her mother are there, then we're going have to attack before that fire spreads. How many men are with you up river from the gate?" He learned there were eighteen men. "If chains need cut, who do you have that can managed that?"

"Imus," Larry said. "He has some tools for cutting iron."

Rex returned to Lou and the upper cannon. "Lou, you have a good view of the up-river gate. Fire at gate and try to smash the gate's hinge supports. Imus grab your chain cutting tools and come with me."

The smoke was becoming noticeable in the jail cell when the door banged open. Four of the tattooed monsters rushed into the cell, shoving the cruel stockade commander, Gene Peter, in front of them. The savages started to grab the Keeney sisters, until they realized their jailer had locked their collar chains to eyebolts embedded in the rock wall.

"Where's the keys," the one called Qua asked Peter. Two of the savages kept glancing out the door, clearly worried about something. A muffled distant boom followed by a nearby loud crash made the warriors step away from the door opening.

"James has the keys," Peter said. "What'd you do with him?"

Qua's response was lost in another nearby loud crashing sound from outside by the gate. The gunshot in the cell was deafening. Peter fell to the floor in a twitching, bleeding heap by Indira. Qua was looking out the cell door, holding a smoking single-shot muzzle-loading pistol. Then the red tattooed killers were gone. The cell door closed.

As her hearing returned, Indira could hear her mother crying and the crackling of a large fire. The air was warmer, the smoke starting to accumulate in their cell. The cannon continued firing and she could hear the sound of what had to be cannonballs smashing things outside their cell. One time, the jail shook violently, and dust fell from the ceiling. Then the cannon fell silent and intense nearby rifle fire started, along with frantic screams and shouted orders to keep firing. Abruptly the warehouse outside door crashed open.

Rex was deeply worried that their efforts to end James Donnelly's reign of terror would endanger the missing Wapiti women, if they were still in the Hinton stockade. But turning back was no longer an option. He needed to enter the fort and search the buildings before the place burned. Lou Jarrell's aimed cannon shots had blown the upriver stockade gate to splinters and scattered the guards. With Rex leading, the Wapiti warriors stormed the stockade. Rex and Imus with his iron cutting tools raced to the stone warehouse with the slave holding cells. Smoke was pouring out of the roof, which meant that something was now burning in the stone warehouse. They encounter no guards at the warehouse.

"We're in here," Indira yelled.

Rex could see them thorough the bars, but he had no keys.

"Where the damn key kept," he asked, trying the cell door and finding it locked. None of the prisoners knew. "Imus can you break the door?"

Imus set to hammering on the door lock bolt to no effect. The women were starting to choke on the smoke and their short chains prevented them from escaping the smoke. Larry Hopkins arrived with more warriors who all started yanking on the bars. It had no effect.

"Larry, get the cannon and bring it here," Rex said. "And an iron ball," He yelled to Larry's back. Then again, there were several iron cannon balls laying on the ground outside the warehouse. "Indira, have everyone lay against the wall and plug your ears."

Ten long minutes later, the cannon arrived and the cell door still resisted Imus's efforts. Rex had changed his mind and found a fence post small enough in diameter to slide into the cannon barrel.

"Larry, use a half powder charge, double wadding, and then the wood post in place of a cannon ball," Rex said. The smoke had his eyes watering as Rex aligned the cannon muzzle. The fence post protruded about a meter out of the cannon barrel. Rex positioned the cannon so the post end was a half of meter from the iron plate protecting cell door lock.

"Ready Indira?"

"Just do it," she cried. "The smoke is killing us."

"Larry, clear a path for the cannon rebound. Fire in the hole," Rex said and touched the red-hot wire Imus had heated to the cannon fuse-hole.

A ferocious bang and cloud of smoke sent the cannon skidding several meters down the hallway from the jail cell door. The cannon shot had left the cell-door a twisted wreck and open. The mangled fence post laid in the middle of the cell. Imus was on the slave collar chains in a moment and cut the chains.

Rex helped Indira and her mother out of the smoke filled cell to fresh air while Larry helped the Keeney sisters. A quick check determined all the Wapiti women had survived.

Epilogue

Rex Knight never resolved who killed James Donnelly. When he entered the warlord's office before the fire consumed it, he discovered the man dead from an apparent bullet in his forehead. The large office safe was open and empty. A careful search after the fire found no trace of Manuel Prado and Friedrich Burgdorf. Rex figured the wily feldwebel had helped the Ichneumon trader escape.

Chief Qua and most of the Cinnabar warriors who had returned to Hinton after their second ill-fated attack on Salt Furnace, managed to escape across the river and had disappeared. All the mercenaries still in Donnelly's stockade died during the Wapitis' final assault.

Indira and the other Wapiti women survived the assault. Rex's young friend had a terrible wound from a knife slash diagonally across her face. Only time would answer whether the scars on her psyche and body would destroyed Indira or make her stronger.

The Wapiti Chief's Council intended to hang Prince Cherukuru for raping Wapiti women, though Rex suspected the council would consider a sufficiently attractive ransom offer. Colonel Paget remained safely locked in the saline works' furnace cell. The IRS agent-accountant Franciscka Weidman, Captain Fritz Caprivi, and Tara Smith remained in Roanoke pursuing the creation of a Wapiti Territory.

Chief Pete Chin was a murderer and traitor, but the council, in their wisdom, allowed him to retire. Then the council conditionally granted Rex Knight a block of unclaimed land in fee. The tract's location was in the upper part of Jarrell River. To claim the five-thousand hectares, Rex had to pacify Cinnabar's murderous band of Clovis living in the highlands and pay the new land tax by the first of the New Year.

As we leave Herr Knight, he's wondering if he should move on or try to satisfy the land-grant conditions.

Follow Rex's adventures in Boilermaker.

www.ingramcontent.com/pod-product-compliance
Lightning Source LLC
Chambersburg PA
CBHW030020180626
46810CB00001B/126

* 9 7 8 0 9 8 3 1 9 0 7 7 6 *